THE Senator's Agenda

Other books by Bob Larson

Fiction

Dead Air
Abaddon

Non-fiction

Satanism: The Seduction of America's Youth
Straight Answers on the New Age

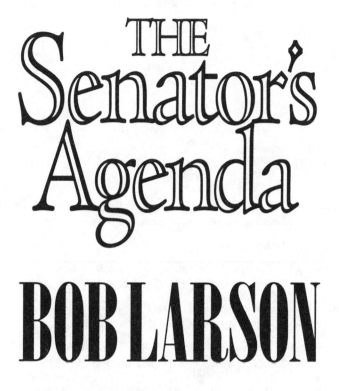

THE Senator's Agenda

BOB LARSON

A JANET THOMA BOOK

THOMAS NELSON PUBLISHERS
Nashville • Atlanta • London • Vancouver

Copyright © 1995 by Bob Larson.

Published in Nashville, Tennessee, by Thomas Nelson, Inc., Publishers, and distributed in Canada by Word Communications, Ltd., Richmond, British Columbia.

The Bible version used in this publication is THE NEW KING JAMES VERSION. Copyright © 1979, 1980, 1982, 1990 Thomas Nelson, Inc., Publishers.

Library of Congress Cataloging-in-Publication Data

Larson, Bob, 1944—
    The senator's agenda / Bob Larson.
    ISBN 0-7852-7879-6
    1. United States. Congress. Senate—Elections—Fiction. I. Title.
PS3562.A747S46   1995
813'.54—dc20   94-49019
                                                           CIP

Printed in the United States of America

1 2 3 4 5 6 — 00 99 98 97 96 95

To Brynne Ann. When you were six months along in your mother's tummy, I started writing this book. When you were born August 17, I was half finished. During your sixteenth week, I finally completed the manuscript. Throughout the writing of this book, I was accompanied by your prenatal kicking and your postnatal cries. Now, as I let go of my writing pen, your tiny fingers reach up to grasp my hand and your smile delights my heart. You are truly God's gift, and you make all my long hours of solitary writing worthwhile. As a first-time father, I want you to know that two parents never loved a child more. Welcome to our world, Brynne Ann.

Acknowledgments

My wonderful wife, Laura, who amazingly edited with a pen in one hand and our new daughter, Brynne Ann, in the other.

Janet Thoma, extraordinary editor, who understood my struggles as a new father and graciously gave me slack on my writing deadlines.

Tim La Haye, a long-time friend, who was responsible for introducing me to my first major book publisher.

Eldred Thomas, who, along with his late wife, Ray Nell, encouraged me to develop my potential as a national radio broadcaster.

Bobb Biehl, a dear friend and advisor, whose words of wisdom helped me keep in sight God's purpose for my life.

My parents, whose love and prayers have constantly encouraged me.

My mother-in-law, Joan, who held Brynne Ann to free Laura's arms so she could edit during those crucial final hours of writing.

1

A booming voice pierced the crowd's murmur. "Ladies and gentlemen, they said it couldn't be done, but we did it! We won the primary election! Bill Baldwin is a candidate for the U.S. Senate from Colorado!"

A huge audience in Denver's lavish Mile-High Hotel ballroom erupted into cheers. Wes Bryant cocked his head sideways and leaned to his left to see past the bushy-haired man in front of him. He pulled his wife, Annette, close to his side to keep her from being jostled in the crush of the crowd.

The tall, square-jawed speaker at the podium continued. "We won by pulling together a coalition of groups that nobody else courted, groups that the *experts* said couldn't deliver the votes. But you did deliver, and in November the party in power is going to find out that Stand for America is a political party of the people, for the people, and by the people!"

Wes felt a sharp elbow jab his ribs as an overly exuberant celebrant flailed his arms in excitement and leaped up and down. He resisted the temptation to give the man a piece of his mind since speaking in anything but a scream would have been inaudible.

"Bill Baldwin wants to thank you, all of you, for working so hard these last three months, collecting names on the petition drive to get us on the ballot, knocking on doors, and telling everyone that Colorado's historic third party, Stand for America, is the wave of the future."

More thunderous shouts mingled with noisemakers. Wes strained his neck as far as possible in either direction to survey his surroundings. Hundreds of metallic red, white, and blue balloons with silver streamers had been released and were bobbing against the thirty-foot-high ceiling. At both ends of the room huge banners proclaimed, "Bill Baldwin, The People's Choice." Low-hanging crystal chandeliers reflected the almost constant camera flashes. Members of a five-piece band waited on an elevated platform in a far corner with their instruments in a ready-to-play position.

"Thanks to you in the Evergreen Club for realizing that Stand for America is the way to save America's forests and streams," the speaker continued above the slightly abated din. "Thanks to you who believe that the privacy of a woman's body should not be controlled by laws that seek to invade her personal choices. Thanks to you who have survived the victimization of intolerable bigotry at the hands of religious zealots and, as a result, want to avoid making our state a hate-filled territory. And thanks to each of you who believes this is a great nation where every man and woman has the right to free expression and liberation from failed dogmas of the past. Our victory is your victory. And the mandate you give to us will be the message our candidate takes to Washington in January!"

With that, any semblance of decorum disintegrated as the band blasted the strains of Billy Joel's "Keepin' the Faith" over a sound system more suited to a stadium rock concert. Everywhere people were dancing and flinging each other around the room. Some exchanged partners to hug and enthusiastically kiss whoever was in their proximity, men with men and women with women. Others celebrated less lustily as they slapped high-fives or punched their fists in the air in accompaniment to the beat. Champagne corks popped so frequently the music seemed to be embellished by a massive, amplified popcorn popper.

"Who is this guy?" Annette yelled into Wes's ear as she grabbed his neck to pull his head closer and then pointed toward the podium.

Wes shrugged his shoulders and fumbled in his pocket for the VIP invitation he and Annette had received. He figured that Bill Baldwin had invited them because he was an old buddy from college. He held his elbows out to fend off the reveling crowd and read:

You are cordially invited to a joyous celebration Friday, April 22, sponsored by the Stand for America victory committee. Opening remarks will be made by Robert Woodall, party chairman. Our winning candidate, William Baldwin III, will greet the faithful who have enabled his message to be heard throughout America. Enjoy all the champagne you can drink and dance until dawn with the music of our Stand for America orchestra in the Mile-High Hotel Grand Ballroom. Be there, and KEEP THE FAITH!

"Robert Woodall!" Wes yelled at Annette, overemphasizing the words so she could read his lips.

"Woodball?" Annette yelled back with an inquisitive look on her face.

"Woodall, Woooood-aallll," Wes responded, drawing out the vowels to underscore his pronunciation.

"Oh," Annette nodded affirmatively, "Woodcall. Thanks," she shouted.

Woodall stepped back to the microphone and tapped it several times to regain the audience's attention. Gradually the merrymaking subsided. The band muted its sound to a soft drumbeat and bass line.

"His name isn't on the program, but I want you to give a round of applause to an important member of our team," Woodall exclaimed. "The man who got Bill Baldwin elected, our Stand for America campaign chairman, David Kelly."

The frenzy resumed. The audience seemed ready to use any excuse to party the night away. Wes's eyes caught an imposing figure who stepped to the dais and waved enthusiastically to the crowd.

"I don't believe it!" Wes exclaimed to Annette. "That's David Kelly, another guy I knew in college. I played football with him. Best nose tackle

I ever saw. Nobody got past him unless he was double-teamed. He was one tough customer."

Kelly didn't say anything but smiled broadly in acknowledgment of the adulation. Wes was amazed to see how little his former football teammate had aged. *That head of dark, wavy hair hasn't lost a strand.*

Kelly's broad shoulders still looked big enough to impose a threat to any opposing lineman. Wes remembered Kelly's huge hands locking around his legs during intrasquad scrimmages. *Last I heard he was headed for the NFL draft,* Wes recalled. *Wonder if he ever made it to the big time?*

Kelly returned to his seat and the band picked up the tempo to the Joel classic until the crowd could no longer match its gyrations with the beat. Abruptly the band stopped, and the guitar player soloed with a series of lightning-fast licks that captivated the attention of the predominantly thirty-something crowd. Higher and higher his fingers flew on the frets until the immense hall was filled with a deafening shriek. A dozen or so air-guitar aficionados mimicked the virtuoso's performance, accompanying their impersonation with wobbly, leg-splitting leaps in the air mimicked from old Pete Townshend videos.

Then, over the public address system, the voice of an announcer, sounding like the ringmaster for a World Wrestling Federation feature match, intoned, "And now, the man you've been waiting for, the man who will take us to victory in November, a man who believes our country is for every American . . . Bill Baldwin!"

Wes watched as the ceiling parted and red, white, and blue confetti rained down on the crowd. Spotlights swiveled in every direction to enhance the drama of the moment. Suddenly the hall darkened except for one glaring spotlight that illuminated the podium. A handsome, slightly graying, thick-haired man confidently strode to the center of the beam. He lifted his arms in the air to form a victory V. His radiant smile sparkled under the normally harsh television klieg lights. Not a wrinkle or crow's foot marred his forty-something face. Once at the podium, he rocked gently from side to side in rhythm, obviously relishing every moment of acclaim. Slowly he leaned toward the microphone and said, "Friends, black and white, liberal and conservative, straight and gay, rich and poor, downtown and uptown, tonight is your night. You have earned the right to celebrate what America is really all about. Freedom!"

"Freedom!" the crowd roared back.

"Freedom!" Baldwin implored again. "Freedom for you to be who you want to be, say what you want to say, believe what you want to believe, and love who you want to love. Freedom, that's what America is all about, and that's the message I will take to Washington if you make me the next U.S. senator from the great state of Colorado! Just keep the faith!"

Baldwin stopped speaking momentarily as the band swung into yet another chorus that Wes concluded might have nauseated Billy Joel if he had to hear the song that many times.

"So that's your classmate at Clarion Community College," Annette yelled in Wes's ear. "The one who took all the girls away from you!" she added with a wink.

"That's him," Wes bellowed back. "Still as gregarious as ever."

Wes's mind went back more than twenty-five years to his college days in Clarion, Indiana. There he was, a freshman, eager to prove his manhood on the football field while Bill Baldwin proved his mettle by garnering votes for student-body president. Wes winced slightly as memories of the injury that ended his football dreams jarred his consciousness: lying on the thirty yard line instead of carrying the ball across the goal line for a touchdown. He remembered the intense smell of wet, October grass as he struggled to move his immobilized left knee.

Bill Baldwin had never stomped a cleat on football turf. His playing field had been campus government, and he had scored every time he carried the political football. Student leadership positions were just the beginning. After those modest accomplishments, it was on to national politics, working summers in the offices of various U.S. senators and running the campus division of the Students for the President campaign.

"Yeah, yeah, yeah, yeah, keepin' the faith," the Billy Joel facsimile droned on.

"So what's Baldwin been doing since you last saw him?" Annette asked.

"Making money, lots of it!" Wes yelled back.

Wes had casually followed Baldwin's career through law school and on to success as a high-profile Indianapolis litigator before his move to Denver. After that Wes had lost contact, until nine years ago when he took over as owner and general manager of KVCE radio, Denver's top talk station. Now Baldwin's ventures were a legend in the Denver business community, and every baby boomer in the state had marveled at his skill in turning one investment after another into a multimillion-dollar portfolio. Politics seemed like a natural move, so Wes wasn't at all surprised to hear that Baldwin had formed a third party to take on the political establishment in a run for U.S. Senate. However, Wes hadn't seen or spoken with Baldwin since college days, so he was surprised to get the VIP invitation.

He probably invited me because of my clout in the broadcasting community and is going to come calling for some free publicity during the campaign, Wes concluded.

Wes was so caught up in his thoughts he hadn't noticed that Baldwin was gone from the limelight and Woodall was back at the podium, announcing, "Those with special VIP invitations please proceed to the left of this platform for a private reception."

Wes took Annette's arm and started toward the ballroom exit.

"Aren't you going back there?" she asked, pointing to the left of the dais.

"What for?" Wes said harshly. "I already heard everything Baldwin has to say years ago. Besides, I have to get up early tomorrow for some appointments at the office."

Annette stopped dead in front of Wes. She shot one of her knowing glances at him as if she didn't need to say a thing to call his bluff.

"What . . . you think I don't want to go in there because I don't want to see Baldwin . . . that I'm jealous of him or something? Give me a break!"

Annette tilted her head to one side, looking prepared for Wes's next excuse.

Wes looked at his wristwatch. Then he gave her a knowing smile and led her toward the reception.

I saw enough of that guy back in Clarion, and I've spent the last five years in Denver avoiding him because I don't want him rubbing in my past failures and his current successes. If Annette only knew what kind of an ego this guy has . . .

"Invitation please," a long-haired campaign volunteer said as he barred their entrance to the reception doorway.

Looks like one of those change-the-world political idealists that guys like Baldwin use to feed their ambitions, Wes thought, sizing up the reception's pseudo-gendarme. Wes fumbled in his coat pocket for a minute, then produced the access notice.

"Thank you, sir," the young man said politely. "And don't forget to vote the Stand for America ticket in November."

Wes feigned a smile as he brushed past the ticket-taker to a meeting room filled with several hundred jovial campaign celebrants. He moved through the crowd, paving a way for Annette, and aimed toward the only available empty table.

"Want something to drink?" he asked Annette as he pulled out a chair for her.

"A diet soda would be fine."

Wes looked around for the hospitality bar, spotted it in a far corner of the room, and headed in that direction. He ordered a diet Sprite for Annette and a Perrier for himself, then proceeded back to the table. He carefully navigated a pathway past people who were gesturing wildly with their arms in animated storytelling of memorable moments on the road to victory. Wes spotted two large, blond, muscle-bound men who wore diamond studs in their ears. They stood near the restrooms and whispered to each other. Just as Wes neared the table where Annette was sitting, he heard the unmistakable resonant sound of Baldwin's voice.

"Wes, is that you?"

Wes turned, drink glasses still in hand. He hesitated for a moment, not sure what to do, and then bent down to set the glasses in front of Annette. He rubbed his hands on the sides of his jacket to wipe off the moisture from the condensation on the ice-filled glasses then put his right hand out. Baldwin gripped it tightly and moved closer. He put his left hand on Wes's shoulder.

"After all these years, I can't believe it's really you. Rah, rah, wanna be cool? Clarion College, that's our school," Baldwin chanted as he clenched his fists to imitate a half-time cheer.

Wes laughed nervously. "Maybe you should have been a cheerleader instead of chasing all those pom-poms."

"Is this your daughter?" Baldwin said, motioning to Annette. "We never saw anything this lovely on campus or I might have given you competition off the football field."

"Annette, I would like to introduce you to Bill Baldwin. Bill, this is my wife, Annette."

"I'm honored you could be here tonight," Baldwin said as he leaned past Wes and took Annette's hand. "It's too bad we haven't gotten together before this," Baldwin added, turning his attention again to Wes. "What a shame we ended up in the same city but were too busy to renew an old friendship. We'll have to get together sometime, although my schedule is going to be hectic between now and November. Maybe I can visit you at the station," Baldwin said while a broad smile exposed his perfect white teeth and lit up his suntanned face.

"Be quiet! Stop! I have something to say!" a voice crackled through the room.

Both Wes and Baldwin were startled by the urgency of the voice that turned everyone's eyes toward the far end of the room where a small platform had been erected to hold a table that displayed campaign literature. A bald-headed man in his early forties stood stiffly at an oak-paneled lectern stationed at the front edge of the platform. His gray suit looked unpressed, and he held the front of the lectern with both fists as if it were his anchor to reality.

Wes glanced at Annette, but her eyes were fixed on this pathetic-looking man. His eyes were opened wide, and his face was bloated and bright red. There was a spongy quality to his complexion.

"That's my press secretary, Alex Lewis," Baldwin whispered in Wes's ear. "I'm not sure what this is about."

"Listen, I told you!" Lewis demanded in a desperate voice.

A mutter of confusion floated around the room as people looked curiously at each other, searching for a person near them who might know what was going on. Wes could see from the looks on people's faces that no one, including Baldwin, knew the reason for the outburst.

Several men started toward the platform.

"Stand back, I tell you!" Lewis warned. "Don't try to shut me up. I've kept silent for too long!"

Confident he had the audience's attention, Lewis leaned forward. "You know me," he hissed. "I'm not crazy. I'm deadly serious. It has to end. It can't go on!" he cried at the top of his lungs. "You can't get by with it. If I know, others know, or they will know!"

The murmur became a rumbling. "Get him out of here." "Somebody stop him." "He's had too much to drink."

The two diamond-studded men Wes had previously noticed looked to Baldwin as if awaiting instructions to rush the stage. Baldwin put his hands forward, palms downward, to indicate restraint.

"Bill!" Lewis cried loudly. "You tell them. And if you won't, I will!"

As all eyes looked in his direction, Baldwin shrugged and gave a pitying look at Lewis.

"I've begged you again and again; now I can't take it any more!"

With that, Lewis was silent. He pulled something from his pocket. All at once a shot rang out.

Wes watched as Lewis's eyes bulged from their sockets and his face seemed to compress and flatten from an invisible force that squeezed it from both sides. Then his head jerked sharply left, and Wes could see the gun fall away from Lewis's right hand that was pointed at his temple.

As his body slumped forward on the lectern, the room went deadly silent. All that could be heard was the discharged gun hitting the floor.

Screams of shock suddenly pierced the room.

Several men lunged toward the platform as others bolted for the nearest exit doors. No one seemed certain whether to run to Lewis's crumpled body or to run for their lives.

Wes immediately threw his arms around Annette with his back to the platform to shield her from the panicking crowd.

"Call a doctor!" a voice cried out.

"It's too late; call the police!" another screamed.

"He's dead!" a deep voice declared above the din.

2

"Wes, I've got to talk with you as soon as possible," Baldwin pleaded. He went on to recount the tragedy of the night before.

Through bleary eyes Wes glanced at the clock radio on his bedroom night stand. It was 7 A.M.

"Is there any chance you could see me this morning?" Baldwin asked.

How can I refuse? Wes thought. *He probably needs to talk to someone he knows outside of his political circle.* "Give me an hour or so to get ready," Wes whispered, hoping he wouldn't awaken Annette any more than she had already been aroused by the ringing of the phone. She stirred restlessly as he continued. "Is 8:30 okay?"

"Fine," Baldwin responded. "Do you still live just west of the city, near Mountain Springs?"

"Yes," Wes answered, pausing for a moment to wonder how Baldwin knew where his home was. Before he could ask, Baldwin concluded the conversation.

"I'll be there at 8:30. And, Wes, let's speak alone at first, like old friends."

Wes rubbed the sleep from his eyes and quietly got out of bed. He closed the door to the bathroom so Annette wouldn't hear him getting ready. After shaving and brushing his teeth, he grabbed some clothes from the closet and made his way to the kitchen where he finished dressing.

Saturdays were a special time for Wes and Annette. They usually slept in, had a leisurely breakfast, and puttered around the house or ran errands that the demands of their weekday routine prevented. He hoped Annette wouldn't mind Baldwin's intrusion once she fully awakened and discovered what the early-morning call was about.

After consuming a glass of orange juice and several bites of a day-old microwaved muffin, Wes settled into an easy chair in the living room to await Baldwin. He tilted back his favorite dark green La-Z-Boy to a lounging position, closed his eyes, and dozed off. Strange, recurring dreams invaded his thoughts as he floated in and out of consciousness. He imagined dark shadows lurking behind him as he walked through the empty streets of an unfamiliar city. These scenes intermingled with the shouts of large crowds pressing toward him, reaching out to touch him, their arms piercing his body as if he were transparent.

The sound of the front doorbell interrupted the threatening dream, and he gripped the arms of the chair to regain his equilibrium. Quickly he collected his thoughts and went to the door.

Baldwin stood there, somewhat hunched over, in a pressed, tan trench coat. With his collar pulled up around his neck he looked like a detective. "Sorry to wake you up so early on a Saturday morning," he apologized.

"No problem," Wes answered. "Annette was so deep in sleep she didn't notice I got up."

Baldwin removed his coat, and Wes reached out to take it. "Last night must weigh heavily on your mind," he said as he turned to hang the coat in the entryway closet. "If I had been through something like that, I'd want someone to talk to."

Wes led Baldwin to the living room. "Have a seat," Wes said, gesturing toward the couch.

Baldwin dropped onto the inviting cushions as Wes sat back down in his recliner. An awkward silence followed as each waited for the other to speak. Finally, Baldwin lifted his eyes and stared into Wes's. "I need your help. After what happened last night, I'm going to lose my bid for the Senate unless you give me a hand."

Wes shifted nervously in his chair. *What does he want? Free advertising on the station? An endorsement of some kind?*

"Help you?" Wes asked. "To be honest, Bill, you probably need a minister or psychologist more than me. I've never had a friend shoot himself, so I don't have the faintest idea how to handle something like that."

"No, no. That's not what I'm getting at," Baldwin said hesitantly, choking on each word. "It's the campaign itself I need help with."

Wes was stunned. He stiffened his back slightly. "Politics isn't my thing. I know football and the radio business like the back of my hands; that's it. Just because I put up a few posters around campus to support your run for the student government doesn't mean I'm some kind of political know-it-all."

Baldwin crossed his legs and leaned back, extending his arms across the couch pillows behind him. "Lewis was my right-hand man. I couldn't have won the primary election without him. I don't know why he . . ." The words stuck in his throat. He tugged at his shirt collar and loosened his tie in what looked like an effort to allow the words to come more easily.

"Can I get you something to drink, maybe some orange juice or coffee?"

"No thanks; I can't stay here long. Let me get to the point." Baldwin looked intently at Wes. "I want you to be my press secretary during the general-election campaign that will be starting in a few weeks."

Baldwin's words took Wes by complete surprise. He opened his arms wide and shrugged his shoulders in disbelief. "What? You want me to do what?"

"Wes, I've thought about it all night. Maybe our meeting last evening had some purpose we don't understand. Maybe you were supposed to be there. Perhaps it was God's way . . ." Baldwin's voice trailed off as he seemed once again lost in thought.

"With all due respect, Bill, I'd need God and all the power in heaven to do what you're asking. I've got a radio station to run. Even if I could find the time, I know nothing about politics. I'd be like a football player trying to kick a soccer ball into the net. Look at me, Bill, this is Wes Bryant talking to you. I can do a talk show and discuss anything with people calling at random, but don't ask me to get up in front of the press and face that crowd of headline-seeking scavengers!"

Baldwin seemed collected, more calm than when he arrived. "I'll lose the general election if you don't take this job," he said with a demanding tone to his voice. "I've heard you behind a microphone. Granted, you don't do talk radio anymore, but everybody knows you're the best communicator in the business. No one else in this state can affect an audience like you."

Wes fiddled with his watch, somewhat embarrassed by the compliment.

"Yeah, I'm good at what I do, but you're asking me to do more than stand at a podium and deliver some canned response to the press. You're asking me to stand for what you stand for. Stand for America? How can I represent you? I'm not even sure what you stand for."

"I stand for what's right!" Baldwin's eyes flashed with conviction and enthusiasm. "Stand for America means standing for what made this country great, the values that gave us our liberties!"

"I'm not asking for a political speech," Wes interjected. "You don't need to convince me about your politics right now."

Baldwin didn't let up. "Look, Wes, our liberties are being threatened by a group of people who want to tell the rest of us how to think and how to act. We've got to stop them."

"Who is this group?"

"That doesn't matter," Baldwin went on. "What matters is that the freedoms of America should be for all Americans, not just those who are politically correct."

Wes figured he shouldn't push Baldwin about this unidentified group because of his state of mind, so he let him off the hook for the time being.

"How can I fill Lewis's shoes? The first thing reporters will want to know is what Lewis was referring to when he shot himself. Do you know what he was talking about?"

"Of course not! But you can't expect people who kill themselves to be very rational, can you?"

"If he was your right-hand man, how can you explain his behavior?"

Baldwin cleared his throat and adopted a sympathetic look. "Lewis was a manic-depressive." Without changing his expression he continued, "He must have let the pressure get to him and forgot to take his Prozac."

Wes heard Annette's soft steps coming down the stairs.

"Sweetheart, you remember Bill from last night," he said, standing and motioning toward Baldwin. "I tried not to wake you when he called."

"Please forgive me, Mrs. Bryant," Baldwin added, also standing chivalrously. "I desperately needed to talk to your husband this morning and . . ."

"It's all right," Annette responded graciously despite her startled expression. "Can I get either of you anything?" she asked as she swept a hand over her waistband and tightened her robe.

"Bill wants me to be his campaign press secretary," Wes blurted out.

Annette folded her arms across her chest but did not reply.

Baldwin broke the awkward silence. "I need your husband's help, Mrs. Bryant," he said softly. "He's the only person in the entire state who's got the ability to do the job, and he's the only person I would trust to handle it."

Baldwin stood up and tugged slightly at the belt of his trousers. He looked at Wes and said, "It wouldn't take much of your time. You could still run the radio station. If you needed help, I'm sure our campaign committee could find someone. Anyway, I wouldn't need your time exclusively until the last couple of months before the election when we blitz the state with personal appearances."

Wes walked over to Annette and slipped his arm around her waist. He tried pulling her close to him, but she stiffly resisted.

"I know your main concern isn't money," Baldwin said offhandedly as he made his way toward the front door, "but the Stand for America committee is prepared to pay you $100,000 for the next six months, plus expenses, and they're very liberal with their expense budget. Like I said, the issue isn't money. I just want you to know that you'll be taken care of.

"I wish I could give you more time to think this over," Baldwin said reaching for the door latch, "but unfortunately these things are beyond my control. The campaign committee has scheduled a press conference at three this afternoon."

Wes looked at Annette, whose eyes were filled with apprehension. "I won't promise you anything, but Annette and I will talk it over, and I'll call as soon as I can, hopefully before lunch."

Baldwin pulled the car keys out of his coat pocket and thumbed through them to find the right one. "I know I can count on you, Wes. Can't I?"

Wes shrugged his shoulders ambivalently. "Be careful that wind doesn't blow you off the road," he warned. "We're having one of those spring chinooks, and you know how fiercely they come down off the mountain slopes."

"At least it warms things up this time of year," Baldwin said as he pulled his coat collar up around his neck. "I hear it's going to be in the low seventies today, not bad for the end of April."

Wes watched as Baldwin opened the door and walked outside. He leaned against the wind, which was bending the tops of the sturdiest pine trees. Baldwin made it quickly to his car and jumped in as a sudden powerful gust nearly swept him off his feet. He slammed the car door, but not fast enough to prevent a few pieces of paper from being sucked off the car seat and blown across Wes's front yard. Wes raised his hand and yelled at Baldwin, who by now had started the car and was headed down the long driveway. He hesitated for a moment and then bolted out of the house, trying to grab the sheets of paper and hail Baldwin who he hoped might look back through his rearview mirror.

Wes darted after the paper that had been blown against branches of pine needles, holding them in place. He reached down, grabbed the papers, and stuffed them into his pants pocket, realizing there was no way he could get Baldwin's attention. The wind cut through his shirt and reminded him that, in Colorado, winter can extend through spring without much warning. As he made his way back to the front door, he pulled one of the papers from his pocket. From its jagged edges, it looked as if the wind had ripped it from a journal since only a portion of someone's scrawled handwriting could be deciphered.

He squinted as the morning sun reflected off the paper, but made out the words: "You can't win if they . . . what really happened to . . ."

3

The wind grabbed at the paper again, but Wes salvaged the note, folded it, and tucked it in his shirt pocket. He went inside and walked to the bedroom where Annette was seated at her dressing table, combing her hair. He placed his hands on her shoulders and gently massaged her neck.

She tilted her head up in appreciation. "I know you like long hair, Wes," Annette said, "but it sure is a lot of work. Boy, what I go through to keep a good man like you happy," she added with a wink.

Wes smiled in response, then stared at her reflection in the mirror. "You really don't like Baldwin, do you? Is it his politics? His background? What bugs you?"

Annette stopped the brush in midstroke. She cupped the lock in her hand and looked at Wes's reflected image. "It's just him," she answered with a shiver. "It's one of those things I can't put a finger on. I don't trust him." She finished running the brush through the strand of hair. "I suppose his eyes bother me the most."

"His eyes?"

"When I look deep into them, something tells me you shouldn't get mixed up with him." Annette let out a sigh and looked at the wedding ring on her finger. She twisted it in circles with the opposite hand, lost in thought. In one movement, she turned around in her chair and faced Wes. "I know I sound too emotional, but after all we've been through, you can't blame me for being skeptical."

"What are you saying?" Wes asked, "Is he the type of guy our dog would growl at if we had one?"

Annette chuckled. "No, I think our imaginary dog might go for his throat."

"Come on, Honey. Baldwin must be doing something right. He's made influential friends, built a financial empire, and talks about freedom for all Americans. He's not a TV pitchman selling synthetic-jewel necklaces on the home shopping channel. Baldwin has built a solid reputation and could not have made it this far without some integrity."

"You make me question myself," Annette capitulated. "Perhaps you're right. All of those people there last night must know what kind of guy he is." Annette looked frustrated. "I don't understand the political process, but I can't imagine so many people standing behind someone as their leader who is . . ." She searched for a word. "Who is . . . evil."

She waved off her growing apprehension with her hand. "You know I trust your judgment, and I'm behind you all the way. If you think you have to help him, I'm only asking that you try to make it for a short period of time, maybe a transition while he looks for someone else."

"Transition, yeah, I like that. It would get me off the hook; I wouldn't be abandoning a Hoosier in need. I'll be his press secretary, but they can add the word *transitional* in front of my title. In fact, I'll insist on it."

Wes held Annette's face in his palms and leaned down to kiss her forehead. "I married the most beautiful woman in the world," he said as his lips touched her brow.

Wes exited off the Interstate 25 freeway ramp, taking the quickest route to the Rocky Mountain Regent Hotel.

"I'm sure glad Baldwin switched the press conference from the Mile-

High Hotel where we were last night," he said to Annette as he turned onto Sixteenth Street. "It would have been eerie, being in the same building where Alex Lewis shot himself."

One block later, Wes and Annette arrived at the towering Regent Hotel. They parked in the underground garage, walked up a flight of stairs, and made their way to the bustling hotel lobby. A freestanding sign near the stanchions pointed people to the registration area where there was a listing of the day's events. "Stand for America News Conference—penthouse level," Wes said to Annette, pointing at the sign. "Looks like Baldwin's people have gone all out to make this a big event."

Wes saw crews of people in the lobby loaded with television cameras. Several had collapsible camera stands balanced on their shoulders. Others pushed dollies with huge metal cases full of equipment. The identification on the sides of the cases heralded the importance of this event: CNN, ABC, CBS, and NBC.

"Looks like this press conference is major news," Wes said to Annette. The wheels on the dollies rattled and clanged against the marble floor as they were being pushed toward the freight elevator. "I don't mind the publicity, but I can think of better ways to get it. It bothers me that this is all in the aftermath of tragedy."

The Regent was an atrium hotel with a soaring central column surrounded by rooms. Glass-walled elevators were located at either end of the massive lobby, which was filled with foliage, a swimming pool, and a children's play area. Wes took Annette's hand and walked to the nearest elevator. When the door opened he let Annette go first and then followed her, taking only one step beyond the closing door. Annette pushed her face to the glass to take in the view as the elevator rose toward the penthouse level. In contrast, Wes stayed as close to the stainless steel entry as possible.

"When are you going to get over your fear of heights?" Annette said, looking over her shoulder and motioning with her index finger for Wes to come nearer.

"Maybe never," Wes answered. "I'm the only one in my family like this, and it's something I've had as long as I can remember. If I went near that window, I'd feel like I was falling through the glass. The last thing in the world I need right now is a panic attack."

"Penthouse level, please exit." Wes hated those impersonal, technological innovations. It seemed too Orwellian to him, having some disembodied voice that wasn't a voice at all telling you where to go and what to do. He remembered the days when elevators were operated by real people, usually polite, old men in smart uniforms and white gloves. They would announce the floor, grab a handle, pull back a steel guard, and open the door with a flourish.

These days everything is too detached and interchangeable. Guess I am too. They're plugging me in this campaign like I'm an interchangeable part of the political process.

The elevator door opened, and Wes saw a hand-lettered sign taped to the opposite wall: "Stand for America News Conference, Room #2510." As they made their way down the hallway, Wes could see it was filled with more equipment dollies. On either side of the hallway, a half-dozen television cables lay like endless snakes.

"Follow those cables," Wes said to Annette. "Wherever they end up is where I face the press."

As Wes and Annette made their way down the hallway, they were passed by workmen carrying television equipment. At times they had to turn their bodies and move sideways, the hallway was so crowded. The noise that rose from room 2510 made it easy to identify. Wes and Annette stepped inside and watched the flurry of activity. A hastily painted "Stand for America" banner hung along a back wall. Reporters who knew each other were sharing gossip tidbits while others tried to find seats unobstructed by one of the half-dozen tripods that held glaring television lights.

Wes recognized many in the pack of reporters as part of the local press. Others apparently represented the national media. "That's Tom Benton," Wes whispered in Annette's ear as he pointed toward a handsome man being fitted with a cordless lapel microphone. "He anchors the ABC network news every night. I don't watch him, but half of America does."

Benton looks more like he belongs on a Hollywood set than at a news event, Wes thought. *Looking and sounding good are a lot more important than gutsy reporting these days.*

Suddenly Wes's eyes caught those of David Kelly, Baldwin's campaign manager. "Wes Bryant," Kelly called out across the room in his booming baritone voice. He grinned broadly as he headed toward Wes, his right arm outstretched. "Give me five! Haven't seen you, in what? Fifteen, no, nearly twenty years. How are doing, and who's this beautiful woman at your side, you old fox?"

Wes and Kelly shook hands, and Wes introduced Annette. *He sure hasn't lost any strength in those hands,* Wes concluded as he pulled back from Kelly's huge palm and inconspicuously rubbed his knuckles from the crush of Kelly's grip.

"I heard you're joining our campaign. Welcome aboard."

"What a coincidence, right?" Baldwin observed as he joined the group. "Three old college classmates from Indiana, all combining forces to straighten out the people of Colorado."

Wes wasn't sure what to think. "So when does this conference get started?"

"Right now," Kelly said. "As soon as I step to that podium. I'll make a brief statement and then introduce you as our interim press secretary."

"Better do it soon," Baldwin said, giving Kelly a firm nudge in the back. "If we run too late, we'll miss getting footage on the evening news. Wes, Annette, please follow me. You'll both be sitting with me behind the podium."

Wes and Annette looked at each other with the same apprehension. "I thought you agreed that this would be low-keyed," Wes said. "I'd prefer not to have Annette involved."

"I understand your concern," Baldwin assured Wes as he led them to the podium, "but I'm sure you can also see the importance of dispelling any anxiety the press has about Lewis's successor. They need to see a family man, someone who is stable, with a solid reputation in the city. Annette doesn't have to say a word. Her presence will speak volumes."

Wes knew Baldwin had a point, so he gently took Annette's hand and moved toward the podium. They were seated, and Kelly tapped the microphone several times to test it. Then he spoke as confidently as Wes remembered him taking on a 215-pound fullback.

"Ladies and gentlemen of the press, welcome. Most of you are acquainted with me. I'm David Kelly, an old friend of William Baldwin and the manager of his primary campaign. I realize last night's tragic circumstances have made you give up a weekend to cover the story, but we'll make this as brief as possible."

Kelly planted his rock-hard frame with a wide stance. He looked indomitable as he placed his hands on either side of the podium. "Mr. Baldwin wants you to know that he is deeply saddened by last night's misfortune and that every effort will be made to uncover why Mr. Lewis chose to end his life under such unusual circumstances. Bill Baldwin also wants the friends and family of Alex Lewis to know that all of us in the Stand for America Party will include them in our prayers during this hour of grief."

At that, Kelly lowered his head and cleared his throat. "In a moment I want to introduce you to Mr. Lewis's replacement, but first I'll take a couple of questions from the floor."

Hands everywhere shot in the air in unison, but no one yelled out. Kelly glanced across the room several times and said, "Albert Mason, of the *Denver Observer,* you can go first."

Mason stood slowly and looked unsure of himself. "That strange monologue Lewis gave before he shot himself . . . do you have any idea what it was about? What did he mean about being silent?" Mason glanced at the pad he was holding to refresh his memory. "And what was he referring to when he said your candidate had to tell something? Frankly it all sounded a little suspicious."

Mason sat down as Kelly shifted his weight nervously and shot a glance at the reporter. "I wish we knew . . . we all wish we knew. To be honest, the whole thing was so irrational I don't think we should put too much stock in what Lewis said. If he was ready to shoot himself, whatever stress he was under could have disoriented him, perhaps causing him to experience paranoia. We'd like to give Lewis's family some semblance of dignity surrounding his death. There are extenuating circumstances, which for the privacy of his family, we are not at liberty to discuss at this time."

Mason raised his hand and started to his feet again. But before he could stand, Kelly looked to the other side of the room. "Mary Ann Kindle of the *Consolidated Press.*"

"Yes, Mr. Kelly," the irascible elder stateswoman of the Denver press corp responded. "Isn't the public going to wonder how stable your campaign is if one of your key people shoots himself while posing some strange, unanswered questions?"

Before she could go on, Kelly snapped back. "That's why this press conference was called today, so you can meet Mr. Lewis's replacement. And that's what I'd like to . . ."

"Mr. Kelly, I'd like to ask a question," a reporter demanded.

Kelly turned slightly to his right and reached out his arm in the direction of Wes as the interrupting reporter continued. "I'm afraid your response leaves some important facts unaddressed. If I may . . ."

"I was about to introduce Mr. Lewis's . . ."

"I realize that, sir, but if I may just ask one more question before you do?"

Kelly seemed irritated, as if he wanted the flow of events to proceed without any unpleasantness. "I suppose you may, but this is an especially painful time for all of us. Please be brief, Mr. . . ."

"Taylor, Stanley Taylor of the *Citizens' Gazette.* It's the official publication of a voters' advocacy group concerned about restoring family values in our state. I'd like to know if your party is going to continue calling for gender-neutral legislation, like homosexual adoption rights?"

Kelly stiffened his body so his large frame seemed to grow by several inches. He looked like a rottweiler about ready to take a bite from someone's leg. He leaned forward. "Mr. Taylor, if you're going to turn this tragic time into a debate about whether a narrow-minded minority can impose their bigotry on the compassionate citizens of this state . . ."

"No need for insults!" Taylor shot back. "Just answer the question."

Baldwin abruptly stepped to Kelly's side. With all the smoothness acquired from years of perfecting the art of political compromise, he said, "Mr. Taylor, we of the Stand for America Party appreciate your concerns, and at another more appropriate time we'll be happy to respond. But right now it appears unseemly to engage in a heated exchange about an issue the courts of this state have decided is best left to competent judges rather than the legislative process."

Baldwin had gained the upper hand and seized the opportunity to continue. "I'd like to introduce a dear old friend who shares much in common with the ideals of the Stand for America Party, Mr. Wes Bryant, owner and general manager of radio station KVCE. He will be assuming the late Mr. Lewis's duties for the remainder of the campaign. On the table in the back of the room you'll find a resumé sheet with complete details on Mr. Bryant's background and qualifications. Now I'd like Mr. Bryant and his lovely wife to stand."

Baldwin stepped back from the podium in deference to Wes and Annette who rose to the sound of polite applause.

Why did Baldwin forget to emphasize, as I requested, that my position was strictly temporary?

Wes had anticipated saying a few words to the press and had rehearsed them in his mind while driving in the car. To his surprise, Baldwin stepped back to the podium and resumed speaking without asking him for a single statement.

"Mr. Bryant will be available for questions at a later date. In the meantime, I ask you to remember the devastating circumstances we've all been through. Please be understanding of our reluctance to discuss things in detail at this time. Thank you for your time."

His words were greeted by shouts of indignation. A dozen reporters rushed the podium and cornered him before he could move. Kelly placed his bulky frame in front of Wes and Annette to protect them from the crush of cameras and microphones. Baldwin tried to excuse himself, but the media wouldn't budge. He finally tossed back a few of their interrogation volleys. Yes, he had noticed Lewis was a little depressed in recent weeks, Baldwin said, but considering the stress of the brutal campaign they had been through he didn't consider that unusual. No, the police hadn't opened an investigation since Lewis's suicide was an act witnessed by hundreds. Yes, he was concerned that the public might recoil from his candidacy because of the traumatic events, but he hoped he would still be judged by his position on the issues. No, he wouldn't be taking much time off before starting the general election campaign, and he would shortly release a report defining his position on every essential campaign issue.

In the midst of the crowd Wes saw Tom Benton, ABC's evening news anchor, motion to Baldwin, who excused himself as courteously as possible. Baldwin edged his way toward a corner of the room where Benton's entourage had constructed a makeshift set, complete with chairs and a false backdrop of the Denver skyline. Kelly took Wes and Annette by the arm and began directing them toward a rear exit.

Wes was glad to be outside the raucous room. "The rudeness of the press was even worse than I expected," he commented. Then he remembered that Baldwin had failed to announce that Wes's position was transitional. "Why didn't Bill do as I had asked and point out my job as press secretary is only temporary? And why wasn't I asked to say something?"

"Things didn't exactly go the way we had planned," a visibly shaken Kelly responded. "I suppose that after that Taylor character tried to disrupt the conference, some things slipped Bill's mind. He also may have thought it was best to avoid putting you in a situation where you might face issues we haven't fully briefed you on yet."

"What issues?"

"No time to go into that now, Wes. You'll get your political education later," Kelly said smiling warmly. "Right now, we need to get out of here before some reporter who spotted us leaving decides to come after us for one last scoop."

The three made their way down a service entry hallway to the freight elevator. "You and Annette take this," Kelly ordered. "You'll be less likely to be spotted since any reporters will expect you to get off one of the regular elevators."

Kelly punched the elevator button on the wall and started back down the hallway toward the press conference room.

"David," Wes called out. "Just one question. What was that Taylor guy so concerned about? What did he mean by gender-neutral legislation?"

Kelly stopped cold and turned around slowly, his eyes flashing with indignation. "Taylor is one of those homophobic fanatics who wants to tell other people what they can do with their bodies, like women who are in need of medical care."

"Medical care?"

Kelly's body went rigid with disgust for Taylor. He doubled his huge right fist and pounded it into his left palm, rhythmically pounding out a cadence of his frustration. "Abortion," Kelly growled, "a woman's right to control her own body!"

"What's that got to do with homo . . ."

"Homophobia!" Kelly interrupted. "Taylor is a bigot. I don't know how he got into the news conference. He thinks we're still living in some kind of puritanical age where religious extremists can dictate what other people do in their bedrooms. He was a leader in the state legislative fight to pass a disgusting resolution that called for the outlawing of adoption rights for loving couples who might live together in circumstances Taylor's kind don't approve of."

"You mean homosexuals, gays?"

"Labels aren't important, Wes. Love is."

Wes wasn't exactly sure how to say it, but he knew how he felt. "Yes," he responded, "but isn't putting children in that kind of environment morally, uh . . . wrong?"

Kelly's expression turned gravely serious, and he took several steps toward Wes until his imposing physique loomed over Wes just outside the elevator door. "Do you have a problem with people choosing who they will love and how they will love?" he asked redundantly.

The elevator alarm rang, and the door started to close. Annette put her hand on the edge of the door while she waited for Wes to enter.

"I can't say I've given the issue a lot of thought, but I guess I am a little worried about a kid being raised in that environment. Yeah, I suppose I have a problem with it."

"Well, then," Kelly said smiling slightly, "that's something you really need to talk to Bill about."

"I'll do that," Wes answered, stepping into the elevator.

Kelly turned to leave, then stopped just before Annette removed her hand, allowing the door to close.

"Wes," Kelly said looking over his shoulder. "There's something you need to know. I'm gay!"

4

As the choir repeated the lyrics "It is well with my soul," Wes felt emotionally lifted by the assurance of the hymn's message.

I've missed church the last couple of weeks. It's good to be here. I've got to cut back on my involvement in the business over weekends.

The song sank deep within his spirit and lodged in a place that needed nourishment. All was not well with Wes's soul, and he knew it had to do with his new role as press secretary for Bill Baldwin's senatorial campaign.

"Will you all stand and sing from your hymnals song number 123, 'A Mighty Fortress Is Our God,'" instructed Jefferson Carson, a stout, well-dressed African-American in his early thirties. "While we sing, the youngsters may be dismissed for their special children's service. Everyone, now, lift your voices in song."

As the words to the hymn reverberated off the dark oak beams of the sanctuary's cathedral ceiling, Wes's thoughts were far away. He held the hymnal in his right hand and wrapped his other around Annette's waist and gave her a hug. She responded with a warm, receptive smile that reminded him how much his life had changed since ten years ago when she had brought her love and her faith into his life.

Wes traced Annette's countenance with his eyes. Her soft complexion hardly showed the trace of a wrinkle from her forty-plus years. Her silky brown hair lay softly on her shoulders, and the vibrancy of her expression demonstrated a woman who found her greatest joy in the satisfaction of relationships with those nearest her.

Wes's fifty-three-year-old frame straightened with confidence whenever he was reminded how much Annette had influenced every aspect of his existence, from his once uninspiring wardrobe to his complacent attitude about life's responsibilities. His receding hairline had called a truce and apparently stabilized for the passage toward age sixty. His six-foot frame still stood erect, thanks to a vigorous physical-fitness regimen that included daily jogs and twice-a-week trips to the tennis court. *Annette is a good woman. I never imagined life could be this good, and it wouldn't be without her.*

He leaned forward slightly and smiled at his stepdaughter, Jennifer, who sat on the other side of Annette. Jennifer was a student at Rocky Mountain Christian College, and they had just celebrated her nineteenth birthday. The three of them had fought some enormous battles that stemmed from Jennifer's past sexual abuse at the hands of her real father.

Jennifer noticed Wes looking at her and smiled back. Her long, blonde hair, which she had spent a lifetime growing and nurturing, had been recently replaced by a more severe cut that reflected her active freshman lifestyle. She dressed in the latest "Generation X" fashions but tempered the usual sloppiness, oversized flannel shirts and billowy skirts, with feminine accessories. At church, she always wore her Sunday finest. God was the most important thing in her life, and she seldom missed attending church and her Spiritual Life classes at college.

The congregation continued singing, "For still our ancient foe, Doth seek to work us woe." But the refrain, "It is well with my soul," from the choir's earlier number, kept repeating in Wes's mind. *So why isn't everything well with my soul?*

Deep inside he knew. It was David Kelly's shocking revelation and Stanley Taylor's probing questions. Above all, it was his commitment to a political campaign in support of someone he knew well from the past but not the present.

"You may be seated," Carson directed.

Wes hadn't noticed the song was finished, so he was still standing as the congregation of several hundred sat down. Annette tugged gently at his suit coat and rolled her eyes sideways, steering him downward to his seat. With his head momentarily above the crowd Wes spotted someone on the church platform.

Taylor? That looks like the guy at the press conference yesterday!

Carson quickly confirmed Wes's suspicion. "Before Pastor Ridgeway comes to deliver this morning's message, we're going to hear from someone most of you know. A man who has taken on a huge task for the Lord. He's a servant of God who has faced unbelievable opposition, standing for the old-fashioned values that most of us grew up with. Put your hands together and welcome our brother in Christ, Stanley Taylor."

Some in the multiracial congregation took Carson's cue to express themselves with uninhibited enthusiasm, rocking from side-to-side as they clapped. Some waved their hands in the air, palms facing upward in exhilaration. Others who were slightly more reserved but equally ardent showed their excitement by the smiles on their faces.

Taylor maintained the same earnest demeanor he had displayed at the Regent Hotel's news conference but seemed humbled by their excitement. Wes could tell this was a no-nonsense man, dedicated to his cause.

Before stepping away from the pulpit, Carson added, "Many of you have supported the efforts of brother Taylor's Restore Our Heritage Crusade. If you want to know what issues currently concern his group, be sure to check the literature he's placed on the table by the back left exit. And remember what brother Taylor keeps telling us," he said as he shook his fist in the air, "register, vote, get involved, and get God back into government. Now, Stanley, take your liberty to share what's on your heart."

Taylor stepped up to the pulpit and thanked Carson. He laid his large, burgundy leather Bible and a small stack of books on the side of the lectern.

He glanced down for a moment as if collecting his thoughts and then looked intently at the congregation.

"Many of you know who I am and what my crusade is all about," he began. "You know that I didn't ask for this responsibility and fought God at first before I yielded to His will. But like Jonah, I had no choice. I had to go to my Nineveh, the state of Colorado, and deliver the message God gave me."

Taylor propped himself on one elbow and stretched across the top of the pulpit to project his message more personally to the audience.

"I'm just an average person, like you. I operate a small carpet-cleaning business and have never wanted to be in the public eye. This mission started when my eleven-year-old daughter, Rhonda, brought home some suggested-reading books that were part of an experimental education program. The school board called it a 'cultural diversity curriculum.' Sounds harmless enough, doesn't it?" Taylor asked.

Wes watched the audience on both sides of him and saw most people nod in agreement.

Taylor grabbed one of the books on the pulpit and thrust it in the air. He leaned forward and yelled into the microphone, "Well . . . this is one of Rhonda's books!"

A murmur swept through the congregation as people strained to see the cover of the book. Those toward the back shrugged their shoulders, but from the front pews several polite gasps could be heard.

"It's called *Dennis Has Two Daddies*," Taylor explained as he waved the book back and forth in subdued anger. "You probably can't make out the small print on the cover, so let me read you the line under the title: 'The story of a different kind of family where love is what matters most.'"

Taylor slammed the book on top of the pulpit. Some members of the congregation flinched, not only from the thud of the hardcover book hitting the wooden pulpit and reverberating in the microphone, but from their disgust at what he had just revealed to them.

Taylor sighed deeply and continued. "The school my daughter attends banned Christmas carols last year and recently shut down an after-school

Bible club that was meeting voluntarily. In contrast they are encouraging the reading of books that suggest the traditional mother-father family of a man and a woman is outdated. Let me read a passage."

Taylor picked up the book and thumbed through several pages. The congregation was so still Wes thought that the proverbial church mouse could have been heard. Older members averted their eyes in slight embarrassment while young adults sat up straighter and perked their ears attentively.

"Here it is, page fifty-six," Taylor went on. "'Dennis is different, but that makes him special. Instead of having a mommy and a daddy, he has two daddies. The daddies love each other, and they both love Dennis. Sometimes, the other children at school make fun of Dennis because he has two daddies, but that is mean and hateful. Dennis thinks he is a special little boy because there is always at least one daddy to take him fishing or to the baseball game. Instead of feeling sorry for Dennis, you might wish you had two daddies too!'"

This time Taylor lowered the book slowly and placed it gingerly on top of his Bible. He gently patted both books and stared determinedly at the congregation. "Friends, we have to make a choice in this state. Do we want other Dennises to have two daddies—or two mommies? Or will we limit adoption and child custody to heterosexuals?"

Wes glanced at Annette, who looked straight ahead without flinching. He leaned back slightly to look past Annette and get a glimpse of Jennifer. She was equally intent and nodded her head slightly in agreement with Taylor's concerns.

"This fall you have the opportunity to make a difference at the polls. I can't tell you who to vote for, but I can tell you to check every candidate's position on gender-identity issues. Oh, by the way, you might also ask them how they feel about abortion. Those two issues usually go hand-in-hand." Taylor took a step back from the pulpit and lowered his voice to a more tractable tone. "My special thanks to Reverend Ridgeway, and you, too, Jefferson," he said, turning to acknowledge both men before again addressing the audience. "If you need more information about our Restore

Our Heritage Crusade, my number is on the brochures on the table, and I'll be there after the sermon to answer any questions."

During the rest of the church service, the phrase "Love is what matters most" haunted Wes's thoughts until it blocked out anything Reverend Ridgeway was saying. *Those are almost the exact words Kelly used,* he reminded himself.

The pastoral benediction startled Wes back to the present. Reverend Ridgeway had finished his sermon and was heading down the center aisle toward the back of the church to shake hands with those leaving.

"Dad, I spotted some friends I haven't seen in several weeks. Do you mind if I take a few minutes to say hello?"

"No problem, Jennifer. We'll meet you at the car."

Annette hung on to Wes's arm, and they slowly made their way toward one of the exit doors as Jennifer headed in the opposite direction. Wes felt uncomfortable sneaking out the back of a church, trying to avoid one man. Behind the radio microphone, he faced criminals and con men. More than once someone had tried to verbally get the best of him and failed. Now he was inching toward an exit to avoid a man in the business of cleaning carpets.

"Mr. Bryant!"

Wes sank back on his heels. He looked over his shoulder to see who had called him.

"Excuse me, Mr. Bryant."

Wes turned around to see Stanley Taylor standing in front of him with one hand outstretched to shake his, the other hand holding a stack of paper.

"I hope you'll not consider my speaking with you to be an imposition," Taylor said confidently. "Someone told me you were present this morning, and I wanted the privilege of meeting you."

Wes reminded himself that this was a minor inconvenience compared to the more dire incidents he had faced before. He shook Taylor's hand, but he felt his face turning red. "It's a pleasure to meet you. This is my wife, Annette," Wes said.

"My pleasure," Taylor responded, dipping his head slightly in Annette's direction. "May I offer you these pamphlets about our crusade?"

"Certainly," Wes answered, taking the pamphlets and placing them in his suit-coat pocket. "Thank you."

Wes cupped Annette's elbow in his arm and gently nudged her toward the door. Seconds later they were outside and walking in the direction of their parked car.

"I wonder what Taylor's literature is about?" Wes mused aloud.

He took a slick, glossy pamphlet entitled *Hard Facts about Abortion* from his pocket. He glanced through the opening paragraph and then turned the page.

"This is disgusting!" Wes blurted out as he stopped abruptly.

"What's disgusting?" Annette inquired.

"Taylor has printed a vivid, color photograph of a bloody, dead fetus. Its arms and legs are mutilated, and it's been decapitated!"

5

The clock read 8:00 on this cloudy Monday morning, April 25, and Wes knew he had to call his office and let the staff know of his plans. He dialed the phone on the desk in his den, and Deborah Jennings, his secretary, answered her direct line.

"Deborah, I don't plan to be in today."

"Wes," Deborah said with a pensive tone, "the entire office is buzzing about what happened over the weekend. Your staff is in turmoil, and I suggest you get things calmed down. Some are wondering if you're resigning from your duties at the station or if you may just sell it."

Wes rubbed his forehead with his outstretched hand. "Resign! Where did they get that crazy idea?"

"At the news conference," Deborah answered. "The suicide and your appointment to Bill Baldwin's campaign were the hottest news items in the state all weekend. Get real, Boss," Deborah said with uncharacteristic boldness. "How are you going to help run a major senatorial campaign and manage the city's number one radio station?"

"It's temporary, Deborah." Wes paused for a moment and then reassured her. "I'm only an interim press secretary. This isn't permanent."

"They didn't say that on TV," Deborah reminded him.

"It was an oversight."

"If it was an oversight, you can tell that to Mr. Baldwin yourself. He called first thing when our offices opened this morning and asked to speak to you," Deborah said. "I wasn't sure when you'd be in. Baldwin said to have you call right away. Something about a strategy-planning session this afternoon."

"This afternoon? At one o'clock I'm meeting with our station's biggest client, Jim Robinson's Honda & Toyota. You know that, Deborah. You told Baldwin, didn't you?"

Deborah paused. "I was so stunned to be talking to the man who may be our next U.S. senator, I was dumbfounded. I said I'd give you the message. Sorry if that isn't the way you wanted it handled."

Wes pushed back his chair and kicked his feet up on top of the old-fashioned rolltop desk. "You did all right, Deborah. Did Baldwin leave a number?"

"Yes, 555-2666. Kind of a spooky number for a politician, huh?"

"Spooky? Oh, the 666 at the end?"

"Yeah, and from what some people say about Baldwin, he's either an angel or a devil!"

Wes didn't want to start a political or religious discussion. After all, both topics were guaranteed to spark controversy with someone as strong-willed as Deborah, and the two topics were sure to keep him on the line longer than he wanted.

"Call Jim Robinson for me. Tell him something urgent has come up and I'll get with him at his convenience tomorrow. Apologize profusely."

"I'll do it, but are you sure you want to risk your biggest account?"

"Please do as I ask," Wes said. "Tell the staff not to worry. I'll explain all of this to them the first chance I get."

"One more thing before you go," Deborah added. "A courier delivered a package about fifteen minutes ago. You've always given me the option of opening any mail I thought might not be personal. Well, there was no return address on the package, so I opened it."

The phone went silent as Wes waited for Deborah to continue. The quiet lasted so long he wondered if they had been disconnected. "Deborah?"

"Sorry, Boss, this is a little embarrassing. I opened the box and inside was a jar. It was full of . . ."

"Yes, full of what?"

"H-h-horse manure!"

"Horse manure?"

"That's what I said, Boss. There was a note inside. Do you want me to read it?"

"No, Deborah, just leave me sitting here wondering why someone sent me a bottle of you-know-what!" Wes retorted sarcastically.

"Okay, don't get irritated at me. Anyway, the note said, 'Enjoy your new job, you gay-loving . . .' Wes, I'd rather not repeat what this person called you. You can read it yourself when you get to the office."

"That's it?"

"No. It says, 'Get away from Baldwin now or you'll end up like Lewis!'"

"Don't touch the jar, the package, or anything else. And don't say anything about this to the rest of the staff."

"That's a little late. Everyone heard me shriek when I opened the box. I suspect by now the whole office knows. But they didn't see the note. I kept that to myself."

"Good. I'll be back in touch later, after I've called Baldwin."

Wes realized that his favor to an old friend was clearly getting out of hand. The choice between Baldwin and business was bad enough, but the death threat affected his family. Wes dialed Baldwin's number. The phone rang, and he recognized Baldwin's mellow voice. "Stand for America executive office. Can I help you?"

"Bill? It's me, Wes. I didn't expect you to answer the phone."

"I gave your secretary my private office number. Wes, we've called an emergency strategy-planning session for 1:30 P.M. I must insist on your attending. Some things have come up we hadn't anticipated, and we need you urgently. In addition, I'd like to talk with you privately beforehand at about 1:15."

Wes confirmed he would make the meeting, hung up the phone, and sought out Annette to inform her of his plans. She was in the kitchen having a morning cup of coffee, seated at her new kitchen table, a late-nineteenth-century English reproduction with artificially distressed scratches and gouges. She had encouraged Wes to get rid of their old maple dinette set in favor of something more traditional.

He quickly told her about his meeting with Baldwin. "I'll stay at home this morning and take care of some personal business, then go directly to meet Baldwin."

Annette pushed the chair next to her away from the table so Wes could join her. "Saturday was the news conference, and today is another meeting. Something tells me this part-time job is going to demand your full-time devotion. Is that what you really want?"

"No, I don't think so, and I'm going to tell Baldwin that today," Wes hesitated for a moment, wondering if perhaps he should tell Annette about the threatening letter. *No sense upsetting her now until I can see the stuff for myself.*

"I'd like to join you at the table, Honey, but with half my day gone this afternoon, I'd best get to the stuff on my desk. I'll check the driveway for the newspaper so you can read it if you'd like."

"Perhaps my number one man will be on the front page," Annette said, smiling as she reached out her hand to touch Wes's. "We should have gotten a newspaper yesterday to see what they said about the news conference. My guess is they will still be playing the story out this morning since a lot of people don't pay attention to the news over the weekend."

Wes walked to the front door. The entry to their home was about fifty yards from the main road, and the paper boy was consistently careless about where he tossed the plastic-wrapped newspaper. Sometimes he dropped it close to the entrance on the main road. Other mornings he'd pedal his bike up the slight incline to send it sailing nearer the house. Wes glanced down the driveway and saw that this time the boy's aim was short.

He paused for a moment on the porch and took in his surroundings.

He loved living in this state, with its crisp spring mornings when green blades of mountain grass were just starting to poke through the ground.

Wes stepped off the porch, rounded the corner of the garage, and stopped dead in his tracks. Laying there, out of view from the house, was what appeared to be a bloody, dead baby. It looked so real Wes thought for a split second it might actually be a murdered child. Its decapitated head was sitting on top of its chest.

After the initial shock, Wes could see that it was a child's doll, splattered with some kind of slime and what he surmised was red food coloring. As Wes knelt down beside the form he noticed an envelope, tucked underneath it. He broke off a stick from a nearby bush and pushed aside the doll. As he did, the head fell off and rolled several feet down the driveway. Even though he knew it was someone's idea of a prank, it sent a chill up his spine.

Quickly he opened the envelope and took out a note inside. It read:

Dear press secretary,

Now that you've joined the abortion baby killers, you need to understand something. Saving the lives of a thousand babies is worth ending your life!

Wes watched the skyline of Denver pass by his window as he navigated the I-25 freeway southbound toward the southeast section of the city. He entered the suburb of Glendale and quickly got off the freeway at the Pine Castle exit, then turned right onto Stalker Street. He glanced at his wristwatch and saw that it was nearly one o'clock in the afternoon. He was still at least fifteen minutes from Baldwin's campaign headquarters, so he called on his car's cellular phone and left a message with the receptionist that he'd be a few minutes late.

Wes's thoughts continued to seek answers to questions about the events of the morning. As he had feared, the *Rocky Mountain Journal's* front page had featured Saturday's news conference and Baldwin's senatorial aspirations. Wes was on the front page, in color, just under the nameplate, standing next to a grinning David Kelly. *Did the guy who sent the jar to the office see that picture in the paper? Did he know about Kelly's private life?*

As far as the decapitated doll was concerned, Wes had never given much thought to the issue of abortion. Now he was being called a baby killer. He thought of abortion like almost everyone else he knew; he didn't like the idea, but sometimes it seemed necessary and he felt it should be available to those who wanted it, though he hesitated about asking taxpayers to fund it. Anyway, who could be against people having the freedom to make up their own minds about such a highly personal decision?

Wes honked at a dump truck loaded with gravel that had pulled in front of his car, interrupting thoughts he realized he must confront. Abortion and homosexuality had been just matters he read about, and topics he heard late night talk show hosts joke about. Now that he had become the object of hate and possible harm, he had to take a personal stand.

Wes eased his steel gray Nexus into the right lane of South Lincoln Boulevard. Just a few buildings away he saw the massive red, white, and blue star-studded sign designating the Stand for America Party headquarters. He pulled into a parking lot next door, dropped four quarters into a numbered honor system slot in a metal box, and headed to the front door.

Wes had envisioned the party headquarters as a storefront operation, temporarily rented, with dozens of young, scruffy volunteers scurrying about carrying stacks of papers in their arms. He had expected to see a bank of phone operators making solicitation calls from makeshift cubicles, and the entire environment, he thought, would reek of stale coffee and cigarette smoke. Instead he looked up at a five-story building with reflective copper-colored windows and stainless steel trim, much like a successful bank building. Even the Stand for America sign was not the usual political placard painted on plywood. It was chiseled into a copper plate, conveying the image that the operation was there to stay.

Inside the foyer Wes was greeted by a smiling receptionist who took his name and asked him to be seated on a plush couch surrounded by the fragrant array of broad-leafed plants. The thick pile carpeting, walnut-paneled walls, and tastefully furnished appointments exuded a sense of serenity and confidence.

In front of him on the coffee table were plastic-bound copies of business magazines and political journals. The decor upstaged even the most opulent doctor's office. On the walls were tasteful pictures of Baldwin campaigning, Baldwin posing with dignitaries, and an entire section devoted to scenes of Baldwin and his family, bicycling, having a picnic, skiing.

"Wes, thanks for getting here a little early." Baldwin appeared out of nowhere and motioned to an inconspicuous door just around the corner from the elevators. "Let's get away to my office for a couple of minutes and have a heart-to-heart talk before the tough part of today's schedule gets started."

Baldwin stepped before an oversized wooden door with a security keypad. He punched in several numbers, a buzzer went off, and the door automatically slid sideways into the wall, permitting their entry. As they stepped through, the door automatically closed behind them. Baldwin led Wes into the most extravagantly furnished executive setting he had ever seen. Even though there was no way to see outside, the office's interior was so big and beautiful Wes felt like it had a window on the world.

A massive aquarium that looked more like it belonged in a marine park covered an entire wall at least twenty feet long. Neon-hued tropical fish darted in and out of brilliantly colored coral. Larger fish, and what looked to be an actual shark, floated lazily through the four-foot-deep tank. The opposite wall was covered with a holographic image that changed shapes as Wes moved across the room. Wes didn't want to be too conspicuous so he only glanced at the image out of the corner of his eye. He noticed it was a series of three-dimensional, interlocking triangles surrounded by a kaleidoscope of colors that changed hues with each step he took.

Baldwin's desk was a baroque Louis XIV-style table. No filing cabinets. No drawers. No staplers, scissors, photocopiers, or fax machines. A single, early-twentieth-century-style phone with a ceramic handle rested in its U-shaped cradle. Whatever went on in this office didn't including shuffling paperwork. And the mirror-backed shelves behind the desk contained only a few selected books, mostly classics.

The conference table at the far end of the room looked big enough to seat a dozen or so people. In the center of the room, a ten-foot-wide staghorn chandelier dominated any upward glances.

Baldwin gestured for Wes to be seated in a large, comfortable-looking chair directly opposite the desk. Baldwin started to step behind the desk but paused halfway and sat down on the desktop, his right foot rigidly against the floor, his left leg dangling off the edge of the desk. He folded his arms across his chest and looked at Wes seriously. Wes locked onto Baldwin's gaze as he sat down.

"I'm afraid the position I planned for you isn't going to work out," he said.

Wes was startled. He was prepared to let Baldwin know his time on the campaign would be limited, but Baldwin was beating him to it. The words, "That's all right, Bill, I feel the same way," were on his lips as Baldwin interrupted.

"Being a temporary press secretary won't be enough. I've got to have you stay on for the full campaign!"

Baldwin unfolded his arms and signaled with his right hand as if to shut Wes up before he said anything. "I know what you're thinking, Wes. You're wondering how I can ask you to serve full time after I gave my word that wouldn't be necessary. Hear me out before you object."

Baldwin moved around the desk and sat down in a high-backed, black leather chair. He picked up a red burl-wood Mont Blanc pen lying on top of a tan pad of paper and flipped it back and forth between his fingers as he collected his thoughts.

"I know it's asking too much of you, and you have every right to turn me down if that's your decision. But if you don't take the job full time, I will lose this election. You're the only one who has the verbal skills to counter the evil, bigoted forces that are determined to stop my senatorial bid. Wes, you have no idea what I'm up against. My enemies will stop at nothing. You've already seen what they did to Lewis!"

Baldwin reached for a picture frame sitting on top of his desk, a photograph of him and his wife lounging at a seaside villa with a Mediterranean charm. "I love Candy too much to risk taking on this task without your assistance. It would be too dangerous. If someone doesn't speak forcefully for me, as I know you can, Wes, things will get out of hand."

Wes sat quietly as Baldwin cradled the photograph. Whatever Baldwin's political persuasions, Wes felt solace for Baldwin and his concerns for his wife.

Wes took advantage of Baldwin's silence to press his case. "Bill, I hear everything you are saying, and I appreciate the confidence you place in my abilities, but I just can't do it. I have a family, too, and I have other obligations to my business that can't be overlooked. I consented to our meeting today because I wanted to tell you I'm resigning immediately as your press secretary. It's not a question of whether it's a permanent or temporary position. I need out now."

Baldwin set the portrait down on his desk, took a deep breath, and walked over to the fish tank. He bent over slightly and peered into the coral, tapping lightly on the glass to arouse several small seahorses that were feeding near one of the coral clusters. Then he walked back to his desk and opened a drawer. He took out a sheet of paper and laid it facedown on the table. He also took out a small Chinese cloisonné box about four inches square and set it in the center of the table.

Baldwin looked at Wes intensely. "Perhaps you need to know why I'm in this campaign. It's not about power or ambition. Money isn't an issue, either; I've already got more of that than I can use from my real estate investments. This campaign is about Rebecca."

Baldwin took the sheet of paper and handed it to Wes. It was a photocopy of a newspaper clipping dated October 30 from the previous year. In the center was a picture of Baldwin, his wife, and his daughter, all skiing in Aspen. The caption read, "Rebecca Baldwin falls to her death while climbing near Centennial Peak area."

"I'm sorry, Bill. I remember seeing this article, and I should have called you last fall when I read about this. She was a beautiful young lady."

Baldwin took a handkerchief from his hip pocket and wiped away tears that were rolling down his cheeks. "She was more than that, Wes. Rebecca was an honor student; she played in the junior symphony orchestra and was looking forward to graduating from college and pursuing a medical career. You never met a more loving, caring individual in your life. She always put others before herself whether it was an injured bird she brought home as a child or some less fortunate friend she brought home for dinner during her college years. Rebecca was a saint and my only little girl."

Baldwin continued wiping the tears as he gained his composure. He reached down and gently picked up the enamel-lacquered box and held it as if it were some kind of precious stone. Then he opened the lid and walked toward Wes, holding the box in front of him.

"Look inside," Baldwin said.

Wes looked closely, but all he could see was a small pile of gray-colored material. "Go ahead; touch it, Wes."

Wes hesitantly put the tip of his index finger against whatever was in the box.

"This is Rebecca," Baldwin explained. "It's her ashes. I keep them in my desk to have her near me."

Wes instinctively withdrew his finger. He felt embarrassed that something so important to Baldwin had been a momentary sense of revulsion to him.

"It's okay, Wes," Baldwin said as he put his hand on Wes's shoulder. "I understand it's not every day you run into somebody who keeps the ashes of his dead daughter in his desk."

A small smile crossed Baldwin's lips. "This is the reason I started the Stand for America Party. Rebecca didn't accidentally fall from that cliff, as the news article describes. Rebecca was a victim of the intolerance and hate of Taylor's Restore Our Heritage Crusade. Taylor hounded her mercilessly and ridiculed her wherever she went."

Baldwin slowly closed the lid on the box and returned it to the drawer in his desk. Then he leaned forward, both fists clenched on top of his desk, supporting the full force of his body. He squarely faced Wes. "Rebecca was the sweetest young lady who ever walked the face of this earth. She jumped to her death. She committed suicide because she couldn't take the harassment from Taylor's people anymore. Rebecca was a lesbian."

6

Every argument Wes had to counter Baldwin's request crumbled. How could he refuse a man who so poignantly pleaded for help over the ashes of his dead daughter? Part of Wes felt emotionally violated by being placed in an impossible position. The other part genuinely felt compassion as he thought of his own stepdaughter, Jennifer, and how he would respond if she had tragically been driven to the brink of suicide.

Baldwin spoke. "You don't have to decide now about resigning or taking the job full time. At least come to our strategy meeting and get a better idea of what our party is all about."

Wes saw no harm in that. Besides, no matter what the decision, he was curious why whoever delivered the manure and doll was so opposed to Stand for America's politics.

"I'll stay, but no promises, Bill."

Baldwin smiled, walked over to Wes, and reached out to grip the sides of his shoulders with both hands. He looked Wes squarely in the eye with a sincerity Wes hadn't seen in Baldwin before.

"I knew God brought us together for a reason," Baldwin declared. "And to think, after all these years, the man on whom I am leaning the most is the man who knows me best by my roots back in Indiana."

Wes felt a little uncomfortable with the compliment, but reached up and squeezed Baldwin's right wrist as a gesture of solidarity.

"Come on," Baldwin admonished as he headed toward a door next to the aquarium. "Everyone is already waiting for us. This afternoon will be the most important meeting of my political career."

He opened the door and led Wes down a tunnel-like, ten-foot hallway to another door. As they neared, Wes could faintly hear voices on the other side. Baldwin knocked on the door with a strange staccato cadence, and it opened inward. David Kelly was the first to greet Baldwin and shake his hand. A woman and two other men quickly stood to acknowledge his entry, and Baldwin headed to the head chair at the end of a conference table.

Then Dave Kelly spotted Wes. "Welcome, Wes. We've all been anxiously awaiting your arrival. Please be seated next to Bill, but first let me introduce you to the others," he said and turned toward the group. "This is Ladonna Gallagher, who handles our scheduling."

Wes leaned across the table and shook Gallagher's hand. Her dark brown hair was carefully trimmed in the latest fashion, and she smiled pleasantly. She had a studied sensuality about her; but in her gray wool two-piece suit her appeal seemed one dimensional, as if it had been contrived on the pages of one too many romance magazines.

"Robert Cusco is our liaison to handle relationships with special interest groups," Kelly explained.

Wes turned to his right and shook the hand of this young political turk whose round-rimmed glasses and tense mannerisms reminded Wes of someone who had political aspirations of his own.

"Ralph Winston is our advertising and public relations director," Dave Kelly added as he directed Wes's attention to a tall, plainly dressed man on his left. *Looks like he belongs in an accounting firm,* Wes concluded.

It was an unpretentious group, sort of what Wes expected from a party formed out of populist discontent: Kelly, campaign manager, handsome and articulate; Gallagher, scheduling secretary, cool and efficient; Cusco, special interest liaison, ambitious and manipulative; Winston, public relations, detached and methodical.

"Let's get started," Baldwin said as he motioned for everyone to be seated. He glanced through some papers that had been set on the table in front of his chair then slipped a pair of bifocals out of his suit pocket and put them on.

"Winston, how's the damage control progressing? Have you pulled the right strings to make sure the story about Lewis gets buried fast before any more questions are asked?"

The PR man grabbed his briefcase and scrambled through a couple of documents he handed to Baldwin. "It's all here in these papers, sir," Winston answered. "The wire services are under control and know where their limits are, and the major dailies in the state have relegated coverage to news briefs. Not a single editorial has called for an investigation."

"The national press?" Baldwin inquired.

"Dead," Winston said. "Not a peep."

"Good job, Winston," Baldwin said. He doubled his fist and twisted it on the table. "Crush anything or anyone you see trying to bring it up again. You know the tack we're taking. It was a suicide, plain and simple. He was on Prozac, stressed out from personal financial problems, and flipped out. Don't even dignify what he said with an answer. It was the ramblings of a mad man. Got it?"

"Got it," Winston affirmed.

Wes was taken back by what he heard. He had expected some kind of discussion about the issues or internal management considerations, not a cold, calculated effort to control the media's treatment of a tragedy. This was a side of Baldwin he hadn't seen, and Wes found it difficult to reconcile the grieving father of a few minutes ago with this dispassionate executive.

"Cusco, is our constituency all in place?"

"Not a single defection," Cusco asserted. "The Abortion Liberty League waffled a little when you gave that speech before the ministerial group last week and asked them to pray that abortion would become more rare in our state. The league figured you were just throwing the preachers a bone. Let's face it, Bill, fifty thousand dollars in campaign contributions from the Reproductive Services Centers is nothing to sneeze at. They want their doors kept open for those fifteen-year-old girls paying cash on the line to get rid of their dirty little secrets."

"Good job, Robert. Tell the centers their money is safe, and I'll use my influence to hold off the parental consent legislation that the Senate will be taking up after the fall election. No arrogant parent is going to tell some kid she can't get an abortion. Which reminds me. Maybe we need to run a few more spots on TV showing those antiabortion protesters screaming at teenage girls trying to enter the clinics."

"I've got you one better," Cusco interrupted with a snide smirk. "We bought video footage from that guy who caught Dr. Flynn's murder on camera."

"You mean the abortion doctor in Alabama who was shot because some nutty pro-lifer was upset about Flynn's performing third-trimester abortions?" he asked.

"That's the one," Cusco confirmed. "We did a commercial showing the murder in slo-mo, frame by nasty little frame. You see the gun going off and the look of horror on Flynn's face as he turns around and realizes he's been shot in the back. Then we freeze-frame the look, and the sound goes dead. We call it 'The Silent Scream.' I've got the vid clip back at my office. I'll send it over this afternoon."

"Fabulous," Baldwin said as he broke into a full grin. "So how does the commercial end?"

"Well, the last thing you see is Flynn's terrified face as the announcer says, 'Don't believe the lies. Now you know who the real murderers are. Keep abortion safe, and legal. Vote for Baldwin, the real pro-life candidate.'"

Baldwin stood, walked over to Cusco, and put his hand on Cusco's shoulder. "That's my man, Robert. You'll go a long way in this organization. Just remember, the other side is well-motivated. Taylor's people don't give up easily, so don't let up the pressure."

As Baldwin returned to his seat Wes could see Cusco beaming like a schoolboy who had been commended in front of the class.

"One more thing, Cusco," Baldwin added as he sat back down. "You need to call Tony Griffin over at the Gay and Lesbian Caucus office and tell them their check was late last month. If they know what's good for them, it won't happen again. I've got debts to cover, and they'd better cover their debt to me first. If they want that letter of endorsement from me in support of their domestic-partners-benefits resolution, which is coming before the county commissioner's board in Pinnacle County, they'd better sign on the dotted line. And don't forget to tell them, as long as they back me all the way, the directorship of the Colorado Educational Planning Office is in the bag. Next year the statewide semiannual textbook selection committee meets, and they don't want to miss out on controlling that process."

Cusco was writing notes as fast as Baldwin talked. Suddenly he stopped and shook the eraser of his pencil in Baldwin's direction. "There is one problem with all of this. Polls show that the gay marriage resolution you said you'd introduce in the senate if you are elected has only about 30 percent of the public behind it."

"Hey, Robert dear," Baldwin said, with a slight lisp as he lifted his right hand and let it dangle limply from his wrist, "we can always tell our 'special' friends that we tried. If we can't get a federal law giving them marriage rights, we'll at least get the state director of medical services to give them free lavender condoms."

Wes noticed that Kelly stiffened slightly at the slur but held his emotions in check. Robert Cusco's eyes darted back and forth between the people in the room as if he wasn't sure whether to laugh at Baldwin's homosexual impersonation. Baldwin led the way by tilting back in his chair and laughing heartily as the others, except Kelly, joined in. Wes looked down and fumbled with the tail of his tie to avoid appearing as though he wasn't going along with their joke.

"Ladonna, sweetie, how does the week look?" Baldwin asked, completing his circuit around the table, except for Kelly.

The scheduling secretary flipped through several pages of an appointment calendar and responded. "Tomorrow you are scheduled for a photo opportunity at the state Boy Scouts convention, and Wednesday the Seniors Rights Alliance has invited you to attend the luncheon at their state convention. The Abortion Liberty League has requested a meeting with you on Thursday of this week. Other than that, there should be time for us to consider whatever pressing issues arise."

Ladonna Gallagher lifted her eyes provocatively in Baldwin's direction. Wes wasn't sure whether it was merely a flirtatious glance or a sign that something more intimate was going on between the two.

"David, that leaves you to wrap things up," Baldwin said as he turned his chair left to face Kelly more directly.

"The others covered things pretty well," Kelly responded. "There are just a couple of items on my agenda. First, Taylor and his crusade. There are over eighty churches in this state with five hundred or more members, and he has pledged to visit every one of them between now and November. If he does, and if he manages to sway their votes, that bloc could mean the difference in the general election."

"What are the options?" Baldwin wanted to know.

"Do nothing. Hope it fades. Personally, I think that's dangerous," Kelly answered. "We could launch a disinformation attack."

"And say what?" Baldwin inquired.

Wes glanced at everyone in the room and sat quietly.

"Throw out all the usual buzzwords and paint him as a radical. I've got several editorial writers in my pocket who could do a couple of columns calling Taylor homophobic, a hate monger, a fascist. You know, the usual."

"That's already been done, and he's still around," Baldwin countered. "You've got to step up the pressure!"

"We could get him on finances."

"He's clean."

"Depends on your perspective," Kelly insisted as he pulled a file out of a leather portfolio resting beside his chair. He tapped the file against the palm of his left hand. "It's all in here: misuse of the nonprofit status of his Restore Our Heritage Crusade, personal profiteering from donations to his cause, a lavish lifestyle funded by good church folks who expect some austerity from their leaders, and the clincher."

Kelly's mischievous smile turned malevolent.

"Can you back it all up with documentation?" Baldwin persisted in knowing.

"I've got a TV investigative reporter just chomping at the bit to do the story. Facts? Like I said, the guilt is in the eye of the beholder, and what he beholds is what he is encouraged to see."

"It'll work," Winston butted in. "I know the reporter David is talking about, and he sees our slant. The right camera angles, a little editing of the interviews we can get from disgruntled ex-employees— and everybody's got them—plus the facts and figures presented in the right context, and we'll nail him. If it's done right, he'll spend from now until November dodging so many accusations about himself he won't have time to raise questions about what we're doing. The press will keep him on the run."

Now Robert Cusco joined the discussion. "Gay Caucus does this all the time to their opponents. First you start with the tabloids. Nobody really believes the allegations, but at least the mud is in the air. Then you find the small-time national magazines, rags with short press runs that are looking for something sensational, a cut above 'Alien Baby Born to Ronald McDonald'"

Everyone burst into laughter again.

"Then you move the story on to the local newspapers. Even if you can't get front-page coverage, you've at least legitimized the story. By now, everyone is convinced something is going on," Cusco explained. "Some mud is starting to stick. People assume with all the smoke there has to be a fire somewhere."

"But the facts," Baldwin demanded. "Isn't any serious reporter going to stop and actually examine the facts?"

"Newspapers want to increase their circulation, and TV stations want to top the ratings," Kelly responded. "Facts used to concern the Walter Cronkites of the business, but those types are disappearing fast. This is the information age, and with information overload, only the most scandalous stories survive."

Ladonna sat back in mock superiority, batted her eyelashes, then said, "Bill, dear, at this point in the attack you bring in the experts. People with supposedly unassailable judgment. You get them to look at the 'facts' and then go on camera. Give them a title, even if it's bogus. People love titles," she said with a condescending smile.

Baldwin got up and paced several times across the length of the room. He loosened his tie with every stride and seemed to release the tension that was filling the room. Then he faced Kelly and pointed his finger directly toward the campaign manager. "What do our legal people say? Have you asked them?"

"No problem. Taylor's people won't sue. Remember, they're on a moral crusade, and in their minds they don't have time to stoop to our level. If they do, we've got the big legal guns. We'll just roll out the $475-an-hour sharks to take a few bites, and they'll back off."

Baldwin walked toward Kelly's chair. "Let me see that file. Everybody take a break while I look this over."

Baldwin headed back to his chair. Everyone except Wes stretched and headed for the silver coffee urn, which sat on a small stand at one end of the room. Wes could hear the others murmuring as they sipped brew from delicate china. He stayed seated and kept an eye on Baldwin's reactions as he turned page after page. Finally he closed the file and shoved it across the table toward Kelly's portfolio.

Wes was frustrated. In spite of the crassness of Baldwin and his people, Wes knew that political campaigns were too often based on cutthroat operatives who controlled what the public was allowed to know about the issues and the candidates. Still he concluded that Baldwin had elevated the art of campaign skullduggery to a new high.

"I was right; he's spotless," Baldwin concluded. "He's led an impeccable life, and his finances are in perfect order. Your spin doctors will have their work cut out for them if they're going to make a shambles of this guy's reputation."

"Except for the clincher," Kelly smirked.

"Oh, yes, the clincher you mentioned a moment ago," Baldwin responded. "Spill it, Dave. What have you got on this guy?"

Kelly's eyes circled the room in excitement as he calculated any hesitation in the resolve of those present. He deliberately avoided looking at Wes. Then Kelly tapped his fingers rhythmically on the contraband file like a cat switching its tail before devouring its prey.

Wes knew that even though Kelly hadn't looked his way, he was the object of Kelly's suspicions.

I don't know why he's worried about me, Wes thought. *I've heard enough in this room today to destroy Baldwin's credibility if I wanted to run to the press. What else does Kelly have that is so dynamite he is uncertain about whether to share it?*

"He's okay," Baldwin said, gesturing toward Wes. "We're buddies from a long time ago, and friends don't betray friends. You can trust Wes with your life, and he's not going to walk from this room and say a word about what he's heard here today. Kelly, you remember what kind of team player he was. After all, he's one of us for the long haul . . . er, uh, at least I'm praying he will be. Go ahead, Dave."

Kelly pulled a sealed envelope from his briefcase and waved it at Baldwin. "Taylor has a few skeletons in his closet that aren't in this file."

"What?" Baldwin asked.

"Sex!" Kelly answered.

"So what?" Baldwin replied. "He wouldn't be the first man who fooled around a little and cheated on his wife. These days that's not an unusual peccadillo. In fact, he could probably turn that into a positive by claiming his God had forgiven him and made him a better man for having sinned."

"Bill, it wasn't a woman," Dave Kelly said soberly. "It was a twelve-year-old boy."

7

Wes was stunned. Everyone stared straight ahead. Only Cusco managed a sly smile. Baldwin was expressionless. Kelly wiped saliva from the side of his mouth. His eyes were wild. The strategy session, as Baldwin had called it, had turned into a manipulative exercise in "politics as usual" of the most sordid variety. Until Kelly's revelation, Wes had been more certain than ever that he wanted nothing to do with Baldwin's campaign. Now, new information about Taylor made Wes wonder if Baldwin, with all of his instincts for the political jugular, might be the lesser of two partisan equals.

Wes decided that getting Baldwin elected might not be so bad once he considered the idea of an accused child molester leading Christian soldiers into battle.

"Can you make the charge stick?" Baldwin asked Kelly.

"It's all in this envelope. The name of the child, even a police report."

Wes concluded it was time to challenge what he had heard around the table. "Why hasn't this stuff been leaked to the press before?"

Kelly tilted his head to one side and in a soft, almost feminine, voice said, "I've been saving it until we needed it."

"But the mother certainly would have said something by now," Wes challenged Kelly.

Wes looked out of the corner of his eye to see how Baldwin was reacting. The candidate put his right elbow on the arm of his chair and cupped his chin in his hand, listening thoughtfully to the exchange.

"Look, I tell you, it's airtight. Taylor will never get out of this one. Don't you see?" Kelly went on. "All the innuendo we can throw his way will soften up the public to believe anything. They'll become weary, hearing one insinuation after another. Gradually they'll be so desensitized about Taylor's reputation they'll be ready to accept the big allegation—pedophilia."

Ralph Winston joined the conversation. "From my standpoint, the key to all of this is not having to prove anything; just the accumulation of charges will start to weigh on people's minds. Then, when they hear the final blow, they'll shrug their shoulders and say, 'See, I told you so.'"

Baldwin threw out the next question. "Won't anyone come to Taylor's rescue?"

"A few," Winston admitted. "But their voices will be drowned by our constant barrage. I think it will work. But we've got to be careful about the timing."

Wes pushed back his chair a little from the table to get a better look at everyone. "Do I hear all of you correctly?" he asked. "You're going to deliberately set out to destroy this man and ignore the truth?"

"The truth is, Taylor is a child molester, a pedophile, Bryant!" Kelly shot back and wiped his mouth again. "Is that someone you want to defend?"

"That's not the point," Wes retorted. "If what you say is true, this is a matter for the police. This should be the responsibility of a criminal investigation, not a political vendetta."

"Wes has a point," Baldwin agreed.

"You're forgetting something," Kelly argued. "We all know there's no justice anymore. If they could get Taylor convicted, he'd be back on the streets in a few months, or a few years. The only justice is to destroy him and what he stands for. We'll kill two birds with one stone. Taylor's criminal acts will be ended, and his crusade to rob others of their civil rights will go down too," he said and snapped his large tanned fingers.

"Then let us all see what's in that envelope," Wes insisted. "Prove that you have the facts you say you do. Then we can make a rational decision, not one based on assumptions."

Kelly jumped up and sent his chair flying across the room. He squared off toward Wes. "Are you calling me a liar, Bryant?" he screamed.

Wes started to get up from his seat when he felt Baldwin's hand on his shoulder. "Wait a minute, guys. This isn't the way to handle this. Sit down right now, Dave!" he ordered Kelly.

Sweat beads formed on Kelly's brow and the surge of adrenaline in his body caused him to breath rapidly. "All right, I'll cool off," Kelly said as he slowly sat back down, "but I won't have my honesty questioned by a political novice." He wiped his mouth with his handkerchief. "Just remember who's running this campaign, Bryant. I'm the manager, and you're the spokesman. You may know how to say it, but I tell you what to say. Got that straight?"

"Dave!" Baldwin shouted. "You're out of line. I'm the boss around here, and I need both of you men. Maybe we're all losing sight of what this boils down to. Our opponent in this campaign isn't another political party. It's a narrow-minded group of hatemongers, Taylor's crusade people. They are the real enemy, and we've got to expend our energy on them, not on turf claims in our own circle. Give me that envelope."

Kelly straightened his shoulders and pulled at his suit coat to steady himself and regain his composure. He relented and tossed the envelope toward Baldwin. "Okay, okay," he said, "but I'm warning you Bryant, if you . . ."

"That's enough, Dave, and I'm not telling you again," Baldwin demanded. "We've got important business to get on with, and saving our state from the likes of Taylor is why we're all in this room." Baldwin tucked the envelope in his open briefcase, which sat on the floor next to his chair. "Let's all take a ten-minute break, then get back to business to wrap things up today . . . all except you Wes. I'd like you to come back to my office."

Everyone stood and headed in different directions: to the coffee, the bathroom, and the main entry door. Baldwin motioned for Wes to follow him back down the secret tunnel to his office.

Once inside the office, Baldwin took off his suit coat and laid it over the back of a chair. He took several steps toward the hologram and stood in front of it for several minutes with his back turned to Wes. He seemed to be completely lost in thought, almost trancelike, motionless. Wes quietly slipped out of his chair and moved slowly back and forth across the room, watching the triangles of the hologram dance about as if they were alive.

Finally, Baldwin jerked as if snapping to attention and calmly turned around to face Wes. "I know that was an abrupt introduction to rough-and-tumble politics," Baldwin said, "but this is the big leagues, and hardball is the only game. Don't let it disillusion you. There are larger issues to consider. For me it's the memory of Rebecca. Imagine how I feel. The man who drove her to suicide appears to have committed acts more despicable than anything he accused my daughter of. Wes, you can't abandon me now. Rebecca's soul cries out to you. I cry out to you. Be the voice for me that I can't be for myself. Stand and declare that intolerance is off-limits in this state and in America. Expose the hypocrites for who they are and how vicious their prejudices are.

"I've heard you behind that microphone, and no one is as articulate. No one can make an audience respond the way you do. You can take our humble, fledgling party and make it into a national force that will silence discrimination of every kind in this nation, once and for all."

Baldwin was either the ultimate con and should be behind bars, or he was a man who passionately believed in his mission and flags should be waving. Wes wasn't sure. Despite his apprehension, what he had seen this afternoon had changed his mind. *If what Kelly says about Taylor is true, Bill deserves my help to expose the Restore Our Heritage Crusade for what it really is. If Kelly is lying, the best place to stop him from destroying Taylor is from inside this organization.* He felt compelled to take on the job of press secretary, but not for any noble political cause. His reason was simple. He had to find out who was lying, either Kelly or Taylor.

"I'll do it," Wes said confidently.

"Permanently?" Baldwin asked almost timidly.

"I'm in this thing until you get elected or defeated," Wes professed. "But there is one condition."

"Anything, Wes; say it and it's yours. Name the price."

"Money isn't the issue," Wes replied. "I'll speak for you, but I want the right to tell the press the truth as I see it. And I must have access to every piece of information that affects this campaign, including whatever is in that envelope about Taylor."

Baldwin smiled, but he didn't look Wes in the eye. He seemed to focus just past Wes's right ear. "You've got it, Wes," he said, "but understand I can't show you the envelope now. I've got to run it by our legal people first. You understand."

Wes hesitated. *Is this a stalling tactic? Do I make my demand nonnegotiable now, or bide my time?*

Wes's argument ended quickly. "All right, I don't have to see it today," Wes agreed. "But before any information is released to the press about Taylor's personal life, you've got to run it by me."

"Absolutely," Baldwin conceded. "Hey, it wouldn't be right for old Clarion College alumni to be any less than totally open with each other. Right?"

"Right."

"Let's head back to the others. They should be waiting."

As they returned to the conference room, everyone but Kelly was seated and busily looking through his or her briefcase. Wes started toward his chair when he felt a strong arm seize him. The former college lineman glowered at Wes and leaned down to whisper in his ear.

"Don't ever cross me again," he said and gave Baldwin an appeasing smile. "You and I have a job to do, and we'll do it because we're on the same team. But I've got your number now like I did back in those football scrimmages. And this time I won't wrap my arms around your legs. It will be your throat!"

Wes stepped out of the Stand for America Party headquarters though the door that fronted Lincoln Street, uncertain of what to do next. He walked alongside his car and noticed a yellow flyer tucked under the windshield wiper. *Another one of those useless advertising flyers that cuts down yet another tree in the rain forest,* Wes thought with a shake of his head. He ripped the flyer from under the wiper and was crumbling it in his hands, when he noticed the stark black headline: RESTORE OUR HERITAGE CRUSADE RALLY.

Taylor's group was right here next to Baldwin's building soliciting recruits. They were either extraordinarily bold or awfully presumptuous!

Wes straightened out the half-crumpled paper and read further:

Do you want your children indoctrinated with gender-neutral education? Do you want your taxpayer's dollars paying for abortions on teenage girls whose parents have no idea they've undergone a medical procedure? Do you want the sovereignty of your state surrendered to special interest groups determined to destroy our Judeo-Christian heritage? Find out how you can fight back. Saturday, April 30, 12:00 NOON, on the steps of the state capitol.

If there were a way to be there undetected, I wouldn't miss that meeting for anything, Wes thought. He folded the flyer and put it in his briefcase. He hopped in his car, pulled out of the parking lot, and glanced at his watch. Wes realized it was so late in the afternoon, there was no point in going to the office. He decided to drive home and surprise Annette. All too often, his workdays turned into evenings, and this would be a special opportunity for them to have a romantic time together.

As his car climbed into the Rocky Mountain foothills, Wes considered his conflicting feelings about Bill Baldwin and Stanley Taylor. On one hand, it was possible that nothing more than a steely game of politics was being played out by both sides. On the other hand, the accusations were too serious to dismiss. Wes realized he could not afford to straddle the fence. His integrity and his professional reputation were hanging precariously over the issues of homosexuality and abortion. Homosexual rights were necessary for

America's social progress, or they were a civil endorsement of deviant behavior. Abortion was a constitutionally protected, private medical decision or a murderous act destroying innocent, unborn life. When it came to Taylor and Baldwin, one was a hero, a defender of what made America great, and the other was a traitor to social decency. Wes realized his conclusion might eventually affect millions of U.S. citizens.

As Wes turned onto the long driveway toward his house, he spotted Annette outside in the front yard. She had her hair pulled up in a chignon and was wearing blue jeans and a yellow-and-green sweatshirt. She was wearing leather gloves and appeared to be collecting wood that had fallen from the trees during the winter. Every year Annette and Wes cleaned up the forest floor behind their house to provide kindling for warm winter fires with a crop of fallen limbs. Wes watched Annette toss one stick after another into a red wheelbarrow and then maneuver it over the uneven mountain ground pocketed with rocks and hardened soil. She strained to keep the wheelbarrow from tipping.

When Annette saw Wes, she brought her cargo to a stop, tossed her gloves into the wheelbarrow, and walked over to meet him as he pulled into the garage. "How's my handsome man?" she asked as Wes turned off the car and opened the door. Her hug felt good to Wes after the tension and conflict of the day. "I didn't expect to see you home so early. To what do I owe this unexpected pleasure?"

Wes grabbed his suit coat hanging on a hook inside the back car door, and said with a wink, "I finished early with Baldwin, and there was no point going back to the office."

Wes wasn't ready to tell Annette he had changed his mind about being press secretary and wasn't sure how he was going to explain. But before he could say anything, Annette asked, "I have a suspicion that you're staying on as Baldwin's press secretary, right?"

Wes felt grateful that she hid any disappointment in her voice.

"How do you women figure these things out?" he wanted to know.

"Radar. It's something God gave us. When you're a wife, you earn a double dose," she said with a laugh. "Actually, I saw you carrying your decision on your brow. You didn't show the kind of relief I expected if Baldwin had accepted your decision and you had stuck by your guns."

"Annette, I really did intend to tell him I was quitting. It's just that . . ."

Annette slipped her arm inside his and gave his hand a reassuring squeeze. "Wes, you don't have to explain if you don't want to. It's okay. I knew you'd make the right decision. Sometimes life presents us with dilemmas that force us to make decisions we wouldn't have anticipated making. That's when you've got to go with your gut. If that's what you did, I'll back you all the way."

As Wes walked through the garage door leading into the house, he heaved an audible sigh of relief. He wanted Annette to know what had gone on but didn't want to bring it up right then. He needed the sanctity of his home to relax and collect his thoughts. Wes quickly changed out of his suit into a pair of sweat pants and lay down on the living room couch.

Annette sat down in a chair next to him and said, "This is quite an evening. I've got a double surprise. You're home early and Jennifer is coming by in a few minutes."

"Jennifer?" Thoughts of an amorous evening faded. "We've hardly seen her since she moved out of the house into the college dorm to get a taste of personal freedom."

"She seemed real excited and said she wanted to share some news about what she's going to be doing this summer. You know, Wes, how concerned I've been about that. This is her first free summer after college, and I was hoping she'd be able to find a good job. We're paying her tuition, and she appreciates that, but there are a lot of extra little things she'd like to have."

Wes sat up and propped his feet on top of the coffee table. "But you know she can work at the radio station. I've always said that."

"Wes, you're acting a little protective. Remember, Jennifer is nineteen and wants to do things on her own. Working at the station would not let her develop her independence. You know how important that is at her age. You do remember when you were nineteen, don't you?" Annette laughed as she walked behind the couch and leaned over to ruffle Wes's hair.

"Nineteen, let's see, which century was that?" Wes said and tried to smooth his hair.

"Mom, I'm here!"

Wes and Annette heard the front door open and Jennifer announce her arrival. She bounded into the living room, flung her well-worn backpack on a chair, and gave Wes and Annette a hug.

"Dad, I didn't expect to see you here this early. Is anything wrong? Your hair's all messed up."

"No, I just finished up some business earlier than expected," he said and looked up at Annette with a playful grin. "Your mother tells me you have some exciting news to tell us. You know you can always work at the station . . ."

"Now, Wes," Annette interrupted. "Let's hear what Jennifer has to say without any interference from you."

"Do you have any Diet Coke in the fridge, Mom?" Jennifer asked as she headed toward the kitchen.

Annette followed after her. "No, but I have some mineral water. That's a lot better for you than straight carbonated caffeine."

Jennifer fumbled through the refrigerator and settled on a bottle of Clearly Canadian. "We'll compromise with this," she said unscrewing the bottle top and gulping down a mouthful. "So, what's going on at the station, Dad?"

"Nothing much. Besides, I'm anxious to hear about your new job."

"Mind if I turn on the TV? The news will be on in a few minutes. There are a couple of stories I've been following I wouldn't mind seeing."

"You can turn on the TV if you want, but your dad and I are excited to hear about your new job. I thought that's what you were coming over here to talk about."

Jennifer nervously fiddled with the TV remote control. "I was, that is until . . ."

"Until what?" Wes asked.

"Dad, I just didn't expect to see you here. I wanted to talk to Mother about this first."

"Look, if this is a woman's thing, I'll be happy to leave the room so you two ladies can hash it out."

"It's not that, Dad. I just thought what I had to say might be upsetting to you, and I felt more comfortable breaking the news to Mom first."

Wes's mind raced. What kind of job could she have that he wouldn't approve of? Jennifer had always been a decent girl, so he wasn't concerned that she might work in an inappropriate place. Perhaps the salary wasn't enough or the hours were too late. In spite of Wes's speculation, he was completely unprepared for Jennifer's explanation.

"I'm spending the summer doing volunteer work for Stanley Taylor's Restore Our Heritage Crusade." She looked with embarrassment at Wes. "Dad, I'd never do anything to hurt you, but this is something I really believe in. I stand for what Stanley Taylor stands for. I'll make sure I don't talk to any reporters who might try to make a big deal out of you and I being on different sides of the fence."

"Stanley Taylor?" Wes took a deep breath and tried to make sure he didn't give away his feelings of dread. It was essential in radio to hide his emotions behind the microphone when he was confronted with a situation that required professional cool despite personal turmoil. The lump in his throat now was very tough to swallow, though he realized he didn't have any actual proof Taylor was a child molester.

"It's all right, Jennifer," Wes assured her, knowing that he would demand she quit if he found out the allegations were true. "You have to do what you believe is right. I'll do my best to make sure it doesn't affect our relationship. All I ask is that you be careful."

"Careful about what?" Jennifer asked.

"Just careful," Wes repeated.

Jennifer got out of her seat, walked over to Wes, and hugged him. "Thanks for understanding, Dad. You don't know how important this is to me. It won't affect our relationship; I promise you."

"When does your job start? I hope it doesn't interfere with the last few weeks of this school year," Annette insisted.

"Oh no," Jennifer assured her. "It will be several more weeks yet before I get involved full time."

Wes sighed in relief. At least there was some time for her to change her mind.

"I'll know more about my schedule after tomorrow night," Jennifer explained. "Taylor has asked me to head up the statewide youth division of his crusade. He's going to tell me all about it when he and I have a private meeting at his house."

Wes hung on to those words, *private meeting*.

"Do you think it's a good idea to meet with him privately?" Wes asked in a halting manner.

Jennifer looked as though her patience was wearing thin. "Dad, you've told me I am an adult now. Either you mean it or you don't. Maybe I should just move back in with you and Mom and have you approve my every move." She finished speaking and defiantly folded her arms.

Wes stared straight ahead. Jennifer looked over at Wes, then at her mother, who did not return her glance.

"I'm sorry," Jennifer blurted out. She dropped her head and looked at the ground. "I'm really sorry. I shouldn't have spoken in that manner."

Wes gave her a little smile and said, "You're right. You are an adult. Let's just forget this whole blowup. Please forgive me, too."

For the next hour everyone exchanged small talk about Jennifer's upcoming finals and the classes she planned to sign up for in the fall semester. They discussed personal interests in the latest movies and news events, but everyone scrupulously avoided any mention of local state politics.

When at last Jennifer said she was getting tired and it was time to go, Wes felt guilty but was relieved to say good night. He wasn't sure what to do, but he knew there was no way he would let her meet privately with Taylor. To Wes, it was better to err on the side of caution. He stood at the living room picture window and watched the headlights of Jennifer's eighties-model slate blue Subaru head down the winding driveway and disappear behind a hill.

8

After a restless night, Wes was up early the next morning to check out the phone directory for Taylor's listing. He jotted down Taylor's address and phone number on a piece of paper and slipped it into his shirt pocket. Then he went round and round thinking about what he should do to throw some water on Taylor's plan. Should he spy on the meeting? Wes kicked the idea back and forth and then let it settle somewhere in the back of his mind. He had the rest of the day to contemplate his actions, so there was no sense making any rash decisions.

Wes's Tuesday morning at the office was filled with tension. He called a staff meeting and tried his best to outline the events of the last three days. He explained that he was not selling the station and his role in Baldwin's campaign would not interfere with his business interests. In spite of his increased workload, Wes declared he was going to handle day-to-day responsibilities. After all, Baldwin's campaign would be over in little more than six months. Wes also pointed out his commitment to the Stand for America Party was based on friendship, not philosophy. Wes told them he hoped the radio station would not become the target of protests from those opposed to Baldwin's ideas. He vowed to let the public know his relationship to Baldwin was personal, not political.

The staff seemed satisfied with Wes's explanation. In fact, some showed enthusiasm because they said they planned to vote for Baldwin and hoped Wes's job would sensitize him to the causes Baldwin championed. Others expressed disappointment that someone of Wes's moral fortitude would be associated with Baldwin's agenda. Regardless of their political persuasion, most of the KVCE employees understood that it was a job, a favor, and nothing more than that.

After the meeting, Wes went back to his office and thought about his more reasonable options for dealing with Taylor that evening. Several times he reached for the phone to call Jennifer and ask her to cancel the meeting, but he resisted.

"Tough day, right, Boss?" Deborah's voice intruded upon Wes's thoughts as he sat shuffling papers at the end of the day.

"I've had worse."

"I'm on my way home and just poked my head in the door to see if there was anything you needed before I left."

Wes looked up from the stack of memos that had accumulated over the last two days and yawned. "Everything seems to be under control. I'll just have to get back here early tomorrow morning and plow through all of this. I'm on mental overload right now and don't think I'll get much further today. I'll lock up the executive suites when I leave. Are the program logs for tomorrow all filled out?"

"Jeff Watkins, who handles production traffic, finished them five minutes ago. They're posted in the studios so there shouldn't be any problem." Deborah paused. "Your meeting with the staff went well, at least from my point of view."

Wes pushed the chair back from his desk and stood to stretch his legs. "Yeah, most of my concerns were alleviated too. I suppose one or two people still wonder why I'm getting involved in politics, but that's to be expected."

Deborah pulled a light coat over her shoulders and looked at Wes seriously. "I should hope they'd be concerned, with that stuff that came in the mail and your taking over the position of a man who just shot himself. Anyway, we all wish you the best, and we'll do our part here to make sure the workload flows smoothly. You do what you've got to do, and let the staff pick up the pieces."

Wes smiled. "Thanks, Deborah; see you in the morning."

The noise of loud voices, faxes, copy machines, and computers had dwindled to the solitary sound of a hallway monitor airing a program feed from Studio A. In the background, through his open office door, Wes could hear the sounds of Harry Zimmermann wrapping up his five o'clock sports talk show with the forecast about the next day's Rockies' baseball game.

Maybe Zimmermann's predictions are self-fulfilling prophesies, Wes thought. *I wish he'd say they're going to win more often. Even if they didn't, at least I'd feel better.*

Wes glanced at the ornate brass clock sitting on his credenza. 5:45. The late-April sun was just above the mountaintops on the western horizon, and the shadows of early budding trees were beginning to lengthen. Within an hour it would almost be dark, and Wes knew this was the worst time of the day to drive westward toward his house. He remembered the many times his light-sensitive eyes were burned by the sun's angle through the windshield. He decided there was no point heading home until the sun dipped behind the mountains. He sat back down at his desk to dictate a few more memos. As he eased himself into his ergonomically designed leather chair, he glanced around the room.

Next to the clock on the credenza was a cut-out photograph, laminated on plastic, of Wes and Annette's wedding nine years ago. They were smiling at each other in the back of a horse-drawn carriage festooned with balloons. Next to that photo was a Shure ribbon microphone, circa 1958, the kind Wes used when he first went into broadcasting. He often looked at it to remember how far he had come since those early days of small-town Indiana radio. His bookcase was filled with popular volumes by authors he had interviewed through the years. Each was inscribed with a special message. At the far end of the room was a leather couch with a glass-topped coffee table. On top, Wes had arranged several volumes of broadcasting-industry reference guides. The thick-bound books were supported at either end by bronzed cowboy boots, the actual ones Wes had worn at age five to gallop astride his stick horse in search of desperadoes. His walls featured tasteful watercolor displays of Colorado nature scenes. One wall, his "brag wall," was filled with plaques and framed letters, accolades for his service in the broadcasting industry.

The walls of his office faded in Wes's mind as he realized that little more than an hour from now Jennifer would be entering the home of a man he had reason to believe dangerous. Part of Wes acknowledged he had stayed late to take care of a backlog of work. He also knew he was killing time to devise a way to spy on Taylor and Jennifer. As the minutes ticked past six, Wes checked his watch every other minute. As it neared 7 P.M., he grew more agitated. Wes busied himself with the stacks of paper on his desk until he realized he hadn't looked at the clock in some time.

It's almost 7:15! That's it. I'll do it! He threw the remaining documents in his briefcase, reached in his shirt pocket, pulled out Taylor's address, and left his office.

Wes walked briskly to his car, breathing in the cool evening air. Once at the wheel, he fumbled and dropped his keys. He leaned over to search the floorboard. His fingers traced the carpet, then he felt the metal keys. In exasperation, he stuck the key in the ignition and started his car, and in one swift shift, pulled out of the parking lot. He drove right past a black luxury sedan parked perpendicular in a parking space.

His car flew down the Sixth Avenue Freeway and headed north on I-25. The business and industrial sections of the city whisked by as he entered the province of convenience stores, mini-malls, and suburbia. He exited on Eighty-ninth Street and within minutes was in the heart of a middle-class neighborhood. He watched carefully as he passed the area street signs to make sure he didn't drive in front of Taylor's house. He seemed to be going through a maze of cul-de-sacs, circles, drives, and lanes.

Lawrence Street! He recognized the street name. *Taylor can't live more than a block or two away.*

Then, out of the corner of his eye, in the dim of dusk he saw Jennifer's Subaru parked in front of a single-level ranch-style brick home a hundred yards away. Wes hit the accelerator and darted past the street entrance, fearful that Jennifer might catch a glimpse of his car. He hadn't seen another car in Taylor's driveway. The porch light was on.

I can't keep circling like a fool. I've got to get near enough to the house to get a look inside.

Wes was revolted by the thought of being some kind of voyeur; however, if what Kelly said was true, Wes feared what might be going on there.

Wes spotted the perfect location to leave his car, next to a neighborhood park about a half-dozen blocks from Taylor's house. The twilight faded and several small children furiously competed to get in their last trips on the slide before their mothers' voices beckoned them home. The reassuring sound of the parents calling to their children reminded him of the innocent days of his own youth. For a minute he wished he were plunging down the slippery chute into the arms of a waiting mother or father who would whisk him away to a warm meal and the security of having someone else handle life's problems.

Dear God, Wes prayed as he tightly gripped the leather-wrapped sport steering wheel, *this may be the dumbest thing I've ever done, but help me find out if Jennifer is in any danger.*

It seemed odd to be seeking divine guidance about such a bizarre objective, but Wes knew he needed direction beyond his own perplexed state of mind.

This time of year the days were warmed by the sunshine, but once night swallowed the mile-high city, the temperature dropped rapidly. When he felt the chilly air, Wes regretted that he hadn't brought a jacket with him. His suit coat would suffice for a few minutes, and he hoped his task would be completed before long. Anyway, he figured his adrenaline would keep him warm. As he got out of the car, he squeezed the remote key lock and heard the click of the doors responding. It was time to head for Taylor's house, though he wasn't sure what he'd do when he got there.

Wes walked briskly, trying to appear as if there were nothing unusual about leaving a luxury car next to a park at night and heading aimlessly down a sidewalk. He hoped no one was watching from a window and was thankful that during this time of year it was too early to find many people in their yards, especially with night approaching. Wes walked slightly faster with each approaching block, anxious to get on with whatever he would do. Then, he turned a corner and spotted Taylor's residence five houses down.

The backyard, was all Wes could think of. *I have to find a way to walk into his backyard and look into a window.*

Wes slowed his pace slightly as he walked by the street light from the next corner. Fifty yards. Thirty yards. Ten yards. He made it! Taylor's house was immediately on his left. He walked slower and glanced out the corner of his eyes, trying not to stare. He made his way toward a slat wooden fence with a gate extended on the left side of the house. Without time to think, he stepped quickly across thirty feet of grass and silently prayed the gate wouldn't have a secured latch. It didn't. He gently pulled it outward. The hinges creaked slightly.

Lights, behind him. They shone like a searchlight casting his dark shadow on the fence as if night had suddenly been turned to day. The illumination gave him an instant glimpse of the large backyard full of trees. He turned quickly and saw a car had rounded the corner. By the time Wes's body was facing the street in panic, the car's taillights were fading into the distance down Lawrence Street.

Perhaps they didn't see me, or maybe they thought it was my house and I was just entering my own backyard.

As he turned around to continue, two other more disturbing thoughts shot through his mind. First, *What if Taylor has an attack dog to guard his house?* The other thought was just as serious. *I'm unlawfully entering his property!*

Wes felt stupid. Why hadn't he considered that before? Whether or not Taylor was some kind of pervert, right now he, Wes, was the criminal. For a split second it didn't matter whether Taylor or Baldwin was right or wrong. If he were caught and Taylor pressed charges, getting fired from Baldwin's campaign would be the least of his problems.

But there was no turning back. Success or failure didn't matter as much now as the thought that Jennifer's welfare was at stake. He would risk whatever was necessary to satisfy his concern for his stepdaughter, and the prayer he prayed back in the car would have to be his protection. He had to go through that gate.

In one swift motion he stepped inside the yard and closed the gate behind him. There was no dog, at least not one that greeted him. He slowly made his way by ambient light from the windows of nearby dwellings. He listened for any sound from inside, but all he heard was the sound of his own steps crunching winter's dead grass under his feet. This side of the house seemed dark. He guessed it was the bedroom end of the building. The most distant portion of the yard, around the corner of the house, was lit by the glow from windows in the back.

Maybe they have a family room in the rear of the house and that's where they are meeting.

"Good-bye, we'll be back in fifteen or twenty minutes."

Wes heard the voice speak clearly. It was an older woman, and the sounds were coming from the front door. It wasn't Jennifer's voice. Was it Taylor's wife?

Wes remembered a joke he once heard with the punch line, "Just because I'm paranoid doesn't mean someone isn't out to get me." Full-blown paranoia was beginning to take over, and it was accentuated by the sounds of Taylor's garage door opening and a car backing down the driveway.

Muted laughter from inside the house didn't ease Wes's mind. *I've got to see in somehow. For better or worse I'm turning the corner to look in the back.*

Wes expected there would be a patio of some kind and he was right. A redwood deck about two feet off the ground was covered by an overhang that shielded a black wrought-iron table and chairs and a permanent built-in brick barbecue spit. The voice that had laughed now shrieked. Was it a cry for help? It sounded too much like Jennifer for Wes to stand still. He leaped onto the patio and landed in a crouching position. As he did, spotlights went on instantly and a shrill siren exploded into the night air.

Before he could plunge off the patio, a door flew open and Wes found himself face-to-face with Taylor, holding a gun in his hand. The two froze in shock. Taylor flicked a switch and the alarm ceased its screeching.

A young woman about Jennifer's age called out, "Dad, what's happening! Is there a burglar out there?"

"It's okay, Honey," Taylor answered. "Stay where you are. Dad has everything under control. Go back to watching that scary video you girls rented."

Taylor lowered his gun slightly. "I was hoping we'd have the chance to meet again outside the boundaries of our own political arenas, Mr. Bryant, but I never expected it would be in my own backyard." He paused and motioned with the barrel of his gun for Wes to stand. "I suppose it's in order for me to ask what you're doing here. This obviously isn't a friendly visit. Before I call the cops, you'd better explain."

What could Wes explain? He decided that telling a man pointing a gun that he's suspected of being a pervert would not be wise.

"I came here to see my daughter." *Well, that is technically accurate,* Wes thought, excusing his stretch of the truth.

"You might have called first," Taylor retorted.

"Uh, I was in the area and thought I'd just stop by."

Taylor cocked his head sideways with a skeptical look. "Well, then, why didn't you come to the front door? Why sneak into my backyard?"

"I wasn't sneaking," Wes insisted. "I, uh . . ."

"We have a doorbell. Why didn't you ring it?"

Wes shrugged his shoulders and mumbled under his breath.

"You're lucky my Doberman is in the kennel overnight getting some laboratory tests," Taylor warned. "If you had come through that gate when he was here, you'd probably still be running."

"I'm sorry. I didn't mean to intrude like this," Wes meekly offered, hoping Taylor would put his gun away.

"How do I know you weren't trespassing to find out some information for Baldwin's campaign? If my security motion detector hadn't gone off, I might not have known you were here. You could have listened in on the discussion your daughter and I and the other young women of the crusade's youth corps are going to be having. This looks to me like a badly bungled stepchild of Nixon's 'third-rate burglary.' Dirty politics, that's how it strikes me. And furthermore, it's criminal. You're trespassing."

Taylor had the upper hand, and Wes knew he'd better swallow a big dose of humility fast if he were going to avoid arrest and evade public humiliation.

"Look, Taylor, I'm a parent, and you are too. I was just concerned about what my daughter might be involved in, and I did a stupid thing." Wes felt better at his admission. "I was afraid the press would pick up on her affiliation with you, and that might compromise Baldwin's campaign. I figured if I could at least get some information without having to ask Jennifer directly it would ease my mind.

"I realize my attempt at eavesdropping was an inept stunt, and I apologize. Please, I've made a fool of myself. If you'll let me go, I'll never tell anyone I was here, and I beg you to do the same."

Taylor's face softened and he snapped the safety on his gun. He laid the weapon on the patio table and put his hands on his hips.

"All right, if you're telling the truth . . . but I'm still not sure I buy what you're saying. If I ever catch you or any of Baldwin's people trying something like this again, I'll tell the whole story about what happened tonight to the press. I'm doing this for you, Bryant, and your daughter, not for Baldwin. It's what he stands for that I find detestable, and I welcome this campaign as a chance for all the voters to decide what they want. I want a fair fight about the issues."

There was an integrity in Taylor's manner under these strange circumstances, and Wes found it compelling. All he wanted at the moment was to make a hasty retreat.

"Get out of here," Taylor instructed. "Your daughter has gone to the store with my wife. They'll be back any minute."

Wes leaped off the patio and turned briefly to face Taylor. Here was the man Baldwin's people hated and were determined to destroy. In gratefulness for Taylor's letting him go he wanted to warn his political antagonist. Inside him, the words screamed out, "Taylor, Baldwin says you're a child molester and is going to destroy your reputation. If you're not guilty, take some defensive action before it's too late."

The words wouldn't come. Wes felt a little cowardly, but his adrenaline was pumping so fast it was hard to focus on anything except flight to avoid further embarrassment.

Vroom! Wes heard the sound of a car racing its motor.

It's Jennifer and the others returning. They're pulling into the driveway!

Wes bolted from the yard and charged through the gate, leaving it wide open. He sprinted across the lawn away from the house as the car stopped in front of the garage door. He hoped they were concentrating so much on their own actions they wouldn't see him running up the street. At his age Wes could still move fast, but not quite as fast as he wanted to.

In what seemed like seconds, he approached his car. Wes slowed his pace to a fast walk and then a more normal gait. He felt so embarrassed and worried that someone might see him running frantically and think he was up to foul play. Wes managed to walk calmly to his car and get inside. He quickly drove away, his hands shaking at the wheel. He felt ice cold. As he headed back to the freeway, he glanced in the lighted visor mirror at his disheveled appearance. He reached in his hip pants pocket to get a comb. It wasn't there, and neither was his billfold!

9

Wes spent a restless night tossing and turning over the loss of his billfold. *It could be in Taylor's backyard. Or maybe some kid picked it up between Taylor's house and where I parked the car. How would I explain that?* Wes hoped that someone would find the billfold and return it to him, no questions asked.

All night long Wes made a mental list of everything in his billfold so in the morning he could go about replacing each item. The thought of making a trip to the motor vehicles department to stand in long lines for a duplicate license made him pull the blankets over his head. Credit cards would have to be canceled. There were security issues to consider. He kept the alarm code of the KVCE office on a sheet of paper tucked inside a small pocket. Would the wrong person find the number, figure out what it was, and attempt unlawful entry?

Fortunately, this situation happened while Annette had planned to be out of town for several days. She had left Tuesday afternoon to attend a women's retreat held at the Mountain Highlands Campground. This was one of the few times they had been apart since their marriage. Wes was lonely without Annette to snuggle up to at night, but her absence allowed him to toss and turn fitfully without explanation.

In the early-morning hours he fell into a deep sleep. He dreamed he ran fearfully across a mountain meadow, pursued by snarling, half-human, half-animal creatures. He awoke to the stark sound of the front doorbell. Half asleep, he threw on a pair of sweatpants and a T-shirt and stumbled to the entry. He opened the door and was greeted by a burly, unsmiling police officer.

"Mr. Wes Bryant?"

"Yes," Wes answered as his bleary eyes squinted from the early-morning sunshine glinting off the officer's badge. "Is there a problem of some kind?"

The policeman stood with his hands on his hips. "I'm Officer Detwielder," the policeman said, taking out his billfold and displaying his credentials. "I'm afraid I need you to accompany me to the county sheriff's office."

Wes was instantly alert. "Why? Has there been an accident in my family? Has my station been broken into?" Wes's mind quickly ran through all the reasons why a policeman would be at his front door.

The officer put his billfold away and responded without smiling. "I can't answer those questions right now. I just do what I'm told, and I've been ordered to deliver you to Sheriff McCormick's office. He's waiting to talk to you right now."

"But you can't tell me to get in your car without a reason. Don't I deserve to be informed of my rights or something? I'm not under arrest, am I?"

"Look, Mr. Bryant, this will be a lot easier on both of us if you'll cooperate." Detwielder rested his right hand on the handcuffs tucked inside his belt. "I'd rather not use these unless I have to."

"Okay, okay, I'll cooperate, but it seems like I ought to be able to call my lawyer first if I'm being arrested."

Detwielder shuffled his weight back and forth from one foot to the other with impatience. "You're not being arrested, unless you refuse my request. In that case, I guess I would have to take you to see the sheriff by force."

Wes shook his head in disbelief. "Give me five minutes to jump in the shower."

The officer reached up to his flat-brimmed hat and tugged it down lower on his brow. "I'll be waiting in the cruiser. Five minutes. No more."

He turned and walked toward the police car. His steps seemed so heavy that every board on the porch creaked with the full force of his weight. He never looked back until he got to the cruiser door and opened it. Then he shot a stern glance at Wes who was still standing in the doorway, frozen in disbelief. The trooper put up his hand and pointed his palm toward Wes with all five fingers spread out. Then he closed his hand into a fist and got into the car.

Wes rushed to the master bath; he didn't wait for the water to heat up completely. *A cold shower will do me good. Perhaps this is all a dream and I'll wake up once the water splashes in my face.*

That didn't happen. Wes was in the shower less than sixty seconds. He dried himself, brushed his teeth, and sprayed into place what was left of a once-full head of hair. He quickly slipped on a pair of loafers, not taking time for socks, pulled on a sweater he guessed would match his slacks, and rushed to the front door.

Wes hoped his neighbors weren't up so early as the patrol car headed down his driveway and out to the main street. *Randall Anderson is usually jogging this time of the morning,* Wes remembered as he shrank lower in the car's backseat.

Fifteen minutes later, they pulled into an empty parking place in front of the Fox Creek County Sheriff's Headquarters. Wes reached for a door handle to get out and realized that it didn't work from the inside. He waited for Officer Detwielder to release him from his captivity.

"Follow me," Detwielder demanded.

Wes remembered all the TV shows he had seen of people being arrested who pulled their shirts or coats up over their heads so no one would recognize them. He wondered if he should do the same, but realized there were no reporters or cameras.

Once inside the front door, Detwielder motioned for Wes to follow him to the front reception desk. "McCormick is expecting me," he said to a uniformed female officer who was busy answering telephone lines. The operator gave Detwielder the thumbs-up signal and pointed toward a hallway. "Come on," Detwielder said, motioning for Wes to follow.

The sound of the officer's heavy boots reverberated off the tiled floor and walls. After turning several corners, Detwielder stopped at an unmarked door and knocked. He paused, then opened it and motioned for Wes to step in. It was a stark room except for a long table in the center surrounded by a half-dozen steel-framed chairs with dark brown Naugahyde seats. At one end of the room Wes could see a door with frosted-pane glass. A goosenecked floor lamp stood in one corner, and the only item on the table was an ashtray full of reeking, smoldering cigarette butts.

"Mr. Bryant," Detwielder said, deferring to a dark-haired, lanky man who was seated in a chair at the end of the table, "this is Sheriff John McCormick."

McCormick had unnaturally dark hair for his age that was carefully combed into a side part, and his jaw seemed clamped shut. His brown eyes squinted at Wes like he was badly in need of a pair of glasses. He pointed to a chair directly opposite him at the far end of the table as he said, "Sit down over there, Bryant."

Wes settled into the chair and leaned forward with his elbows and forearms resting on the table. He cocked his eyebrows, looking first at Detwielder and then McCormick, and asked, "Would you mind telling me what this is all about?"

McCormick took a pack of Marlboros out of his shirt pocket and tapped on one end, slowly extracting a cigarette. He rolled it between his fingers for a few seconds before finally unlocking his jaw and clamping down on the cigarette. Then he struck a match and in one swift motion raised it to his cigarette. He paused for a moment and looked up at Wes as he shook the match and the blue sulfur smoke rose. "You don't mind if I smoke, do you?"

It seemed like a ridiculous question. It was just after seven o'clock in the morning, and he had been taken to the county sheriff's office without knowing why. Now his captor was extending an irrelevant courtesy. Wes shrugged his shoulders.

McCormick took a couple of deep puffs of his cigarette. "Missing anything, Mr. Bryant?"

"Just breakfast," Wes said with a slight note of sarcasm.

McCormick grinned with clenched teeth. He turned his cigarette sideways, looked at it, then shot a hateful glance in Wes's direction. "Perhaps if you knew why you were here you'd take my inquiry a little more seriously, Mr. Bryant," McCormick retorted. "Like I said, missing anything?"

Wes instinctively reached back with his left hand to pat the hip pocket where he normally carried his billfold. As he did, McCormick flung Wes's billfold on the table. Wes started to reach for it when Detwielder, who had been standing over Wes with his legs spread at shoulder width and his arms crossed, reached down his strong arm and grabbed Wes's wrist before he could touch the billfold.

"Just leave it there, for now," McCormick instructed. "Perhaps you'd like to know where we found it?"

I thought Taylor was a man of his word. Obviously he found the billfold and turned it over to the cops, Wes concluded.

McCormick got up from his chair and began to circle the table slowly and deliberately. "Several of our boys in the narcotics unit busted some drug dealers in a small mountain cabin last night," he said as the soles of his cowboy boots shuffled slowly across the floor. "That rich Hollywood crowd up in Aspen and Vail do a lot of drugs, and an enterprising group of fellas from the Canyon Creek area have been all too willing to meet the demand. Seems they fly the stuff in from somewhere down south after it's dropped over the border. Cocaine, Mr. Bryant, the purest coke you ever saw. But I'm not telling you anything new."

Sheriff McCormick continued to pace around the table. "You know what my boys also found at that cabin?"

Wes shrugged his shoulders.

"They found this," McCormick said pointing to the billfold.

Wes couldn't imagine how his billfold ended up at a mountain cabin in the possession of cocaine smugglers, but at least he understood what he was doing here and why Detwielder and McCormick had played hardball with him.

"How do you suppose your billfold got to that little cabin?" McCormick asked in a mocking voice. He stopped on one side of the table, put his hands on top, and leaned toward Wes.

"I have no idea, Sheriff McCormick," Wes responded. "I discovered it was missing last night and was hoping someone would find it and call me."

McCormick looked up at Detwielder as they smirked at each other. Wes knew they didn't believe him and were going to continue their intimidation tactics to get at what they perceived was the truth. For a long pause, no one said anything. Then McCormick looked at Detwielder and nodded toward the door. Detwielder returned an acknowledging nod and exited through the door. McCormick took a small pocketknife from his pants pocket and began to methodically clean his fingernails. He finished his left hand and started on the index finger of his right hand without saying a word when Detwielder returned with a manila folder. Detwielder laid the file in front of McCormick and reassumed his militaristic position behind Wes.

For a few moments, McCormick flipped through pages in the file. When he seemed satisfied, he took out a single sheet, closed the file, and laid the sheet facedown on the table. He sat silently, nodding his head as if in agreement with something. "It's all in order. Tell the boys they've done a good job," he said to Detwielder.

McCormick slowly lifted his head and looked Wes straight in the eye. He reopened his knife and began to work on his right index finger again. "You're in a whole heap of trouble, Mr. Bryant," McCormick said. "Getting involved with small-time drug dealers doesn't seem your style, but maybe you have some private indiscretions we know nothing about."

Wes wanted to pound the table in disgust. He was angry at this kangaroo court and was infuriated by McCormick's innuendo, but he tried to keep his head. He breathed deeply to help him remain calm.

"This will go a whole lot easier for all of us if you'll cooperate," McCormick said as he patted his hand on the paper he had taken from the file. "This is a warrant for your arrest on charges of drug trafficking."

Wes couldn't sit still anymore. He jumped up and sent the back of his chair into Detwielder's shins. "What? I don't even do drugs. I never have. I have no idea what's going on. I want to talk to an attorney!"

Wes heard Detwielder's groan and then felt the officer's huge hand on his right shoulder, pushing him slowly down into the repositioned chair. He wanted to resist but knew it was best to cooperate.

"Maybe you don't get it, Mr. Big-Shot Radio Station Owner," McCormick said sarcastically. "That billfold was found with the drug stash we confiscated last night. According to Judge Russell Hoffman, who signed this warrant, we've got enough evidence to detain you under a hefty bail and keep you off the streets until we find out what's going on."

McCormick tilted his chair back on two legs and resumed cleaning the fingernails of his right hand as if it were the most important task before him.

What a fool I was! Taylor was just setting me up. No wonder he capitulated so easily. He was waiting to put this noose around my neck. Boy, was I taken in by him. Wes rolled his eyes and hit the table with his opened hand. *Baldwin was right! The guy's a snake. I wonder if Taylor's got this sheriff on the take.*

"Well, Bryant, what's it going to be? Are you going to cooperate and talk to us or do I handcuff you now?"

"Cooperate? What do you mean cooperate? I don't know anything about the drugs you found or how my billfold got there."

McCormick slowly finished his little finger and thumb, folded up the knife, and put it back in his pocket. "You tell us what you know about the dealers we busted last night, and we'll see what kind of a deal the district attorney is willing to make."

Instinctively, Wes started to get up again but Detwielder's hovering bulk forced him to sit back down before he could stand. "I've told you the truth, and I'm not telling you anything more until I talk to an attorney."

McCormick shoved his chair back from the table, stood, and adjusted his holster belt to a more comfortable position on his hips. "Have it your way," he responded, "but there's someone else you may want to talk to first."

McCormick motioned to Detwielder, and both of them headed for the door. They stepped out, leaving Wes alone. Seconds later, the door opened and Wes looked up to see Bill Baldwin entering the room. Baldwin had a genuinely sympathetic look on his face. He walked toward Wes and reached out his hand.

"Don't get up, Wes. You've been through a lot, and you'll need all the strength you can muster."

Baldwin pulled up a chair a few feet away from Wes and went on. "You don't have to tell me anything if you don't want to. I'm not your lawyer. But if you're honest with me, it will help me to get you out of this."

Wes clenched his fists in frustration. "There's nothing to get me out of. I haven't done anything. I lost my billfold, and somehow it turned up at this drug bust McCormick is talking about. Somebody is trying to frame me."

Baldwin looked at Wes with a slight hint of skepticism. "I assure you, Wes, nothing you tell me will leave this room. We're friends, remember? Old college buddies. We don't rat on each other. Hey, I experimented with drugs a little back in college, you know, pot parties, that sort of thing."

Wes jumped up from his chair. "You don't believe me, do you?"

"Sit down, Wes. I'm not here to pass judgment; I'm here to help."

Slowly Wes eased himself back into his chair. "What *are* you doing here, Bill?"

"A friend on the police force gave me a quick call. Wes, this sort of thing could ruin my campaign if word got out. My political enemies like Stanley Taylor would have a field day with this. They would link me to what's happened to you, and by the time the press got done with it, I'd be the one accused of trafficking in drugs."

Wes stiffened his back and shook his finger at Baldwin defiantly. "I'm telling you for the last time, Baldwin, I haven't trafficked in drugs, I don't do drugs, and I have no idea where this cabin is that the bust took place. Someone's out to get me . . ."

"Or me," Baldwin interrupted. "If you're telling me the truth, Wes, Taylor is the one behind this. It wouldn't surprise me if dealing drugs is the way he's getting the money to finance his crusade. We can't let a word of this leak to the press. I've got to use my influence to get you released immediately."

Wes couldn't sit still any longer. His facial muscles twitched. He pushed his chair back and began pacing the length of the table. "Right now, I don't care what it takes to get me out of here. You ought to have seen the look in McCormick's eyes. There's no question in his mind I'm guilty."

Baldwin slumped down in his chair and braced one knee up against the edge of the table. "It isn't going to be easy for me to talk him into letting you go. I may have to owe a big favor. But, Wes, it's worth it."

Wes had his back toward Baldwin and turned around slowly to look his old college friend in the eye. "I'll be grateful for anything you can do. I don't expect you to put your political career in jeopardy over this, but I'm sure you realize if word of this gets out, not only will your campaign be destroyed, but my radio station will also go down the tubes."

Baldwin stood up and headed toward the door. "It's settled," he said. "McCormick has had his job a long time. Maybe we can work out a promotion to U.S. marshal or a Federal Emergency Management Agency job. Either position would double his pay. No matter what the price, I think he'll deal."

Baldwin left. After the door closed, the room felt so cold and stark, Wes shivered. He folded his hands and sat there looking at the walls as a pervading sense of loneliness crept into his bones.

Five minutes later, Baldwin poked his head inside the door. "I think we've got a deal," he said. "You don't have to stay in here. Wait for me outside the building."

10

Wes wasn't sure how Baldwin might obtain his release, but he was relieved to be outside breathing clear Rocky Mountain air. Sheriff McCormick's oppressive interrogation room had looked and felt like something out of a Kafka novel. Wes was concerned about how Baldwin might be playing politics with police work, but didn't that happen all the time? He weighed any abuse of the justice system against the fact he had been falsely accused. So what if Baldwin was in there pressuring McCormick to bend the rules a little? He was on his way to being a free man and that's what mattered.

Wes was sobered by the reality he owed his freedom to Baldwin. Despite who was right in the dispute between Baldwin and Taylor, Baldwin was the one who came through to avert a tragedy. Wes knew he was now in debt to the Stand for America Party.

Wes sat down on the steps of the entry to the sheriff's headquarters and waited for Baldwin. The morning sun warmed his face as he sat. Ten minutes passed by, then fifteen, and twenty. After nearly half an hour, the doors to the sheriff's office flew open and Baldwin emerged smiling.

"Let's go, friend; you're a free man. I'll bet you're anxious to leave this place."

"Not at all," Wes said, standing up and brushing the dust from the steps off the seat of his pants. "I was beginning to like it here."

The two men laughed, and Baldwin put his arm around Wes's shoulders as they walked to the parking lot. "I know you're concerned about heading home right now, but sometime soon we need to discuss nailing Taylor for putting you through this misery. Perhaps we can do that after we take part in the parade," Baldwin said as he opened the passenger side of his black Mercedes and motioned for Wes to enter.

"Parade?" Wes asked as he settled into the elegant leather seat. "Did I miss something? I don't remember your mentioning a parade."

Baldwin pulled out of the county courthouse parking lot. "It's the annual Gay Respect parade two weeks from Saturday. It will wind through the center of the city. I've scheduled you to ride with me in an open convertible as part of the honor guard to show our support for Proposition 16."

"Isn't that the referendum that calls for full recognition of adoption rights for homosexuals?"

"That's the one."

"I haven't had a chance to read the resolution, and I'm not sure I want to give my endorsement without knowing more."

Baldwin gripped the steering wheel tightly as he stiffened his arms. "Perhaps you don't understand your role as press secretary," Baldwin said tersely. "Your being there isn't an option. The gay community in this state is one of the biggest voting blocs. They also pack a lot of financial clout. Turning down their offer to ride in the parade would be political suicide."

Wes found it difficult to question the persuasions of a man who had just gotten him out of jail. Still, no matter what debt he owed for being freed, Baldwin was calling in his IOU a little too early to suit Wes.

"I told Dave Kelly I would be in the parade. If you're not there, Taylor's people will make it look like there's a division in our camp."

Wes turned sideways in his seat to get a better look at Baldwin. The would-be senator sat looking forward without an expression on his tanned face. His hair was shining from the reflection of the sun, and his white polo shirt contrasted against the black leather interior of the Benz. "What will happen at this parade? Have you been to one before?"

"Sure, several times. It's no big deal. There'll be lots of happy people, some in costume, marching, displaying banners, and riding on floats."

Wes looked at Baldwin to challenge his description. "That's it? Bill, let's not kid ourselves. This is a homosexual parade, and I've heard some pretty wild things go on. Wasn't there a big controversy last year about a video that showed the parade?"

Baldwin doubled up his left fist and slammed it against the padded center portion of the steering wheel. "Lies! All lies! That video was the work of Taylor's people. They took pictures of the lunatic fringe at last year's parade and tried to make people think that's what the whole event was like." Baldwin kept his fist doubled and pounded rhythmically on the steering wheel, softer this time. "You can blow anything out of proportion if you take an extreme example and make that represent the whole. I told you before; you can't trust Taylor's people. They're filled with hate and prejudice! Look what they've done to you."

They rode the rest of the way without saying a word. When they arrived at Wes's house, he thanked Baldwin again and went inside. His early morning interruption had exhausted him, and within minutes he collapsed on the couch and fell into a deep sleep.

Suddenly something touched his forehead, and he slapped at it instinctively. He awoke to see Annette leaning across the back of the couch.

"That's a fine way to greet your wife when she kisses you on the forehead."

Wes rubbed his eyes and waited for his pupils to adjust to the light. "I'm sorry, Sweetheart. I dozed off and I thought a bug was crawling on me."

"A bug? How dare you," Annette chided Wes with a mischievous laugh. "Maybe I should really bug you," she added as she rolled over the top of the couch and landed on top of Wes, tickling him playfully.

It was just what Wes needed to forget the unbelievable events of the day. It was hard to picture himself, only a few hours before, being held by the sheriff and facing an indefinite stay in jail. Now, he was safe at home with Annette curled up next to him on the couch.

"I didn't expect you back this soon. Weren't you supposed to return Saturday?" Wes asked, still trying to clear the cobwebs out of his head.

"Yes, but I decided to come back early. Did I intrude on something? You weren't planning on having the boys over for an all-night poker game, were you?"

Wes laughed. "Of course not. I don't even know how to play poker. In fact, I'm glad you're back. That means I won't have to go alone."

Annette stood to straighten out the wrinkles in her skirt. "Just exactly where were you going?"

"Stanley Taylor's group is having a rally Saturday. I thought it would be a good idea to check him out, especially since he'll probably be talking about the parade I'm going to ride in."

Annette put her hands on her hips and looked seriously at Wes. "Wait a minute. You're throwing all this at me too fast. First there's something about Taylor and then you've jumped to a parade. I don't know about either of these events. It might be nice if we could have a husband-to-wife discussion about what's going on."

Wes explained to Annette about finding Taylor's rally flyer and suggested they both attend to check out what Jennifer was involved in. Annette was hesitant at first; she didn't want it to appear they were spying on Jennifer. Finally, Annette relented.

"Well, this isn't my idea of a date," Annette said, "but if you'll promise me a romantic evening at my favorite restaurant in exchange, I'll be happy to join you."

Wes grabbed the flyer and jerked it from Annette's hand as if he were disgusted. "Bribery, so that's how you operate," he said in mock disgust.

Annette shook her finger at him and said, "Better be careful, Mr. Wes Bryant, or I'll have you back down on this couch tickling you until you can't stand it."

Wes and Annette both laughed, and Wes continued. "Just wait a minute; I want you to check out my costume for the rally."

Wes went to the bedroom closet and rustled through a couple of beat-up boxes on a top shelf. From the trousers rack, he grabbed an old pair of blue jeans that were reserved for yard work. Then, from a corner of the closet floor, he retrieved a tattered pair of old tennis shoes, soiled with years of mud, grime, and paint. He put on a faded madras shirt and donned a floppy denim fishing hat. Fully attired, Wes returned to the living room.

"Excuse me, sir," Annette inquired. "I don't believe we've met before. What's your name?"

Wes pulled the hat a little lower until it touched the bridge of his nose, obscuring his eyes. "Clem," he answered in his best hick accent.

"What are you doing in these here parts?" Annette asked, adding a nasal twang to her voice to play along with the ruse.

They laughed, and Wes took off his hat and tossed it on a chair. He sat down next to Annette and took her hand. "This really isn't a joke. I'm caught in the middle of Baldwin and Taylor's politics, and at some point I'll have to make a choice. I smell a stench, but I can't tell which direction it's coming from. When you separate the personalities from their platforms, it's easier for me to pick and choose who and what I stand for. The problem is that we have to pick a package. Then there's the personal aspect of my involvement with Baldwin's campaign and Jennifer's commitment to Taylor's crusade. Election Day in November is a long way away, and this whole campaign is getting increasingly complicated, beginning with the parade I mentioned. Baldwin expects me to ride with him. It's the Gay Respect parade."

Annette searched Wes's face to see if he was serious. "Wait a minute," she said. "Are you telling me my husband, who is all male, is going to be smack in the middle of those . . ."

Wes reached out to touch Annette's arm. "Don't worry, Sweetheart, I know how you feel; but there's no way around this one. There's got to be some good people who are gay. Look at Dave Kelly. In spite of our differences, he seems pretty normal. On the other hand, there are straight people whose lives are a lot worse. Look at Taylor . . ."

Wes caught himself in midsentence. He didn't want Annette to know about Kelly's accusation. He was afraid she might worry too much about Jennifer.

"Taylor? What about Taylor? What's wrong with him? Do you think he is gay too?"

"No, he's . . . I mean . . ."

"Wes, just spit it out," Annette implored. "I spoke with our pastor about Taylor, and according to Pastor Ridgeway, Taylor is a solid, sincere, and bold man. Do you have any information to the contrary? Whatever you're holding back, I deserve to know because of Jennifer."

Wes sighed deeply. He rested his body deep in the cushions of the couch and summoned strength to speak. "I've been told that Taylor is a child molester."

11

Saturday morning, April 30, Wes relaxed around the house, caught up on some neglected reading, and waited for Taylor's rally at noon. In a week, Wes felt as though his world had turned upside down. His attention had shifted from KVCE's program scheduling to subjects he would have otherwise glanced over in the daily papers. Now he couldn't stop thinking about abortion and homosexuality. Both issues were being played out in the newspapers and on radio and TV. He wondered if it was coincidence or whether it was just his focus that made these topics glaring, you-can't-ignore-this news.

Wes had written in his diary that Thursday and Friday, April 28 and 29, wouldn't end. They had dragged on because he had felt he was simply marking time waiting for Saturday's Save Our Heritage Crusade rally. He and Annette shared a leisurely brunch and at 11:00 left the house for the thirty-minute drive downtown.

Wes expected a few hundred people gathered for the rally on the front lawn surrounding the capitol. When he arrived downtown, he was amazed to find that all the streets within a three-block area bordering the capitol had been cordoned off and that traffic cops directed cars to a parking area several blocks away. After following a series of hand-lettered signs and yellow traffic-control devices, he finally found a place to park.

It was a warm midspring day with the temperature in the low sixties. Annette draped a sweater about her shoulders, and Wes put on an old denim jacket that perfectly matched his floppy hat. Annette poked Wes with her elbow and said, "Come on, Clem, it's time for us'n folks to skedaddle outta here."

A steady stream of people with a festive attitude made their way toward the gold-domed capitol. Many carried banners and posters with slogans such as "God hates sin but loves the sinner," "A baby is a terrible thing to waste," and "Restore Our Heritage before we become Sodom."

Many couples had two or more kids in tow. Toddlers were wheeled in strollers while younger children bobbed to and fro in backpacks. The teenage crowd looked unusually well-scrubbed and clean cut. Wes searched among them for a single tattoo, nose ring, obscene T-shirt, or torn pair of jeans. This was middle America at its best, and Wes couldn't picture any of these youngsters spray-painting graffiti or coming home drunk. If these were Baldwin's enemies, Wes couldn't see what America had to fear.

The closer they got to the capitol, the more congested the crowd became, yet the ever-present police seemed unnecessary. The orderly crowd respected every stop-and-go signal and seldom strayed from the confines of crosswalks. A few passing cars honked in protest, and passengers hung out the windows to yell obscenities. Those attending the rally smiled back, waved, and repeatedly yelled "God loves you." At one point, a car swerved toward the sidewalk, and a passenger hurled a bucket of water through an open window. A dozen or so pedestrians were doused, but they didn't seem to mind. They laughed and waved at the car as it sped away, seemingly unconcerned by the insult.

As they neared the capitol, the crowd-control crusade volunteers wearing red, white, and blue vests grew in number. They cheerfully gave directions and pointed out the best route to the rally staging area. Wes heard the sounds of music filtering through the noise of the crowd and traffic. From the rally stage, a high-energy gospel group churned out hand-clapping music that had pedestrians swaying to the beat. Police barricades created a large gathering area of at least several acres. Thousands had already assembled. Some hoisted small children on their shoulders while others lounged around the edges on lawn chairs. There wasn't a can of beer in sight. The tart smell of freshly squeezed lemonade from nearby concessions replaced the usual odor of fermented malt at large, public gatherings. A massive phalanx of speaker boxes blared forth the sounds of the band that concluded with a soulful finale.

Wes was confident no one would recognize him in his costume. He was surrounded by men who wore casual slacks, knit shirts, and light nylon jackets. Still, he thought it was wise to stay out of sight and nudged Annette toward the rear of the designated area. They leaned against a police barricade on the outer perimeter. The crowd grew rapidly, and Wes estimated they numbered at least ten thousand or more in front of the temporary platform that had been erected near the steps of the capitol. Despite their distance from the stage, Wes could clearly see who was gathering on it. The governor, mayor, and other high-ranking officials were notably absent.

A few policemen on horseback made their way around the outer perimeter. Parents held their children up in outstretched arms so that they could pet the horses as they passed by. The cops smiled. Wes figured they were probably used to confronting far more unruly crowds. As the band finished, a man stepped to the podium.

"It's Reverend Ridgeway," Wes whispered in Annette's ear.

The minister's voice thundered above the gathering and echoed off the walls of the towering office buildings nearby. "Dear God," he intoned, "we're gathered here in Your name to celebrate life, to celebrate decency, and to celebrate hope for this state. We ask You to heal our land and forgive the sins we have committed against You. We have transgressed Your holy law and failed to be a voice for the unborn children. Bring back the days when our children were safe from murderers and molesters, when a man was a man, and a woman was a woman, and we knew the difference."

Reverend Ridgeway was interrupted with shouts of "Amen" and applause that seemed ready to break into a thunderous ovation had he paused a little longer.

"Revive us, oh Lord, and make us once again a people proud of our heritage. Amen."

The prayer's conclusion signaled it was time for the crowd to release their pent-up enthusiasm in one tumultuous roar. As their cheering died down, a tall, stately man in his late fifties stepped to the podium and said, "Before the crusade's leader, Stanley Taylor . . ."

When the crowd heard Taylor's name, many enthusiastically waved their arms while others emitted ear-splitting whistles. As the shouting diminished, the man continued. "Mister Taylor will share his vision for the future of our state in just a few moments. First, I want to introduce myself. My name is Zachary Broe, and I am a Colorado state representative from the eleventh district. As your representative, I have worked closely with Stanley Taylor to promote pro-family and pro-life values in pending legislation. I pray that someday all Americans will find hope in these ideals, just as we have here in Colorado."

Broe fumbled with some papers and then went on. "Now we're going to hear from members of the Save Our Heritage Crusade youth corps. First, let's welcome the college division leader, a young woman named Jennifer."

Wes and Annette looked at each other in astonishment. They knew Jennifer fervently believed in Taylor's crusade but never expected her to take such a public position. Wes felt a sense of pride as well as consternation at the thought of his daughter being the first one to address the gathering.

Gradually the crowd hushed, and Wes saw Jennifer climb several small steps at the side of the platform and stride toward the podium. Annette stood on her tiptoes to see over the crowd. Zachary Broe shook Jennifer's hand and scooted a small wooden box behind the podium for her to stand on. Jennifer stepped onto the box, leaned over the podium, and nervously tapped the microphone several times.

Every amateur does it, Wes thought. *There must be some universal instinct that if we start talking without checking the microphone first, it's not going to work.*

The crowd was so quiet that the microphone picked up Jennifer rearranging the papers containing her speech. The only other sounds were the steady roar of distant traffic from the freeway and the ordinary bustle of downtown, big-city life.

Finally Jennifer spoke. "I've been asked to address you today because people my age are the leaders of tomorrow. Many of us will soon cast our first vote, and we deeply believe that this fall's election will be the most important in the history of our state. You have a clear choice. You can stay true to traditional values, or you can support a social experiment that will cast aside all gender distinctions and ignore reverence for unborn life. This is the platform of candidate Bill Baldwin."

When Jennifer said Baldwin's name, the crowd spontaneously booed in unison, and she dropped her head and looked at the podium. She paused for a few moments in what looked like an effort to compose herself.

Standing there, she seemed to realize she had struck a responsive note, and Jennifer laughed nervously. She stopped smiling and continued, "How we treat unborn life will be the measure of who we are as a people."

The audience cheered uproariously. Jennifer knew the audience liked what she said, and she responded to their encouragement with the skills of an experienced speaker. "To those who are gay, let me emphasize that we don't hate you, but we hate what you do. If you live together and want all the rights of marriage, the young people of our generation say to you boldly, you are not a family and your union is neither matrimonial nor holy!"

The crowd cheered again. Wes felt a flush of pride at Jennifer's natural oratory skills and squeezed Annette's hand to let her know how he felt.

Jennifer's speech continued. "You don't have to live a homosexual lifestyle or cover up your sexual sins by abortion. I know from experience."

The audience hushed. Wes and Annette looked at each other out of the corner of their eyes, not sure what Jennifer meant by that statement.

Jennifer lowered her voice nearly to a whisper and her shoulders shrank. "I've struggled with lesbian feelings. My real father abused me, and for a long time I hated all men. Sex to me was something dirty and unnatural. Every man, except my wonderful stepfather, seemed to be an animal who only wanted one thing. Men made me feel like an object, not a person. I questioned who I was sexually."

The audience hung on her words. "I never actually made love to a woman, but I came very close several times. My faith in God and the love of my parents kept me from stepping over the line. But if Bill Baldwin's ideas had been more popular when I struggled with feelings of sexual confusion, it would have been more acceptable in society for me to try lesbianism. I might have stepped over the line."

Jennifer paused dramatically. "Young people like me look to adults to be our example. If you say it's okay for a man to have sex with a man or for a woman to do the same with a woman, that message tells my generation there are no rights and wrongs. Young people need to be protected by laws that encourage good morals, not laws that grant special rights to a minority whose identity is determined by their abnormal sexual behavior."

The crowd exploded into applause. Wes couldn't believe his ears. His stepdaughter, Jennifer, was delivering a stemwinding speech that any politician or any talk show host would have relished.

As the cheering subsided, Jennifer spoke softly. "If William Baldwin has his way, many young people in our state will also turn to abortion as a way to hide the consequences of their immoral actions. They will kill innocent babies because Bill Baldwin will tell them it's legal and therefore normal. He wants the government to pay for teenagers' abortions and prohibit rules about parental consent. More young people in this state will kill their babies and have blood on their hands!"

The crowd was so quiet, Wes heard the sounds of the police horses' hooves click against the pavement. Slowly and emphatically, Jennifer concluded, "One of the hardest things in life to deal with is knowing you've made a terrible mistake by getting illegitimately pregnant and then compounding it with the even greater mistake of murdering your baby.

Without my parents knowing, at the age of seventeen, I aborted my baby. God has forgiven me, but it's very hard to forgive myself."

Wes and Annette looked at each other blankly. In a public setting like this, there was no way they could react verbally or emotionally. Annette had been leaning against Wes, and he pulled her more tightly to his side. Wes felt her body quivering slightly, and he gently rubbed her arm to ease the distress.

Wes knew Jennifer had every right to speak her mind and reveal her innermost secrets publicly. Still, it hurt that this large gathering knew what he and Annette hadn't been told. Was it easier for Jennifer to bare her soul in front of a crowd?

"My own parents still don't know what I did," Jennifer told the audience. "If I had gone to the hospital to have stitches or any other kind of minor medical attention, I would not have been admitted without signed parental consent. And yet, I was able to kill my baby without anyone knowing, except the doctor who wanted to be paid in cash."

A slight gasp rippled through the crowd.

Jennifer continued. "No one at the abortion clinic asked a single question about my prior medical history, and no one asked to see me again. They weren't concerned about my long-term health. They were only concerned about my *reproductive rights* and filling their pocketbooks!"

By now, the crowd was hushed to total silence. Wes could hear Jennifer sniffling into the microphone, and he saw her lift a hand to brush away tears from her cheeks. "The abortionist never explained what happened that day, and it wasn't until last Tuesday evening that I found out what goes on during an abortion. Stanley Taylor showed me a video that finally made me realize how cruel and selfish my actions were."

Jennifer waved a videocassette in the air with her right hand. "This video shows an actual abortion. If you know anyone who is pro-choice, show them this video. It's called 'The Terrible Truth about Abortion.'"

Jennifer laid the video back on the podium and rustled through her notes to continue. As she did, Wes heard the distant sounds of yelling. At once, the mounted policemen galloped their horses in the direction of

Civic Center Plaza two blocks away. Before Jennifer could speak again, the shouts grew so intense that most of the audience turned away from the stage toward the direction of the tumult. Wes saw what looked like an unruly mob of several hundred protesters charging past police officers and barricades chanting, "We're queer, we're gay, we're here to stay!" Many in the mob carried boards and baseball bats, which they flailed in every direction.

12

Jennifer stumbled back from the podium. She looked frightened and held her hands to her face. A policeman moved toward the stage.

"Annette, let's get out of here!" Wes shouted as he grabbed her hand and pulled her away from the crowd.

Parents grabbed small children and ran. Within seconds, the spot where Wes and Annette had been standing was overrun with a force of protesters, and the police barricades were smashed. Wes's denim hat flew off and was trampled under foot by the fleeing crowd.

Wes heard police whistles screeching in vain to stop the chaos. The mounted policemen seemed helpless to do anything as they fought to keep control of their horses. Those who had been seated on lawn chairs were toppled over and trampled mercilessly. Screams from those who were beaten indiscriminately mingled with the wailing of children who stumbled around trying to find their parents. Some in Taylor's crowd fought back, countering blow for blow in self-defense.

"What about Jennifer?" Annette cried as she and Wes neared their parked car. "Will she be safe?"

"Don't worry," Wes assured Annette as he fumbled in his pocket for the keys and flung open the passenger door. "Did you see the cops by the stage? Also, the demonstrators are outnumbered. They'll do a lot of damage, but I doubt they'll be able to storm the stage."

Wes ran around the back of the car to get in the driver's seat. The wail of sirens was intensifying. Ambulances, police cars, and hook-and-ladder trucks demanded the right-of-way to any thoroughfare near the capitol. As Wes closed the car door, he put down the window so he could look up at the helicopters with logos of TV stations circling overhead. His nostrils faintly picked up the acrid smell of teargas. He started the car and headed in the opposite direction from all the excitement.

Wes took Annette's hand to assure her. "I'm confident Jennifer will be okay," he reassured Annette. "We'll leave a message on her answering machine at the dorm and tell her to call us as soon as she gets there."

Annette silently shook her head. Wes could tell she was fighting back tears of worry and shock as she repeatedly sawed her index finger against her lips.

"Wes, what Jennifer said was awfully brave. I had no idea."

"Neither did I."

Annette reached across the center console with her left arm and squeezed Wes's shoulder. "We've got to talk to her about this. We must tell her we were here today and that we know. Even though she's on her own, she needs us now. She must understand we love her no matter what's happened, and we need to help her through this. My concern is that . . ." Annette paused.

"You're concerned about what?" Wes asked gently.

"I've never known anyone who had an abortion. I'm not sure what you say. Surely there are people who counsel young girls who've been through this sort of thing. Who do we turn to?"

Taylor, Wes thought. *He would know, or someone in his organization could tell us. No wonder Jennifer is so attracted to his crusade.*

Wes's thoughts were interrupted. "The baby! I was almost a grand-mother," Annette said, her voice half in shock and half sobbing. "What do you suppose it was? A little boy? A little girl?"

Now Annette's voice broke into full-fledged weeping. Her chest heaved deeply, and Wes reached over with his right arm to comfort her.

Annette collected herself and went on. "Am I a failure as a mother? Jennifer didn't feel she could come to me."

The emotional intensity was too much for Wes to handle while navigating his car. He pulled into a parking space along the street. As he shifted into park, he leaned over to hug Annette.

"Kids today grow up in a world where they're told too often that their parents are enemies. We played an ad like that on our station the other day. I didn't think about it at the time, but now I'm angry we ever sold them the time."

Annette reached in her purse and pulled out a tissue to wipe her tears. She flipped down the visor to look in the mirror and straightened her makeup. "Ad? What ad?"

"It was an ad by the Child Planning Federation," Wes explained. "The voice of a young girl kept asking, 'Who do you go to for advice about sex and personal matters? You can't go to your parents.' The thrust of the ad was that parents can't be trusted, that they're not reliable sources of information. The ad told young girls to consult the Child Planning Federation for straight talk." Wes slapped his hand against the dashboard and resisted muttering a curse under his breath. "Those are probably the people Jennifer went to for an abortion. And to think they have the audacity to call themselves a child planning organization!" Wes exclaimed as he slowly opened and closed the fingers of his left fist to release the anger inside him.

Annette flipped the visor back in place and regained her composure. "Why didn't Jennifer need parental consent? She wasn't of age."

Wes settled back in his seat and sighed deeply. "I'm just beginning to learn all about this abortion business, but I followed the news enough to know that last fall the legislature passed a law that said minors couldn't receive any medical procedure, including abortion, without the signature of a parent or guardian. A judge said that was an unconstitutional invasion of privacy. When I first heard about the ruling, I thought it was a good idea because some underage girls who want an abortion might be victims of incest. Now I wonder. Let's face it, the abortion clinics must rake in a lot of money from desperate, frightened young girls like Jennifer who are too ashamed to face their parents."

"Wes, can we go back to the stage and try to find Jennifer? I've got to be sure she's safe, and I want to be near her now."

Wes questioned whether there would be any hope of getting near the staging area. Then he remembered—his press pass. He carried it in the glove compartment at all times, never knowing when there would be some major news story he needed privileged access to. He hadn't used it in months but assumed it was still valid. He flipped open the glove compartment, and there it was.

Wes slapped the pass in the left corner of the dashboard, facing the front window, and made a U-turn out of the parking spot. "I'll do my best," he said to Annette as he pushed the speed limit racing back toward the capitol.

Minutes later, Wes approached several police cars sitting sideways in the street, their lights flashing. An officer put out his hand motioning for Wes to stop. The sober-looking policeman walked slowly toward Wes's car and leaned down to the window. He looked in the backseat and glanced around the interior before addressing Wes. "You'll have to turn your car around, mister," the officer said sternly. "There's been a disturbance and no one is allowed past this point."

Wes pointed toward his press pass.

"Look, I don't care if you're here from the *New York Times*. It's too dangerous to go in there until we've got things under control."

Baldwin! Wes wondered if he should play that trump card. If Baldwin had enough influence with the police to get him out of jail, maybe invoking his name would make the difference now.

"My boss isn't going to be happy if I don't get in there to see what's going on," Wes insisted.

"Boss? Who cares who your boss is? I'm the sergeant in charge of this detail, and I say you're not going in there, and that's that!" The officer slapped his hand against the opening of the driver's-side window.

"I'll pass that on to my boss, Officer . . ."

"Adams, Barry Adams," the officer said with increasing frustration. "You can tell your boss . . ."

"Bill Baldwin," Wes interrupted. "I think you know who he is."

The officer leaned back and straightened up. "Bill Baldwin? Are you sure he's your boss?"

"I'm his press secretary."

The officer backed away from the car slowly and walked to one of the parked patrol cars; he reached inside the window to use the radio. Adams nodded several times, handed the receiver back to the officer in the car, and returned.

"Go ahead," he said motioning Wes to drive forward.

Wes slowly crept past Officer Adams and weaved his way between the patrol cars to the street adjacent to the capitol. He was slightly bemused at the irony of the situation. He was on his way to the main staging area for a Stanley Taylor rally, assisted by the political power of Taylor's sworn enemy, Bill Baldwin.

As he neared the capitol, other policemen gave his car the once over, wondering what he was doing there. Wes passed ambulances that were being loaded with prone and bandaged people. He had left his window down, and he heard many of them wail in pain. Some had IV bottles hooked to their arms while others stumbled in the direction of the ambulances on the arms of paramedics. Dozens of people were handcuffed and responded to the questions of officers who took down information on small pads. Most members of the gay mob were shirtless, wore earrings, and sported tattoos. It was obvious that Taylor's crowd did their best to cooperate while the demonstrators assumed a more haughty posture.

Wes drove until he spotted the stage. He pulled past a police barricade, the last remaining obstacle. Scores of people scurried about as vans and passenger cars loaded as many as possible and pulled away from the site.

Wes stopped the car. "Let's get out and see if we can find Jennifer."

Wes rushed around the car to take Annette's hand, and together they ran toward the center of activity. There was so much confusion, no one noticed Wes and Annette as they elbowed their way past the dazed spectators and crusade officials.

"There she is!" Annette shouted. "That's her standing by those speaker cabinets."

Wes sprinted toward Jennifer, who was frantically speaking to a half-dozen people gathered around her. She waved her arms in every direction, and Wes figured she was reiterating what she had been through. Suddenly, Jennifer saw Wes, and she stopped cold. Wes jerked to a near halt as he and Annette took several slow steps in Jennifer's direction. Then Jennifer bolted from the group and ran toward Annette's outstretched arms, embracing her mother with heaving cries of relief.

"Mother!" Jennifer cried over and over. "It was awful! Little children were trampled, people were bleeding. They had baseball bats . . ."

Jennifer's voice trailed off as she erratically described her ordeal. Annette stroked her hair and hugged her tightly.

"It's okay, baby," Annette said reassuringly. "Wes and I were here. We saw the whole thing. Oh, Jennifer, you're such a brave girl to tell the crowd what you did."

Jennifer pulled back from her mother. "You heard? Mother, I meant to tell you, but I just couldn't. Please don't be ashamed of me. I made a terrible mistake, but I've learned."

Annette took Jennifer's outstretched hands and squeezed them tightly. Wes put an arm around her shoulder, and the three of them shared an embrace. After a few moments, Annette tugged Jennifer in the direction of the car. Once there, she opened the back door for her. Jennifer practically fell into the back seat. Annette and Wes quickly got in the car. As Wes started to drive away, a young girl came running toward them.

"That's Ashley Marie," Jennifer said. "She's the secretary of our youth organization."

"Jennifer! You forgot these!" Ashley Marie cried out as she waved a video tape and some papers in the air.

"Oh my goodness!" Jennifer opened the car door and took the items from Ashley Marie. "Thanks, Ashley," she said. "Call me tomorrow."

Ashley Marie slowly backed away from the car as Wes turned and headed away from the staging area.

"I told them they couldn't give my last name," Jennifer explained. "You heard that, didn't you? All they said was Jennifer."

Wes reached over the seat with his right arm and patted her arm. "It's okay, Honey. I'm not worried about anyone knowing who you are, I'm just thankful you're safe."

Wes slowly weaved his way back through the ambulances and police cars. They drove past several demonstrators who were handcuffed together and posed defiantly in front of their captors. One of them turned and recognized Jennifer through the windshield. He jerked his head and spat at her. The spittle splattered on the window and trickled down as Jennifer cringed and curled into a ball with her feet on top of the seat. Wes angrily shifted the car into park, threw open the car door, and leaped at the offender. As he doubled his fist and drew his arm back to punch the man's face, the strong arm of an officer restrained him. The demonstrator looked at Wes fiercely, then broke into hideous laughter.

Wes wondered why the man was laughing. He took in the full measure of the young man's appearance and guessed that he was in his early twenties. A small silver cross dangled from his right ear, and his hair was cropped short on the sides. Blond curls spilled off the top of his head and across his sweaty forehead. He was bare from the waist up, except for nipple rings that pierced both sides of his chest. His 501 jeans were slung low, the top button undone, exposing his genital hair. His body was muscular, and his athletic build was obviously the result of hours spent pumping iron. He cocked his head to one side and sized up Wes. "Well, if it isn't Wes Bryant."

Wes was stunned. After all his efforts to remain in disguise, he had been recognized.

"So what if you know who I am?" Wes responded.

"It's who I am that ought to concern you," the young man said sarcastically, his eyes narrowed and his gaze changed from arrogance to anger. "You were one punch away from ending your career in politics and radio!"

"All right, that's enough," the restraining officer said. "Let's move on." He tapped the young man on his shoulder with his nightstick and motioned for him to head toward one of the paddy wagons.

The demonstrator flung his arm at the nightstick and shoved it away defiantly. "You better be careful who you're pushing around," he said to the officer. "If my father finds out you're the one who arrested me, your career will be worthless."

13

Wes decided not to even offer Jennifer a ride back to the dorm. Without saying a word, he drove straight for home. The silence captured by the closed windows made everyone feel safe and miles away from the cries, flying punches, and profanities they had just encountered.

Wes turned on the radio and hit the pre-set button tuned to the classical station. The soft strains of Vivaldi filled the car as Annette held Jennifer's hand tightly. Jennifer rested her head against the leather seat. Within minutes, she closed her eyes, her breathing slowed, and she was asleep. Wes glanced in the rearview mirror at his stepdaughter, who was almost childlike in her ability to quickly put behind her the horrible events of that afternoon and find solace in slumber.

Thirty minutes later Jennifer awakened a few hundred yards from the Bryant household. "Where am I?"

"Home," Annette said, "where you belong right now."

Jennifer nodded with a faint smile on her face and looked out the window. Wes could tell she knew she needed her parents at a time like this. As the car pulled in the garage, Jennifer gathered her things and followed Wes and Annette inside.

"Mom," Jennifer said, "you may think this is a strange request, but I'd like to show you something." She pointed to the video she was carrying in her right hand. "I want you to see what made me get up in front of those people today."

"Jennifer," Annette responded, "you've been through so much today, I'm not sure you should put yourself through another emotionally stressful situation."

"Please, Mother?" Jennifer asked. "That quick nap did me a world of good. I'm feeling a lot better now. You and Dad need to see this video if you have any doubts about whether abortion is wrong."

"I think it would be best for you to get some rest; maybe we could look at the video tomorrow," Wes commented. "But it's up to you, Jennifer."

Annette seemed to sense that Jennifer wanted closure on the events of the day; looking at the video was her way of convincing her parents that her public pronouncement was a kind of redemptive act to counter her personal tragedy.

"Let's look at it now," Annette said as she took the videocassette from Jennifer's hand, walked to the TV, and put it in the VCR. Annette picked up the remote control and settled on the couch with Wes. Jennifer sat on the floor with her legs crossed, her elbows on her shins, and her head resting in the palms of her hands. The room was silent as the image of the FBI copyright warning flashed in red on the screen. Then against a stark black back drop were words in white: "The scenes you are about to see are graphic and may disturb some. Please use discretion regarding younger children seeing this video." Then the screen went black again and the deep resonance of an ominous chord provided the audio background for the narration.

"Abortion is an abhorrent act of violence that kills a baby," the announcer said. "In the next few minutes you will see babies who were killed as a result of nine- and ten-week abortions. In each of these cases, the babies' hearts were beating and their brains were producing brainwave activity. In some instances you will see babies killed in the second and third trimesters. Their bodies were removed from garbage found in a dumpster behind an abortion clinic. While you watch these scenes remember two things. First, the majority of abortions are performed because of decisions regarding convenience. Second, current laws permit such abortions to take place throughout all nine months of pregnancy."

Wes looked at Annette and grimaced.

The announcer continued. "Is a video like this necessary? Remember the films of the Nazi holocaust that were used to teach the world about the Third Reich's secret agenda against the Jews? The pictures of gas chambers and ovens and of bodies stacked like cordwood were used to educate the public because the deeds of Hitler's henchmen were so atrocious there were no words to describe what they had done in the death camps. The evil of Nazism was not completely understood by those outside of Germany until the world saw the graphic photographs showing Hitler's final solution. It's the same with abortion today. After seeing this video you will finally understand the horror of terminating the life of the unborn as a means of birth control. If what you are about to see seems too horrible to watch, consider whether it is also too heinous for a civilized society to permit."

As the announcer's voice faded, pastoral music provided the sound track and the first scenes of an egg being fertilized in the uterus filled the screen. Gradually the uniting of egg and sperm gave way to the first images of a baby, clearly distinguishable as human. Wes saw the head, appendages, and body.

"That baby is about eight weeks old," Jennifer said in hushed tones. "Look, Mother, you can actually see its facial features."

Annette nodded her head. Wes realized that what they saw on the TV was too intense to interrupt with talk.

Abruptly, the tranquil scene of a fetus gently floating in amniotic fluid was interrupted by a view of an abortion's aftermath. Steel forceps were seen invading a mother's body and gripping a bloody mass of indistinguishable tissue. Then the forceps turned and Wes realized he had been looking at the back of a baby's decapitated head! Now the unborn fetus's nose, mouth, and bulging eyeballs were detectable. A long metal probe stabbed the head and held it up like some gruesome, savage ode to victory. Next, tweezers sorted through tiny limbs, arms, and legs so small they fit in the plastic-gloved palm of the attending nurse. The appendages had been ripped from the baby's body so no piece of the baby would be too large to scrape from the mother's uterus. At one point, little fingers seemed to grip a scalpel as if the listless hand were reaching out in desperation, clinging to life. Then the camera panned to buckets containing the fully intact bodies of late-term abortions.

"Those were probably performed at somewhere around the seventh or eighth month," Jennifer explained. "Believe it or not, Dad, those babies will be shipped to fetal research labs where their body parts will be sliced off and harvested for medical research. Mr. Taylor refers to the labs as 'clinical Cuisinarts.'"

The horrible scene was replaced by camera shots of abortion protesters sitting in front of clinics. Some sat silently while others prayed. Suddenly police appeared and began clubbing the protesters indiscriminately. One after another the protesters, some of them wearing clerical collars, were beaten, grabbed in twisting headlocks, and dragged to waiting vans. Bibles were ripped from the ministers' hands. Some protesters were trampled by the police who seemed intent on arresting as many as possible without any consideration for possible bodily harm.

Wes looked out the corner of his eye and saw Jennifer clench her fists angrily. "Baldwin," he heard her mutter under her breath as she softly pounded the carpet.

"Who?" Annette asked as she wiped the tears from her face.

"I was just thinking about a law Mr. Taylor told our youth corps about," Jennifer said. "A law originally designed to strike back at organized criminals is now being used to shut down demonstrations that oppose this butchery. They've even passed a statewide Reproductive Facilities Ingress Act that makes it illegal to get within twenty feet of one of these slaughterhouses unless you are there to receive 'health services.'"

The biting sarcasm in Jennifer's voice cut through the heavy atmosphere of the room. Wes was taken aback by her vivid language and blunt evaluation, but he couldn't argue that what he saw on the TV screen deserved a less passionate response.

The camera returned to the abortion scene as instruments clutched the pieces of an aborted baby's body and reassembled them against the stark background of white gauze. It was like a methodical constructing of a jigsaw puzzle, first an arm, then a foot, next a leg, and finally the head and a piece of the torso.

"They're doing that to make sure they didn't leave anything inside," Jennifer continued with her biting narration.

Now the spectacle of mangled babies' bodies alternated with camera shots of police violently manhandling protesters. The intent of the video producers was obvious: to show the similarity of the brutal savagery of the abortionists and the corresponding severity of the treatment of the protesters.

Wes wasn't sure he could take any more as he watched a policeman ruthlessly beating a protester juxtaposed against the sight of a baby's crudely severed head floating in a jar of formaldehyde.

The video concluded with shots of dozens of babies taken by late-term abortions. They were not mutilated. The announcer explained they had been removed by a hysterotomy, the abortive equivalent of a Caesarean section. Their bodies, extracted intact, lay lifeless, their legs tucked against their stomachs and their arms crossed on their chests. Their facial features were fully human, and their bodies were fully formed. Some had their eyes open in an eerie gaze of death. Others had their tongues protruding. A few had the umbilical cord still attached.

Their tiny ears look as if they can hear. Their little mouths seem ready to open and speak—or scream at their tormentors. They could have been born alive! Instead, these innocent lives were . . .

Wes couldn't complete the thought. His throat choked, and his eyes misted over. As the video production credits slowly rolled up the screen, he and Annette let out quiet sighs of relief. Now he understood. Part of him had slightly resented Jennifer's speech at the rally because he feared its impact on his own reputation. Now he realized that Jennifer's brutal honesty was necessary for her own inner healing.

Annette clicked off the TV and hit the VCR rewind button on the remote. Jennifer sat motionless. As the VCR clicked, indicating the rewind phase was finished, she stretched her legs in front of her and reached out with her arms to touch her toes. "I don't even know who it was," Jennifer said with her eyes slightly downcast. "I was invited to a fraternity party, and the last thing I remember was drinking a glass of pop. Then the next thing I knew, I came to in one of the bedrooms. I was lying there . . ."

"It's okay," Annette said reassuringly. "You don't have to tell us anything you don't want to." She got up from the couch, walked over to Jennifer, and kneeled down next to her.

Jennifer whimpered as one tear after another traced the contour of her cheek. She did nothing to wipe them away until Annette reached in the pocket of her skirt and took out a small handkerchief. As she handed it to Jennifer, Annette gently stroked her daughter's back.

Jennifer gained her composure and went on. "I suppose I should have gone to the police and reported what happened, but I was too ashamed. Anyway, there were no witnesses, and even I didn't know exactly what had happened. It could have been any one of a dozen or more guys at the party."

Wes felt uncontrollable anger building inside him. He wanted to say something, hit something, or somehow release the aggression he felt toward the nameless person who had drugged and raped Jennifer.

"I pushed the whole thing out of my mind and never thought about it for weeks, until one morning I threw up," Jennifer continued. "I went to the drugstore and got one of those home pregnancy test kits. It tested positive. That's when I told Ashley Marie. She suggested I call the Child Planning Federation."

Jennifer suddenly erupted into heavy sobs, clenched her fists tightly, and pounded her hands against her thighs. "What a lie! They don't plan children; they kill them! They never said a word about adoption or any other alternatives. The woman I talked to had one thing in mind—getting me to that office to talk me into an abortion!"

Jennifer's whole body shook as her weeping turned into dry spasms of grief. She gripped Annette's right forearm tightly. "I would have told you, Mother, but the Child Planning people said you'd be angry, that you would reject me and force me to have a child I didn't want. They said that rape is what abortion is all about. Mother," Jennifer cried, "they said I was three months along and had to act quickly. They insisted I shouldn't worry. According to them, all I had inside me was a bloody chunk of tissue, like a tadpole; that's how she described it!"

Jennifer's frustration got the best of her. She jumped to her feet and paced frantically back and forth across the room, flailing her hands in the air with her lips moving silently as if she were conversing with an invisible enemy. Finally, she turned and stared directly at Wes with deep sadness in her eyes.

"Dad, I'll never forget the sound of that vacuum pump. I felt as if my insides were being sucked out, like my own life was flowing through that tube, along with my baby."

Wes started to get up but hesitated. He felt it was best to hold back until Jennifer had undergone the full catharsis of her soliloquy.

She stood there still staring at Wes. "The rape was wrong, a violent criminal act. But was that the baby's fault? Should the value of that baby's life have depended on who the father was and why he impregnated me?"

As she spoke Jennifer threw her hands open in a questioning gesture. Wes wasn't sure whether her inquiry was rhetorical or whether he should answer. The questions thrust deeply into his heart like porcupine quills that penetrate farther the more one tries to remove them.

Jennifer sat back down on the floor. Her body was limp, and she seemed exhausted from all the energy spent releasing her pent-up feelings. She lifted her head slowly and looked at Annette and then at Wes. "Don't ever let anyone tell you the unborn child isn't a living, separate human being. I felt my baby's soul leave my body."

As she said those words, Jennifer fixed her eyes on Wes. He knew what she said was more than the distraught fervency of an angry young woman who had been violated. He felt pinned to the couch as if a wrestler were on top of him, holding his reasoning and logic to the mat for the count.

Jennifer suddenly lost all composure. She let out a shriek that was half a scream and half a wail. "I heard them talking in the next room as I was getting dressed," Jennifer blurted out. "They were talking about reassembling the parts of my baby, just like in the video, to make sure they got everything out before I left their office. I'll go to my grave remembering the voice of the doctor saying, 'That's the other leg; we got it all!'"

14

Wes walked over to the VCR and hit the EJECT button without looking at Annette or Jennifer. The VCR spit out the videocassette, Wes retrieved it, and he held it in his shaking hands. He slowly turned to see the expressions on his family's faces. Wes knew that words could not begin to ease the viselike grip on his heart. Jennifer averted Wes's gaze and looked at the palms of her hands. Annette winced as she shared a glance with Wes. She rolled her eyes closed and shook her head.

"I feel like I'm going to get sick. I can't believe I did that to a little baby," Jennifer said as tears streamed down her face again. "The abortionist acted like it was just a growth on my body similar to a wart. That nurse told me that it was a very simple procedure, and it was not a life that I was taking, because life begins at birth. And if the baby was never born . . . she said the government would never sanction murder, now would they?"

Jennifer paced in a circle around the room. Without looking at her parents, she carried on a monologue with herself. "I could scream. I wish I would have watched this video before they strapped me down for the abortion." She waved her right hand in the air and then rubbed her forehead. She walked toward one end of the room and talked to the ceiling.

Then she turned toward her parents and spoke in their direction for a moment. Finally she pivoted on her heels and went the other direction. "Why didn't they tell me? Why? How can they do this to thousands of girls every day? I just don't see how they sleep at night, knowing that they not only squelched these little lives, but that they tortured them before they died."

Annette and Wes stood near Jennifer, but didn't speak. Her last comment brought tears to Annette's eyes. Wes could tell she wanted to hold Jennifer and make things rights. Yet she somehow sensed that Jennifer needed to let her emotions flow without having someone try to take care of her. Wes believed she was coming to grips with herself as a woman, a woman who had made a painful mistake.

Wes knew that any words of reassurance would have hung in the room like a cheap greeting card, so he stood there, holding back the tears that welled in his eyes.

"How can you forgive me?" Jennifer asked her parents. She walked over to them and looked meekly at Wes, then Annette. "How can you forgive a crime of this magnitude?" she asked, looking through eyes that were red and swollen.

Annette reached out and held Jennifer's hand. In a comforting voice, Annette responded. "God will forgive you, and you need to forgive yourself. It goes without saying that you don't need to apologize to us. We love you, and we know that you are a good person who would never purposely hurt anyone or anything."

Jennifer started to cry, and Annette put her arms around her. Wes stood by, not knowing what to do. Jennifer reached out for him between sobs, and then he held her. "My heart just aches," she cried out. "All I can think about is what I've done."

Jennifer slowly pulled away from Wes and grabbed some tissues to wipe her eyes. She blew her nose and said, "I need some time alone to sort some things out. I think I'll write in my journal and get on my knees in prayer."

Annette smiled at her daughter and asked, "Why don't you stay with us tonight? I don't think you should be alone after what you've just been through. Your old room is just like you left it."

Jennifer finished wiping her eyes. "Sure Mom. I'm extremely tired, and the sooner I get to bed the better. Thanks for your offer. By the way, what time is it?"

"Almost 7:30," Wes answered.

"Wow! It seems like just a couple of hours ago I was standing on the stage and . . ."

Annette put an arm around Jennifer's shoulder and began walking with her toward the bedroom. "I'll put some fresh sheets on your bed while you're getting ready," Annette said. "Wes," she added, "would you mind bringing that small kitchen TV to Jennifer's room in case she wants to watch something to help her fall asleep?"

"No problem," Wes answered as he caught up to Annette and Jennifer in the hallway to plant a good-night kiss on Jennifer's forehead. "I need to check on some things in my den first. Then I'll bring you the TV."

Jennifer put her arm around Annette's waist, and Wes watched the two walk down the hallway. As they did, he thought about the countless nights that Annette and Jennifer had shared mother-daughter talks at the end of the day. Such innocence seemed years away from today.

Wes turned back and walked to his den. His briefcase was still sitting where he had left it Friday night. He picked it up and went through his routine of switching on the halogen lamp, booting up his computer, and turning on the copy machine. As he started to put his briefcase on the desk, he noticed a sealed package with a "Same-Day Delivery Service" label. Attached to it was a note in Annette's handwriting: "This was delivered to the house on Friday afternoon."

In the hectic events of today she must have forgotten to tell me about this. Wes picked up a sharp-edged letter opener and slit the top of the flap. Inside was a Stand for America red, white, and blue folder with a note stapled to the front. It said:

Wes, inside you'll find memoranda and newspaper articles arranged topically according to campaign issues. I need you to develop a brief position statement about each topic. You'll also find enclosed a copy of our party platform to help guide you. Sorry for the short notice, but I'd like to meet with you to discuss this Monday night, May 2, at 7 P.M. at my house, 1676 Aspen Lane, City View Estates. See you there.

  Thanks,

  Bill

Wes tossed the folder back on his desk. He was frustrated that Baldwin would ask him to do something so important on such short notice. Wes had no idea as to the political intricacies of the issues, and the stack of Baldwin's papers was nearly two inches thick. He'd have to read through everything and then summarize what he thought Baldwin believed about each subject. He didn't relish the job, but the possibility of facing time in jail under the long arm of Sheriff John McCormick reminded him of the debt he owed Baldwin.

Wes arranged the paperwork into neat stacks. True to Baldwin's word, the organizing had already been done. Each section had its own cover memo stating the topic and what documentation was attached. Wes had expected to see abortion and gay rights included, but he was surprised to see the other issues Baldwin had incorporated: crime control, deficit reduction, gun control, health services, political redistricting, population regulation, religious liberty, term limitation, trade treaties, welfare reorganization, and racial justice sentencing. *He wants this by Monday night?* Wes wondered. *If I had a month I couldn't get all this properly digested and draw intelligent conclusions.*

Wes tried to put aside his annoyance. This task would give him a chance to get inside Baldwin's head to find out what made his political soul tick. Also, the slant he could put on each issue would allow him to affect the political inclination of Baldwin's campaign.

He read slowly through the list, making mental notes about what he thought Baldwin's position would be. Then he turned to review the alphabetized, detailed cover memoranda. Glancing through the memos gave him a fast political education.

"Abortion should be lawful, safe, and infrequent," read the opening line of the first cover sheet.

Seems to me that if there's an exceptional effort to make something available, that's the wrong way to make it scarce, he thought.

"Prevention should be the priority when dealing with violent antisocial acts," read the crime control synopsis. *Fine,* Wes concluded, *but what about imprisoning career criminals who roam our streets without fear of punishment?*

Wes picked up the deficit-reduction file. The summary read, "Government financial integrity demands that all spending be subject to a rigorous test of whether it reduces the deficit without abandoning the country's neediest citizens."

Wes concluded that providing a social safety net was admirable, but doing so, at the expense of greater government debt, mortgaged the financial future of all citizens.

He picked up a pen and started writing notes on the cover sheets. He didn't bother to read the gay rights synopsis. In large letters he penned: "Abandon support of Proposition 16!"

The gun-control section sounded reasonable enough. Who wasn't concerned about keeping dangerous weapons away from criminals? Wes laid that briefing alongside the party's position on crime control and noticed a glaring contradiction. While the gun-control section limited the rights of ordinary citizens to bear arms, the crime-control category evaded mandatory sentencing for those who committed a violent act with a gun.

I can guess what he says about health services, Wes thought. Sure enough, Baldwin promised cradle-to-grave benefits for both the employed and unemployed. *I don't need to bother checking if this one is covered under "deficit reduction,"* he thought sarcastically.

Wes glanced at the trade treaties file and discovered Baldwin's position would compromise America's sovereignty by surrendering all trade decisions to international tribunals. *Any unfriendly country would potentially have an economic stranglehold on the United States!*

Wes leaned back in his chair and sighed at the thought of wading through Baldwin's politically inconsistent propaganda. He realized Baldwin wanted him to make the mercurial seem steadfast and the incongruous appear consistent. To do so he'd have to artfully describe Baldwin's policies as if they represented the political mainstream, a task Wes concluded would require outright lies.

In his heart Wes had suspected that Baldwin was a consummate politician. The paperwork in front of him was black-and-white evidence to Baldwin's perfidy. What troubled Wes the most was Baldwin's rhetoric that indicated his willingness to surrender any principle in favor of his political goals.

Wes looked at his wristwatch. *It's almost 8:30. I let the time get away while I was reading this stuff.*

He immediately went to the kitchen where he kept a five-inch portable TV on the counter. Wes used it to watch the early news every morning when he had his orange juice and cereal.

Before I take this in to Jennifer, I might as well catch what's on.

Wes flipped the TV to channel 5. The tiny screen instantly illuminated in the middle of a commercial. Out of the corner of his eye, Wes watched a basketball player leap twenty feet in the air and land on top of the backboard. The sneaker-clad star nonchalantly dropped the ball through the hoop and winked into the camera as several scantily clad cheerleaders cheered his heroics. "Scoring is easier when you're wearing Court Siders," a female's sultry voice said.

The ad's mixture of sports and sexual images irritated Wes. *It's bad enough we have kids shooting each other over expensive tennis shoes,* he thought. *We don't need to tell them that they can get sex as easily as a pair of shoes.*

"We interrupt our regular programming for a special report." The serious voice of the news reporter, Gerald Slavinger, caught Wes's attention. He leaned across the kitchen counter to get a closer view of the tiny screen. The camera zoomed in on the local correspondent who held a microphone and stood in the middle of an open grassy area. In the background, the state capitol's dome illuminated the dark sky.

"Earlier today, this was the site of a riot provoked by a well-known anti-gay group. At last count, the injury toll had risen to nearly two hundred. At least fifty are in serious condition. There are no reported deaths yet."

Wes picked up a dish towel and slammed it on the counter top. *Provoked by an anti-gay group! Jennifer was the only speaker, and she didn't start that riot! The homosexual demonstrators attacked the crowd!*

The TV camera cut away to scenes of subdued pro-gay protesters being led away by the police. They appeared to be cooperating fully with the officers. A few smiled at the camera and waved. The report suggested the protesters' rights were being violated. Wes remembered the obscenities they screamed and the baseball bats they flailed in every direction. The TV camera caught none of that. Several hospital scenes showed people being treated for lacerations and bruises. To Wes's amazement, every victim was a demonstrator, identified by T-shirts that read, "We're here, and we're queer!" A nameless announcer's voice reported the list of injuries suffered by the pro-gay activists.

Next an explanatory message scrolled across the bottom of the TV: "Live news conference coverage." As Wes watched, the camera focused on several people huddled behind a podium. Over their heads a banner read, "Gay and Lesbian Caucus." As the group broke up, a man stepped to the podium and motioned for the others to move aside.

"My name is Tony Griffin, president of the Gay and Lesbian Caucus. Today was a sad day for our state," the clean-shaven, athletically built spokesman said, looking earnestly into the camera. "A small group of religious zealots known as the Restore Our Heritage Crusade staged a homophobic, fascist rally. Their bigotry enraged many oppressed citizens who tried to defend their views. When they did, the crusade crowd furiously turned on them, resulting in a melee during which scores were seriously injured. Our sympathies go out to those who were violently assaulted by these hatemongers. Today's event has underscored the necessity of passing Proposition 16 and affirming the right of everyone to pursue his or her chosen lifestyle without fear of intolerance and hate.

"Our caucus can't let the matter stop there. Gay adoption rights aren't enough! We have petitioned senatorial candidate Bill Baldwin to introduce federal employees' rights legislation that will enforce criminal penalties on any employer who discriminates against gays. More than ever, we must work for the election of Bill Baldwin."

The speaker's audience broke into applause as the TV cameras panned the room.

Dave Kelly! I might have known he'd be there! Wes thought as a camera showed Kelly standing in the front row, clapping his hands and shaking his head in agreement. His gloating smile filled the camera's screen. Wes shook his head. *Kelly looks so clean-cut and respectable.*

Kelly's complicity with the lies about the rally, and the indirect attack on Jennifer, infuriated Wes. He wished that last Monday's confrontation in the Stand for America meeting room were happening now. This time he would let his fist smash Kelly's face.

The idea of the caucus pushing for employment antidiscrimination rights incensed Wes. *If Congress passed that sort of legislation, it would be a field day for lawyers,* Wes realized. *Any gay employee could claim discrimination based on his or her sexual behavior and find a free Individual Liberties Union attorney to file a lawsuit. The employer would be forced to settle because he'd be in a no-win situation. How would the employer know an employee was gay unless he snooped into the private sexual lives of the employees, something he shouldn't do?*

As Wes continued watching, the camera focused again on the podium. "From now until November, our rallying cry will be, 'Remember April 30,'" Griffin said, reaching into his suit pocket. He held a rainbow-colored lapel button in front of the camera. It read, REMEMBER APRIL 30! "If you believe in freedom for every Coloradan, wear one of these on your left lapel."

They must have planned the riot in advance and manipulated the news media to give them this time. Those buttons weren't created today.

"Thank you for caring about our country and defending the rights of those you may not agree with," Griffin said with an everybody's-brother eloquence. "Remember, if they came after our politically unpopular ideas today, they will trample your beliefs tomorrow."

Wes reached over to turn off the TV when he noticed Slavinger back on the screen. The reporter held a stack of papers in his hands. "The Gay and Lesbian Caucus enjoys a wide range of support in Colorado," he said.

That was more like a free infomercial than a news report, Wes angrily thought.

"The following are a few of the organizations and individuals who back the efforts to pass Proposition 16," Slavinger added as he began reading from the list.

The entries didn't surprise Wes: the Colorado Court Lawyers Association, the Individual Liberties Union, the Child Planning Federation, the Evergreen Club, the Colorado Educators Association, the Ecumenical Pastoral Council, and the Rocky Mountain Endowment for the Theater. Then Slavinger started reading a list of local luminaries, heads of corporations, politicians, artists, entertainers, sports figures, and even members of the clergy.

Slavinger paused and said, "Most of those involved in politics back Proposition 16, including the following." He continued listing state legislators, congressional representatives, and candidates for public office, including Baldwin. "Finally," Slavinger concluded, "we in the media have to come out of our own closets and proclaim our support for human dignity. Here are some of the radio and TV stations, along with their ownership and management, who urge you to support Proposition 16."

Slavinger mentioned channel 5 and the other network affiliates that had given their endorsements. As the reporter droned on with his media list, he cited radio stations and their owners' names. Wes's ears perked up and he froze to hear which of his colleagues were backing gay rights. The list was made up of predictable supporters because of their past involvement in liberal social issues. Then Wes heard Slavinger announce, "KVCE owner Wes Bryant."

15

Wes shifted his car into second gear to climb the road that led to the summit of Outlook Mountain's eight-thousand-foot tabletop. The peak, a level foothill plateau that cropped up just beyond Denver's city limits, offered an ideal setting for real estate development. In fact, enterprising builders had envisioned their elite dream in the 1960s and had created City View Estates. The rambling lots of three-plus acres were reserved as building sites for the million-dollar-plus residences of Denver's high rollers. The Mile-High City's well-to-do settled either in Deer Creek Village, adjacent to the Western States Technological Park south of town, or in City View Estates a half-mile above the city.

Real estate agents marketed the Estates as the development that offered the best of both worlds. The landscape was dotted with native pine trees and rock outcroppings that gave a sense of mountain living. The views of Denver's skyline and the spreading metropolis reminded residents they were minutes away by freeway from all the amenities of big-city life. Wes considered the area where he lived a cut above suburbia, but City View Estates sported a crowd that moved in faster circles than his neighborhood. And, of course, the Estates was a gated community.

"I'm here to see Bill Baldwin," Wes said to a crisply uniformed security guard who was ensconced in a small building at the entrance to City View Estates. The guard bent down to check out the interior of Wes's car, and he asked for identification. Wes pulled out his driver's license, with its criminal-looking mug shot. The guard glanced at it and then stepped back into his post to check his paperwork, which was attached to a clipboard that hung from a string. Wes watched the guard check off something and then punch the button opening the reinforced steel gates. The guard gave Wes a salute from the bill of his cap and motioned for him to pass on by.

Wes had seen some big and beautiful homes in his lifetime, but nothing matched this grandeur. Each had a long, circular driveway leading to an entrance that was expensively landscaped. Wes drove slowly, taking in the overstated opulence of each residence. Finally he spotted Baldwin's house. It was larger and sat on what looked like the best lot. Most of the homes featured mountain architecture and landscaping, but Baldwin's place looked like it had been lifted out of antebellum times and deposited in late-twentieth-century Colorado.

Wes slowed his car to a crawl to get a better look. *That house must be at least twenty thousand square feet!* Wes thought as he tried to take in its immensity.

The front of the house was dominated by a half-dozen massive white pillars that stood two stories high. They supported a large porch that extended off the third floor. The front of the house spread out at least one hundred feet beyond either side of the pillars. To one side of the dwelling there was a sunken tennis court; on the other, there was a glass and wood laminated enclosure that covered what looked to be an Olympic-sized swimming pool. About a hundred yards behind the house and off to the left was a horse stable that was almost as big as some of the other houses in the development. In the twilight of dusk, Wes estimated the entire estate was at least twenty acres.

He turned into the driveway and dozens of lights came on, brightly illuminating the expansive front entry. Baldwin had landscaped the front of his home with intricate rock designs and a meticulously placed variety of trees with rows of hedges. The approach gave the feeling of entering Xanadu more than driving to the front door of a house.

As Wes pulled under the portico Bill Baldwin, dressed casually in crushed cotton slacks, a polo knit shirt, and loafers, stepped out the front door and waved. He looked like a friendly real estate agent about to make a showing or a golf pro welcoming his next student.

Wes turned off the motor and stepped out of his car. "How did you know I was here?" he called out to Baldwin and squeezed his remote car lock button.

"The security system alerted me," Baldwin responded. "Anytime someone starts up the driveway, it beeps inside the house. We have invisible electronic guards around the property. It's good to see you. Please come inside."

Wes felt like he was entering a grand palace. His own home wasn't too shabby, but Baldwin's entry was as big as his entire living room. A massive, dust-free crystal chandelier hung from steel supports that were surrounded by a green-and-blue Tiffany glass dome. Both walls of the entry were decorated with massive oil paintings, each twenty feet wide by ten feet high. Their pastoral landscapes looked like baroque classicism pieces. Wes was sure the paintings had profound artistic significance, but he didn't know enough to comment on them.

Baldwin paused between the canvases, then motioned for Wes to step into the living room which looked big enough to hold a small convention. The stark white carpet was offset by an enormous upholstered couch with big claw feet. A black grand piano sat in one corner, next to a copper embossed fireplace. In the opposite far corner sat a magnificent gold harp.

"Candy plays the harp," Baldwin said, smiling warmly. "When we're finished with our business, I'll see if I can get her to play for us."

"That would be very nice," Wes said, somewhat overwhelmed by the museum quality of the room. He glanced down at his shoes, hoping that he hadn't tracked any dirt on the carpet.

Baldwin caught his gesture and leaned over to whisper in his ear. "The cleaning people are here twice a week. Frankly, I wasn't crazy about this carpet myself, but the idea of a pristine white room was all Candy's, and I love her so much I just couldn't say no. Come on, let's retire to the study where we'll be more comfortable."

Baldwin turned to his right and directed Wes down a marble corridor leading to the far south wing of the house. He could hear his footsteps reverberate off the highly glossed floor. Wes anticipated the study would be a cozy little room, like the one in his house where he and Annette shared quiet moments reading and talking. Baldwin's study, however, was nearly as big as the living room, with high, vaulted ceilings framed with light aspen wood and outlined with a dark ebony trim.

The far wall featured a home entertainment center with a video projection screen that was at least twenty feet high by twenty feet wide. On either side were huge speaker cabinets, big enough to provide the sound for a small rock concert. In one corner a modified circa-1950s Wurlitzer nickelodeon was stocked with the latest CDs. Beside it sat a large, comfy leather chair that faced a panel of electronic wizardry, which resembled the cockpit of a science fiction space ship. A pair of strange-looking goggles lay on the seat.

"It's a virtual-reality machine, a real trip into the mind," Baldwin said, responding to Wes's puzzled look. "Want to try it? Just put those goggles on, sit down, and place your hands in those plastic finger forms, and you can experience hallucinations, sexual stimulation, euphoric emotions, even spiritual insights. Let me plug you in."

Wes resisted Baldwin's tug on his arm. "No thanks, Bill; the only trip I want to take is through the stack of paperwork you sent me."

"Ah, the paperwork," Baldwin nodded in agreement. "That is what you came here for. Pick a seat, and we'll get started. Can I get you something to drink?"

Wes lowered himself into an inviting leather chair. "Maybe later. Not now."

Baldwin walked to a small desk at one side of the room and picked up a pad, pen, and clipboard. He sat down opposite Wes and asked, "Have you had a chance to prepare a few brief statements about the topics in my packet?"

Wes swung his feet up on the ottoman in front of his chair, and the leather creaked. "Not exactly. I've read through everything and collected my thoughts. I figured I could put something in writing once you and I resolved a few issues tonight."

Baldwin smiled. "Good, that's what I hope to accomplish this evening. Did you have a problem with any of the topics?"

Wes hesitated. "Yes . . . all of them."

Baldwin had been writing on his pad, but his pen stopped in midsentence at Wes's answer. He looked up seriously. "All of what?"

"All the issues. I read the synopsis sheets, and I can't find even one of your party's positions that I agree with," Wes said as he gave Baldwin a steady gaze.

Baldwin put the top of his pen to his mouth and slowly rubbed his lips with it. "I didn't expect you to unanimously support all of our party's platform, but don't you think you're exaggerating when you say you disagree with all of them?

"Give me a few examples, and let's explore the misunderstandings."

Wes had Baldwin's packet in a soft leather pouch. He opened it and took out the stack of papers. For a few seconds, he leafed through them. It would be best, he decided, to avoid the more obvious issues, abortion and homosexuality, and concentrate on less controversial matters. "Welfare reorganization," Wes said. "Your position paper says you want to end the current unworkable system. Yet the legislation you propose would keep current welfare recipients on the dole for at least another three years."

Baldwin put his clipboard on the arm of his chair and stared intently at Wes. "Yes, that's right, but during that time the recipient would receive job training, and if she's a mother with children, we'd provide free healthcare and childcare. Three years later, she would hopefully be in a position to get off welfare. If not, we'd continue the payments for two more years or until such time as she could secure gainful employment."

Wes looked at Baldwin in disbelief. "Bill, how can I support that? What incentive would there be to get off welfare? You're giving welfare mothers more free services than most single mothers who are working full time. That would create greater dependency on the system, not less."

Baldwin's eyes flashed with irritation, but true to what Wes had seen in the past, he kept his cool. "You've got a point, Wes, and I suppose there are some modifications we could take under advisement. Later we can discuss your ideas in more detail, but for right now we need your best effort to put our proposed plan in writing so it seems palatable to the public. You understand what I mean, don't you?"

Wes understood all too well, and it frightened him. He was expected to lie about what the plan would cost, mislead the taxpayers about any real effort to get people off welfare, and pay no attention to the economic consequences. Baldwin wanted Wes to do what was politically popular now and forget about who would pay for it later. All that mattered was how many votes would be affected.

Baldwin played the diplomat and picked up his pad and jotted down a few notes. "I like your ideas, Wes," Baldwin said. "In fact, I'll direct our platform committee to revisit this issue later in the fall before election day. Now, are there any other issues particularly troubling to you?"

Wes thumbed through the paperwork again. "Racial justice sentencing," he said. "If I understand the theory correctly, it suggests that some people on death row should have their cases reconsidered based on the percentage of death-row occupants in their racial category."

Baldwin shook his pen affirmatively. "It's the only compassionate position to take. Do you have any idea how many death-row inmates come from racial minorities?"

"No, I don't know, but isn't the issue whether or not they committed the crime, not the color of their skin?"

Baldwin shook his head. "Wes, you should speak with one of our Individual Liberties Union lawyers. You'd be stunned to hear about the unacceptably high percentage of death-row inmates who are there because of racism. It's a disgrace, I tell you."

"Perhaps, but it seems to me the solution is strengthening the conviction rate of all criminals, not letting some murderers off the hook. Isn't that combating inequality by creating another injustice?"

Wes could tell Baldwin was getting increasingly upset the more they talked. This time, Wes decided he'd pick a more confrontational issue. "I've read what your party says about abortion, and on the surface it sounds good. You make all the politically correct references to rape, incest, and pregnancy health problems, but that's not the majority of people who walk into abortion clinics."

Baldwin laid his pad back on the chair's arm, took his pen in both hands, and tapped it rhythmically with his index fingers. "Please don't use the term 'abortion clinic.' To us, they are family planning health centers. Language, Wes, means everything. It's how you say it."

Wes distracted himself for a moment by flipping through Baldwin's paperwork. He wanted to choose his words carefully. "When does life begin?" he asked. "Isn't that the real issue?"

Baldwin laid down his pen. "I don't concern myself with deep philosophical questions like that. I only know that women who want to see a physician for reproductive health services should have the legal right to do so without interference."

"But if life begins at conception, isn't any termination of that life an unjustifiable act of homicide?"

Baldwin slammed his hand on top of his clipboard. "The average woman simply needs to take care of a mistake. It's her body, Wes, and she can do with it what she wants. As men, you and I have no right to tell her otherwise."

"But what if it isn't her body? . . . If that life inside her is a separate human being, wouldn't it be murder to terminate it?"

Baldwin jumped to his feet. "Look, I'm trying to uphold the law, and the courts say that abortion at any time is legal. I will not yield to a bigoted minority who try to deprive others of their privacy rights. Besides, the polls in this state show that 53 percent of the electorate favors elective abortions. Fifty-three percent means 53 percent of the vote, and that's a tide you don't run against!"

Wes slowly stood to his feet. "Are you telling me that the ethical questions about life and death don't matter? Are you saying that votes in the ballot box are all that count?"

Baldwin flashed a threatening glance in Wes's direction. "You sound like Stanley Taylor and his self-righteous crusade crowd. If it weren't for me, you'd be spending time with Sheriff McCormick. Or did you forget so soon?"

This was a Bill Baldwin Wes hadn't seen before, unyielding, controlling, blackmailing.

"Taylor," Wes said between clenched teeth. "I'm glad you brought him up. I've been meaning to ask you about that envelope."

"What envelope?" Baldwin responded as he walked over to the Wurlitzer and peered at its playlist.

"The envelope Dave Kelly had at the meeting a week ago. You said you'd show me the contents when the time was right. Bill, that time is now. If I'm going to be your press secretary and confront the Restore Our Heritage Crusade people, I've got to know what proof you have that Stanley Taylor is a child molester.

"I'm grateful you got me off the hook with McCormick, but my personal debt to you doesn't override finding out the truth about Taylor. I told you a week ago I'd be your press secretary if I could tell the truth. Bill, I can't tell the truth if I don't know what the truth is."

Baldwin looked up from the Wurlitzer. "All right. I'll show you what's in that envelope if you insist."

Baldwin stepped over to a small bookcase behind the desk. He pushed aside several volumes and with his right hand reached behind a large, leather-bound family Bible. He pulled out a key and put it in the lock of the center desk drawer. He turned the key, opened the drawer, and took out the gray envelope Wes remembered seeing a week ago.

"This is it," Baldwin said, shaking the envelope at Wes as if it were a loaded gun and Wes was about to be zeroed in its sight. Then he tucked the envelope under his belt as if to taunt Wes, walked to the other side of the room, and sat down in the virtual-reality chair. He grabbed hold of its steering yoke and turned it from side to side as if he were navigating a small aircraft. All the while, Baldwin said nothing. He stared at the computer gadgetry for several minutes and then looked at Wes seriously. "If you see what's inside this envelope you will be held accountable for information that could change your life forever."

Baldwin took the envelope out of his belt, held it in his right hand, and flapped it against the other hand as if tapping out some kind of warning. Slowly he walked toward Wes.

"Dad! I'm home! Whose car is that in front of the house?"

Baldwin stopped abruptly. He looked past Wes's shoulder in the direction of the voice. Wes turned around and saw a handsome young man with blond hair enter the room. Wes literally rocked back on his heels. The sudden, unannounced entry had caught him off guard just as he was about to take possession of the envelope. But Wes's sense of shock went deeper than that. Standing before him was the pro-gay protester who had spat at Jennifer.

16

W̲es, I'd like you to meet my son, Henry."

"I'm very pleased to meet you, Mr. Bryant," Henry said and reached out his hand to shake Wes's with no hint of recognition.

Wes hesitated before extending his hand. *What kind of charade is this? I nearly punched out this guy on Saturday, and now he acts like he doesn't know me.*

"Are you sure we haven't met somewhere before?" Wes inquired as he shook Henry's hand.

Henry firmly clasped Wes's palm. Wes diverted his eyes hoping he wouldn't be seen giving Henry the once-over. He noticed the hair and facial features were those of the same young man under arrest at the capitol rally riot. However, Henry's expression was now soft and polite, unlike the scornful look Wes recalled seeing just two days ago.

"Yes, I think we have met before," Henry responded soberly.

Wes caught his breath as he thought Henry remembered Saturday's confrontation.

"I used to work at Bernito's Clothing Store in the ladies fashion design department. They considered doing some advertising on your station, and

I accompanied our sales manager to your offices one day. I remember seeing you briefly in the hallway."

Wes's meetings with potential clients ran into the dozens on a monthly basis. His mind raced back over the last few weeks, trying to remember Henry's appearance at the station, but nothing came to mind.

Henry turned to his father and said, "I'm on my way to meet some guys for a drink at the Mesquite Grill, and I just stopped by the house to pick up a couple of books. I didn't mean to barge in like this."

"No problem, son," Baldwin said. "Are you still coming by party headquarters?"

"Sometime this week," Henry smiled warmly. "So glad I got to meet you, Mr. Bryant. I'm sure our paths will cross again."

"I'm sure they will."

Henry slapped his father on the shoulder and walked away. As his steps faded down the marble hallway, Baldwin remarked, "Hank is a good kid. He's in his last year of study at the Northern Colorado Institute of Art. If things continue as well as they are going, he'll graduate at the top of his class. He's a sensitive kid, just like his sister, Rebecca, was."

Baldwin looked up at a photograph on the paneled wall by his desk. There was a hauntingly beautiful picture of a frail-looking girl with delicate features and an aimless expression. Embarrassed, he turned his face away and put his right hand to his face to steady his quivering lower lip. His emotion seemed genuine, though Wes still questioned Baldwin's sincerity. Wes thought William Baldwin III seemed to be two people. One Baldwin would say or do anything for votes to further his senatorial aspirations. The other Baldwin appeared to be a sensitive family man who missed his daughter, doted on his wife, and was proud of his son.

Baldwin pulled the envelope out from under his belt and laid it on top of the desk. As he did, he turned around to face Wes.

Before he could say anything a voice echoed from the hallway. "Bill, Sweetheart, where are you?"

"I'm in the study, Candy," Baldwin answered.

Wes heard footsteps coming nearer to the door. He was beginning to wonder if a smoke-and-mirrors trick had been contrived to keep Baldwin from handing over the envelope. The interruptions seemed far too coincidental.

"There you are," a beautiful woman said as she walked toward Baldwin and threw her arms around his waist. "And this must be the incredible Mr. Bryant you've told me so much about," she said, drawing out the word *so.*

Baldwin slipped his right arm around Candy's waist and gestured toward Wes with his left hand. "Candy, this is *the* Wes Bryant. Wes, meet my wife, Candy."

Wes took several steps forward and stretched out his hand to shake Candy's right hand. She was as stunning as Wes had remembered when he first saw her photograph in Baldwin's office. Long, dark hair fell upon her shoulders, and she bore the unmistakable elegance of a woman accustomed to weekly beauty treatments. Her long, red fingernails were immaculately manicured, and her skin glowed with a healthy tone Wes guessed had been acquired with regularly scheduled Hungarian mud baths. There wasn't a crease in her black silk blouse, which clung to her perfect figure. A southwestern-style silver belt topped her gray linen slacks. Every other finger displayed extravagantly large diamonds and jewels, and her pierced ears were accented with large pearls surrounded by at least a dozen diamonds. Yet, for all her opulent elegance, her smile conveyed a warmth that disarmed Wes.

"I can't begin to tell you how grateful Bill and I are for your willingness to serve in the campaign," Candy said. "When Alex shot himself, I thought our hopes of bringing a new vision to American politics were gone." Her left arm was wrapped around Baldwin's waist, and she patted his chest with her right hand. "Alex was like a brother to Bill, and the loss was devastating. It was like losing a family member as well as a trusted business confidant. I don't know anyone but you, Mr. Bryant, who could have filled Alex's shoes. If you had said no, well, Bill would have never been the same."

Her compliment seemed genuine, and Wes lowered his head slightly, a little embarrassed by her effusive comments. "You're very gracious to say those things. Bill and I go back a long time, and I could hardly say no when he first called."

"Candy, would it be asking too much if you played a selection on the harp? I want Wes to know what a brilliantly talented wife I have."

"Why, I'd be delighted. Please join me in the living room," Candy said, motioning for Wes and Bill to follow her.

With each step down the marble corridor, Wes knew he was getting further away from what Baldwin had on Taylor in that envelope.

"Allow me a moment to tune, since I haven't played in several weeks," Candy asked as Wes and Baldwin were seated.

In less than a minute, Candy's nimble fingers stroked the strings with professional deftness. Strains of Edvard Grieg filled the room as Wes relaxed against the back of the couch. Candy's fingers glided across the strings as smoothly as the strokes of a master painter brushing strokes on a canvas. The almost spiritual beauty of her performance struck Wes as a strange contrast with everything else he knew about Baldwin and his family.

Twenty minutes later, Candy's fingertips gently plucked the final strains of the Peer Gynt Suite. Slowly and gracefully, Candy dropped her arms at her side. Wes took a deep breath. He would have clapped, but that seemed out of place, a response too crude for such mastery. Baldwin grinned from ear to ear. He seemed deeply touched by his wife's performance, though Wes surmised he must have seen her play like this hundreds of times.

"Beautiful, Mrs. Baldwin. I feel like my ears have been touched by angels."

Candy stood, tilted the harp back into its stand, and rubbed her fingers to relax the muscles. "You're too kind," she responded. "Now, if you gentlemen will excuse me, I have some things I need to do upstairs. Mr. Bryant, it truly was a pleasure to meet you," she said, extending her hand one more time.

Candy exited the room leaving Wes and Baldwin standing there awkwardly. *We're both thinking of that envelope,* Wes thought.

Baldwin spoke first. "We have some unfinished business back in the study, right Wes?"

"Right," Wes replied firmly.

Without another word, Wes followed Baldwin back down the hallway to the study and proceeded toward the desk. With his back to Wes, Baldwin picked up the envelope in his right hand and slowly turned around.

"You question whether Taylor is as bad as Kelly claims?" Baldwin inquired.

Wes decided it was his turn to stall, so he walked over to the Wurlitzer and checked out the playlist on the old nickelodeon. He bent down and scanned its selection of songs.

"What does this thing take? Quarters? Dimes? Nickels?"

"Nothing," Baldwin said, smiling. "We had it modified when we updated it to play CDs. All you have to do is pick out what you want to hear and hit the button."

Wes ran his finger across the orange-colored buttons and settled on B-26. The modified chrome-plated lever, which used to reach out for old 78s and 45s, firmly grasped a CD and placed it on the spindle. The CD started spinning as the speakers squeezed out the James Taylor classic, "You've Got a Friend."

Rip!

Wes turned around quickly to see Baldwin slitting the envelope open with his finger.

"You look inside and tell both of us what it says," Baldwin said, handing the envelope to Wes.

Wes took it. "You mean, you don't know what's in there?"

"No. I took Kelly's word for it. I've never had a reason to question his integrity. If he says the name of Taylor's molestation victim and his mother are in this envelope, that's good enough for me."

Wes glanced at the cryptic envelope with its contraband contents. With an index finger he traced the roughly torn edges of the flap. Then he handed the envelope back to Baldwin. "Taylor is your nemesis, and the privilege of finding out who he wronged should be yours."

"If you insist," Baldwin said, regaining possession of the furtive information.

Slowly he removed a sheet of paper and opened its trifold. Baldwin didn't say a word at first, but Wes couldn't mistake the look of shock on his face.

"No! It can't be." Baldwin doubled his right fist and came down hard on the desktop. He threw the paper at Wes and leaned on his desk for support.

Wes looked at the page and read: Melissa and Benjamin Lewis.

Baldwin stood erect, turned around, and folded his arms across his chest. Wes had seen Baldwin look threatening before, but this time his eyes flashed with a frightening, murderous hatred.

He regained his composure and put it on like a mask. Baldwin spoke in a clipped, deadly calm voice. "Melissa Lewis is the wife of Alex Lewis, and Benjamin is Alex's son!"

Baldwin stood motionless for a moment. "Taylor will pay for this," he said with steely resolution. "I won't go after him right away. I'll wait until he is most vulnerable. Then I'll strike without mercy." Baldwin punctuated his resolve by doubling his left fist and slamming it against the palm of his right hand.

"But what if this information isn't true?"

"Isn't true, Bryant?" Baldwin shot back. "Kelly wouldn't lie about something like this." Baldwin took several steps toward Wes as if to silence any further objections. "Alex is dead. Don't you get it, Bryant? One way or another, Taylor murdered him." Baldwin shook his head. "I thought he might have had an adverse reaction to the Prozac he was taking to treat his depression." He walked slowly across the room, mumbling with each step. "Alex tried to talk to me so many times, but I was always so busy planning my political strategy I never had time to listen."

When he reached the far side of the room, Baldwin slammed the bottom of both fists against the textured wall and sent a framed picture crashing to the ground. "God only knows why Alex didn't expose Taylor himself. Perhaps he figured nobody would believe him."

Part of Wes wanted to comfort Baldwin in his grief, but something held him back. The performance quality to Baldwin's display of emotion made Wes feel uncomfortable.

Baldwin looked again at Wes. "Why did you have to know? Why couldn't you leave well enough alone?"

The invective seemed unfair to Wes. He did deserve to know, and if what was written on that sheet of paper was the truth, it was better for both of them to find out now.

Baldwin's face softened. "I'm sorry, Wes. I shouldn't blame you for this. In a way I wish we had never opened that envelope. But I know it's best to get the truth out before our campaign goes any further."

Baldwin walked over to the chair he was sitting in earlier, collapsed in it, and spun it around to face Wes. He shook his finger at Wes. "Not one word of this gets out of this room! No one but Kelly, you, and I must know what was in that envelope until I decide on a strategy to silence Taylor once and for all. I'm not going to tell Candy, and for heaven's sake, don't tell Annette. I'm not even going to tell Kelly that I opened the envelope. I don't want him pushing me to take action prematurely."

Baldwin rested both elbows on the arms of the chair and relaxed his body a little. He seemed totally exhausted. "If you don't mind, Wes, I'd like to be alone now."

"No problem," Wes said. "I'll see myself out."

As Wes headed for the door leading to the den Baldwin called after him. "The weekly strategy session we usually have on Mondays was postponed until Wednesday. I trust you can make it at 1:30 P.M. at party headquarters. We've got a lot to talk about before the "Gay Respect Parade."

"I've still got to give that issue more thought," Wes responded.

Baldwin stood and said, "All right. I also need some time to work through the shock of what I've just learned tonight. Remember, Taylor is responsible for the deaths of two of the most important people in my life."

Wes said nothing as he turned once again to head toward the front door. He let out a sigh of relief when he got into his car and drove to the City View Estates exit. The efficient security guard gave him a parting salute as Wes aimed his Lexus down the hill toward the freeway.

As he drove toward home, Wes tried to recall the words Alex Lewis said moments before he shot himself. *You can't get by with it.*

After the scene at Baldwin's house, Wes wanted to make sense of Lewis's words. He switched on the cruise control so that he could take his mind off the speedometer and concentrate on the evening's events. Why did Henry Baldwin refuse to recognize him? Did Baldwin know his son was gay? Surely he wouldn't have been naive about his son's lifestyle after what had happened to his daughter, Rebecca.

Wes closed the garage door, walked in the house, and called for Annette. There was no response, so he went from room to room until he found her in the master bedroom, curled up against some pillows, talking on the phone. Annette gave Wes a big smile, put her index finger to her lips, and silently mouthed the words, "Just one minute."

He went into the walk-in closet and took off his suit coat and tie and started to remove his shoes when Annette came up behind him and announced that she was off the phone. Shoeless and tieless, Wes followed Annette from the closet into the bedroom.

"Tell me about your evening with Mr. Baldwin," Annette asked.

"I'd like to, but first I'd like to put on my robe and get something to drink. Who were you talking to?"

Annette waited until Wes finished undressing, threw on his favorite terry-cloth robe, and stood by the bed. "I phoned someone who may be able to help Jennifer get over her abortion."

"A minister or a counselor?" Wes asked as he reached out to help Annette off the bed.

"A lay counselor who specializes in post-traumatic stress disorder, what some women go through after an abortion," Annette answered. With that, she and Wes walked hand-in-hand to the kitchen.

Wes got a can of soda out of the refrigerator, popped the top, and took two long gulps.

"Tell me all about the evening with Bill Baldwin."

Annette didn't seem very anxious to talk about her phone call, and that made Wes curious. "So, who is this lay counselor?" he asked.

"Someone with Project Baby-Save," Annette responded as she pulled out a chair from the kitchen table and sat down.

Wes set his soda on the table and joined Annette. "The group that's involved with the antiabortion demonstrations? The last I heard, the federal Justice Department had sent a U.S. marshal to check out these people. The newspaper article I read said they're dangerous and violent."

"Not according to . . ." Annette caught herself saying something she obviously didn't want to say.

"According to who?"

Annette sighed. "Oh, I might as well tell you. I got their number from the Restore Our Heritage Crusade."

Wes slugged down another sip of soda. After the incident at Baldwin's house, he was filled with anger at the mere mention of Stanley Taylor's name.

"Did you have to contact Taylor's people?" he asked, restraining his feelings. "Couldn't you just look in the Yellow Pages?"

Annette stared at him inquisitively. "Look under what? The phone company doesn't allow antiabortion organizations to advertise. They are forced to sneak in their advertisements under pseudonyms or align themselves with adoption agencies, thanks to the Criminal Conspiracy Investigation Act."

"Whoa!" Wes said. "Suddenly, you're awfully knowledgeable about this sort of thing."

"Since I found out about Jennifer's abortion, I've been reading everything I can get my hands on. I've had a quick education about the pro-life movement."

"What did these Project Baby-Save people tell you?"

"We need to have a memorial for Jennifer's baby."

"A memorial? You mean a funeral?"

"The counselor said Jennifer needs closure. Women who have an abortion never get an opportunity to say good-bye to their babies. You saw that video. Once a woman realizes what she's done, she needs a way to deal with the guilt and put the past to rest."

Wes had never thought about it, but this made sense. If Jennifer genuinely believed she had killed her baby, she couldn't brush aside the emotional consequences of her actions. Yet the thought of having a memorial for a person who had only existed as a tiny identity inside Jennifer's body made him feel a little uncomfortable. It made him think about when life really begins and who was right—those who said life begins at conception or those who argued life begins at birth. The video Jennifer had brought home made him sick. Commemorating the passing of this unborn baby would acknowledge that the abortionist had in fact destroyed a human being.

"How do we go about this?" Wes inquired.

"The counselor suggested that we keep it low-key. The three of us could gather in a pleasant setting, outdoors somewhere. We need to give Jennifer time to talk about her feelings and then encourage her to say good-bye to the baby, as if the baby could hear and understand her words."

"When?"

"As soon as possible. I'll call Jennifer tomorrow morning and explain it all to her. Then it's up to her if she wants to go through with it."

Wes crushed the pop can in his hand, stepped on the release for the trash compactor, and threw the can inside. He started to leave the kitchen when he realized his account of what happened at Baldwin's house had been waylaid. "Baldwin asked me not to tell you something, but I'm going to anyway. I didn't promise him I wouldn't, and I think you need to know. It's about the accusation that Stanley Taylor is a child molester."

Annette put her chair back under the kitchen table and walked toward Wes. "I've already told you my opinion. I don't believe it. I don't know who made up that story, but it simply isn't true."

"You may be right, but Baldwin and Kelly claim they have evidence.

They say the child Taylor molested was Alex Lewis's son, and that the boy and his mother are willing to come forward."

Annette looked shocked, then she seemed to concentrate on something. All at once she hugged Wes and looked up into his eyes. "I can't imagine what it's like, Sweetheart, the way you've been pulled back and forth the last couple of weeks. Frankly, it looks to me like Kelly and Baldwin are trying to manipulate you with this story."

Wes appreciated Annette's warmth and her reassurance that she understood the struggle he was having to determine who was telling the truth.

"The antiabortion movement isn't the only thing I've been checking into lately," Annette revealed. "I've also looked into Baldwin's background. I'll bet Baldwin never told you how Alex Lewis got his job."

"No, as a matter of fact he didn't. But then, I never had reason to ask. The issue seemed so emotionally sensitive, I didn't want to do any probing."

"Then maybe it's a good thing I did some investigating. The maiden name of Melissa Lewis is Baldwin. Alex Lewis married Bill Baldwin's sister."

17

Tuesday, May 3, Wes woke up in a cold sweat. His dreams lately had made his sleep fitful at best, once he finally got to sleep. He looked over at Annette. She was turned away from him and sleeping on her side. He watched for a moment as she slowly breathed in and out. Then he stared at the ceiling fan, which made a whistling sound as it whirred above the bed. If going without sleep over Baldwin and Taylor wasn't enough, Wes hadn't been getting much work done at the office.

The office. The thought made Wes sit straight up in bed. He had to be there by 8 A.M., on the nose. He slipped out of bed and made great time rushing through his morning routine. He was out of the house and on his way to the office by the time the clock hit 7:58. He spent the entire morning catching up on work and instructed Deborah, his secretary, to hold all calls and allow no interruptions unless there was an emergency. He made it through the morning without any intrusions, except for Deborah, who delivered a tuna salad sub sandwich for an eleven o'clock lunch. It was the longest period of time Wes had to think since the night of Lewis's suicide, and he took advantage of the opportunity.

By noon, Wes had waded through the most important issues related to managing the station. A huge stack of business memoranda still awaited his inspection, but none was urgent enough to require immediate attention. When all those documents had been sorted out, he placed them in a single pile and dumped the stack into a file folder to take home so that he could get to them at his convenience.

What interested Wes most had nothing to do with station business. It was a stack of conservative political journals he had asked Deborah to collect for him. The foot-high pile of periodicals consisted of everything from independently published, right-wing patriotic newsletters to four-color magazines. Wes hadn't realized there were that many journals devoted solely to political analysis from a right-of-center perspective. Some were obviously desktop periodicals, spit out by home computers catering to a regional audience. Others were national in scope and featured sought-after writers who espoused their views on slick paper.

Abortion was clearly the hot topic. One article entitled "The Slippery Slope of Assisted Suicide" connected euthanasia and abortion in a revealing piece of logic. The writer suggested that court documents from dozens of judicial cases showed that mercy-killing and termination-of-treatment incidents were legally upheld by the statutory right to an abortion. The writer said, "The so-called 'right to choose' trumpeted by abortionists, is the same argument offered by those in favor of assisted suicide. There is definitely a connection between the two issues."

Wes put the magazine down and thought about what he had read. If the writer was correct, Baldwin's appeal for unhindered personal freedoms was really a smoke screen for an immoral agenda. In the past, Wes had always felt that abortion was acceptable in the cases of rape and incest. Now he wondered if these cases were used to attract sympathy so society would adopt a quality-of-life ethic rather than protect all unborn life. Certainly Jennifer's sorrow over her loss was no less grievous because of how her baby was conceived.

Wes grabbed another magazine and from the front page saw that this issue focused on crime. One article described the crime problem this way: "Life has been so devalued in the eyes of some that they can blow others away on a whim. Today's lawbreakers are driven by contemptuous greed, and their only code of behavior is gangster bravado. Criminals must be made to understand that their deeds will lead to public shame, quick retribution, and prolonged punishment. Their incarceration must be based on deprivation and discomfort."

Wes grabbed his briefcase, pulled out the Stand for America Party platform, and read the opening statement on crime control. Its analysis sharply contrasted with the article he had read. The summary stated, "Antisocial behavior should not uniformly be condemned. To do so would damage the self-esteem of the criminal, who is himself a victim. We of the Stand for America Party are committed to behavioral enhancement based on job skills training, exposure to the arts, and therapeutic intervention."

Wes threw the platform papers back in his briefcase. Did the idiots who wrote this political babble really think that a trip to the Louvre and a glance at the Mona Lisa would reform drug dealers and street hustlers? He swallowed deeply as he realized the "idiots" were his political partners.

Disgusted, Wes kept thumbing through the magazines. The arguments for and against "political redistricting" stunned Wes. He vaguely knew about court challenges to the concept of tailoring voting districts to satisfy racial quotas. Wes hadn't realized that such gerrymandering actually created artificial boundaries and carved up the electorate for the sake of righting past racial wrongs. Baldwin's platform said, "Such apportionment is an admirable attempt to create voting blocs to increase the representation of minorities in government." An opposition writer concluded, "Race-based redistricting is a form of reverse political apartheid, and unconstitutionally creates voting districts according to the color of skin instead of shared geographical interests."

Wes had never been troubled much by issues of religious liberties until now. He had always assumed that the first amendment was pretty clear: the Constitution sought to protect religion from government intrusion, not protect the government from any influence of religion. What he read frightened him: a school principle was fired for reading his Bible during lunch hour; a small rural community was forced to chisel the Ten

Commandments off a stone marker in the city square; a graduate was refused his diploma because he offered a voluntary prayer at commencement.

Wes felt betrayed by the mainstream media for covering up so much information that affected his freedoms. And he felt deceived by Baldwin who had made his job as press secretary seem so functionary. He stared at the pile of magazines. He identified too many times with Baldwin's opposition to make his position as press secretary effective. He had to go beyond his allegiance to an old friend and the debt he owed for escaping McCormick's cement playland. His conscience and honor were at stake now.

The office intercom buzzed. "Boss, I apologize for interrupting," Deborah explained, "but I just went through the mail, and there's something I think you should see."

Seconds later, Deborah knocked on the door and stepped to Wes's desk, holding a videocassette in her hand. "It wasn't marked personal so I followed your usual orders of not wasting your time to forward something to you that hasn't been checked out first. I went to the conference room VCR and popped it in for a few minutes. It's produced by some outfit called Citizens for Ethical Government."

"What's it about?"

"Baldwin. And it isn't very complimentary."

"Doesn't surprise me," Wes said. "It probably won't be the last piece of political dirty work we'll see from all sides once we get closer to November."

"You know more about this sort of thing than me," Deborah said condescendingly, "but what's on this video is scary. Some guy named Andrew Patterson says he used to work for Baldwin and that Baldwin was a womanizer and liar."

"I'd expect that," Wes said, a little bored by the conversation and irritated that his intense study had been suspended for a muckraking video.

"There's more to it," Deborah added. "The video shows proof that Baldwin has been involved in drug smuggling, influence peddling, and extortion. It also says that his son, some kid named Henry, is part of a child-pornography ring."

Deborah brought the video to Wes, who immediately put it in a VCR. White letters on a black screen read: "Citizens for Ethical Government presents Bill Baldwin—The Senator's True Agenda." The screen faded to black, then the camera framed a man in his forties, seated in what looked to be a library with bookshelves as a backdrop. The studious ambiance was accented by the man's green cardigan sweater, which gave him the feel of an intellectual Mr. Rogers, a thoughtful friend in your neighborhood. The video wasted no time getting to the point.

"My name is Andrew Patterson," the earnest-looking gentleman said peering directly into the camera. "For five years I was employed by Bill Baldwin as his personal business manager."

Here it comes. Another disgruntled employee gossiping about a boss he betrayed. Wes had his share of people he had fired who later trumped up false accusations to file a potentially embarrassing lawsuit. They were usually the type that had to blame someone else for their failure.

Apparently Patterson was different. "I'm not suing Bill Baldwin," he explained, "and I'm not looking for any money. I'm doing this as a patriot. I don't want to see my country sold out to evil forces that will destroy the foundations of our republic."

Wes's noticed that Patterson's eyes were watering.

"Do you swear that the statements you are about to make are the truth, the whole truth, and nothing but the truth?" an off-camera voice said. The single camera of this low-budget video tilted down slightly to show Patterson's hand spread out on top of a Bible as he responded, "I do."

The camera tilted back up and zoomed in closer to Patterson's face. "I audited Bill Baldwin's books and traced the transactions for his real estate purchases, which were funded by loans from now-bankrupt savings institutions. None of those loans were ever repaid, and most were later written off the books shortly before these institutions became insolvent. I watched Mr. Baldwin curry favor with the federal regulators who tried to trace these transactions and who eventually gave up because there was an insufficient paper trail. Any remaining debt on those properties was later paid off by untraceable infusions of cash, which I believe were the result of drug-smuggling operations."

For the first time, the screen showed something other than Patterson's face. A shaky camera with a grainy picture, obviously taken from a distance in poor lighting conditions, zoomed in on an airstrip. A single-engine plane landed and was met by four burly men with rifles slung over their shoulders. They quickly unloaded a dozen or so large burlap-wrapped packages and stepped away as the plane took off again.

The camera followed the men as they carried the packages to a shed. Patterson's voice announced, "The aircraft you just saw was registered to Baldwin III Associates, an international trading commodities company. It's my belief that those packages contained cocaine and were part of an operation centered in the Canyon Creek area, supplying Aspen and Vail with drugs during the winter ski season."

Canyon Creek! Were these the people Sheriff McCormick supposedly busted? All along, Wes had thought Stanley Taylor was the one who had planted his billfold. If there was any validity to this video, Baldwin himself could have done the dirty work.

Only minutes into the video, Wes was already sick with speculation. Was Baldwin's much-vaunted real estate success actually the result of illegal money laundering? Did Wes really owe Baldwin a debt of gratitude for freeing him from McCormick? Was Wes a gullible pawn in a more serious charade?

Patterson held a stack of papers in front of the camera. "These are top-secret files from the Colorado Bureau of Investigation. They were leaked to me by a fellow patriot who fears that Baldwin's election will turn our beloved state into a law-free zone that will be a haven for South American cocaine cartels. These files document the dates, times, and places of plane shipments when huge quantities of illegal drugs were flown into our state. Nothing has been done about this because powerful people want Bill Baldwin elected. My fellow Americans, Bill Baldwin owes his soul and his political campaign war chest to the scum who peddle drugs to our children!"

As the screen returned to Andrew Patterson, the camera moved back for a wide shot that showed him sitting in a high-back leather chair, his right leg over his left knee, and his hands folded in his lap. The scene was less intimidating than the tight shot of his eyes. But what he said was just as forceful.

"I have two children, a boy and a girl," Patterson started out. "As a parent, I would never want to say or do anything harmful to another parent, but larger issues are at stake here. When I decided to do this video, I had to make a choice between protecting Bill Baldwin's right to privacy and protecting the future of our state." Patterson looked down for a moment, averting his eyes from the camera to collect his thoughts, then looked back up with sadness on his face. "It was no secret to those of us in Bill Baldwin's inner circle that his children went astray. Instead of trying to remedy their behavior, Mr. Baldwin excused their conduct. In the end, he exonerated their lifestyles and defended their unsavory practices."

Patterson drew out the word *unsavory* with a tone of disgust and reluctance. Patterson genuinely found this part of the video hard to deal with. He swallowed several times and reached for a sip of water from a glass sitting on a small stand next to him. He leaned forward and spoke softly.

"It's no secret to anyone that Baldwin's daughter, Rebecca, was a lesbian. What he did hide from many people was her involvement in activist organizations with a militant feminist agenda that would establish a matriarchal society headed by lesbian avengers. Those women actively recruit young girls for lesbianism. They are also connected with the vampire lesbian movement, whose practices are so unspeakable, modesty forbids me to address them on this video. But as bad as Rebecca Baldwin's behavior was, her brother, Hank Baldwin, carried things much further. Hank Baldwin belonged to the American Boy Lovers Association, also known by the acronym ABLA. ABLA's slogan is 'sex by ten, with older men.'"

The screen shifted to a photo of marchers in some kind of public protest. Some in the group were shirtless, displaying nipple rings. Others, dressed as drag queens, were decked out in long, flowing boas and large, pastel prints. A young man in the center of the group held high a poster that read "Freedom, equality, pederasty." Slowly, the camera lens zoomed in, and Wes saw the protester was Hank Baldwin.

The camera returned to Andrew Patterson. He had gotten out of his chair, leaned against the bookshelves, and held a single piece of paper in his hands. With all the seriousness he could muster, Patterson declared, "According to this report, Hank Baldwin's involvement in ABLA goes deeper than public protests. Six months ago, an apartment he was living in was raided, and pornographic videos of male minors were confiscated."

Patterson folded the document and sat back down in the chair. He looked back at the camera. "I'm asking candidate Bill Baldwin of the Stand for America Party to withdraw from the campaign until the issues surrounding his character and that of his son are resolved."

As the address of Citizens for Ethical Government and the video credits rolled, Wes looked at his watch. The entire presentation had taken less than ten minutes. Alex Lewis's last words flashed again through his mind. This time, Wes wondered if Lewis was referring to Hank Baldwin.

Wes rewound the videotape and threw it in his briefcase, along with the other unfinished paperwork he had organized earlier. He reached for his suit coat, which he had left hanging on the door. As he did, the intercom buzzed. He picked up the phone and heard Deborah's voice.

"Boss, if you've finished with the video, I've got a message for you. It came in earlier today, but you asked not to be disturbed so I didn't pass it on. Then when I saw the video, I deliberately held the message until you had a chance to view it. Hank Baldwin called about two hours ago and left a number."

Wes froze with one arm through the sleeve of his suit coat. He took his arm out of the coat and laid it across the top of a chair. "Give me the number, Deborah."

"555-1617," Deborah responded.

Wes sat back down in his chair and cradled the phone between his shoulder and ear. *Should I wait to return the call until after I've confronted Bill Baldwin with these issues? Should I stay out of this whole thing completely and resign from the campaign?*

Wes dialed Hank's number.

A soft-spoken young man answered. "Hello, this is Hank Baldwin."

"Wes Bryant here. I'm returning your call."

Wes heard an audible sigh of relief. "Thank God you called me back. I was afraid after what happened at the rally you'd hate me so much I'd never hear from you. Then, when I pretended I didn't know you at my father's house, I thought that might turn you away completely." Henry Baldwin's words were followed by a long pause. "Look, Mr. Bryant, if you don't want to talk with me or ever see me again, I'll understand. My actions last Saturday were inexcusable. I've been thinking a lot about what happened that day, and I'm truly sorry for my actions. Your daughter is a very brave woman, and what she said has haunted me ever since."

Wes was skeptical. "What do you want from me?"

"I've made a lot of mistakes in my life, Mr. Bryant, but I'm not as bad as you think I am. I want your help. I want out of everything I'm involved in, and I don't know of anyone else I can turn to."

Wes wanted to hang up the phone and pretend the conversation had never taken place. "Why should I believe you?" he asked.

"I know all about the threats, the horse manure that was sent to your office, and the decapitated doll that was left in your driveway. All I ask is that you promise my father will never know about this conversation or any other conversations we may have."

"I'll give my word I won't say anything about this phone call," Wes assured Hank. "I can't give any assurances about what might happen in the future."

"Fair enough," Hank responded. "I know you're scheduled to meet at party headquarters tomorrow. Can I see you secretly before then?"

"When?"

"Tomorrow morning? You name the time and place."

"Let's make it nine tomorrow morning at the Sagebrush Health Food Restaurant just west of town on Route 36."

"I know the place," Hank responded. "I'll be there."

18

Curiosity about Henry Baldwin's call made Wes anxious to leave the office, get home, and ask Annette what she thought about his meeting the next morning. *I'll take Annette out to dinner tonight and keep the promise I made about a romantic evening. I'll get her some flowers from that guy on the street corner outside the office. He's always hawking carnations to people stopped at the light.*

Thud! Something slammed into Wes's office door. He opened it and saw Ansel Lowe, KVCE's news director, pushing a large blue, shock-resistant case down the hallway. Its wheels made tiny tracks in the carpet.

"Hey! What's going?"

Lowe stopped and stood up straight. Both arms were draped with long rolls of microphone cable he had slung over his shoulders. He huffed and puffed for a moment trying to catch his breath. "Sorry, Wes, this Comrex tipped over and banged into your door. I checked, and there are no scratches. I was in such a rush."

"I hope you didn't damage the equipment. Why are you in such a hurry? You haven't used that remote broadcasting Comrex in months. It's not only heavy, but it's a pain to hook up. It was so expensive, it makes me angry just to see it!"

Wes had approved the purchase of the Comrex remote broadcast board several years ago to cover important news events on location. It connected to a standard telephone line and enhanced its sound quality by boosting the kilohertz of its transmission. Consequently, the normally thin sound of a voice over a phone line could be enhanced to approximate broadcast quality. Delbert Pike, KVCE's chief engineer, had rigged the Comrex to connect with the cellular phone in the company van. He had also adapted the Comrex to run on DC current from special batteries stored in the vehicle. These adaptations allowed KVCE to broadcast live from any place that could be reached by cellular service.

Wes had mixed feelings about seeing the Comrex in action because, along with its original cost, it was expensive to operate. He had restricted its usage to paying events, like special advertising promotions. In fact, he remembered it was last used when Jim Robinson's Honda/Toyota dealership held a week-long sale extravaganza, and they parked the van smack in the middle of the used-car lot.

"I just got a call from Chris Beale, the kid from broadcasting school who's doing an apprenticeship with us," Lowe explained. "He reported in from the scene of those abortion protests at the Reproductive Services Centers clinic in South Foothills. Stanley Taylor's crusade people have been camped out nearby for three days and have kept an around-the-clock prayer vigil. The police are getting edgy about possible violence. You know how tense things have been since that abortion doctor named Flynn was shot a few weeks ago."

Wes remembered the gleam in the eye of Robert Cusco, Baldwin's special interest groups liaison, when he talked about the video footage of Flynn's murder. *Baldwin has probably got someone at the South Foothills protest with a video camera rolling.*

"Let me help you," Wes said. He grabbed his briefcase and threw on his suit coat. As he did, he patted the pocket of his coat to be certain he had his pocket-sized Dictaphone tape recorder. He always kept it handy to record memos and notes as ideas came to him.

Wes took a roll of microphone cable off Lowe's shoulder and slung it over his own. "Let's go," he said as he held the front door open for Lowe. "I'll help you get that Comrex in the van and then follow you in my car."

As Wes followed the van out the parking lot, he spotted a flower vender and motioned to him.

"Only six dollars for half a dozen," the man called out.

Wes leaned out the window, motioned for the man to approach his car, and took a deep whiff of the carnations. He pulled out a five-dollar bill.

"Six, sir, not five. Smell them. Your lady like them very much. She be very nice to you," he said with a Middle Eastern accent and a wink. He shoved a bouquet of flowers toward Wes.

The light turned green, and Wes saw Lowe pull away from the intersection. He put his car in gear and started moving. "Okay, okay, for you, special price of five dollars," the man said running alongside Wes.

After a quick exchange of flowers and cash, Wes floored his Lexus and sped after the van. He wasn't certain which abortion clinic the protesters had gathered in front of and needed to follow Lowe closely. Ten minutes later, they entered a residential neighborhood bordered by convenience stores and a sixties-style mini-mall. At one corner of the complex was a small brick building surrounded by police barricades and patrol cars.

Lowe parked, and without waiting for Wes, threw open the back door of the van. He slid out the Comrex and dialed KVCE's main studio. Then he unstrung the microphone cable as Wes took in the surroundings.

The main staging area for the protesters was a small park about fifty yards away from the abortion clinic. A few camping tents had been erected, and the fifty or so people who had gathered, talked and prayed. The steps leading to the clinic were guarded by a uniformed U.S. marshal. Three women, dressed as nurses, stood at the door ready to escort any women who approached. On the sidewalk, about fifty feet away, a dozen people knelt quietly, their heads bent in prayer. Several had Bibles by their sides. Wes looked closely and saw Stanley Taylor.

The silence of the protesters was contrasted by several women who stood on the clinic's front lawn, screaming taunts. "Choice, choice, choice," they chanted between profanities.

The protesters seemed unfazed by the verbal assaults, and they kept praying. Another group of about twenty rounded the corner of the block and headed toward the clinic. The noisy crowd angrily countered the clinic's defenders with slogans of their own. "Baby killers go away; you deserve to die today," one screamed. A man with a clerical collar, who appeared to be a priest, held aloft a sign that pictured Adolf Hitler with the caption, "Reproductive Services Centers' Founder."

As they neared the clinic Ansel Lowe reported in a more animated manner. *There isn't another microphone or camera in sight,* Wes thought. *Whatever happens, we've got the scoop.*

A frail, blonde-haired girl Wes guessed as no more than sixteen-years-old stepped from a car that stopped in front of the center. She slowly made her way toward the clinic's entrance. She hung her head, and her long, straight hair fell about her face like a camouflage. Everyone focused on her. For a moment, no one spoke.

The sound of weeping interrupted the silence, and Wes saw a lady next to Taylor break into open sobs. The marshal became more attentive. His hands nervously fingered his belt, and he rubbed the palm of one hand against the leather of his handgun holster. His eyes shifted rapidly from the protesters to the young girl and then to the clinic personnel.

The girl stopped momentarily and glanced at the weeping woman whose hands reverently clasped a rosary. For a few seconds, it seemed as if the girl might not enter the clinic. She ran the fingers of one hand up and down the strap of the purse hanging from her shoulder. Her hesitation froze everyone except Lowe, who continued his unbroken banter.

Then all eyes turned toward the clinic's door as it opened and a tall, lanky man dressed in white stepped out. "Molly, we've been expecting you," he said to the girl. He stretched out his arms.

Molly looked at him and took a halting step forward.

"Baby murderer!"

Wes wasn't sure where the scream came from, but it triggered instant reactions from everyone. Molly ran toward the clinic, followed by the priest with the Hitler sign. He lunged at Molly, knocking her onto the clinic's front lawn. Taylor sprang from his crouched position and entered the fray, trying to restrain the priest. Police came running from every direction as a chorus of screams and verbal invectives filled the air. Within seconds a riot erupted with the battle lines drawn so hastily it was hard to tell who was attacking whom.

Those who had prayed with Taylor stepped back in surprise. Members of the priest's group moved in and slapped and slugged the clinic defenders. What amazed Wes was the way the police responded. He watched in disbelief as they waded into the group of Taylor's people with billy clubs and started swinging. One after another, the crusade protesters dodged the onslaught of blows, but many fell to the ground clutching their bloody and bruised heads. They were immediately manacled with quick-tie plastic handcuffs. Some had their arms violently twisted behind their backs by the officers while others cowered as their forearms, raised in protection, were battered again and again. The sound of bone-crunching blows, mingled with cries of anguish from the protesters, was marked by cheers of encouragement from the unmolested clinic staff and their supporters.

Ansel Lowe stretched his microphone cord to its maximum length and shouted every graphic detail to KVCE listeners. Wes was getting his scoop, but it was a broadcast exclusive he wished he were without.

Crack! The sharp report of a gunshot brought the melee to an abrupt halt.

A woman near the entrance screamed. "Dr. Bowman has been shot!"

Wes saw the man who had welcomed Molly slump against the doorway. Blood covered the front of his smock. Molly got up from the ground, ran toward the car that had brought her, and jumped inside. Taylor tried to get up, but he looked stunned. The priest pointed at him and yelled, "He did it! I saw him shoot the doctor. Baby-killer Bowman deserved to die. The blood of innocent babies is on his hands. God bless Stanley Taylor!"

A handgun lay next to Taylor.

The cleric stood and pointed toward the fallen doctor. "He's the murderer. He's the one condemned by God. This is a noble deed, one worthy of praise to the Almighty!" The priest picked up the gun and pointed it first at Taylor, then at the marshal. He waved his hand toward the police. "Back off! Stanley, run! Escape while you can!"

Taylor stood, looking like he wasn't sure what to do. The marshal motioned for his fellow officers to remain calm.

"You've done God's work. Now, in His name, run!" the priest yelled. He pointed the gun menacingly at Taylor as if he might be shot next.

Taylor bolted from the scene. He ran down the street and disappeared into an alleyway. Once he was out of sight, the priest dropped the gun and embraced his followers. Police sirens blasted and two officers ran after Taylor, who, Wes surmised, was well beyond their grasp. As all eyes turned toward Taylor's pursuers, Wes caught the priest out the corner of his eye. The priest backed away from the action, slipped around a corner of the clinic, and fled.

One of the clinic nurses knelt beside the doctor and put her hand on his neck to feel for a pulse. "He's dead," she said quietly.

19

The Sagebrush Health Food Restaurant was one of Annette's favorite eateries, so Wes had been there many times. It was a cross between a New Age cookery and a leftover sixties Alice's Restaurant upstaged by the polish of nineties decor. The menu offered a variety of southern and ethnic foods as well as natural, organic dishes. In Wes's opinion, the restaurant's saving feature was its delicious baked pies. What the health food dishes lacked in butter and fat, the pies supplied.

Wes arrived early on that Wednesday morning in May and settled himself in a secluded booth in the far corner of the restaurant. He waited fifteen minutes past the appointed time and began to wonder if Henry Baldwin had chickened out or if the entire conversation had been a cruel hoax by someone with a Rich Little talent for mimicry. Wes drank two cups of Angelic Aroma tea, sagebrush spice flavor, and was about to leave when he saw Henry Baldwin at the hostess desk. Wes waved to catch his attention. Henry smiled, waved back, and headed toward the booth.

"Sorry I'm late, Mr. Bryant, but I wasn't as sure about the location of this place as I thought. I'm glad you didn't leave."

"No problem," Wes responded as he slid a menu across the table toward Henry. "I can recommend anything, so long as it doesn't have sprouts or an overabundance of wheat germ. Their breakfast muffins are fantastic. Believe it or not, they actually put sugar frosting on them—if you ask. Personally, I've been known to have a piece of their pie for breakfast, just to be a nonconformist."

A fortyish-looking woman in a sixties-style granny dress with sandals and her hair pulled back into a ponytail hovered over them, looking like a temporarily employed Grateful Dead follower. "Are you guys ready now or should I come back later?" she said with a tone of indifference.

"You go ahead, Mr. Bryant. This is on me. I need just a second to check the menu."

Annette's constant chiding about his cholesterol count, and the guilt from having had one too many pieces of pie in the past, influenced Wes's decision. "I'll take two of your bran and raisin muffins, along with a piece of that brussels sprouts breakfast quiche."

"A cinnamon roll, heavy on the frosting, and two fried eggs over easy with sausage," Henry said without a second thought to Wes's order. "A Coke to drink."

Wes remembered when he was Henry's age. He was amazed by what he put in his stomach back then and wondered how he ever managed to survive on fried foods, sugary desserts, and caffeine-laced drinks.

Henry glanced over his shoulder at the two adjacent empty booths and looked out of the corner of his eye to see if anyone was within listening distance. Satisfied that their privacy was secure, he clasped his hands and leaned across the table. "If the wrong people knew I was here, my life would be at stake," Henry said as his face grew serious. "The people who want my father elected will stop at nothing to make sure he represents their interests." Henry relaxed slightly and leaned back against the wall in his corner of the booth.

The waitress stopped by their table to deliver Henry's Coke and carried a pot of hot water to refill Wes's teacup. An awkward silence prevailed until she walked away.

"I don't know why you wanted to talk to me," Wes said. "You claimed you had some information, like who sent that horse manure and who put that decapitated doll near my front steps. Let's start there."

"Dave Kelly. Well, maybe not him personally, but someone representing him. It was his idea to hire you in the first place, not my dad's. He thought that since the three of you were college buddies, you could be controlled easily. To make sure you were loyal, Kelly wanted you to think that Stanley Taylor was the man you should fear. The truth is, David Kelly is a man without a conscience. He will destroy anyone who gets in his way. I don't expect you to believe me, but just hear me out. Ask me anything. I swear I'll tell you the truth."

"Rebecca, your sister. Why did she commit suicide?"

Hank's hands shook and his voice quivered as he said softly, "Rebecca didn't commit suicide. It's true she was a lesbian, but she was tormented by the moral conflict about her behavior. She didn't want to be that way. Her friends convinced her that she had to be like that. They told her she was born gay. Unfortunately, Rebecca believed their lies and got involved in the most militant factions of the lesbian movement. It was her way of running further and further away from what happened to us as children. If it hadn't been for our neighbor, Mr. Albright, who babysat both of us, a lot of things would have been different."

"Which of you ordered the cinnamon roll?" the waitress asked, her short-term memory obviously impaired.

Hank motioned that the order was his, and she set the plate in front of him. Wes took one look at the sausage and eggs and held his breath as his much healthier dish arrived.

Henry took a big bite of his roll and went on. "Rebecca was murdered. That much I know. I'm not sure who did it, but I'm determined to find out. That's one reason I've come to you."

"Me? What has my involvement in your father's campaign got to do with solving a murder case, if you are right about what happened to her?"

Anger flashed in Henry's eyes. "I'm right," he said gripping the handle of the fork in his hand and slamming his fist on the table. "I knew my sister. A brother and sister were never closer. If she had been that despondent or had planned to kill herself, I would have known. I saw her earlier that day. Sure, she was depressed, but no more than normal. In fact, she talked about getting some help for her lesbianism. She asked me if I knew a counselor or someone she could talk to. My dad tells people that she was so tormented by Stanley Taylor and his group she couldn't take it anymore, but it's a lie!"

Wes took a couple of bites of his breakfast. "You make it sound like Dave Kelly is some kind of Svengali who orchestrates what your father thinks and how he lives his life. Are you saying your father doesn't believe in the political philosophy he espouses?"

"He believes it, all right, or at least he's convinced himself that he does. Look, my father is charming, intellectually bright, and as smooth as they come when making a business deal. You can be with him five minutes and he'll convince you you're the most important person in his life. He never forgets a name, and he never loses his smile in front of the camera. Politics is an easy trade for him. It's what he's always wanted. But why should I be telling you that? You remember what he was like back in college."

Wes nodded his head in agreement. He was surprised to see how candidly this young man saw his own flesh and blood.

"Solving Rebecca's alleged murder. Is that why you're here?" Wes asked.

"That's part of it, but it's more personal than that. It's true I've been involved in the gay rights movement for the last couple of years, but I've never had sex with a man. The same sexual identity problems that plagued Rebecca have bothered me, all stemming back to Mr. Albright," Henry said as his bottom lip trembled.

He looked at Wes with a sincere expression and went on. "I'm truly sorry for my behavior at the rally on Saturday. You've got to understand the only reason I acted that way is that I was so drunk I didn't know what I was doing. Frankly, Mr. Bryant, I was scared of what they'd do to me if I didn't cooperate. So I downed a six-pack, took a couple shots of whiskey, and played the most convincing role I could. Now I'm ashamed of myself."

Henry reached up with his left hand to wipe the moist corners of his eyes. Wes still wasn't convinced, but if this young man wasn't telling the truth, he deserved a Tony Award for a Sagebrush stage performance.

"Is there any truth to the allegation you were involved with the American Boy Lovers Association?"

Henry was so taken aback he dropped his fork, and it clanged against his plate. "How did you know about that?

"I won't deny it. I even marched in one of their demonstrations. You've got to understand, Mr. Bryant. If you think you're homosexual and you get involved in the gay rights movement, you have to justify all kinds of perversion. All I can say is that something took over my mind and twisted it."

Henry picked up his fork again and slowly licked some of the frosting off, acting as if this part of the conversation was so distasteful he couldn't continue eating.

"Do you know anything about a group called Citizens for Ethical Government?"

Hank grinned slightly and nodded his head knowingly. "I get it. You've seen that video, and that's why you're asking me questions like this. I suppose you want to know about the pornography bust."

Wes said nothing. His silence answered the question.

"I was bunking with some guys I met in the movement. It was the low point of my life, and I felt I had no one else to turn to. They accepted me as I was, or as I thought I was. It wasn't my apartment, though it was registered in my name. I did that because they didn't have the money for the deposit. I swear, Mr. Bryant, I had no idea they had that filth stashed there."

"Would you mind telling me about Albright?"

Henry seemed embarrassed. "There's not much to tell. My father wasn't all that wealthy when we were growing up, and we lived in a modest, middle-class neighborhood. Albert Albright wasn't married and lived a few houses down the street. He seemed like a good man. He went to church every Sunday and was always handing out candy and presents to kids in the neighborhood. He was an electronics engineer, and most people thought his strange ways were the result of his being a bachelor and spending all of his time with wiring schematics and oscilloscopes. Several times, my parents wanted to be alone for an evening, and Albright offered to look after Rebecca and me. Nothing much happened the first couple of times he was alone with us. But one night . . ."

"I get the message. You don't have to talk about it. Why didn't you tell your parents?"

"I was just a kid of five or six, Mr. Bryant. He was such a nice man and explained what he was doing to us in such a pleasant-sounding way. Frankly, I blocked most of it out of my mind. It wasn't until our midteen years when Rebecca and I started questioning our sexuality that bits and pieces of what he did started coming back. Rebecca never could deal with it. That's why she turned to sex with women.

"Even though I never became sexually involved with a man, I felt safe around gay people. That way, I wasn't challenged to prove my heterosexuality and didn't have to deal with my shyness toward women. I'm sorry to say, it was an easy way out. In the process, I got mixed up in the gay rights movement. Over the last couple of months, I've had my doubts, and Saturday was the turning point. As drunk as I was, what Jennifer said affected me deeply. Not only that, I found her . . ."

Henry looked down at his food and saw that it was getting cold. He quickly took several mouthfuls of sausage and washed them down with a drink of Coke.

"Go on. You found her what?"

"I'm embarrassed to say . . . after all, you are her father, and I don't want you to get the wrong idea about this conversation."

"Go ahead, man; spill it."

"Mr. Bryant, your daughter is beautiful. Just watching her speak that day brought out feelings in me I've never had before . . ."

Before Wes could respond the waitress approached their table again. "I'll leave the check right here," she said, scribbling on a pad, ripping off the sheet, and laying it on the edge of the table. "You can pay on your way out. Let me know if you want anything else."

Wes reached for the check, but Henry beat him to it. Henry pulled a credit card out of his wallet and slid out of the booth. Wes followed and waited at the front door while Henry's card cleared and he signed the receipt.

"I realize you have no reason to believe a word of what I've said this morning," Henry continued as they walked toward his car, a bright red Corvette. He pulled a pen from his pocket, ripped off the end of his credit card receipt, and scribbled a number on it. "Here's my phone number. It's an apartment I keep near the campus."

Wes took the paper and stuffed it in his pants pocket. "Over the phone, you said something about my life being in danger. Are you talking about the threats that came with the manure and the decapitated doll?"

"That's not what I'm talking about. When you first became press secretary, they thought they could control you. Now they're getting worried. They see you as a threat, a man who knows too much and may find out a lot more."

"They?"

"This isn't the time or place to talk about it. Anyway, I've got to do more investigation myself before I point fingers."

"One more thing. How can you be so certain that Rebecca's death wasn't a suicide? Wasn't there an investigation?"

"Yes," Henry said as he opened the door to his Corvette. "Sheriff John McCormick went through the motions, but he's not to be trusted. Neither is the judge who signed off on the report."

"What judge?"

"Judge Russell Hoffman."

20

As Wes pulled into the Stand for America Party headquarters at 1:15 P.M., he wished the meeting with Bill Baldwin and the discussion with Henry Baldwin had been held on different days. He feared that by the time Wednesday was over, he would experience Baldwin overload.

Before the conversation with Henry, Wes had planned to make today's party meeting a knock-down-drag-out session to get to the bottom of any questions he didn't yet have answered. Now he decided to play it cool. If murder and lies were part of Baldwin's political aspirations, Wes determined he could do a better job of finding out the truth from inside the organization. Wes knew he was involved in something a lot more serious than the plot of a trite airport newsstand novel. If Henry was right, whoever murdered Rebecca wouldn't stop at killing anyone else who got too close to the truth.

Wes nodded to the receptionist, who greeted him by name, and walked down the hallway leading to the meeting room. The door was slightly open. Wes saw that it was empty except for Dave Kelly and Robert Cusco, the liaison to special interest groups. They were seated at the far corner of the room, deep in conversation. Wes lightly rapped on the door to announce his presence. Kelly, dressed sharply in a dark navy, double-breasted suit, jerked around quickly with an angry look on his face. Then he broke into his synthetic smile and stood.

"Come on in." He stepped toward Wes and put out his hand to shake Wes's. "Robert and I were going over some last-minute details about the Gay Respect parade. The others will be along shortly. Have a seat, and we'll get started as soon as Bill and Ladonna join us."

Wes glanced around the plushly furnished room. At one end was a small desk with a telephone, a fax machine, and remote controls for the multimedia entertainment center that sat in the far corner. The silver coffee urn at the other end was joined today by a steamer that bubbled with the smell of fresh cappuccino and warm milk. On the walls on both sides of the length of the conference table were contemporary oil paintings featuring abstract swirls of brilliant colors.

Wes sat down in a chair at the opposite end of the table from Kelly and Cusco and laid his soft leather briefcase on top. He noticed that Cusco was as intense as he was during the last meeting. Cusco constantly poked at the bridge of his glasses. As Wes started to take out some papers, Ralph Winston, director of advertising and public relations, came through the door. Winston still assumed an unimpressive posture and wore the same dull gray suit and pale blue paisley tie as the week before. He greeted Wes and waved hello to Kelly and Cusco. Neither acknowledged him. Wes strained his ears to hear what Kelly was saying, but could only pick up a few comments about speaking schedules and parade routes.

At exactly 1:35 P.M., the door from the tunnel leading to Baldwin's office opened and Ladonna Gallagher, scheduling secretary, stepped into the room, followed by Bill Baldwin. Both had flushed faces and looked like teenage lovers aglow with the flush of interrupted passion.

"Dave, Robert, Wes, Ralph," Baldwin said as if conducting a roll call, "glad you're all here. Ladonna and I were going over some last minute details. Sorry to keep you waiting."

Cusco stood to pull out a chair for Ladonna. Wes noticed that she looked at Baldwin from the corner of her eye when he made his reference to "details."

Baldwin donned bifocals as he glanced through several documents that lay on the table in front of his chair. "Let's start with a status report."

Baldwin took off his glasses and set them on the table. He leaned back in his chair and brought his hands together in front of his face, thumbs and little fingers together, while the other three fingers of each hand tapped rhythmically against each other. "Ralph, you go first."

Winston seemed flustered for a moment as if he hadn't expected to be first on the docket. In seconds he gained his composure and checked off several items on a list he took from his coat pocket.

"The major media seem to be under control. I don't think the big three networks will be any problem, and CNN isn't likely to pose a threat. A couple of nosy reporters from Fox acted like they were after a Pulitzer, and we had to put a spin on a couple of things they were checking out."

"Like what?" Baldwin asked.

"Just old stuff. We've dealt with it before and know how to handle it."

"Rebecca and Hank?"

"Yeah, but I don't want you to worry, Boss. Our people have taken care of it."

"Anything else?"

Winston ran his pen down the edge of his checklist and stopped near the bottom. "There have been some questions about a couple of your real estate deals, and some nosy freelancers have looked into your personal life, but I handled that," Winston said as he shot a harsh glance in the direction of Ladonna. "Let's face it, if you were a TV evangelist or a priest or some far-right patriot politician, we wouldn't be able to keep the news hounds away. But the media like you, Bill. They want you elected, and the only thing they are likely to do is kick up enough fuss to make it look like you're getting the scrutiny a senatorial candidate deserves."

Baldwin relaxed a little and put his bifocals back on to review his own list. After several moments he looked up. "Any other problems I should know about?"

"Just the video," Winston said as he reached his right arm over the side of the chair and pulled a VHS cassette out of his briefcase.

"I've seen it! The question is what do we do about it?" Baldwin said curtly.

"You could issue a series of denials, point by point," Cusco suggested.

"When you answer those kinds of accusations, your response only invites more inquiries," Baldwin explained. "Besides, Patterson has a lot of credibility in the business community."

Dave Kelly stared at the video in the middle of the table. "We could rough Patterson up," he said coldly and deliberately.

For a moment, no one said anything. Most importantly, no one dismissed the suggestion.

"Suppose that only makes him madder and encourages his resolve?" Baldwin asked.

"I might be able to handle him," Ladonna said with a smirk on her face. "It wouldn't look very good for someone of such high *ethics,* especially a married man with two children, to be found in a compromising situation."

Again there was a brief silence. Wes was getting uneasy. Obviously, immoral and violent actions were acceptable solutions to everyone else in the room but him. Without indicating he knew what was on the video, he spoke. "Assuming the allegations on this video are lies, why not hold a press conference and issue a general denial, then take a handful of questions to elaborate and leave it there."

Wes didn't expect his suggestion to taken seriously. It was.

Baldwin pushed his chair back and stood up to stretch. "I like that idea, only it won't be a press conference; it'll be a carefully staged interview. We'll get a local investigative reporter who owes us a favor and prearrange the questions. We'll do it at my house, with Candy at my side. You know, home and hearth, that kind of aura. Candy can tell how much these allegations have hurt her as a woman and then do her Tammy Wynette stand-by-your-man routine." Baldwin sat back down, feeling energized by the scenario he had formulated. "I'll admit I've made some mistakes, but who hasn't? I'll push the buttons of the 'there but for the grace of God go I' defense."

Wes noticed Winston's broad grin as he said, "Good thinking, Boss. The voters wouldn't want this happening to them, and everybody has a few skeletons in their closets. You can ignore the specifics and deal with people's emotions. All they'll remember is you telling them that you're sorry you've disappointed them and all you want is a second chance to do what is right for America. It might even improve your standing in the polls."

Kelly was still expressionless. "Who can we get to cooperate?"

"Alice Peckman. She's looking to get out of town and land a network anchor position. I think we can arrange the ticket for her. I'll prepare her questions in advance, and I'll coach Candy on how to look at you, Boss, when the camera is taking a wide shot. Trust me, she'll be the most adoring wife in political Disneyland." Winston chuckled like a cynical acting coach who was about to direct a command performance.

Everybody seemed ready to move on except Kelly, who held up his hand to get attention. "Before we settle this, I still think we should let Ladonna do her thing." He squared his jaw and looked across the table at Ladonna, who shifted her weight in the chair and lifted her left leg over her right knee, showing an ample portion of her thigh.

"I'll take care of it. But just remember," she said, tilting her head down and looking at Baldwin from the corner of her eyes, "I may need a little extra compensation for overtime."

Only Cusco seemed a little unnerved by the conversation. Beads of sweat had formed on his brow, and he reached in his coat pocket for a handkerchief to wipe them away. Everything had been done very businesslike. No emotions, no scruples, no regrets.

"Now, Robert, how are our friends in the Abortion Liberty League and the Gay and Lesbian Caucus handling things? Any wavering?" Baldwin asked.

Cusco's expression turned serious immediately. Wes could tell he was happy to see the agenda shift his direction.

"For one thing, they're in our camp because they have nowhere else to go. The pro-choice people are still banking on your support of that no-parental-consent law. They know that's where the big money is, teenage girls who don't have to ask their parents. Kids in trouble pay in cash, and they don't ask a lot of probing questions. Guarantee the league that legislation, and they are yours all the way to November 8."

"Are our gay friends that solid?"

Cusco twisted his face slightly, indicating he wasn't so sure about that voting bloc. "The key to our success is presenting an image that gay rights has broad public support. I've done a good job selling that message to civic leaders, the business community, and the media."

Wes butted in. "Using my name without my consent!"

Cusco shot a shocked look back at Wes. "You do support gay rights, don't you?"

"Did you bother to ask me?" Wes said soberly.

"Well, not exactly, er . . . I just assumed that . . ."

"Assumed you could speak in my name without giving me the courtesy of obtaining permission to do so?"

"You assumed correctly, Robert," Baldwin said abruptly. "Wes is one of us, and he backs this campaign all the way. He supports everything the Stand for America Party represents. Isn't that right Wes?"

Baldwin had cajoled, coaxed, manipulated, and lied in the past, but this was the first time he had forced Wes to submit. Baldwin reached for his briefcase and pulled out a manila folder and laid it on the table. He looked firmly at Wes and shoved the folder in his direction. It slid across the table and all eyes were on it.

"Open it!" he ordered.

Wes laid back the cover of the folder and saw a single sheet of paper, the warrant for his arrest that Sheriff McCormick had given him.

"That has never been rescinded and is still available for enforcement at any time," Baldwin explained.

No one in the room asked what was on the paper. Wes figured they either knew or knew to keep quiet.

Wes looked back at Baldwin with equal determination. Then he glanced again at the paper and noticed the judge's signature. This time the name, Russell Hoffman, meant something to him.

Baldwin stood up and walked over to where Wes was seated. He leaned down, picked up the file folder, and handed it to Kelly. The room went silent. Wes sat perfectly still. Baldwin looked down his nose at Wes and said in a singsong voice, "Mr. Bryant is getting upset. We wouldn't want him getting into any nasty trouble, now would we?" Baldwin let out a laugh and everyone in the room joined him except Wes.

Baldwin cleared his throat, and the room fell quiet again. He stood behind Wes and grabbed his shoulders. "Wes thought this was a college scrimmage. But this is the pros." Baldwin paused. "And we play for keeps."

Baldwin walked deliberately back to his chair, sat down, and winked at Ladonna.

Wes locked his gaze on Baldwin. He was deep in thought, checking out some papers, until he lifted his eyes and stared arrogantly at Wes. *Good. He thinks he's got me right where he wants me. Maybe he'll show more of his agenda.*

"Now that we've got the media and Andrew Patterson taken care of, what are we going to do about Taylor?" Baldwin demanded. "While he's on the run from the law for *allegedly* shooting that abortion doctor, we've got a chance to finish him off for good."

"You know what's in that envelope, don't you?" Dave Kelly asked Baldwin.

"Yes, but do you think it's time to play that card? Should we wait until McCormick's men hunt him down and then add this icing to the cake?"

"If Melissa's ready to tell her story, there's no sense in waiting," Kelly suggested.

"Will Benjamin cooperate fully?" Baldwin probed further.

"Benjamin will do what *we* tell him to do," Kelly said with calculation.

"Then let's move on it. When?"

Kelly thought for a moment. "Let's do it before the parade. I've got a lawyer who could put together a news conference with Melissa and Benjamin by Friday."

Winston raised his hand to get Baldwin's attention. "I don't mean to be presumptuous, but if I'm going to handle PR, don't you think I ought to know what's in that envelope?"

Baldwin shrugged his shoulders in an unconcerned manner. "Sure, Taylor molested my nephew, Benjamin. Melissa and Benjamin will both testify publicly about what happened."

Ladonna was expressionless, but both Winston and Cusco registered shock.

"Suppose someone says that because Melissa is your sister that compromises the integrity of the accusation?" Cusco asked.

Wes was struck by the nonchalance with which Baldwin seemed to be handling the conversation. He remembered the distraught routine Baldwin had put on at his house on Monday night.

"Melissa knows what to say and how to say it. By the time she's evoked the memory of her dead husband, the press will paint a picture of Taylor that's so ugly people will almost think Taylor pulled the trigger on Lewis, as well as Dr. Bowman."

Everyone but Wes was all smiles.

"Just make sure you get the press conference over early in time for the story to hit the evening news, but don't end it too soon so the reporters will have a chance to check things out," Winston counseled. "Make it a last-minute headline. Once that message is planted in people's minds, it won't make any difference what further investigation uncovers."

Kelly nodded in agreement. "We'll do it at three o'clock on Monday at the Mile-High Hotel. We'll return to the scene of the crime," he said with a grin. "Maybe Lewis's ghost will be around to encourage us."

Now that Baldwin saw no reason to maintain a semblance of political modesty, Wes saw the ruthless, ugly side of Baldwin's brand of politics.

Relieved to have that bit of skulduggery over with, Baldwin relaxed his body, leaned back in the chair, and looked at Kelly. "Is everything in order for the Gay Respect parade?"

Cusco jumped in first. "Everything. You'll be riding in an open convertible with . . ."

Baldwin quickly interrupted. "I'll be by myself."

Why the switch? He made such a big deal of my riding with him. What's he up to now? Wes thought.

"However you want it," Cusco agreed. "The parade organizers would like you there about nine o'clock in the morning at the staging area behind the state capitol building. The parade kicks off at ten o'clock sharp."

"What's planned?" Baldwin asked as if he were inquiring about a Rotarian gathering.

Cusco snickered slightly and put his hand to his mouth as if he were embarrassed. Kelly shot him a dirty look. Cusco quickly got control of himself and said, "A hundred topless lesbians kick things off with a bike ride down Broadway. They call themselves . . . ," he paused, darting his eyes about the room, "Dykes on Bikes."

This time it was Ladonna who snickered. Baldwin showed no emotion.

"It should take about fifteen or twenty minutes for the *ladies* to get their bikes out of the way before the marchers and floats follow," Cusco explained.

"What's this event called?" Winston wanted to know with a keen eye on the publicity value.

"Day of the Dyke," Cusco answered. "The lesbian faction of the homosexual movement feels like it has been discriminated against and that most of the attention to gay rights has been given to male homosexuals. This is their coming-out declaration," Cusco emphasized as he rolled his eyes.

Baldwin was scribbling notes on a sheet of paper when he casually said, "I presume the police have things under control so there won't be any incidents with Taylor's people."

"Well, that depends on what you consider *under control*," Kelly interjected. "Main Street will be a law-free zone Saturday. The police chief knows not to arrest anybody for public nudity or indecency. I can't guarantee what Taylor's people might do, but if anybody runs afoul of the law on Saturday, it won't be the marchers."

"Where is my place in the parade?"

Kelly snapped his fingers as if ordering a servant and pointed toward a piece of paper in front of Cusco. He motioned for Cusco to hand the paper across the table. "Let me look at this list for a second." Kelly's eyes slowly moved down the page. "You are scheduled to ride toward the end of the parade. After the Dykes on Bikes comes the PHP group—that's Proud Homosexual Parents—then a group called Loves Knows No Boundaries, and preceding you is ABLA."

"ABLA?"

"It's a gay activist group fighting for their rights to have legal, consensual sex," Kelly explained.

Wes was furious that Kelly had described pedophiles so harmlessly. Baldwin continued his nonchalant attitude, not bothering to probe Kelly further.

"And who's following my car?"

"Mountain States Telephone is sponsoring their Lambda Ladies organization, a lesbian employees division of the phone company."

"Is that the only corporation represented?"

Kelly looked down the list again. "It appears from this parade permit registration list that there are about a dozen major companies in this state that encourage homosexual hiring and are sending special contingencies to march."

Baldwin nodded his head affirmatively. "Good. That translates into lots of votes and lots of corporate political action committee money. We're depending on those PACs to come through for us." Baldwin paused. "Are there any other government officials or candidates who have agreed to take part?"

"I can answer that," Cusco responded eagerly. "The governor said no. He's conveniently out of town over the weekend, but he did push the mayor to see we got a parade permit."

"Is anyone showing up from the national political scene?"

Winston jumped in. "I handled that one. The White House was most cooperative. The president is sending one of the top lawyers from the Justice Department, plus one of his own personal aides from the White House staff, Hal Hatfield."

Ladonna, who had been quietly filing her nails, looked up. "Isn't he the guy I read about who's dying from AIDS?"

"He's HIV positive, if that's what you mean," Winston responded, "but he's not dead yet. In fact, he's very much alive and one of the most influential people in Washington."

"What about the lawyer from the Justice Department?" Baldwin asked. "What's his name?"

"Jan Renault. Remember last year when they held that International Conference on Human Rights in Washington, D.C.? He's the guy who granted special permission for foreigners afflicted with AIDS to bypass the immigration laws that prevent anyone with a communicable disease from getting into the country. He filed a legal brief redefining *communicable diseases* to exempt AIDS."

Ladonna, who seemed bored by the whole conversation, reached over to run her finger around the curve of Baldwin's suit-coat shoulder pad. "Bill, don't you think we ought to finish up some of those details we were getting to before this meeting started?"

"Yeah, in a minute. I just want to make sure I know what to expect at the parade." He looked straight at Kelly. "Could anything happen that would embarrass our campaign?"

"Not a chance. If some of the marchers step over the line of good taste, we'll make sure that the sound bites on TV and the follow-up stories in the newspaper are sanitized so that things are palatable for mainstream America. Let's face it, the average voter isn't going to be there. All they will know is what they see on TV that night and what they read in the headlines the next day. You don't think for a minute that local TV stations are going to show any scenes unsuitable for family viewing, do you?" he asked with a smirk. "As for the newspapers, the headline has already been written: CIVIL RIGHTS MARCH HIGHLIGHTS INJUSTICES."

Ladonna put her nail file back in her purse and started to take out a bottle of fingernail polish. A harsh glance from Baldwin stopped her in midmotion. As she put the nail polish back with a slight huff of disgust she asked Kelly, "What is the point of this parade? I read somewhere that gays in this state have an average income over sixty thousand dollars a year. They're not exactly impoverished, and no one's throwing them in jail for what they do."

"Approval," Kelly responded. "The marchers don't really want equality; they want endorsement. The real issue isn't equal rights; it's special rights, just like Taylor claims. And they're not going to stop until they get it. This march will soften up the opposition and show that gays have numbers and power on their side. They won't stop until everyone in America is forced to accept them as leaders in their Scout troops, preachers in their churches, and teachers in their schools. The marchers on Saturday are to America today what the protesters in Selma, Alabama, were to their generation."

That logic disturbed Wes. He couldn't imagine Martin Luther King Jr. riding a Harley in the midst of Dykes on Bikes.

21

Sunday mornings were Wes and Annette's favorite time of the week. They typically slept in and went to the later church service. Afterward they usually had brunch at a nearby restaurant, a place called the Delectable Egg, which served Wes's favorite omelet with mushrooms, cheddar cheese, and Italian sausage. Jennifer joined them that Sunday, May 8, for church and then to hold a memorial for the baby.

Unlike the Sunday two weeks earlier when Stanley Taylor had surprised Wes, there were no special guests at church for the Sunday's service. Pastor Ridgeway had reclaimed the pulpit, and his message was entitled, "The Healing of Hurts." Ridgeway kept repeating the words of 1 Peter 5:7, "casting all your care upon Him, for He cares for you."

Wes felt the pastor's sermon was providential, considering their plans after the service. He noticed that Jennifer listened and made notes in the margin of her bulletin. Wes could see that her eyes were red, and the folds under her eyes were moist with tears. It seemed like God had been listening to Wes's prayers and that Jennifer would be healed.

Pastor Ridgeway's words energized the church, and members of the congregation added "Amens" aloud each time he emphasized a point about

God's grace. Wes noticed that his family was not alone in the need to be healed. When Ridgeway finished and gave the benediction, several dozen in the congregation approached the altar requesting prayer for restoration.

After a short stop for brunch, the three drove toward the mountains through Spruce Valley. Annette had suggested a spot near the elegant old Humphrey estate, a turn-of-the-century mountain retreat established by a gold baron who consolidated mines in the southwest sector of Elkhorn County.

For the first few miles, Wes, Annette, and Jennifer carried on small talk about the weather and the return of spring to the Rockies. Small blades of new green grass cropped up on the hillsides amidst delicate blue wildflowers, larkspur, skullcaps, and chiming bells. It was hard to believe that these mountainsides, buried in so much snow for most of the year, could yield such an abundance of beauty. The lower foothills had sparse forest coverage, but as they climbed, the small pine trees thickened. To the right of the highway was a sheer wall of rock. To the left of the road was the river, swollen with melt-off from the snow fields in the high country.

Jennifer steered the conversation to the purpose of the afternoon. "Were there any specific things the counselor suggested?" she asked.

Annette turned around halfway in the passenger's seat to look over her shoulder at Jennifer, who was riding behind Wes. "For one thing, she recommended that we name the baby. How do you feel about that, Jennifer?"

Jennifer thought for a moment and responded. "I've always felt the baby was a girl. I have no proof, but that's what my heart tells me. Perhaps we could choose a Bible name."

Annette paused. "How about Tabitha Dorcas Bryant?" she said with a little laugh.

Jennifer's face softened. Annette's effort to lighten the mood had worked. "What are some other Bible names?" Jennifer inquired.

"Well, there's Rachel, Rebecca, Elizabeth, Mary . . ."

"Rachel Elizabeth Bryant," Jennifer said. "I like the sound of that."

Wes glanced in his rearview mirror for a glimpse of Jennifer's face. He could see that personalizing the baby's identity was having a positive effect on her.

"Were there any other things the counselor said that would help?" Jennifer asked.

Annette reached down to the floorboard where she had set her purse and pulled out a small, white leather Bible. She held it up for Jennifer to see. "Recognize this?"

Jennifer grinned broadly. "Where did you get that? It's my baby Bible. Isn't my footprint in there somewhere?"

Jennifer flipped open the cover and there was the small, black imprint of a baby's foot. Underneath it was the date of Jennifer's birth and the name of the hospital where she was born.

"The counselor suggested reading a scripture about children. The rest of the memorial is pretty much up to us, but I think we'll know what to do when the time comes."

The car rounded a sharp turn in the road and ahead of them was the Humphrey estate. It was on the other side of the stream and was reached by a small bridge. The meticulously landscaped yard seemed out of place with the rugged natural surroundings, but at the same time it lent a sense of well-tended beauty to the rugged rock. Huge blue spruce trees shaded the front side of the dwelling. The back of the mansion was built into the natural granite canyon walls so that the entire edifice seemed to be part of the mountain. A small guest house reached by a shale rock pathway was located no more than thirty yards from the main building. The river had been dammed just above the estate, and the water around the property flowed gently in a huge arc before it continued its decent, cascading over giant boulders. The dam formed a pond with a sign that read "Private Fishing."

Wes slowed the car as they looked out the window to take in the grandeur of early-twentieth-century craftsmanship.

"Does anyone still live there?" Jennifer asked.

"I'm not sure," Wes responded. "The last I heard, the grandson of the original Humphrey family retired here during the summer months. It looks well kept. I understand they have a full-time gardener who lives in that smaller house. He keeps up the property year round."

As the Humphrey estate disappeared in the rear window, Wes spotted their destination, a park area no more than a quarter-mile ahead. He slowed and turned left across a steel-girded bridge that was topped with wooden planks. Most of the planks were loose, and they rattled noisily as the car's wheels turned over the top of them. On the other side of the bridge was a small picnic area with tables, a stone barbecue pit, and public toilet facilities.

"A lot of people from Denver come up here on weekends to have family get-togethers," Wes explained. "Looks like it's still a little early for people downtown to brave the chill. I don't think anyone else is around."

"That will make it extra special," Jennifer said. "I'd like this to be a very private affair with just us and Rachel Elizabeth."

Wes parked the car under a tall Ponderosa pine tree and all three put on light jackets to ward off the cool breeze. The full bloom of spring was still several weeks away at this altitude.

"Why don't we all climb on top of that big rock over there?" Jennifer said. "It will give us a beautiful lookout on the river."

"Sounds like a winner to me," Wes said.

Jennifer and Annette climbed over several smaller rocks and scurried on all fours up the side of the massive boxcar-sized boulder. Within minutes, Wes had joined them. They sat there for a moment, breathing in the fresh mountain air and relaxing.

Then Annette reached in the pocket of her jacket and pulled out the white baby Bible. She thumbed through it slowly and then traced with her finger across a page. She stopped. "'Behold, children are a heritage from the LORD, / The fruit of the womb is a reward.' That's Psalm 127:3. The counselor said this scripture illustrates that children are a gift from God and they belong to Him."

Jennifer was quiet for a few moments, and Wes felt it was best for Annette and him to leave her alone. He motioned for Annette to follow, took her hand, and helped her off the rock. Slowly, they walked about fifty yards to a sheltered spot where a small stream flowing down the steep mountainside made its way toward the river. Wes embraced Annette, and they held each other tightly, wishing there was something they could say or do to help Jennifer.

Wes looked over at Jennifer to see where she had perched on the rock. She appeared to be safe. He sat down with his back to Jennifer and faced Annette in a cross-legged position with his head in his hands. It was then that he thought about his grandchild for the first time. He wondered what it would feel like to be holding that little life. A newborn would smell clean and sweet like baby powder, he imagined. *The baby would probably be so fragile sitting in my big hands,* he thought. Wes looked up at Annette, who was crying. He realized that tears were streaming down his own face too.

"This is really tough. I can't imagine how Jennifer feels."

"It must be devastating," she agreed. "At least Jennifer has us to be there for her to help her heal. Just think of the countless other young women who have no one to turn to and who let this terrible pain fester in their lives." She paused. "Jesus has their little babies in His hands. He is loving them and taking care of them until their moms get to heaven."

"I've been thinking a lot about our granddaughter," Annette said as she wiped her eyes with the back of her hand. "I wish I could hold her in my arms. I would spend hours rocking her and singing baby lullabies. I can't wait until we get to heaven to see our little angel. I want to hug her and make up for all the time we've lost."

"Just think, our granddaughter's body will be made whole again in heaven," Wes said with a smile. "How do you think the baby will forgive Jennifer?"

"I don't know, but God will make a way."

They looked over and saw that Jennifer was sitting motionless. She looked frail up on top of the rock with her knees bent, tucked against her chest, and her hands wrapped around her shins. Her chin rested on her knees. At one point, Jennifer seemed to gesture with her hand as if she were talking to someone.

Wes and Annette said nothing. The only sounds were the gentle flow of the mountain stream falling from some unseen snow bank above and the chirp of mountain wrens that flitted from branch to branch collecting small twigs and pine needles to prepare a nest for their spring eggs.

Wes glanced intermittently at his watch and after ten minutes spoke to Annette. "Perhaps she's had enough time to be alone. What do you think?"

Annette nodded in agreement, and they walked back to the rock and scaled its short summit. Jennifer smiled and reached out to touch their arms in a welcoming gesture.

"Would you think it was strange if I talked out loud to Rachel Elizabeth and told her how I feel?"

Wes and Annette looked at each other and shook their heads no.

Jennifer stretched her legs for a moment, then pulled them back up against her chest. She closed her eyes. "Rachel Elizabeth, I hope you're listening to me up in heaven, because your mommy has a few things she needs to say." She took a deep breath. "I'm sorry that I . . . killed you. It's not what I really wanted to do, but I was scared.

"Nothing like this had ever happened to me. Then after I was raped and you came into my world, I was too frightened to deal with it rationally. I thought about everyone and everything except you.

"I wish I had let you live. Are your eyes brown or blue? What color is your hair? Do you miss me? Do you sometimes ask God why I didn't let you live? Are there other little children you can play with? I know there are no tears in heaven, so you aren't crying, but I would like to know what you feel when you think about me."

Wes looked at Annette and tears were again streaming down her cheeks like they were his own. Jennifer unfolded her hands and wiped her eyes. "If God ever allows me to have another little boy or girl, I'm going to tell them all about you. Please tell God I'm sorry. I was young and foolish and took the easy way out. It won't happen again."

By now Jennifer was reduced to full-fledged sobbing, and she stuttered her way through her words. "More than anything . . . I'd like to take you in my arms and cradle you . . . hold you . . . kiss you, let you know how much I love you.

"Just so you'll know me when you see me, I'm five-foot-six, have long blonde hair, and a little pug nose just like yours. Look in the mirror, and when you see yourself, imagine me just a little older. I'm going to say good-bye for now . . . until someday I say hello forever."

Jennifer let loose a wail. Annette and Wes moved close to her and encircled her with their arms. Wes spoke softly, "We're here for you. We want you to heal from your pain."

Jennifer's sobs shook her body; her cries started out softly and would crescendo into high-pitched wailing.

Annette soothed her by saying, "It's going to be okay, Sweetheart. You can cry and let it all out."

Jennifer pulled them closer, and they all sat on the boulder and cried. Finally, Jennifer sat up straight and wiped her nose and eyes with a tissue. She silently stood to her feet and began to make her way down off the rock, feet first, steadying herself with her hands pointed behind her back. She jumped the last few feet to the ground and strolled slowly alongside the river.

After walking about thirty feet, she knelt down near a small clump of mountain flowers. An early-blooming, brilliantly red Indian paintbrush caught her eye. She pulled it from the ground and stood up. Jennifer held the flower in one hand and gently stroked its petals with the fingers of her other hand. Then she stepped on a boulder at the edge of the creek and inched her way toward the water. Once she had securely settled her weight, she knelt down into a squatting position and stared for a moment as the icy cold, crystal clear water dashed in front of her.

"Rachel Elizabeth, you were a flower I never let bloom. Now you are God's flower." She leaned forward and gently laid the flower in the creek. Then she watched it flow downstream, bouncing over the top of one rock after another, disappearing for a moment and then rising again like some brave swimmer caught in a current. At last the crimson petals faded from view around a bend. Jennifer stood and walked back to Wes and Annette, who were waiting near the car.

"I'm a mother, and I always will be a mother. No one can take that away from me. All the lies about abortion, that it's not really human, that it's part of your own body you can discard if you wish, will never convince me that my little Rachel Elizabeth was anything other than a precious baby, a gift from God."

22

The Monday afternoon sun dipped lower on the horizon, and the wind gently blew the newly budding leaves on the trees. People milled in front of the Mile High Hotel, and a blonde woman barked orders to the bellmen surrounding her limousine. They dutifully unloaded her ten or so Louis Vuitton bags as they mumbled under their breath.

"Coming back to this hotel gives me a creepy feeling," Annette said with a shiver.

"Me too," Wes agreed as he took Annette's hand in his. They were near the door when they heard a shriek. Wes looked behind him and saw the woman's little fluff of a white dog running freely between the tires of the cars. She screamed for someone to retrieve Gio.

Once Wes and Annette were inside the hotel lobby, he spotted the wall-mounted directory of daily events. The Melissa Lewis news conference was scheduled in a main-floor meeting room opposite the registration area. Wes recognized several representatives of the local media headed in that direction. He and Annette followed them.

The conference room was small, no more than forty feet by sixty feet, with a skirted six-foot table at one end and three dozen seats facing it.

Several technicians were setting up TV lights, and cameraman were spotting the best positions for their tripods. Annette followed Wes to an inconspicuous seat in the back corner of the room. No one checked his credentials. Either security was lax, or those in charge recognized him and figured he had a right to be there.

In the next few minutes, two-thirds of the chairs were filled with reporters carrying Dictaphones or small spiral pads; they looked like they were hungry for the scoop of the century. Several recognized Wes and nodded at him or waved in his direction. Calvin Reynolds, the owner of a competitor station, shook Wes's hand and greeted Annette by name. He and Wes were locked in a duel for the top slot in the spring Arbitron ratings so Wes didn't take the expression of friendship too seriously.

At precisely three o'clock, the TV lights illuminated a thin man with wire-rimmed glasses and a prematurely receding hairline. As he stepped into the room, he poured himself a glass of water from the pitcher at the head table and stepped behind the mini podium, which was sitting on top of the table. The front of the podium displayed the hotel's seal: a snow-capped mountain peak rising next to steel-and-glass skyscrapers. The man laid some papers on the podium, cleared his throat several times, and bent his six-foot frame to speak into the microphone that was attached to a goosenecked stand.

"Thanks for joining us this afternoon. My name is Jonathan Baumgart-ner. I'm Melissa Lewis's attorney. Mrs. Lewis is in an adjoining room. She asked me to read a brief statement to you."

"Can you speak up a little?" One of the reporters called out and waved his pencil in the air as if it were a beacon.

"Is this better?" Jonathan asked as he moved in closer to the micro-phone.

"Yes," a chorus of reporters answered.

"On Friday, the twenty-second of April, here in this hotel, Alex Lewis, the press secretary of the Stand for America Party, committed suicide. The cause of this tragic occurrence has been the object of conjecture by many of you. The purpose of this conference is to end the speculation by letting you know what drove Alex Lewis to his death. Because of her husband's courageous involvement in the Stand for America Party's efforts to promote justice, equality, and human rights, Melissa Lewis feels the truth must be told. Alex Lewis was driven to commit suicide because of an unspeakable crime against his only son, Benjamin."

Jonathan took a sip of water and turned over the first page in his stack of papers. Wes noticed two people enter the room and take seats toward the front of the room. He couldn't believe his eyes. It was Henry Baldwin and Wes's stepdaughter, Jennifer. Wes nudged Annette and pointed to where they sat. In shock Annette grabbed Wes's forearm with her left hand. She gripped so tightly he could feel the pressure of her fingernails through his jacket.

"I hope she's doing okay after that emotional memorial we had yesterday," Annette whispered in Wes's ear.

Baumgartner resumed his remarks. "You are all aware that child abuse is a growing problem in America. According to the latest statistics, 85 percent of all crimes committed against children are sexual in nature. The typical child molester abuses an average of nearly four hundred children in his lifetime. Behavioral scientists estimate that the ratio of girls who have sex forced upon them by a relative or other adult is one out of every three. For boys the estimate is one out of every ten."

These startling facts weren't shocking to news-hardened reporters, but their expressions indicated that at least they were appalled. More than anything, they looked puzzled, wondering what this litany of facts had to do with this hastily called news conference. They were searching for a headline.

"Every two minutes, somewhere in these United States, a child is molested!" Baumgartner exclaimed with indignation. "Thirty percent of the male victims go on to become molesters themselves!" Baumgartner pounded the podium like a righteous evangelist provoking the faithful to moral outrage.

The lawyer took another drink of water and lowered his voice from its shrill tenor. "Mrs. Lewis believes that her husband's death will not be in vain if those who abuse our children can be brought to justice. One of these contemptible criminals is the man who viciously assaulted Benjamin Lewis. In effect, he was the man who killed Alex Lewis!"

Baumgartner looked up from his notes. "In a moment I will present to you the widow of the late Mr. Lewis. She will be joined by her twelve-year-old son, Benjamin. Mrs. Lewis will first issue a statement and then give you a brief opportunity for questions."

Baumgartner smoothed the papers in front of him and spoke softly. "Ladies and gentlemen, when you ask questions, please be sensitive about their grief. For the first time, Mrs. Lewis will publicly reveal the name of her son's molester."

That announcement sent the reporters into a quiet frenzy. They whispered into dictation machines and microphones.

"After this conference I will be meeting with the District Attorney who is prepared to file formal charges today." He picked up a sheet of paper from the podium and waved it at the audience. "This is a warrant for the arrest of this despicable individual."

Baumgartner held the paper vertically so the cameras could get a shot of the warrant. His free hand covered the portion indicating the name of the charged individual. Many reporters moved forward, and the cameras zoomed in to catch what he was concealing.

"Melissa Lewis will tell you the name of the guilty party, but you can plainly see this is an official warrant signed by Judge Russell Hoffman. And now, I'd like to introduce Mrs. Melissa Lewis to you."

A door to Baumgartner's right opened, and a frail, blonde-haired woman stepped in the room. Her left hand held a black Chanel clutch purse, and her right hand held on to a sandy-haired boy.

Melissa Lewis was dressed in a black suit offset by brightly polished brass buttons, and gold braid; her A-line skirt reached modestly to just below her knees. She smiled politely. Then she leaned over to whisper in her son's ear as she motioned for him to sit in a chair behind the table. The boy moved slowly without looking at anyone in the room. His neatly pressed tan wool suit clung tightly to his angular body. His jaw was set, and he clenched his teeth, pulling the corners of his mouth even farther down his face.

Baumgartner stepped back. With one hand he held his papers to his chest, with the other hand he motioned Melissa toward the podium. She leaned across the table and stretched to reach the microphone. She cleared her throat several times and gripped the podium on both sides as if she would fall from her teetering position. Her deep blue eyes gazed across the audience. Finally, she spoke.

"Thank you for coming this afternoon. This isn't an easy thing for me to do, and your interest in finding out the truth about my husband's death encourages me that justice will be done."

Some reporters scribbled notes furiously while others were captivated by the drama of the moment. They seemed more interested in watching than documenting the event on paper.

"Alex Lewis was a strong man. You may have heard rumors that overmedication drove him to suicide. That's not true. In fact, if he hadn't been taking medication, he might have cracked much sooner. Until you have experienced the sexual abuse of your own child, you cannot imagine the horror of knowing that one you love has been cruelly violated."

Her slowly measured words held the audience at rapt attention. The reporters leaned forward and most laid their pens down or held them motionless. Mrs. Lewis spoke softly, but no one dared ask *her* to speak up. She was a fragile china doll sitting on the edge of a precipice, and the assembled journalists held their breath lest the slightest interference would topple her.

"My son, Benjamin," she said motioning with her right hand toward the young lad, "is our only child, and Alex doted on him. Alex wanted Benjamin to have every chance in life to excel with his God-given talents. Until six months ago, Benjamin was at the top of his class and participated in every athletic endeavor his private school offered. He studied music, dance, and took part in special programs provided by the museum to broaden his cultural interests. Then . . . ."

Her lower lip quivered, and she gripped the sides of the podium until her knuckles turned white. Baumgartner started to get out of his seat to steady her.

"Then we learned that our precious Benjamin was molested by an evil man. To make things worse, this foul crime was committed by someone of high standing in the community, a man who would never be suspected of such a horrible deed."

Mrs. Lewis swayed to one side and looked like she might fall down. This time, Baumgartner came to her side, steadied her, and poured her a glass of water. Her hand shook as she lifted the glass to her lips and slowly sipped. When she regained her composure she continued.

"You may wonder why we didn't come forward sooner. Well, for one thing we didn't know what happened until a couple of weeks before Alex's death. All we knew was that Benjamin's life was falling apart. At first, we blamed ourselves, thinking we were failures as parents.

"Then we consulted a counselor, and he uncovered the secret that Benjamin had hidden in his soul. The news broke Alex's heart. He wanted to kill the man who did it, but he knew that was wrong. He considered going to the authorities, but he wondered whether anyone would believe him. The counselor warned us that when children are molested by powerful authority figures, the victim may live in constant fear of a repeat offense if the effort to incarcerate the perpetrator fails."

Mrs. Lewis looked at Benjamin, who sat with his shoulders slumped over and his chin against his chest. His sandy locks fell off his forehead and hung over his eyes. He fiddled with the corner of his suit jacket, nervously twisting it one way, and then the other.

Mrs. Lewis turned back to the audience, this time with a defiant look on her face. "The man who molested my son and tormented his soul was . . ."

"I know what you're going to say, and it's a lie!" a male voice cried out loudly.

Mrs. Lewis fell backward and Baumgartner leaped to his feet to catch her. Benjamin jerked his head up quickly, an intense look of fear on his face. The reporters turned their heads in an effort to find out who had shouted.

Suddenly Henry Baldwin was on his feet walking toward the front of the room. As Henry neared the table, he turned around to face the crowd. He waved both of his arms for people to be quiet.

Then he gestured in the direction of Mrs. Lewis and spoke. "I know Mrs. Lewis means well and believes what she was about to say. But she doesn't know who molested her son. She and her husband were lied to. The man who gave them the false information was my father, Bill Baldwin III."

Wes listened as the murmuring in the room ceased. A few gasps could be heard. Others put their pens into action and began writing furiously. This *was* a major scoop and the most important headline of the political season.

Baumgartner opened his briefcase and pulled out a small portable cellular phone. He turned his face aside and cupped his hand over his mouth to conceal his conversation. Reporters began shouting questions and waving to get Henry's attention.

"Please, please, let me continue," Henry pleaded. "Mrs. Lewis believes that Stanley Taylor is the man who violated her son. The people who want my father elected to the U.S. Senate want her to believe that. I know who molested Benjamin Lewis, because the same man molested me. And it wasn't Stanley Taylor! Furthermore, I don't believe that he shot Dr. Bowman."

With that, Henry headed toward Jennifer, reached out to her, and the two of them, hand in hand, ran from the room with reporters in hot pursuit.

23

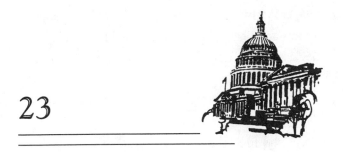

Ⓘt's Jennifer!"

Wes barely comprehended what Annette said. His bleary eyes were trying to focus on the bedside alarm clock. *What's she doing calling us at 6 A.M.?*

All at once, Wes sat up in bed. "Jennifer! Where is she?" He remembered how worried he'd been the night before over not knowing Jennifer's whereabouts.

"She and Henry are in hiding," Annette whispered with her mouth away from the phone receiver.

Wes sat up in bed. "Let me talk to her."

"Just a minute; your father wants a word with you."

"Jennifer," Wes said, taking the phone, "where are you?"

"Up in the mountains at a cabin. I'm talking on a mobile phone. Henry's with me. He wants to lie low a couple of days until the fallout from the news conference is over. He's also fearful of what his father might do after what Henry said there."

"You mean you're alone with . . ."

"Dad, I'm nineteen and perfectly capable of handling myself. And no, we're not alone."

"Then, who . . ."

"Stanley Taylor. He's been hiding out here since that abortion doctor was shot a week ago."

"How did you hook up with Taylor? He's the most sought-after man in the country. Every paper is running a front-page story on him, and the news media can't get enough. The national press has blown this thing across the nation. I never thought he'd be capable of murder. You had better get out of there now!"

"Dad, he didn't shoot Dr. Bowman. You were there. Didn't you see what happened?"

"Yes, but I didn't see who fired the gun. If Taylor didn't do it, who did?"

"It's too easy to tap cellular phones, so I can't say much. Can you come get me? Henry is going to stay here a few days with Mr. Taylor."

"Sure, I'll come get you. When?"

"Today. Now."

"Where?"

"Not here. I'll have Henry drive me to a gas station a couple of miles away. Remember where Highway 34 intersects the jeep trail to Lake Lomond? There's a filling station next to one of those tourist trout-fishing ponds."

"I know the place."

"Shall we meet in an hour?"

Wes ran a hand through his disheveled hair, which always stood straight up first thing in the morning. "Jennifer, I just woke up. Give me two hours. I've got to shower and alert the office I won't be in this morning. And you know how slowly your mother moves this time of the day."

"Dad, please don't bring Mom. Henry tells me that technically we're harboring a fugitive. It's bad enough to involve you without also dragging Mom into this."

An hour later, Wes was out the door alone. He drove down Interstate 70 and exited on to Highway 34. As he approached the trout pond, he saw

Jennifer sitting by the bank, huddled in an oversized gray flannel shirt. When she saw Wes's car, she jumped up and ran to meet him.

"Oh, Dad, you don't know how good it is to see you!" Jennifer threw her arms around his neck. "Hurry, Henry is waiting, and I know he'll worry while I'm away."

The Lake Lomond jeep trail wasn't designed for luxury cars; only 4 x 4s ever dared to travel its unmaintained surface. Wes put his Lexus in the lowest gear and barely touched the accelerator. He tried to steer around any rocks that would hit high center. Slowly the car crept up the steep trail.

"Sure hope nobody saw us," Wes commented. "Lake Lomond is still frozen this time of year, so we aren't likely to encounter any sportsmen. I've hiked back there in June and still had to chip ice to find a fishing spot."

"Yes, and that also means no one is using this road this time of year. That's why Mr. Taylor picked this spot."

"So, how did you two hook up with Taylor?"

"It wasn't all that difficult," Jennifer answered. "Henry wanted to stay out of sight, and we knew Mr. Taylor did too. I've become close with the whole Taylor family because of my crusade involvement. They trust me, and when I contacted Mrs. Taylor to find a place to hide Henry, she arranged for us to meet at this remote cabin."

Thunk! A front wheel rolled over a football-sized rock, and the car lurched sideways. Wes grasped the steering wheel tighter and tried to stay on either side of two ruts, old tire tracks that had been further deepened by the rushing water from snow banks on up the road. A hundred yards ahead, Wes spotted a metallic green Chevy pickup.

"That's Taylor's truck," Jennifer explained. "He usually keeps it parked behind those trees over there." Jennifer pointed toward a thickly forested area.

The pickup was parked next to a split-log cabin like those left behind by 1890s miners. The logs had been felled from the nearby forest, as evidenced by the dozens of decaying stumps that dotted the surroundings. Each log was notched and fitted with such precision that the cabin had survived hundreds of storms and winter winds with little apparent damage. The corrugated-tin roof and solid-core front door bore testimony that some dweller had remodeled the cabin after its initial construction.

Henry Baldwin stood outside waving. As Wes pulled his car to a halt Jennifer threw open the door and ran to meet Henry. He hugged her warmly and motioned for Wes to come inside.

"I thought you said Taylor was here," Wes said as he surveyed the decrepit interior and breathed in the musty smell of the aged wood walls and the earthy odor of the furnishings' damp upholstery.

"He's gone for a morning walk," Henry answered.

"How did you come up with this place?" Wes asked as he walked around the cabin's cramped confines.

"Taylor used to come here on fishing trips as a kid," Henry answered. "It belonged to his aunt. Believe it or not, that thing still works," he said, pointing to a potbellied stove that was set on bricks in the middle of the room.

The stove's soot-blackened exterior looked like it hadn't been cleaned in a hundred years. Wes's eyes followed the makeshift pipe that protruded out the top and angled toward an opening in the side of the wall. The pipe was suspended by a single wire that hung from a foot-thick ceiling beam.

"Sit down while we wait for Stanley," Henry said as he patted the arm of an old stuffed chair, which sent out a cloud of musty dust into the room.

Wes declined the invitation.

Suddenly the front door opened, and Stanley Taylor, Bill Baldwin's arch enemy and the law's most-wanted man, stood in the entry. "Welcome to our humble abode," Taylor said extending his hand.

He looked tired and had several days' growth of beard, but his eyes were bright and friendly. Wes shook hands politely, though he was a little nervous at his proximity to a fugitive from justice. The circumstances for this meeting were much different from their last in Taylor's backyard.

"I didn't do it, Mr. Bryant," Taylor said as he set his walking stick in a corner. "I was framed. I don't know where that gun came from. Maybe

Father Vitali did it. He's an evil man. His own church has defrocked him for advocating what he calls the 'justifiable homicide' of abortionists."

"But the gun was on the ground next to you."

Taylor walked over to the cabin's only window, which had cracked glass in each of its four panes. He leaned down to look outside. "I was trying to make Vitali let go of that girl. I don't believe in abortion, but it's just as wrong to forcefully interfere with someone else's free will. Persuading people is one thing; violently confronting them is another. It's Vitali's people who scream at the women getting abortions and block their pathway on private property. Crusade protesters always stay on public property and never use violence. Ours is a spiritual mission."

"Then why did McCormick's officers treat your people so brutally?"

"You tell me!" Taylor shot back with fire in his eyes. "It's your boss, Bill Baldwin, who calls the shots for McCormick."

Wes saw that Jennifer was tense, so he walked over and put an arm around her shoulder. "Why was it necessary for you to protest? If your people had never been in front of that clinic, this wouldn't have happened."

"Listen, Mr. Bryant, that's not all we do. Our crusade helps sponsor birthright organizations that provide shelter and comfort for young girls like Molly. We help these young women learn about adoption, and we help them every step of the way if they can't keep their babies. We make sure they find loving homes. When they go through the postpartum phase, we counsel them and let them know they are loved and cared for. And if they go through with an abortion, we provide free post-abortion counseling so they can deal with the guilt and trauma once they realize what they've done. Our mission is to bring healing to these young women, not to brutalize them emotionally. We offer them a real *choice*. We've never raised our voices toward a girl entering Bowman's clinic, and we've never used coercion to stop anyone from going in."

"Then why was that U.S. marshal there?"

Taylor spoke calmly and earnestly. "The pro-choice people wanted to provoke a fight, and the politicians went along with it. That scene was politically staged. You saw who the police attacked. We believe we are civil rights protesters. Unfortunately, unlike the noble cause of civil freedom for blacks, we don't have the press on our side."

"What about Vitali?"

"Our crusade repudiates everything he stands for. The media play up the radical fringe of the pro-life movement so everyone thinks that people opposed to abortion are willing to kill to stop the killing."

"Dad," Jennifer said, "I'm ready to go, if you are."

Wes started toward the door. He still wasn't sure if he believed Taylor, but it seemed somehow tragic to leave him and Henry behind in that broken-down cabin. "Are you sure you two will be all right here?"

"Thanks for your concern," Taylor said. "We've got enough canned food to get by, and I've got my cellular phone in case of an emergency. I have an adapter and keep it charged up with the pickup cigarette lighter so my wife can call and stay in touch."

"Why not turn yourself in and let justice take its course?" Wes asked.

"Justice?" Taylor asked with a touch of anger in his voice. "Sheriff John McCormick and Judge Russell Hoffman are the justice in this county, and there's too great a chance I might have an *accident* behind bars if I let them incarcerate me. Besides, if I'm in custody, I can't prove who really ordered the shooting of Dr. Bowman—your boss, Bill Baldwin."

24

Wes slowed down his car, turned off the freeway, and proceeded down Fifteenth Street toward the state capitol building. He glanced down at his wristwatch. It was 8:45 Saturday morning, and there was still plenty of time to check out the staging area before the Gay Respect parade started at 10:00.

"You're worried, aren't you?" Wes asked Annette.

"What mother wouldn't be?" she responded and gave Wes a serious look. "First, Jennifer speaks out on abortion and a riot takes place, then she befriends an accused child pornographer and a wanted fugitive. This must be the hottest story in town with every available journalist fast on the trail. You know how callous reporters can be. I've read stories about those news hounds even going through the garbage of people they're writing about. I've almost gone crazy wondering what they might do to Jennifer. It's bad enough they know she's hooked up with Henry, but what if they found out she's also helping to hide Taylor?"

"I'm glad she's safely back at the dorm, and we don't have to worry— for now anyway," Wes said.

Wes patted Annette's hand reassuringly. "You don't mind walking a little distance to the parade area, do you? I'm concerned about parking in designated areas. If there's a disturbance like at Taylor's rally, I want to be able to get out quickly."

Annette seemed lost in thought. "You do whatever is best."

Eight blocks away from the capitol, Wes looked for street-side parking. He found a vacant spot with a meter saying "no charge Saturdays, Sundays, and holidays," and parallel parked. He reached in the back seat, grabbed his camera, and slung the strap over his shoulder. "Are you ready for this?" he asked Annette in a sober tone.

Annette shook her head with uncertainty. "I have no idea what we're in for, so just stay close to me. If violence breaks out, I'm depending on you to get us out of here fast."

Wes and Annette opened their car doors and stepped into the bright, warm sunshine. For a mid-May day, it was exceptionally warm with the temperature in the high seventies. Wes started to get a jacket out of the trunk, but changed his mind. What strange irony, he thought, that such a bright day would set the stage for such dark circumstances. He took Annette's hand, and they walked briskly toward the capitol. Its gold dome gleamed majestically in the distance.

They had gone no more than two blocks when they heard the sounds of motorcycle engines. From every direction, Wes saw women on motorcycles as they headed toward the makeshift staging area behind the capitol. Wes was shocked. Dozens of women, more than half stark-naked, rode proudly down the street. A few wore skimpy S & M garb. Some feigned modesty with see-through body stockings.

A few couples rode in tandem, the drivers accompanied by their lovers who clung indiscreetly to their private parts. One woman traveled with her preteen daughter who held a sign saying, "I love my mommy, and so does her girlfriend." Wes spotted an obese biker accompanied by her lover who wore a wedding dress.

As Wes and Annette arrived at the staging area, the roar of motorcycles swelled. A tall man holding a clipboard and pad checked off the names of the Dykes on Bikes brigade who filed into formation. The male organizer was dressed head-to-foot in black leather and had handcuffs dangling from one belt loop and a leather whip hanging from another. As he took down each woman's name and motorcycle license number, he pointed in the direction of her preassigned position. The bikers pulled into place, dismounted, and joined the scores of other women who were laughing, drinking, smoking marijuana, and engaging in indiscrete foreplay.

Annette yanked at Wes's arm and pulled him toward her to whisper in his ear. "This is worse than I thought, and the parade hasn't even started yet!"

"Try not to show your shock," Wes responded. "Let's hold each other's hand. That way we can signal what each of us is noticing without being too conspicuous."

Annette nodded an okay. Wes calmly removed the protective lens cap from his camera and started taking pictures. To his amazement, no one minded. Many of the women posed seductively. He snapped one picture after another: A stately redhead dressed head to foot in nothing but fishnet mesh. A muscle-bound butch whose body had dozens of bruises that Wes assumed resulted from her violent love quests. An attractive girl in her twenties with a hat of plastic bananas, oranges, and apples, and a sign that said, "Fruits on Parade." A three-hundred-pound woman who held a sign saying, "Mothers, we're after your daughters."

The entire scene was outrageous. No conduct seemed forbidden, and no display of flesh or perversity brought embarrassment. On the outer edge of the motorcycle gathering, a half-dozen policemen stood watching in disbelief. Normally, this kind of public indecency would have brought immediate arrests. It seemed the police were under orders to keep their distance.

Just around the corner, TV affiliates from the four major networks had set up satellite facilities. Cameramen checked out their equipment, but none took a picture of the provocative behavior. Wes presumed the cameramen had been given instructions to capture only the palatable aspects of the parade.

Wes took Annette's hand and led her through the alcohol-hazed crowd. A few of the female riders wore motorcycle jackets, emblazoned on the back with slogans like "Lost Babes," "Hell's Belles," and "No Guilt." One group had dressed in nuns' habits that included leather halter tops that partially exposed their breasts. Wes saw a woman in a crew cut carefully fasten a dog collar around the neck of her shaven-headed lover. When the collar was in place, she yanked on the chain attached to it and led her lover down the street like an animal in tow. The submissive partner had her hands tied behind her back to indicate her obeisance. Annette squeezed Wes's hand to get his attention and pointed to a woman dressed in a gestapo uniform who held a baby in one arm and with the other hand held a sign aloft that read, "I can't even think straight."

Wes noticed a group farther off to one side and pulled Annette in that direction. A sign said "Vamps" and within seconds Wes realized they had intruded on a gathering of the vampire lesbians he had heard about. Most were dressed in medieval garb, including suits of armor, mail, and steel mesh along with lances and metal hats. Almost all had fangs protruding from their mouths.

"Are those fake?" Wes walked up and boldly asked one woman.

"Are you talking to me?" a mannish-looking woman answered. She turned around to defiantly stare at Wes. Older than the others, she seemed to be the leader. Her long hair, dyed bright red, lay against a leather-and-metal jacket that was laden with four-inch-long spikes. She was completely naked from the waist down. "Igor is my name, and I've had my front teeth cosmetically altered by my dentist. He filed the four front teeth to sharp points, and these fangs are porcelain caps."

"What for?" Wes asked, realizing as soon as he said it that it was a dumb question.

The other vamps standing by all laughed. "Let me demonstrate," the leader said sarcastically.

With a quick motion she drew a knife from a scabbard on her belt and looked menacingly at a young blonde girl standing next to her. The blonde, nude except for a bikini bottom, smiled compliantly. Igor grabbed the blonde by her hair and forced her to her knees. Once Igor had subdued her victim, she yanked the girl's head back to more fully expose her neck.

Igor snarled and put the sharp blade to the blonde's throat. The girl smiled as if she welcomed being a mock victim.

Then Igor bent down, opened her lips wide, and tightly clasped her mouth on the blonde's neck. As Igor withdrew her mouth and stood back up, Wes saw two small rivulets of blood trickle down the blonde's neck. In spite of the agreement between Annette and Wes to appear nonchalant, Annette put her hand to her face and recoiled in horror.

Igor smirked with delight at the disgust she had evoked. "Let me know, Honey, if you need a little of my special loving."

Wes doubled his fist. To him, Igor was more like an animal than a woman, and he would have had no chivalrous doubts about punching her out. Annette felt his anger and gently took his fist in her hand and caressed it.

The idea that the police would more likely arrest him for starting trouble than they would detain any of the marchers who violated all public indecency laws struck Wes as a hypocritical irony. But before he could think about it any longer, the voice of the motorcycle traffic coordinator called out, "To your positions! The parade starts in two minutes."

The cyclists quickly mounted their bikes and revved up their engines. The parade coordinators, identified by their "Remember April 30!" buttons, pushed all spectators aside to make room for the motorcycles to proceed down Main Street. Then they were off, their engines roaring.

Wes and Annette walked from the staging area toward the main route and were surprised to find that thousands of people had already gathered to line both sides of the street. The Dykes on Bikes were greeted with thunderous cheers as they waved and threw kisses to the crowd. It was a festive occasion, the kind of atmosphere Wes remembered back in Indiana on Memorial Day and the Fourth of July. The America of this May 14 celebrated behavior that small-town Indiana never knew existed.

There were no hostile gawkers and no anti-march demonstrators. The handful of observers who appeared to be straight seemed to take no offense at the displays of homosexual liberation and affection. The attitude of the gay community seemed to be one of sticking out its chest in full pride for all to see its unity and brazenness.

"Let's find a place that's not so crowded," Wes yelled at Annette as they ran block after block, looking for an opening in the throng. At times their dash slowed to a fast walk as they pushed their way past hundreds of men dressed in drag and homosexual couples engaged in various kinds of sexual acts. Wes moved so quickly that he could hardly take everything in, but there was no mistaking that the obscene homosexual displays on the sidewalk rivaled the immorality in the parade.

Finally Wes spotted a break in the crowd and made his way to the curb for a clear view. Annette stood next to him and clung tightly with both arms around his waist. The last of the motorcycles passed by, and they were followed by a half-dozen tall men dressed in extravagant evening gowns. They held a huge banner reading, "Queers on Parade: The Day of the Dyke."

Wes got his camera ready and began taking pictures of the marching contingents that followed. First was a group of male cheerleaders, complete with pom-poms. They swayed down the street exhorting the crowd with obscene chants while they blew bubblegum bubbles from their pink-lipsticked lips. Next came a fire engine with a sign, "Gay and Lesbian Firefighters, Keeping Your City Safe." The firefighters, with their dalmatian dogs on leashes, marched next to the engine, waving at the crowd. Behind them were police officers holding a sign saying, "Gay cops uphold the law."

Next Wes saw dozens of baby strollers full of children being pushed by gay couples who held hands and kissed each other as they walked. Annette looked at Wes with fire in her eyes. As a woman and a mother, this part of the parade seemed particularly disgusting to her.

Various organizational groups followed, each with its own banner describing its gay and lesbian affiliation: Gay Teachers Association, Lesbians and Gays of African Descent, the Lavender Veterans of Foreign Wars, Parents of Gays and Lesbians, Gay Witches, and Queers for Abortion Choice. What really shocked Wes was what seemed to be the public endorsement of homosexuality by major corporations. Gay employees from banks, computer firms, oil companies, and manufacturers and retailers of all sorts were present. Even some religious denominations proclaimed their acceptance of gay clergy.

Some groups held signs with slogans calling for various kinds of political action: "Legalize Gay Marriages," "Authorize Gay Adoptions," "Repeal Sodomy Laws," "Support Domestic Partnerships," "Promote Gay Guardianship," and "Back Gay Foster Parents."

Several government officials rode in open convertibles, including Hal Hatfield, the gay personal aide to the president of the United States. Signs on the sides of the cars clearly identified who each participant was and what public office he or she held. The crowds cheered wildly as they passed by, obviously emboldened by this display of political clout.

"We love our lesbian daughter," read one sign held by a middle-aged woman. Next to her marched her daughter, holding hands with her lover. Another set of parents, marching with their gay son and his partner, called out in rhyme, "We raised our child with love and pride, and on this day we're on his side. With his lover we march today to tell the world we're proud he's gay."

Some groups had their own chants. "Two, four, six, eight, how do you know your grandmother's straight?" called out a bunch of homosexual senior citizens. A group claiming to represent gay and lesbian psychiatrists intoned, "Two, four, six, eight, don't assume your shrink is straight." Other marchers were less poetic, shouting, "Get your whole family out of the closet," "Homophobia is not a traditional value," and "I'm gay and I'm in the military."

There were special interest groups representing transsexuals, transvestites, and sado-masochism advocates, each appropriately attired. Following them was a frail man in a woman's dress. He clutched a purse and was being pushed down the street on a hospital gurney. An IV tube went from his skeletal frame to a plastic bottle suspended on a pole. He looked as if he were near death. A sign at the foot of his bed read: "Stop the Killing! Fund AIDS Research." His lover walked alongside the gurney holding the dying man's hand.

He just doesn't get it, Wes thought as he closely observed the man's feminine attire and his affection for his lover. *It's his own moral choices that are killing him. He's not saying stop the behavior that transmits AIDS.*

Then the parade stopped. Two barely-clad women stepped into the middle of the street. One of them posed seductively, while the other, decorated in leather chaps and body tatoos, unraveled a bullwhip and snapped it in the air. Her potential victim yelled, "Do it now, Marina, don't tease me!"

This is disgusting! Wes thought. *And there's not a single member of the media here to report it!*

Wes moved past several people to get an unobstructed photograph. As he did, he felt a fist jam sharply into his stomach. He momentarily lost his breath and looked to his side to see who had hit him. A husky woman, nearly six feet tall, stared at him with her clenched fists resting on her hips.

"Hey, Buster, watch who you're bumping into!"

Wes was taken back by her brazenness. "I didn't bump you," he said.

"Not me, her—my wife," the woman responded, pointing to a frail teenage girl clinging to her waist.

"Your wife!" Wes exclaimed with a tone of disgust.

"You heard me, my wife. You have a problem with that?"

Wes stopped for a moment. He did have a big problem with such behavior, but he wasn't sure if he should say so now. Before he could temper his aversion with reason, he felt powerful hands grip both his arms from behind. He looked over his shoulder at a towering, muscular man who leered down at him. The man, dressed head-to-toe in black leather, looked like he should have been cast as a torturer in a World War II concentration camp film. Wes saw the look of evil in his eyes.

"Is this straight guy giving you a problem, sister?"

"Yeah, he ran into my wife, and he was taking pictures of the other sisters who were having a little fun. He's probably one of those Restore Our Heritage Crusade people spying on us."

"Is that so, buddy?" Wes's captor asked as he clamped Wes's arms harder to show his dominance.

"Hey, this is a free country, and this is a public street. I have a right to be here if I want. Lay off!" Wes shot back in an attempt to bluff his way out of a violent confrontation.

Pow! Wes felt the side of a huge hand crack against the back of his neck. Everything went black, and his body slumped. Annette screamed. The muscle man jerked Wes's camera from his hands, ripped the film from inside, and sent it sailing somewhere into the crowd. He slammed the camera against the pavement and stomped on it with the heel of his boot.

"Leave him alone, you monster!" Annette cried out and flung her tiny fists against his massive biceps.

Wes came to in a haze and saw an angry woman lunge for Annette. He was helpless to intervene. Just as the woman embraced Annette in a crushing body hug, the crowd, which had been watching the fight, broke into cheers. Everyone turned away from Wes and Annette to scream in delight at whatever was happening in the street. People jumped up and down and waved their arms in the air.

"It's him!" Annette's adversary declared as she released her grip.

Wes's foe also let go of him. The captor shoved people aside as he forced his way to the street. Amid the shouts of acclaim, Wes fell to his knees and tried to collect his thoughts. *Glad I have the other six rolls of film in my pockets,* he thought to himself. Wes slowly stood up and reached out to Annette who was weeping from terror.

"What's happening?" Annette cried out.

"I don't know, I can't see."

When Wes regained his strength, he stood fully erect and raised on his toes to see what part of the parade had rescued them.

The crowd knocked over the steel parade barricades and spilled into the street. They ran screaming with delight toward a shiny red BMW convertible and reached out to the man sitting on the top of the backseat. The man in the convertible grinned broadly and waved both arms in the air, the fingers of his hands signaling the *V* for victory, just as he had at the victory celebration after his nomination as the Stand for America candidate for the U.S. Senate.

25

Wes stood on the side of the street, groggy from the blow to the back of his head. He realized in an instant that he and Annette were targets for violence. They had to get out of there quickly. The same mob that cheered Baldwin would turn on them again once the convertible passed.

Wes took Annette's hand and they started running. With his free hand, he stiff-armed his way, as if he were warding off opposing linemen in his college football days. Adrenaline pumped through his veins, and his heart thumped so hard it seemed to bang against his rib cage. Sweat poured everywhere, and he kept readjusting his grip on Annette's hand because his palms were slippery with perspiration. Annette was not in as good shape as Wes, and he felt sorry for what she had to go through.

After running, pushing, and shoving their way past hundreds of parade spectators, Wes spotted a portion of the street where the buildings were set back farther and the sidewalk widened. It provided just enough room for them to slip behind the massive crowd.

When Wes thought they were safe, he stopped and leaned against the front door of an antique store that was closed for the day. The door was recessed between window displays of nineteenth-century Victorian furnishings. Annette almost hyperventilated, and Wes pulled her close to his chest to hold her steady.

At first their gasps for air were so intense, neither one could speak. Once Wes had taken enough deep breaths to get his heart rate down, he said, "I think we're out of danger now. I didn't keep track, but we must have run ten or twelve blocks. We've got to be near the end of the parade route."

After spitting out those few words between breaths, Wes gulped in deep lungfulls of air. Annette said nothing, and her body shook. Her arms were wrapped around Wes's waist, and the side of her face was flat against his chest. Perspiration soaked her hair, and the wet strands spotted Wes's shirt.

"I doubt they'll come after us. There must be somewhere between fifty to a hundred thousand people lining the streets, and locating us would be almost impossible. Besides, they've got more important things on their minds right now than hassling two straight people." Wes took a couple more deep breaths. "Are you all right to start walking again?"

Annette nodded her head. She was still shaking, and Wes sensed it was hard for her to speak. Gently, with one arm around her waist, he stepped out of the doorway, and they resumed walking away from the main parade route. As they neared the end of the block Wes heard the sounds of music.

"The exhibit and concession area must be straight ahead," Wes said to Annette. "I remember seeing some parade plans that Dave Kelly was going over. The perimeter of Roosevelt Park is supposed to be lined with all kinds of booths and small stages where various kinds of performances will be taking place. It's supposed to include food concessions, displays of products and services, and various impromptu presentations."

As they continued walking, Wes caught the distinct strains of a salsa band whose rhythms challenged the more energized beat of dance and disco music that permeated the parade. Both came from opposite directions and created a cacophonous stereo effect.

By now, Wes and Annette had both calmed down and their breathing was back to normal. "I wouldn't mind checking this place out," Wes said. "If you're too fearful of being spotted, we'll head toward some side streets and make our way back to the car. It's up to you."

Annette still held Wes's right hand, and she leaned into his side as they walked. "I agree, it will be a long time before those creeps who attacked us get down to this area, and there are so many people I doubt they could ever find us. If you want to take a few minutes and look around, go ahead. But please, let's not stay too long."

"We'll take fifteen or twenty minutes max to check things out. Then I'll find a safe place for you and run back to get the car."

By now, the salsa music was overwhelming, and it was joined by the sounds of a live gay country band performing near the entrance to the park. The Nashville-sound musicians performed on the flatbed of a truck. They were accompanied by a half-dozen dancers outfitted in dude-ranch clothing—jeans, boots, rodeo shirts, and bandannas tied around their necks. With one arm, they waved their Stetson hats in the air, and with their other arm they held the hand of their partners as they Texas two-stepped. All the dancers were men who paired off in more than plutonic duos. A small crowd of slightly inebriated lesbians and other gay men gathered around the edge of the truck bed for a rollicking version of "Achy Breaky Heart." The dancers clicked their heels and every few steps leaned toward each other for an affectionate kiss. This homosexual hoe-down seemed almost innocent compared to what had gone on at the parade route.

Wes and Annette turned left and started walking past a series of small tent booths that sold various kinds of merchandise and hawked the literature of various interest groups. One booth offered variations on the AIDS-awareness red lapel ribbon. The samples included simple, standard ribbons at the low price end; the costs gradually increased, depending on how elaborate the design. At the top end was an enamel loop of ribbon laced with fourteen-karat gold and inlaid with small diamonds.

The next booth offered a cornucopia of condoms. Wes was surprised to see the incredible variety of colors, designs, scents, sensitivities, and sizes available in the name of safe sex. The booth was staffed by one of the cheerleaders. He had exchanged his pom-poms for a wooden folding chair and sat disinterested, caught up in reading his latest issue of the gay publication *Out and Proud*. Wes tilted his head slightly to see the cover of the magazine. Two muscular men were photographed wearing nothing but leather wristbands. They stood with their back sides to the camera holding small whips in their hands and grinning over their shoulders.

The next several booths dispensed food, candies, hot dogs, nachos, and flame-broiled hamburgers. The concessionaires went about their business efficiently, but they all seemed a little irritated by the booth on the far side, which was staffed by a long-haired young man dressed in drag who screamed so much his voice had gone hoarse.

"We'll all be dead in five years! Don't you get it? The government is murdering us. They want us to die. We need a Manhattan Project for AIDS research, or we'll all be dead!" the young man screamed. "Hey you," he yelled at Wes. "Mister Straight, with your wife there, why are you killing us? Why do you want us to die?"

Wes's curiosity got the best of him, and he decided to find out what the distraught transvestite had to say. He noticed that the guy wore a long, print dress that looked like it was salvaged from the sixties; it was accented by a huge blue plastic handbag that hung over his shoulder. The man's light brown hair had been permed at the tips, and it bobbed at his shoulders in tangled curls. His eyeliner and bright red lipstick were something Wes expected to see worn by Madonna for campy effect in a rock video.

"My name is Mark Sissyqueer," he said, handing Wes a business card. "I was called that my whole life, so I went to court and had it legally changed. It sort of fits me, don't you think?" He cocked his right knee outward, pointing the toe of his high heel shoe downward and thrusting one hip forward.

Wes looked at the card. At the top, it read: "Fags for Life." The line underneath it was: "A cure for AIDS or else." Below that was an address and phone number.

Wes looked up from the card. "Are you serious?"

"Dead serious," Mark said with a more sober tone to his voice. "The people in our group have decided to flaunt every stereotype people have about gays. We're militant too. Remember the uproar when the Pope came to town and someone broke into the cemetery next to Holy Name Cathedral and put condoms on top of all the Virgin Mary statues?"

Wes nodded his head.

"I don't think the Catholic bishops did that, do you? See, we engage in guerilla theater and outrageous acts of vandalism to get the attention of the press. If America put a man on the moon, we can end AIDS now," he said as he waved his arms in the air and his voice rose to a shrill tenor.

"Calm down, calm down," Wes said. "If you don't mind my asking, do you have gay sex?"

Mark seemed unoffended by Wes's blunt inquiry. "Of course!" he shouted defiantly. "I have sex any time and any way I want it. That's my right. Your responsibility is to find out why what I do is killing me. Did straight people stop breathing because they got tuberculosis? Did they stop walking because they got polio? Did they stop going to the tropics because they got malaria? No!" he yelled at the top of his lungs as he doubled up both fists and pounded them on the table in front of him. "You found a cure and kept on doing what you were doing. That's what we demand— sex the way we want it and enough government money to mobilize every medical researcher in America to find a cure for AIDS. The Manhattan Project ended World War II by building a bomb because America was committed to it. If we could build a bomb to kill, why can't we find a pill to cure AIDS?".

Mark started screaming obscenities at Wes as he held out a small glass bowl that contained a few one-dollar bills. He shook the bowl and demanded a contribution. When Wes didn't comply, his obscenities grew more graphic. Wes stuffed the business card in his pocket and walked away from Mark's epithets.

As Wes and Annette hurried past more booths, they heard the sound of singing. At a far corner of the park, a small temporary stage had been built, and a theatrical performance was taking place. Wes and Annette headed toward the noise and saw that it was a staged minidrama with actors and actresses dressed in costumes depicting various gay stereotypes. Signs at the foot of the stage designated the role of each performer.

Above the sign saying "Butch Dyke" was a tough-looking woman wearing a Nazi SS hat, thigh-high boots, and a scanty leather bodice to cover her bulk. Next to her was the "Basic Suburban Lesbian." Her role was played by a ladylike woman wearing Anne Klein-style slacks, a silk blouse, and pearls. She looked like she had just been to a PTA meeting. To her left was the "Athletic Lesbian." A muscular woman in shorts and a tank top strutted back and forth on the stage, alternately swinging a tennis racket, golf club, and a baseball bat. Next to the lesbians stood four men in long, flowing dresses. Their heads were topped with straw bonnets accented with plastic flowers. The sign under them said "Drag Queens Supreme."

All at once, the four gay men broke into song, and Wes immediately picked up on the satirical use of the word *supreme,* as their falsetto voices, accompanied by a prerecorded soundtrack, broke into a medley of tunes by Diana Ross.

After the medley of Supremes classics, the singers switched to an a cappella takeoff on the song "My Country 'Tis of Thee." "God is a lesbian, God is a thespian, God is a dyke," they sang to the first line of the familiar song. In rhyme and rhythm, true to the meter of the original words and tune, the drag singers proceeded to substitute perverse descriptions of a lesbian God engaging in sexual relationships with women.

Annette started walking away and pulled Wes's hand in her direction. He moved toward her without hesitation, disgusted that the humorous caricature had turned into a blasphemous display. The blow to the back of his head ached and gave him further cause to leave.

As Wes and Annette walked away from the booths toward an area of the park where they saw a flower garden, they heard the sounds of a scuffle that came from a small knoll surrounded by bushes. People were yelling, but Wes couldn't make out what they were saying. Other people nearby heard the commotion and started running in that direction.

Then the air crackled with screams. "Leave him alone! Don't hurt him!" a woman's voice cried out above the disarray.

"Wes!" Annette yelled and yanked hard at his arm. "That's Jennifer's voice."

Wes was stunned. *Jennifer? What's she doing here?*

He heard her voice scream out again. "He was only trying to help! Someone stop them, please!"

"That *is* Jennifer. Wes, you've got to do something!"

"Stay here," Wes said to Annette. "Stand by that tree," he added pointing to a huge oak about thirty feet away. "I'll be back as soon as I find out what's going on."

Annette ran toward the tree, and Wes bolted toward the screaming. The top of the knoll was less than fifty yards away, and his long strides got him there in seconds. He dashed past the bushes to a small clearing at the top of the hill. In the distance, Jennifer stood outside a small group of people. She repeatedly screamed in a panic, "Stop it! Take your hands off him!"

Then, Wes saw a blond man with his hair covering his face push his way through the crowd and fight off those who tried to hold him back. As the man broke free from the crowd, he staggered, trying to regain his balance. The man had run only a few yards when the air was split with the sound of a gunshot. The desperate man staggered first to one side, then the other. Finally he lunged forward.

Wes was so startled by the shot and distracted by the crowd, he hadn't gotten a good look at the injured young man. He ran to the victim's side and got there just as Jennifer knelt beside him in the grass. Jennifer sobbed hysterically and for a moment she didn't realize that it was her stepfather who knelt next to her. When she recognized Wes, she cried out, "Dad, they've shot Henry!"

Wes rolled Henry Baldwin on to his back. Blood streamed from his nostrils and the side of his mouth. Wes pulled back the sleeve of one arm and grabbed Henry's wrist with his hand. Wes looked up at Jennifer and said, "He has a pulse. It's weak, but he's not dead."

26

Wes and Annette drove quickly through the trash-littered streets to Denver City Hospital. Wes tried to explain to Annette what had taken place. He remembered kneeling with Jennifer beside Henry's body, waiting for someone to help. When a police cruiser and ambulance finally arrived, Wes was shoved aside as the paramedics went to work. He watched as the medical technicians cut through Henry's bloodstained shirt to locate the wound. Wes remembered the gnarled, gaping hole in the right side of Henry's chest and the speed and precision of the medics who placed Henry on a stretcher. The paramedics were on the way to the hospital with Henry in less than five minutes after they had arrived on the scene. Jennifer had gotten into the ambulance with Henry. Wes tried to call the hospital on his cellular phone but could not get any information from the hospital staff. An hour later, they still didn't know whether Henry was dead or alive.

When they finally arrived at City Hospital, Wes dropped Annette off at the front door, parked in the underground garage, and ran to the emergency entrance. A bored receptionist, who had obviously seen her fill of human tragedies, ignored Wes at first.

"Excuse me, but someone has been shot, and I need to find where he is right now!"

The receptionist kept typing at her computer and didn't bother to look up from her video terminal. "Someone is always looking for somebody who's been shot. You're the third one today. Relax, what's the name?"

"Baldwin."

"First name?"

"Henry! Hey, can you hurry this up a little? He could be dead before you get through this routine!"

The receptionist stopped typing to shake her finger at Wes. "People die here every day. Your friend is just one more. If I stopped what I'm doing to respond to every person who hysterically walks up to this desk, I'd never be out of here by five o'clock."

Wes could see that rushing this gatekeeper would backfire. He calmed himself and spoke as politely as he could. "Forgive me if I've intruded with something important like an attempted murder, but I really would like to see my friend before they bury him!"

The receptionist looked back at her terminal, punched a couple of buttons, and reached forward with her finger to trace down through several entries. "According to the information I have, he hasn't yet been released to post-op. He must still be in surgery. Now, if you'll just take a seat over there . . ."

"I'm not sitting down anywhere. My daughter is somewhere in this hospital with the patient, and she's probably in shock." Wes felt himself losing his patience again. Annette stood there silently. "You're crazy if you think I'm going to wait here while you fill your work quota so that you can walk out of here at the end of the day! Where do they perform surgery around here?"

The receptionist sighed with a huff and pointed down a long hallway. "Most of the operating rooms are in that direction, but you can't . . ."

Before she finished, Wes grabbed Annette's hand and ran down the hallway. Both sides of the corridor were lined with people seated in wheelchairs; others reclined on beds. They were so overcome with their own suffering and desensitized by the indifference of the overworked hospital staff, they barely noticed Wes and Annette's frantic dash. Wes didn't want to charge into every operating room and frighten surgeons in the midst of delicate procedures. He peeked through the tiny windows in each door, hoping to see someone or something that would give him a clue. All he saw were groups of masked people dressed in green scrubs as they hovered over their patients.

The more he looked, the more frustrated he got. Annette, who had gone back and forth with him looking in one room after another, finally stopped near an empty gurney and leaned against it. Wes walked over and put an arm on her shoulder. Just then, they heard, "Mom and Dad? Is that you?"

Wes wheeled around and saw Jennifer walking down the hallway. Her face was puffy from crying.

"Jennifer!" Annette called out and rushed toward her daughter to give her a hug.

"I've been sitting in a waiting area just around the corner," Jennifer said and pointed to the far end of the hallway. "Henry is in that room," she added and pointed to the last door at the end of the hallway. "He's been in there over an hour. About fifteen minutes ago a doctor came out and told me they're not sure he's going to make it."

Jennifer wasn't crying now, but her eyes were red and swollen. Wes guessed she had probably cried so much she was numb.

Wes motioned in the direction of the waiting area, and they shuffled down the hallway. "Come on, let's all sit down. We haven't stopped for a second since early this morning."

A couple of hours later, the sounds of steps and a deep voice speaking softly awakened Wes. He had slumped in a waiting-room chair, and Annette had curled up on a couch. She was still sound asleep. Wes rubbed his eyes and stretched to restore blood to his constricted limbs.

Jennifer was awake, and she talked to a tall, gray-haired doctor in a white coat. The doctor's back was to Wes so he couldn't clearly hear what they said. He did see the doctor shake his head, and he saw Jennifer start to cry. The doctor leaned over and patted Jennifer on the shoulder and left. Jennifer reached in her purse for some tissues and dabbed at her eyes. Wes got up from his blue plastic chair, sat down next to her, and put his arm around her.

"He's in intensive care," Jennifer explained. "The doctor said he'll be coming out of the anesthetic in another hour or so. They're still not sure he'll make it."

Wes pulled Jennifer closer to him and she rested her head on his shoulder. "We'll just have to leave it in God's hands," he said.

"Do you really mean that, Dad? Don't say it just to console me. The doctor said it will take a miracle for Henry to come out of this."

"I do mean it, with all my heart. Why don't you lean back and try to get some rest. I'll stay awake and watch for the doctor so you can see Henry as soon they permit it."

Jennifer nodded in agreement and laid her head back on the top of the chair. She closed her eyes, and within minutes was asleep. Wes thumbed through a stack of old *Time* and *Newsweek* magazines that had been read so many times the corners of almost every page were curled. As the minutes passed, he found it more difficult to concentrate on what he was reading. But it didn't matter. It was a distraction, and anything that got his mind off where they were and why they were there was acceptable.

One hour quickly turned into two hours. By late afternoon, Wes wanted to find some food for the three of them but didn't dare leave. Annette hadn't moved the entire time, and Jennifer squirmed every few minutes but managed to remain asleep. Nearly five hours had passed since they had arrived at the hospital, when the doctor again stepped into the waiting area. He paused at first, not wanting to awaken Jennifer, but her sleep was fitful as she waited for someone to bring news of Henry's condition. She opened her eyes.

"You can see him now," the doctor said. "They've moved him into a private room. He's barely conscious. Come with me."

Wes reached over and gently touched Annette's leg. For a moment she resisted being awakened, then her body jerked and her eyes were wide open.

"The doctor is going to let us see Henry," Wes explained.

He helped Annette from the couch. They followed the doctor and Jennifer, who were a few steps ahead of them, and turned into a room that had a sign on the door: "Special Care Unit. Immediate family and doctor-approved visitors only."

Wes and Annette stepped inside and heard the doctor say, "I'll leave you alone with him, but understand he's in a great deal of pain and probably doesn't comprehend very much right now."

This wasn't a typical convalescent ward. Being the son of Bill Baldwin had automatically granted Henry some extra privileges. The hospital room looked more like a hotel room, oversized and decorated with signed prints on the walls. A twenty-five-inch TV was accompanied by a VCR, and there was a couch and two lounging chairs for visitors. Wes glanced around the room and saw that the bathroom had a Jacuzzi. Instead of the usual sterile off-white paint, the freshly wallpapered walls gave the room a comforting feeling.

With Baldwin's influence so obvious, Wes wondered why he hadn't bothered to check on his son.

Jennifer reached for a chair and pulled it alongside the bed on Henry's right side. To his left, an IV bag slowly dripped glucose into his veins. Above his head, the standard hospital room equipment panel blinked its lights. Digital readouts on a small video screen monitored Henry's vital signs.

Everyone stood there silently, not knowing what to say. Then Jennifer saw the sheets move slightly as Henry attempted to bend his leg. His eyelids parted momentarily, then closed again. Over the next ten minutes, Henry's eyes alternately opened and closed in an uneven rhythm. Finally, they stayed open briefly. He sensed someone was at his side and turned his head to the right. When he saw Jennifer, his eyes focused and a slight smile crossed his lips.

"Don't say anything," Jennifer whispered. "We just want you to know that we're here and that we care."

Jennifer took Henry's right hand in one of her hands, and with her other hand she gently stroked his forearm.

Henry's breathing was slow but steady. At times his face winced in pain. Each time his body tensed, Jennifer instinctively rose out of her chair as if responding to his agony would ease it.

Henry lapsed into a deep sleep again and Jennifer spoke. "I suppose you're wondering how he was shot," she said to Wes and Annette. "Looking back on it, we probably shouldn't have been at the parade. But Henry was so curious to see what might happen, he couldn't stay away. We were ready to go home, and we stopped by the booths for a few minutes. As we started to walk away, someone recognized Henry and started yelling obscenities. Henry did his best to ignore the man, and we kept walking toward the garden area. Soon, the man who recognized Henry yelled at several other people, and they joined him. The group followed us and grew larger as people realized Henry was there. Before we realized it, the crowd had formed a circle around us, and we couldn't get away."

In spite of her fatigue, Annette was on the edge of her seat. Wes also listened intently, but since he couldn't see the door from where he was sitting, he kept one ear open for the incoming footsteps of a doctor or nurse.

Jennifer continued. "Henry told me to sneak away and run for help. I managed to make it out of the circle, but just as I did, things turned ugly." Jennifer nervously wrung her hands and spoke more slowly. "The obscenities turned into serious threats. They said they would kill him because of what he did at the press conference. I couldn't take it anymore and screamed in his defense. Then someone's arm thrust from the middle of the crowd and pointed a pistol. Henry saw the gun, forced his way free, and ran down the hill. The gun went 'pop.' I expected it to sound louder. At first, I hoped it was a joke. But I saw Henry stagger, and then I saw all of the blood."

Suddenly Jennifer froze and stared straight ahead at the doorway to the room. Wes thought she had gone into shock, but her eyes were too focused. She tried to speak but couldn't. Finally, she stuttered, "It's, it's . . . you!"

Wes stood and stepped forward to see who was at the door.

"If you don't mind, I'd like to come in," Bill Baldwin said.

27

Wes was amazed that it took Baldwin so long to make it to the hospital. No one was sure what to say, but they all had their reasons for finding his presence distasteful. The silence in the room was interrupted by a paging call for hospital staff members to come to the trauma ward.

Jennifer spoke first. "Of course you can come in, Mr. Baldwin. Henry's not conscious right now, but when he comes around again I'm sure he'll want to see you."

Baldwin stepped hesitantly into the room with his shoulders drooped and his head hung down. "Hello, Annette and Wes," he said politely. "I'm sorry I couldn't get here sooner. The police tracked me down at a private reception after the parade. Seems that my security people had my whereabouts too well guarded. My wife, Candy, is out of town, and the police are still trying to contact her."

Baldwin stopped at the foot of the bed and stared silently at his son. "When I heard the news I could not believe this was true! I hoped it was a case of mistaken identity," he said. Slowly he raised an arm as if reaching out to Henry. Then he dropped his arm at his side, and his eyes filled with tears.

Jennifer walked to Baldwin's side and touched him. When she did, a pang of anger and bitterness surged through Wes. He remembered that day when Baldwin seemed so grief stricken about his daughter, Rebecca. He also recalled Baldwin's acting performance at his house when he faked learning about Taylor's alleged molestation of Benjamin. Wes figured this was another one of Baldwin's tricks, and he was furious that Baldwin would try to manipulate Jennifer in this way.

"It's my fault. They shot you because of me," Baldwin pleaded. "Someone from Taylor's bunch tried to kill you because of my political ambitions. Please, forgive me, son!"

Wes stepped toward Baldwin and grabbed him by the shirt collar with one hand while he pushed Jennifer aside with the other. With the full fury of his anger, Wes faced Baldwin. Wes doubled his right fist.

Just as he pulled his arm back to land a punch, Henry mumbled, "Dad? . . . Is that you? . . . I . . . I can't see very well."

Wes released his grip on Baldwin and stepped back. Jennifer hurried around the side of the bed and took Henry's hand.

"Please don't let me die, Jennifer." Henry's chest heaved with deep breaths, and he rolled his eyes to focus on Jennifer. Then he lapsed back into unconsciousness. Baldwin crouched closer to his son. He firmly clasped Henry's left hand with both his hands.

"We won't let you die, son. God won't let you die."

Baldwin threw his head back, looked up at the ceiling, and his face flooded with tears. He thrust his arm into the air as if he were reaching toward heaven and cried out, "Don't let my son bear the brunt of my enemies' anger."

Wes stood stiffly. He looked over at Annette, who was seated on a couch. She raised her eyebrows.

"Mr. Baldwin," Annette said, "why do you say it was one of Taylor's people who tried to kill Henry?"

Baldwin turned to face Annette. His facial muscles were relaxed, and there was a softness in his eyes. "Who else would do something like this?

Certainly not those in the parade. They're the most peaceful people I've been around."

Wes had his hand on Annette's shoulder, and he felt the tension in her body. Somehow, Annette remained calm.

"It had to be Taylor!" Baldwin insisted as he glanced at Henry's languid body. Baldwin bit his lower lip to hold back tears and continued. "I suppose things might have been different if my father hadn't pushed me so hard to succeed politically."

Baldwin sat down slowly on the edge of Henry's bed. "He was a well-to-do businessman who laid out a career path for me when I was ten years old. He's dead now, but I'll never forget his saying almost every day of my life, 'Son, when you grow up, be a politician because they are the people who run our world.' When friends were around, he'd introduce me as 'my son, the future U.S. senator.'"

There was such a remarkable sincerity in Baldwin's eyes, Wes found himself being sucked in by his emotion.

Baldwin's jaw clenched and his fists doubled with tension. "My mother never objected to my father's demands. Nobody opposed my father. Whatever he wanted, he got. On his deathbed, he made me swear I would someday run for public office. At his graveside, I promised myself that when I became financially independent, I would launch a senatorial campaign and win."

Wes wanted to grab Baldwin again and finish what he'd started. But this wasn't the time or the place. This was Baldwin's territory, the hospital room of his son. Wes sensed that Baldwin knew he had the upper hand.

"My father's wish became my obsession, and Henry and I developed the same distant relationship I had with my father. I never really understood Henry's sensitive, artistic nature. Consequently, I wasn't the father he needed." Baldwin reached in his pocket and took out a handkerchief to wipe his eyes. "I've often wondered if that's why he yielded to his homosexual urges. I can't do anything about the fact he was born gay, but I do feel guilty that my lack of affirmation may have forced him to look elsewhere for masculine approval."

This last soliloquy was too much for Jennifer. Her reaction was fiery and abrupt. "Henry is not a homosexual, and he wasn't born that way!" she said with such firmness she nearly shouted. "Yes, he had those feelings, but he never gave in to them. You're right about one thing; it's your fault he got involved in the gay rights movement, but not for all the sappy reasons you've given."

Jennifer was delivering the blows Wes had wanted to give, and her tongue was doing a better job than his fists could have.

"Young lady, you're wrong," Baldwin responded with contrived calmness. "You talk like I wanted Henry to be gay. I just wanted him to be who he really was. Gay or straight, it didn't matter. I wanted him to be true to himself."

Jennifer pointed at Henry's lifeless body. "That's a man lying there. A real man. More of a man than you are. At least Henry knew that homosexuality was wrong. That's why they shot him." She paused long enough to take several deep breaths. "It's your sick friends, people like that Kelly character, who are responsible for him being in this bed."

Baldwin stood up straight as if to intimidate Jennifer. "Now see here, Miss Bryant, you have no right to march in my son's hospital room and make those kinds of accusations. I love my son, just like I loved Rebecca before Taylor drove her to suicide. I've already lost one child to bigotry and homophobia, and I'm not losing . . ."

"Oh, cut the act," Jennifer said as she walked around the bed toward Baldwin. Wes readied himself to protect her. "Admit the truth. Rebecca was murdered, and you know it. You don't want to admit it any more than you want to admit that you've demonized Stanley Taylor to find a scapegoat for your failure as a parent." She folded her arms in defiance and stood less than three feet away from Baldwin. "You nearly fooled me a little while ago. I'm disgusted to think I was almost taken in."

Baldwin clasped his hands nervously. He was laboring to control his anger. "If you don't stop I'll have you removed from this room, young lady."

"Why?" Jennifer demanded to know. "Because your political ambitions mean more than the life of your son? Everything you do is driven by one of two motives: How will it affect your image? Or how will it get votes? Every speech you give, every commercial you air, every position paper you write is doctored and manipulated to satisfy some special interest group."

Wes wanted to cheer. He looked at Annette from the corner of his eye and saw that she was beaming with motherly pride.

Baldwin shot a glance at Wes that said, "You're going to pay for this one." He seemed unsure of what to do. It was the first time Wes had seen him so discomfited.

Jennifer squared off against Baldwin. "Fortunately your kind hasn't disillusioned all young people. Some of us are determined to fight against your political machine."

A gentle rapping on the door to the hospital room kept Baldwin from replying. "Excuse me, but I need to speak with a member of the patient's family," said the teenage girl wearing an "In Training" button. Her crepe-soled shoes, crisply pressed uniform, and effervescent smile were telltale signs of her newness on the job. She had not yet become cynical from the sights, sounds, and smells of big-city hospital life.

"I'm the patient's father. How can I help?" Baldwin answered.

"Dr. Johnston has requested that the patient be left alone so he can run some tests. Would it be possible for everyone to clear the room in ten minutes or so?"

"That will be no problem," Baldwin responded.

"Thanks," the aide said with a warm smile as she walked out the door. "You all have a good day, okay?"

Jennifer had Baldwin cornered, and Wes hated to see this interruption spoil her chance to completely demolish him; yet Wes wanted to do the right thing for Henry. Wes reached forward to clasp the hands of Annette and Jennifer and walked with them toward the door.

"Wes, I presume you'll not let this little altercation with your daughter interfere with your duties as press secretary," Baldwin said stiffly. "I'll overlook your outburst toward me as the reaction of a protective father."

Wes responded matter-of-factly. "Of course not. Business is business.

You don't need to worry about my missing the regular Wednesday meeting at party headquarters."

"Glad you mentioned that. Some things came up, and that meeting has been called off. I'll be attending a Stand for America executive conference that day, mapping out summertime strategy for the Labor Day campaign kickoff."

Wes opened the door to the room and held it for Annette and Jennifer to exit. "Fine. Just tell me when and where you're meeting, and I'll be there."

"That won't be necessary," Baldwin responded quickly. "I'll update you afterward."

"Whatever you say."

As they exited Henry's room, Wes turned to Annette. "I'm thirsty and need something to drink. I'll meet you and Jennifer at the emergency entrance after I track down a vending machine. Just don't get into any discussions with that receptionist who probably still wants to turn us in for trespassing."

"There's a pop machine at the end of this hallway and about twenty feet to the left," Jennifer offered. "I saw it when I was walking around before you got to the hospital."

"Thanks," Wes said as he headed in the direction Jennifer indicated. He glanced over his shoulder and saw Baldwin leave the room and heard his footsteps retreat down the hallway. Thirty paces later, Wes turned left; as he rounded the corner he glanced back down the corridor, and he noticed it was empty. Then he saw a man in a white coat enter Henry's room. Wes assumed it was Dr. Johnston.

Wes dropped three quarters in the slot and punched the selection marked Diet Coke. He listened as the can rumbled through the internal apparatus of the machine and dropped into the slot below. With the Diet Coke in his hand, Wes walked back to join Annette and Jennifer. On the way, he passed Henry's room and noticed the door was slightly ajar. He paused for a moment and listened, but there were no sounds. After another quick sip of Coke he continued down the hallway. Twenty feet farther down the hall he stopped again.

The events of recent weeks had heightened his paranoia. Almost everything made him leery. He debated whether he should keep on walking or look in Henry's room. Perhaps Dr. Johnston would be finished with his examination and could give a report on Henry's condition. Wes turned around and walked to Henry's door. He silently nudged it open and stepped inside. The man dressed in white stood beside Henry's bed with his back to the door, and he hadn't heard Wes.

"Excuse me, Dr. Johnston?"

The man jerked around sharply and stared at Wes with a terrified look in his eyes. His thin, angular features were accented by horn-rimmed glasses and a half-full head of sandy blond hair. His expressionless face was dominated by blue eyes that narrowed with piercing intensity.

Wes waited for the man to respond. When he didn't, Wes spoke again. "Forgive me if I interrupted your examination. I'm a friend of Henry's and thought you might be able to tell me something about his condition."

Suddenly the man sharply thrust an elbow into Wes's ribs and ran out the door. Wes noticed that Henry's left arm dangled off the side of the bed, and the bandages holding the intravenous needle laid on the floor. The tube hung in midair, and its contents dripped into a small puddle of fluid on the floor.

Wes dashed out the door as he heard Henry's monitor beep loud and clear. He sprinted down the hallway toward the emergency entrance, past the receptionist's station, and out the front door. He could see the man in the white coat as he fled down the street a block away. Just as Wes charged after him, a black automobile, whose make Wes couldn't see in the dark, pulled around the corner and the man jumped inside. The car, its tires screeching, accelerated down the street.

Wes stood in the cool evening air and sucked in deep breaths. He wiped sweat from his brow with the sleeve of his shirt, and stepped back in the reception area. "Annette, Jennifer, come with me quickly!"

In the corner of his eye he saw that the receptionist who had given him a tough time earlier was gone, replaced by a husky middle-aged woman who looked even more stubborn. Without saying a word, he walked past her and motioned for Annette and Jennifer to follow. The new receptionist did nothing. Wes figured she had seen him running outside and assumed there was some kind of emergency.

Wes was first to arrive at the room. Henry's bed was surrounded by doctors and nurses who frantically tested his vital signs. One of them rolled up Henry's sleeve and injected a long needle. The medical assistants were so busy they hardly noticed Wes, Annette, and Jennifer enter the room.

"What's happened?" Jennifer cried out.

"He's in shock!" one of the nurses answered. "His IV got ripped out, and the drop in electrolytes nearly killed him."

Jennifer started weeping and buried her face on Annette's shoulder.

"Could you wait outside for a moment?" the nurse requested. "We'll let you know his condition as soon as we can get him stabilized."

Wes nodded his head in agreement, put an arm around Jennifer, and started to leave. "Can I ask one question?" he said before stepping out of the room.

"Sure. How can I help you."

"I just wondered if Dr. Johnston could talk to us."

"Dr. Johnston? I'm sorry, there's no Dr. Johnston in this hospital." She pointed to the white-haired gentleman they had met earlier. "That man, Dr. Robert Chapman, is Henry Baldwin's attending physician."

28

The first couple of days after Henry Baldwin was shot crept by slowly for Wes. He was the only one who saw the man in Henry's room, so no investigation of the incident had been launched. There were plenty of strange people hanging around big city emergency wards, so Wes guessed the hospital staff filed it away as a random act. The hospital administration did permit him to hire a private security company to keep watch on Henry's room twenty-four hours a day. Only approved personnel were permitted access.

Except for nights, Jennifer spent all her time at the hospital. Wes and Annette provided her with transportation and stayed by her side as much as they could. Henry improved slightly hour by hour, but full consciousness eluded him. In his semi-comatose state, he responded to Jennifer's presence and opened his eyes for brief moments.

Baldwin didn't call to find out how his son was doing, nor did he visit. Wes wasn't sure whether Baldwin even knew about the second attempt on Henry's life. Candy didn't come at all to see her son. Wes gave her the benefit of the doubt: She was out of town, as Baldwin said, and had not been informed of the shooting. According to Jennifer, Baldwin finally phoned on Wednesday morning, May 11, and spoke with a nurse who told him what had happened.

By midday that Wednesday Wes was exhausted. He had gone four days with only a few hours' sleep. He constantly wondered who the man was that pulled out the intravenous tube. Wes wasn't surprised that one of the people at the Gay Respect parade had tried to harm Henry, but what happened in the hospital was different. That was a methodical attempt at first degree murder.

At 3:00 Wednesday afternoon, Wes left his office and drove to the hospital to see how Henry was doing. Annette had taken Jennifer there earlier that afternoon, and he hoped to see both of them. When Wes arrived, he found Jennifer and Annette standing outside Henry's room. Jennifer leaned against the wall with a sullen look on her face and her arms folded across her chest.

"How's Henry?" Wes asked quietly as he approached.

Jennifer shot back a disgusted look. "Why don't you ask *him?*"

Wes wasn't sure what she meant. Jennifer saw his puzzled expression and explained. "Bill Baldwin is in Henry's room. Mom and I didn't want to stay around while he was there, so we came out here."

"Has Henry's condition improved?"

"He's doing better," Annette responded. "His low blood pressure has started to rise, and his breathing is more stable. That bullet missed his lung by a hair's width. If it had been on the other side, it would have struck his heart." Annette looked down, deep in thought. "It's hard to understand why God let something like this happen, but I am grateful He didn't allow Henry to be killed."

"How much longer do you think Baldwin will be?" Wes asked Jennifer.

"Not long. He said something about a meeting he had to attend," Jennifer explained.

The executive conference. Wes thought of following Baldwin to see who he was meeting. More important, Wes was curious about why he had been excluded. If he left now, he could wait outside, and Baldwin would never know he had been to the hospital. The notion was too tantalizing to pass up.

"Annette," Wes said softly, "I'm leaving. Don't tell Baldwin I was here."

"Where are you going, Dad?" Jennifer asked. "You just got here. You're up to something, aren't you? If it involves Henry, I'm coming too."

Wes leaned down and kissed Annette goodbye. He walked briskly down the hallway toward the entry. Jennifer ran after him. "Dad, you've got to take me with you."

Wes was slightly irritated. "Would you hush? If you don't keep quiet the whole hospital will know what's going on." Wes walked as fast as he could and swung his arms as a counterbalance. Jennifer skipped sideways down the hall in front of him, trying to navigate without falling while she looked Wes in the face. Her pleading was incessant, and she wouldn't give up.

"All right, you can go; but if any trouble develops, you're getting out fast. Understand?"

Was slowed his pace and Jennifer stopped hopping beside him. "What will Mom say to Baldwin about my being gone?"

"I'm not sure. I just know we have to get out of here fast before Baldwin sees me. Your mother is a resourceful woman. I'm sure she'll think of something."

In seconds, Wes was out the front door and running with Jennifer toward his car. They jumped in, and Wes drove toward the parking lot ticket gate. He handed five dollars to a smiling attendant, told her to keep the change, and waited impatiently for the exit bar to lift. Once his car cleared the gate, he made a sharp right turn and drove until he almost lost sight of the emergency entrance. He pulled a U-turn and parked by the side of the street. The location gave him a clear view of everyone coming and going from the hospital but still positioned him at an angle that put him out of the line of sight of anyone leaving the building. Less than five minutes passed before Baldwin emerged.

"Where is he going, and why are we following him?" Jennifer asked.

Wes shrugged his shoulders. He didn't have any answers. Right now he was following a hunch to an unknown destination. A plain white Caprice Chevrolet pulled up to the emergency entrance curb, and Baldwin got in. The spotlight by the driver's door and the long antenna sticking out the back gave away that it was a police car.

"Here we go," Wes said to Jennifer as they followed Baldwin down Colfax Avenue.

"It seems strange, Dad, that we're following a police vehicle, rather than the other way around."

Wes grinned in response, but where they were going, and what he would do when they got there, deeply troubled him. The people surrounding Baldwin had shown their willingness to resort to any means to get what they wanted. His concerns increased when the car pulled onto the Sixth Avenue Freeway and drove toward the mountains. He had expected them to head east in the direction of party headquarters.

The car phone rang, and Wes picked it up. "Wes, Honey, I'm glad I reached you. After you and Jennifer left I went to the restroom—you know, the one that's opposite Henry's room on the other side of the hallway. Just as I was about to come out, I heard Baldwin's voice. He was walking down the hallway talking on a pocket-sized cellular phone. I waited and listened."

By now, the white Caprice had turned onto Interstate 70 and was climbing into the foothills west of Denver. The phone crackled in Wes's ear as the cellular service faltered from the interference of the mountains they were entering. Annette's voice faded in and out.

"It's hard to understand you, Annette. The last thing I caught was something about overhearing Baldwin's conversation."

For a moment the line cleared. "Baldwin was talking to someone about meeting at the Trading Post Lodge in Vail."

Wes glanced at the orange-colored readout on his dashboard clock. It was almost five o'clock, and Vail was over an hour's drive away.

"Thanks, Sweetheart," Wes said as the cellular signal became more noisy.

"You will be careful, won't you?"

"You bet," Wes answered as he looked at Jennifer. "I have some important cargo with me and I intend to deliver her home safely. Besides, I can't break my leg skiing at Vail this time of year!"

Annette chuckled, then her voice faded until the phone clicked, indicating that the signal had been lost.

"Mom's worried, isn't she?" Jennifer said. She looked out the window as they topped the crest of a hill and the snow-capped eastern side of the continental divide loomed in the distance. The last pink glow of daylight reflected off wisps of clouds, which looked like pieces of cotton candy that had been torn and their frayed ends flung into the sky. "Don't forget someone was willing to kill Henry to silence him," Jennifer warned.

"Well, according to Henry, they've already threatened to harm me because I know too much. If that's the case, I'd rather follow them than have them follow me."

Wes looked in his rearview mirror. He had spoken too soon. They were being followed by a police car with its lights flashing. He pulled to the side of the road and watched the white Chevrolet disappear from sight.

"Were you going too fast, Dad?"

"Not according to my speedometer," Wes responded. "If I have broken a law, I don't know how I've done it."

Wes's heart pounded as he waited for the officer. Years ago it was considered courteous to get out of your car and approach an officer as a polite gesture. With the increasing crime rate and rampant violence these days, Wes had read somewhere that it was best for a driver to stay in his car. Any other action could be construed as too aggressive and spook the officer.

Nearly five minutes passed before a stocky patrolman wearing dark sunglasses walked up to Wes's window, bent down, and peered inside. "Good evening, sir. May I see your driver's license and car registration?"

Wes had them ready to hand over and did so instantly. The officer took them, walked back to his patrol car, and called on his phone. Minutes later he returned. "Thanks for your cooperation," he said as he handed Wes back his license and registration. "Drive carefully. I understand the high country is getting a late spring storm. Supposed to snow tonight above eleven thousand feet. They may not let you past the tunnel at the divide without snow tires." He started back to his car.

Wes leaned out his window. "Excuse me, officer," Wes said. "Would you mind telling me why I was stopped?"

"Routine," the patrolman responded. "You'd be amazed how many stolen cars we find this way. You're the tenth car I've stopped this afternoon. One was a couple on their way to California. Stole the car in Nebraska. They were eloping. Guess I spoiled their honeymoon," he said with a sarcastic grin. He touched the brim of his hat in a salute of sorts. "Like I said, drive carefully. If I were you, I'd turn that car around now. It just wouldn't be safe to keep heading west into those mountains."

Wes waited as the patrol car drove off, still wondering if the officer's interruption was a routine stop or a concealed threat.

"You're the ski bum in the family, so I guess I'd better ask you," Wes said to Jennifer as he pulled back on the highway.

"Ask me what?"

"Have you skied Vail lately?"

"A couple of times last season. Is that all you wanted to know?"

"No, have you ever heard of the Trading Post Lodge? Your mother said that's where Baldwin is headed."

Jennifer's face had a baffled expression. "That doesn't make sense," she said. "The Trading Post Lodge is where skiers stop to eat. It's at the top of Vail Mountain."

Wes feared he was on a futile journey. If the Trading Post Lodge was a skiers' destination, holding a meeting there was out of the question. Colorado's ski areas had shut down weeks ago. At this time of year most resort communities were in a state of limbo, awaiting the warmer weather of summer. Perhaps Annette missed something Baldwin had said, or maybe she didn't hear correctly and Baldwin's destination was a lodge by another name.

Wes tried to recall other hotel or food establishments that used the word *lodge*. He could think of at least a half dozen and knew there wouldn't be time to investigate each of them. He decided to continue driving to Vail and look for a phone directory once he got there to check one or two locations. If nothing else, the trip would give him a chance to talk with Jennifer, something he had been wanting to do for days.

Wes put the car on cruise control and leaned back in the seat. "Can we talk about you and Henry?" he asked. The words were no sooner out of his mouth than he realized the question was too abrupt. "I'm sorry. That didn't sound right, and this may not be the best time, so say no if you want to. What I mean is . . ."

"You want to know if Henry and I are involved. You're scared that he's still gay and my relationship with him could ruin my life."

"Well, that's not exactly . . . yes, that is what I meant. I guess I needed you to put it bluntly for me."

Jennifer stretched in her seat and patted the legs of her jeans to relax. "I suppose no time would be a good time, and you and I don't get to see each other that much, so let's go for it. Where would you like me to start?"

Wes found the subject so uncomfortable he wasn't sure what to say next. He followed Jennifer's lead and got right to the point. "Are you and Henry in love?"

Jennifer responded coolly. "What makes you think that?"

"When I had lunch with Henry he raved about how attractive he found you. He said you were the most beautiful woman he'd seen, or something like that. And then you two have been making a team out of going after Baldwin and defending Taylor."

Jennifer blushed and dropped her eyes. "Is that all he said?"

"He didn't go into a lot of details. He just said you brought out feelings he had never known before. At the time I thought he was speaking in generalities about his struggle with homosexuality. Then when I saw how tenderly you looked at him lying in the hospital bed, I wondered if, well, there might be more going on than I originally suspected."

Jennifer couldn't conceal the smile on her face. "If you're asking whether we're lovers, the answer is no. If you want to know how I feel about Henry, I would say I have strong feelings for him."

"Strong feelings?"

"It could be love. I don't know. We really haven't talked about it. I just know that I'm more comfortable around him than I have ever been around any man . . . that is, except you, Dad."

Wes looked at her with mock seriousness. "You'd better not leave me out," he said with a smile.

"Henry and I have a lot in common. We've both been hurt badly and have struggled in our own separate ways to overcome sexual problems. His difficulty was gender identity confusion; mine was fear of the opposite sex. Talking about our feelings has made us realize how much we need to be near someone who understands."

"And Henry understands?"

"More than . . . I mean, almost as much as you, Dad."

"That's sweet of you Jennifer. Look, I think your relationship with Henry is great. It's just that I'm not sure someone who has been in that lifestyle ever gets over it."

Jennifer's soft look hardened slightly. "You're starting to sound like the people from the Gay and Lesbian Caucus. They're the ones who say, 'Once gay, always gay.' I don't believe that, and neither does Pastor Ridgeway."

"You and Henry have been talking to him?"

"Yes, and Pastor Ridgeway has referred us to some wonderful people in an organization called Coming Out. Their name refers to coming out of the gay lifestyle, not coming out to say you're gay. They teach account-ability principles, that the homosexual who wants to be free must submit himself to a group of Christian men who pray for him and monitor his progress weekly. They also believe it's important to find out the root of one's homosexuality to promote healing."

"What difference does that make?"

"Well, for some men the cause of being gay was a dysfunctional child-parent relationship. For others it was pornography, bad information about sexual matters at a developmental age, or curious experimentation with same-sex eroticism. For those like Henry, it was a childhood moles-tation experience. They must understand that no matter what caused the orientation, continuing in an active homosexual lifestyle is a behavioral choice. Behavior involves morals, and morals require spiritual help. Don't ask me too many questions because I'm not an expert on this yet. We've just gone to one meeting."

"You went with Henry?"

"Sure. After the rape, I thought it would be good to help me get over my fear of being near men. That one meeting made a major difference in my life. I understand now the irrationality of blaming all men for the negative conduct of those few creeps who violated me."

Jennifer went on. "Falling in love isn't something you plan. At least that's not what Mom told me about you and her. From what I hear your relationship was pretty passionate." Jennifer playfully punched Wes's arm to drive home her point. "Just trust me that I'll be careful with my heart and my body. Henry is a very special man and I really want to know him better. Right now, the important thing is that we pray he'll fully recover, and we get on with the job of seeing Bill Baldwin defeated in November. That's what you want too, isn't it?"

"Yes, I want that, too."

As he said it, Wes realized it was the first time he had actually stated his convictions about Baldwin's agenda. Wes might still officially be the Stand for America Party press secretary, but he was now in complete opposition to everything the party stood for.

"Suppose we actually find Baldwin," Jennifer said. "Wouldn't it be a dangerous situation?"

Wes had been so wrapped up in thoughts about Jennifer's welfare, he had almost forgotten why they were traveling toward Vail. "I guess that depends on who he's meeting and why they're meeting."

"Henry told me the people backing Baldwin have threatened your life. If that patrolman wasn't telling the truth, they know we're on their tail. This could be a trap." Jennifer's voice grew serious. "Dad, someone I care about has already been shot, and I don't want . . ." Jennifer could say no more.

Wes took Jennifer's hand. "We'll turn around now if you'll feel better about it."

"No, I believe it wasn't an accident you came to the hospital when you did. Maybe we're supposed to be following Baldwin. It's just that I'd feel a lot better if someone else were with us."

"I agree," Wes said. "But who? There's no one between here and Vail who could join us."

Wes lowered the sun visor to shut out the glare of the sun, which was barely above the distant mountain peaks.

"Yes, there is."

Wes glanced at Jennifer inquisitively.

"The Echo Lake exit that leads to Highway 34 and the Lake Lomond trail is just a few miles ahead," Jennifer said. "He could meet us there."

29

S tanley Taylor? You've got to be kidding," Wes said.

Wes was stalling to try to put into words why he was cautious about Taylor. Aside from the obvious, that he was a fugitive, Wes still didn't completely trust Taylor. He had been accused of child molestation and murder, and while the charges were unsubstantiated, the whole thing made Wes uneasy. But the thought of facing a group of unsavory characters alone made Wes reconsider.

Jennifer pointed to the car phone. "I've got his cellular number and know the code to reach him."

"Code?"

"Sure. He only answers a call when the phone rings in a certain pattern. We've also arranged in advance to use secret names. That way, anyone who eavesdrops won't be able to positively identify who is talking."

"Suppose you reach him. Then what?"

"We're not too far away from the cabin, and I know the perfect spot to rendezvous."

Wes shook his head. "You've got this all figured out, don't you?"

"Not really, but I was thinking about this possibility while we were driving. Even if this isn't a trap, I feel like you're walking into a dangerous situation. This doesn't sound like a regular party meeting, and you might have more than you can handle. Plus, it might be the chance Mr. Taylor has been waiting for to clear his name."

Wes smiled. His stepdaughter was clever. She believed in Taylor and actually made her idea difficult for Wes to refuse. "You're just like your mother," he said, laughing. "Good thing you're gone from the house. It's hard enough keeping up with her, but if you were still home, with a college education added to that brain of yours, I'd be more than outnumbered two to one."

Jennifer smiled back. "Will you do it?"

Wes momentarily let go of the steering wheel and threw up his hands in mock frustration.

Jennifer reached for the car phone. Her face was earnest, and she looked older than her years in her clean jeans, white turtleneck, and herringbone sweater. She dialed and hung up several times. "I'm letting it ring the proper number of times, twice in a row. He'll answer on the third attempt." A long pause followed, then Jennifer spoke. "Eagle, this is Osprey. We're just a few minutes away from the sanctuary. Falcon is with me. Could you meet us to dredge up some old issues?"

Wes raised his eyebrows. He didn't understand the code language and wasn't sure how much he resembled a falcon. *Sanctuary? Must be the cabin. But what old issues was she wanting to dredge up?*

Jennifer continued. "Eagle, I can't explain, but it's your chance to corner Jackal. Let's not stumble over rocks in the way. Thirty minutes, okay?"

Wes watched Jennifer out the corner of his eye as she nodded her head in silent agreement and hung up the phone. "He'll meet us. Turn off at the next exit and go west on Highway 34. It parallels the freeway and then goes back into the mountains. That's where Mr. Taylor will be waiting."

Wes knew the area. He had mountain-biked there several summers ago. It was part of the old Sky Hawk mining district that was one of the richest spots on earth during the Colorado gold rush. Most mining in those days was done underground by shaft access to a lode or with hydraulic methods, pressurized jets of water aimed by a gigantic nozzle that washed the mining material into a series of sluices.

In contrast, the Sky Hawk region had used dredging methods. Mountain streams were dammed, and huge barges, with a boom on each end, floated on a pond. The dredges were equipped with a chain of buckets that would continuously scoop up mouthfuls of earth while the dredge pivoted. The excavated material was conveyed by the front boom to an internal concentrating plant, and the tailings were sent to the rear boom, leaving spoil-banks of hundreds of tons of river rock.

The environmental impact was atrocious. The landscape was ravaged, trees and foliage were uprooted, and pile upon pile of barren rocks were dumped haphazardly. Today, over a hundred years later, the rock-strewn river beds were still without undergrowth of any kind. Worse yet, the terrain was dotted with the rotting hulks of the monstrous dredges.

Dredge up some old issues! Now Wes understood. He was a falcon flying in his car down Highway 34 toward an abandoned mining dredge.

"Pretty astute of you," Wes said to Jennifer as he guided his Lexus around the mountain curves of the road to Sky Hawk. "Now all you've got to show me is which mining dredge."

"You're a clever guy yourself," Jennifer said. "I guess that's why Mom picked you." She leaned forward to get a better view of the road. "Quick! Turn here." She pointed to a mining trail that veered off the main road. It looked rocky and uneven. "Don't worry; it's not as bad as the Lake Lomond trail."

After a bumpy first one hundred yards, the path smoothed out and wound next to a river. In the distance, the Lexus headlights shone directly on an old dredge that was listing slightly and sitting in the dry bed of what once had been a pond. It sat about fifty feet high and thirty-five feet wide. Pieces of rotted wood had fallen in marble-sized chunks onto the ground. Wes remembered once exploring an abandoned dredge that had an internal operator's compartment about ten feet wide by twenty feet long.

Wes and Jennifer got out of the car and proceeded on foot. They navigated by the light of a half-moon and a flashlight Wes carried in his trunk.

"Don't come any farther! Stop there!" Wes and Jennifer heard someone order.

"Eagle?" Jennifer said. "It's Osprey and Falcon."

"Be careful. These rocks are slick when they're wet with ground frost. Come inside."

Wes pointed the flashlight down as he and Jennifer cautiously maneuvered over the rocky surface. The edge of the dredge's platform was several feet off the ground. Wes jumped up first, and then extended his hand to pull Jennifer aboard. He turned around and was confronted by Taylor, who once again pointed a pistol in his direction. "Hey! Put that thing away," Wes demanded.

"Sorry, these are dangerous times. It's for our protection," Taylor said and put the gun in his coat pocket.

The floorboards of the old dredge creaked with their every step, and Wes worried that the rotten planks might not sustain his weight. The smell of decaying wood mingled with the aroma of spring pine needles carried in with the evening breezes. Wes shined his flashlight upward so its beam bounced off the ceiling and provided maximum light. The ambient illumination from the flashlight cast eerie shadows on the interior walls that were weathered and warped from ten or more decades of exposure to the bitter mountain elements.

Wes imagined what the inside of this dredge had been like in its heyday. He envisioned grizzled, bearded, unbathed miners huddled in sheep's-wool coats. They sipped hot coffee from tin cups and laced their conversations with descriptions of the nuggets they hoped to unearth the next day.

"We can't stay here long," Taylor warned as he stepped deep inside the dredge to a place Wes recognized as the center of operations. The bucket ladder's cast-iron gears, at least five feet in diameter, still seemed to tug against the line of giant buckets that were halted years ago on their way to dig another load. Taylor leaned against one of the enormous gears.

"Get to the point," he said gruffly, looking directly at Wes. This was an attitude Wes hadn't expected, but he figured that a week of being on the lam had spent Taylor's patience.

Wes wasn't sure what to say. After all, this wasn't his idea. Jennifer said nothing, so he started to explain. "We're following Baldwin to some kind of secret meeting."

"Following? You can't follow anyone out here," Taylor said as he motioned to their surroundings.

"We know where he's going. It's a lodge at the top of Vail Mountain."

Taylor pushed away from the gear and walked a few feet toward a smooth, massive pulley wheel. Wes was surprised to see the pulley, though frayed, was still taut against the wheel after all these years.

"Why would they go to the top of a ski mountain? And how would they get there this time of year? Are you sure this isn't some kind of trap?"

Wes gazed at Taylor. "Maybe, but I'm too curious to turn back. Baldwin didn't want me near this meeting, and there's got to be a reason."

"Whose side are you on, Bryant? Perhaps that's what you most need to decide," Taylor said and readjusted the gun in his pocket.

"Not Baldwin's. I never really was, but after hearing what happened to Jennifer and seeing that antiabortion video and the Gay Respect parade, I'm on . . ."

"Yes?" Taylor said, coaxing Wes to respond.

Wes wasn't sure how to express himself. Taylor was right. It wasn't enough to be against something. He had to be for something. "I guess I'm on your side, Stanley," Wes said softly. "That is, if you're not a child molester or a murderer. I need your word on that!"

"Before Almighty God, I swear I've never done any of the things Baldwin's people have accused me of. Even if you doubt my words, I've proven it to you with my actions. Why do you think I'm still here in Colorado and not bound for the Mexican border?"

"One more thing," Wes said. "The night I sneaked into your backyard, I lost my billfold. I thought you turned it over to Sheriff McCormick. Did you?"

"No, but after you ran away, a policeman, who heard my security alarm, stopped by to see what had happened. I told him I ran off some neighborhood pranksters. He looked around the yard before he left. Maybe he found it and turned it over to McCormick."

The answer made sense. Wes glanced at Jennifer, and she put an arm around his waist and hugged him.

Taylor stepped forward and put out his hand. Wes shook it firmly.

"Welcome to the battle, friend. But let's get something straight. This isn't about being on Baldwin's side or my side. It's about being on the devil's side or the Lord's side. When you take a stand against perversion and speak out for the unborn, you've declared war on Satan and joined forces with God."

Wes wasn't used to such explicit spiritual language, and he didn't normally think of things in such stark terms, but Taylor's words gave him a sense of freedom. For weeks he had been controlled. Controlled by his obligations to an old college buddy. Controlled by Baldwin's threats following the encounter with Sheriff McCormick. Now, he was liberated!

Taylor smiled broadly as he continued to clasp Wes's hand. Suddenly, Taylor embraced Wes. "Brother, you're one of us now. If there's a job to do in the name of what's right, let's get on with it. My pickup is hidden behind a clump of trees just beyond this dredge." He patted his pistol. "I'm riding shotgun in your car now!"

The last ten miles to Vail was all downhill. The grade was so steep the highway department had constructed escape ramps for trucks with failed brakes. The ramps veered off to the right and were built up the mountainside at a sharp incline. They were covered with a thick layer of gravel to slow the careening trucks. Wes turned on his bright headlights to see if there had been any evidence of use and saw deep grooves in an escape ramp where a runaway truck had plowed its way to a safe halt.

As the trio neared Vail, they saw thousands of city lights twinkling in the distance. They drove down the narrow valley with ski slopes on the south side and groves of Aspen trees on the north slope. The road flattened out, and they passed a golf course with slender fairways that hugged the Gore River. The river was filled bank-to-bank this time of year, swollen by the melt-off from distant peaks of the Gore Range. The water flowed westward on the Vail side of the divide, which started its journey toward the Pacific Ocean or the Colorado River.

They passed the East Vail turnoff and continued toward the main Vail exit. Wes crossed under the freeway, turned left at a stop sign, and made his way down a service road. He spotted a parking lot and pulled in. "This looks like as good a place as any to start," he said as he stopped the car and turned off the motor.

The lot was empty, and there was a vacant ticket booth. He had heard that Colorado ski resorts were deserted this time of year—mud season—but he couldn't believe that the population of December and January would completely disappear.

Taylor leaned over and peered out the window. "I wouldn't want to run out of gas out here," he said and slipped his coat on. "By the way, do you have a full tank of gas?"

"Yes, I just filled it up before we left." Wes looked at the fuel gauge. "We've got about three-quarters of a tank."

"This time of the year, you probably couldn't get even AAA to come out here," Taylor said. "But I'm not complaining. I wouldn't want a nosy reporter or a local sheriff, for that matter, breathing down my neck."

As they began walking toward the main village, store after store had hand-lettered signs in the window announcing their closing until after Memorial Day. Not a single store or restaurant was open, and there was no one in sight. The usual spectacle of the enormous crowds with their clumsy ski boots clunking against the cobblestone walkways had turned into a modern ghost town.

They passed by the landmark clock tower and through a small covered bridge that led across a tributary of the Gore. Finally, Wes spotted a phone booth and stepped inside. The Yellow Pages directory was tattered, and the sections under R for restaurant and H for hotels were both missing, probably torn out by self-centered tourists who didn't care about the next person needing information.

Wes found a quarter in his pocket and dialed 411. The quarter popped into the slot. "This is information. What city are you calling?"

"Vail. I'm looking for the number of the Trading Post Lodge."

"One moment please."

Wes could hear keys clicking as the operator searched. "There is a listing, but that number is disconnected this time of year. Are you familiar with Vail?"

"No, I'm not."

"The Trading Post Lodge is at the top of Vail Mountain and is open just during the ski season because the only way to get there is by gondola. Sorry."

"Thanks."

Wes hung up the phone and stepped dejectedly from the booth. "Well, Jennifer, you were right about the location of the Trading Post Lodge, but your mother must have misunderstood something Baldwin said. It's not open this time of year, and you can see for yourself this place is shut down."

Wes put an arm around Jennifer's shoulder and the three of them started walking. "Let's go a little farther and see if we can find a place to eat. You must be starved." He took a couple of steps and continued. "And you, Stanley, are probably even more famished. I imagine that diet of canned food back at the cabin has you longing for a good meal."

"Now that you mention it, some angel hair pasta, garlic bread, and lasagna sound great." Taylor smiled at his ridiculous request.

"I'll settle for a convenience store hot dog," Jennifer chimed in.

Wes laughed and put his hands in his pockets to ward off the cool breeze coming off the mountain. They walked several blocks and turned down one winding pathway after another until they spotted a bar called the Double Diamond. Miller Lite neon signs flashed in the front window, and inside they saw a guitar player seated in a far corner.

"Hey, this looks like *the* night life of Vail in the month of May," Wes said. "It's not my kind of place, but for the sake of our stomachs, I'll go in and scope things out. You two wait here."

Wes opened the door and was hit with the full impact from the sound of two oversized amps, which advertised the musician's lack of talent. The singer-guitarist wasn't exactly Michael Bolton, but that didn't prevent him from attempting a badly executed version of "I Told You I Loved You, But I Lied." There didn't appear to be any waiters or waitresses, so Wes approached the bar.

"Excuse me," he yelled at the bartender who looked like he'd rather be somewhere else. "Do you have any food here?"

"Just cold cuts and hot dogs," the disinterested bartender yelled back and went on pouring beers.

"Two Buds over here," a long-haired man in a partially torn flannel shirt hollered at the top of his lungs.

"All right, all right. Just wait a minute," the bartender screamed back. "And you, sir. Want a hot dog or what?"

"Yeah, three hot dogs. And three soft drinks, whatever you have."

"Pepsi or 7-Up. That's it."

"Three Pepsis."

Wes waited while the bartender grabbed a fork and stabbed three hot dogs rolling round and round on a warmer. He slapped them on buns, doused them in mustard and ketchup without asking which Wes preferred, and topped them with mounds of relish. Then he filled three paper cups from the Pepsi dispenser and handed the order to Wes. "That'll be twenty-five dollars and forty-five cents."

"You're serious?"

"Look, mister, mud season or no mud season, this is Vail. Just because the snow is off the slopes doesn't mean my rent on this joint goes down."

"Okay," Wes said as he handed the man a twenty and a ten. "Keep the change. With the way the town looks this time of year, you need all the help you can get."

"Thanks, bud. Let me know if you need anything else."

"I do need one piece of information," Wes said as he paused with hot dogs in both hands and the paper cups held against his chest by his arms. "How do people get to the Trading Post Lodge?"

"This time of year they don't. During ski season they ride the Bear's Head gondola."

"I've never been on a gondola. It might be interesting to see what they look like. Where do I find it?"

"Two blocks west of here, next to the Aspen Tree ski rental shop. Turn left when you go out the door, then go right on Gore River Lane. Can't miss it."

"Thanks."

Wes slowly made his way past a dozen drunks who looked like they were young construction workers taking advantage of the building boom during the day and drinking away their paychecks at night. Once outside, he handed what he referred to as "heartburn on a bun" to Jennifer and Taylor.

"Dad, I was kidding about the hot dog. You know I hate to eat anything that's made of unidentifiable mulch."

"Sorry, it's the best I could do. Eat heartily; we have a couple more blocks to walk. I want to check out the gondola that goes to the Trading Post Lodge."

Wes, Jennifer, and Taylor walked and ate as the mustard, ketchup, and relish goo squeezed out from between the buns onto their hands and their mouths. Some dripped down the front of Wes's shirt. "Glad I brought along these," Wes said as he reached in a pocket and pulled out a handful of napkins. Jennifer laughed at the spectacle of three adults stuffing themselves with the most horrible hot dogs any of them could remember.

Wes wiped off his shirt and drank the last of his Pepsi. "Whew, I could sure use another drink to wash that stuff down. How about you, Stanley?"

"Sure."

"And you Jennifer?"

Jennifer was silent. She stood frozen, dead still in the middle of the walkway. Wes looked ahead in the direction she was staring.

"What do you see?" Wes asked as he strained his eyes in the dim light.

"A gondola. Dad, I just saw a gondola."

"So? That's what we came here to see."

"Dad, the cabins were moving. I swear, the gondola is running!"

Wes saw nothing. He crushed his paper cup and added it to the refuse from the hot dog wrapper. Jennifer and Taylor also handed him their leftover paper, and he glanced around for a garbage can. He found one about twenty feet ahead at the corner, next to the Aspen Tree store. As he dropped the rubbish in the trash, he heard a creaking sound. Jennifer was right. A blue gondola cabin with a gold painted bear's head on the side was gently swinging from the haul-rope cable and moving slowly in the direction of Vail Mountain.

"I wonder how they got the ski area to start up the gondola," Taylor asked. "Maybe Sheriff McCormick threw his weight around." He narrowed his eyes and looked up the mountain where the gondola disappeared over the first ski run.

Wes cautiously approached the gondola boarding area and motioned for the others to follow him. A large sign about ten feet off the ground read: "Bear's Head Gondola. Please remove skis. Hand skis and poles to attendant as you board. Children under 10 must be accompanied by an adult."

In the distance a gondola cabin swayed back and forth as it made its ascent.

"I thought gondolas had a whole bunch of cabins moving all at once up the mountain," Wes said in a hushed voice.

"During ski season they do, one after another. I supposed when the gondola isn't being used for regular ski traffic they can use just one car at a time as they need to," Jennifer answered.

Wes looked around to see where the car had come from. The cable disappeared into a covered terminal. Slowly he walked up the steps leading to the elevated platform where skiers boarded the cars during the ski season. He paused at the top of the steps and looked around. The only light was the glow from a street lamp fifty yards away. The dim lighting made him feel safer to advance undetected, but it made seeing anything difficult.

Satisfied that there was nothing to see from where they stood, Wes looked at the overhead haul-rope and followed it. It led to a section of the terminal where dozens of idle gondola cabins dangled by their hangers from a rail that curved off to the right side of the cable. Wes guessed that this was where the cabins were kept in storage and pushed onto the haul-rope as they were needed. He walked closer to the cabins and strained his eyes to see how they operated. The hangers by which the cabins were suspended were attached to a clamp, which Wes surmised gripped the cable as the cabin slipped off the rail.

He reached in his pants pocket, took out the keys to his car, and handed them to Jennifer. "You run back to the car and stay there. Lock the doors and wait for Stanley and me."

"You two aren't getting on that thing, are you?"

"You don't worry about what we're going to do. You just wait and pray. Keep an eye on your wristwatch, and don't fall asleep."

"Dad, I'm coming with you!"

"Not this time. I brought you this far, but no farther. Go on. Leave now."

Taylor touched Jennifer's arm gently to restrain her. "Your father is right," he added. "This is risky enough for the two of us."

Jennifer kissed Wes on the cheek, took the keys, and ran toward the car.

"C'mon, Stanley, let's heave one of these gondola cabins on to the haul rope."

Taylor leaned against the cabin with his back as Wes bent forward to push with his hands. Slowly the cabin slid off the rail and gripped the haul-rope. The cabin moved toward the boarding area where the doors would automatically open. When they did, Wes realized that he and Taylor had seconds to decide whether or not they would get inside.

For a brief moment Wes came to his senses and realized where they were and what they were attempting to do. Suppose the gondola didn't fasten properly to the haul-rope and the cabin popped off the cable somewhere halfway up the mountain? Suppose someone had seen them, and Baldwin had a welcoming party at the gondola's drive terminal on top of Vail Mountain?

If Wes had been thinking sensibly he would have turned around when the patrol officer stopped him. And he never would have rendezvoused with Taylor, an accused murderer. Wes took a deep breath and jumped inside the cabin. Without saying a word, Taylor followed him. The doors closed, and the cabin jerked forward. For a few seconds it swayed dangerously on the cable. Its pendulum motion gradually decreased, and Wes leaned back on one of the two bench seats. He sat with his back facing the mountain and watched the lights of Vail fade slowly into the distance.

"We did it Stanley!" he said with a sigh.

"Yes, but what we've done down here is the easy part." Taylor pointed toward the top of the mountain. "It's what we'll do up there that will determine if this was wise."

30

As the gondola climbed over the first ridge of the mountain, the lights of Vail diminished and then disappeared from view. The ski runs they passed over reminded Wes of the crisp, cold mornings years ago when he had buckled on his old Lange ski boots and prepared to hit the slopes. Those were the days, he reminisced, before high tech and hard plastics turned skiing into an expensive sport where the competition for the best was not only determined by how you skied on the slopes but by how you looked in the lodge as well.

Wes hadn't skied in almost thirty years, since his college days, and this gondola seemed centuries away from the poma lifts and T-bars he used when he and a few of his buddies would make their annual ski trip to Colorado. Indiana was no place to perfect the art in skiing, so Wes never got beyond the basics of the stem-christie and the snowplow. Then his college football injury ended once and for all his dreams of learning how to navigate moguls and schuss through fresh powder.

Crunch! The gondola jolted in the darkness and interrupted Wes's thoughts. "Another support tower," Wes said to Taylor, who sat opposite him.

Taylor seemed calm. "My family and I take this gondola all season, and I never even noticed how much noise the gondola cabins make when they pass over the towers. I love to ski, but I've never liked the ride up the mountain. You get cold, and your muscles get stiff. I like it even less in the dark."

Taylor went on. "Every time the haul-rope passes over the guide wheel sheaves, it jerks. Hope we've got this cabin fastened tight enough to keep it on the cable."

Wes couldn't stand to look down but managed to peek with one eye open. The distance between towers varied from a hundred feet or so to fifty yards, and the terrain underneath changed drastically. The smooth beginner runs were flat and open. At other times the gondola traversed huge chasms that plummeted hundreds of feet below, where no one dared to ski. The cabin didn't have comfortable seats, and Wes's frayed nerves intensified everything. At the speed this gondola traveled, Wes figured they'd be at the top in less than fifteen minutes.

"Who do you think is at this meeting?" Wes asked.

"My guess is someone from the Order of the New Alliance. Ever heard of it?"

Wes shook his head.

"It's a shadow government that manipulates international monetary cycles. Whether it's boom or bust times, they profit from inside information. In fact, they orchestrate events that the general public thinks are random occurrences—wars, stock market fluctuations, currency devaluations, the rise and fall of political regimes. I've long suspected Baldwin was under their thumb."

"Sounds like that far-right conspiracy stuff to me," Wes countered skeptically. "If they're so powerful, why do they need a guy like Baldwin?"

"To control every aspect of society. In this state, for example, McCormick is their link to law enforcement, and Judge Russell Hoffman—"

"You know about Hoffman?" Wes interrupted.

"Sure. Practically every decision he's made has benefited the Alliance's agenda. He's their connection to the justice system. What they lacked was someone who could influence national legislation. That's why they set up an independent party and picked Baldwin to front their schemes."

"It seems like we're missing something," Wes interjected. "There has to be a bigger purpose behind all of this political maneuvering."

The haul-rope jerked with a powerful thrust and threw Wes sideways into the cabin door. "Must have passed over another support tower," he said as he rubbed his left elbow. "Guess the cable wasn't aligned too well on that one! . . . You were saying?"

"It's simple. If you can regulate law enforcement, sway judicial decisions, and influence legislation, you have a three-pronged way to control society. It's like having three perfectly interlocking . . ."

"Triangles!"

"Yes," Taylor agreed. "But the Alliance's agenda depends on more than that. Members of the Alliance overpower the minds of those they exploit. Take Baldwin for example. You knew him years ago. Would you have expected him to defend abortion and homosexuality? Considering his Indiana roots, I doubt it. Somehow they took over his mind. He was already a weak individual who didn't stand for much of anything. But to get him to stand *for* something, like gay rights and abortion, they had to . . ."

"Brainwash him?"

"Sort of," Taylor said. "I would describe it more like seizing his mind at will whenever they wanted to."

"This may sound like a crazy question, but could they do that with an object or a symbol of some kind?"

"Like a talisman? Possibly, if the emblem were powerful enough," Taylor answered.

Now Wes understood the meaning of Baldwin's trancelike state when he stared at the hologram just before going into that first party meeting.

Taylor faced uphill, so he was the first to see the warning beacon on the top of the gondola summit terminal. "We're only a few minutes from the top," Taylor observed.

Two more jolts and their cabin hung between the towers supporting the final span. Wes looked over his shoulder and could see that the interior of the gondola terminal was dimly lit by what he figured were various lights from the control panels of the equipment room. It was there that the gondola's continuous haul-rope reached its zenith, wrapped around a massive, steel bull-wheel ten feet in diameter, and headed 360 degrees back down the mountain.

Clunk! The cabin hit a rail guide on the floor and slowed automatically as it entered the terminal and inched along. The doors slid open, and Wes stepped out first. He wasn't sure whether to stand there and get his bearings or run for cover in case anyone was on guard. He decided to walk toward the exit where, during the season, skiers fastened their skis to get ready for their descent. In the moonlight he saw gleaming white patches of hard-packed, leftover winter snow.

Taylor stepped onto the ground and pointed to a sign with an arrow: "Trading Post Lodge, 100 yards."

"Watch out for the exposed rocks and icy patches," Wes whispered. The sharp chill reminded him that the temperature dropped about three degrees for every one thousand feet of elevation. He guessed that the summit of Vail Mountain was at least twelve to fifteen degrees cooler than at the base, and his bones felt it. He rubbed his bad left knee for a moment, then bent it and stretched it out a few times to make sure it wouldn't seize up on him.

Wes and Taylor followed the trail as it narrowed from forty feet across to no more than twenty feet in width. The path was shielded on either side by tall Douglas Fir trees that thrived in this moist, high altitude environment with nine months of snow cover. They could see the moon peek out from between the trees as they walked. The moon hid behind the tip of first one tree, then another, as if it were some heavenly eye that watched their progress.

Beyond a curve in the trail, Wes saw a massive log building, the most magnificent he had ever seen. The huge beams of the structure towered above the surrounding forest. It looked like an Old West trading post enlarged in size about a hundred times.

"What an inviting place for cold skiers," Wes said to Taylor. "I could use a cup of hot cider or coffee myself, right now."

Wes stepped into a clearing in front of the lodge, an open area where skiers rested and took off their skis before going inside. They could have easily been spotted in that location by a guard, but Wes wasn't sure there was much they could do if they were detected. So they walked along the edge of the clearing, slightly hidden by the trees, toward the double-door entrance to the lodge.

The doors were unlocked and unguarded. Wes swung one side open and stepped into an air lock. The second set of doors in front of him sealed off a small foyer so that cold and snow from outside would have to pass through two entrances. A grate below their feet, which rattled when they stepped on it, was designed to allow the snow to fall into a foot-deep well below. Inside this passage Wes saw flickering light reflect off the ceiling beams of the main room inside the lodge. He opened the second door and realized that the reflection came from a crackling fireplace at the other end of the room. He couldn't see the actual fire because he hadn't walked far enough inside.

What he did see clearly was the cafeteria section, located directly in front of him. The design made perfect sense to entice tired and hungry skiers as they walked into the lodge. In the distance Wes heard muted conversation that was barely audible above the crackling logs in the fire. Somewhere beyond, he knew he'd find a group of people warming themselves in front of a fireplace. Determining who was in that group was their purpose for being there.

Wes was amazed that such an important meeting was so poorly guarded until he realized how ingenious it was to meet there. They didn't need conspicuous security. After all, who would expect powerful political leaders to gather at the top of a mountain during a time of year when such a location was supposedly inaccessible? And who would think anyone was crazy enough to crash the gathering by hijacking a gondola?

Wes leaned toward Taylor and spoke quietly in his ear. "The service kitchen must have direct access to the main section of the lodge. Maybe we can slip in there and take a peek at what's happening."

Cautiously, Wes and Taylor moved past stacks of trays that, during the ski season, would be piled with pastas, pizzas, and hot chocolate. The light from the fireplace gave them just enough illumination to see past the large hamburger grills and the deep fryers into the bowels of the kitchen where the ovens and dishwashers sat. Once inside, it was totally dark except for a sliver of light from under a door. Wes and Taylor silently approached the door. It was held on swinging hinges. Wes took a deep breath to steady himself and nudged it slightly open, just enough so they could see and hear. Wes peeked through a top section of the tiny crack while Taylor knelt and peered out a lower portion.

Beneath a log-beam ceiling forty feet above was a wall-to-wall rock fireplace at least sixty feet wide. Its opening was the size of a garage door, and it was filled with four-foot sections of logs and a fire that blazed furiously. Overstuffed chairs and couches surrounded the center of the fireplace, which looked like it must be a favored spot for après-ski conversation and refreshments. Tonight, the seats were occupied by about a dozen men. The three interlocking triangles of the hologram Wes had seen in Baldwin's office seemed to float above the fire, projected by what appeared to be a laser beam. There was no doubt about it now. This was a meeting of the Order of the New Alliance.

The conversation was spirited, but Wes couldn't hear clearly enough to understand it. Everyone seemed to be talking at the same time. A single bartender dressed in a suede vest, black pants, and white shirt kept everyone supplied with a constant flow of alcohol. Unlike the sweaters and casual attire normally associated with this setting, those gathered were dressed in business suits. Occasionally Wes saw a part of someone's face as he turned sideways, but at first he couldn't identify anyone.

Baldwin! There he is. Wes spotted Taylor's nemesis at the far right side of the fireplace, talking intently to a group of four men. *Kelly! I might have known he'd be here,* Wes thought as he saw the gay-rights defender seated at the far opposite side from Baldwin.

The rest of those present chatted with first one person, then another. At times, loud laughter could be heard, but for the most part the talk was serious. Wes wished he could hear and see more of what was going on in the room, but opening the door any further would most certainly give them away. For now, he and Taylor had to settle for an eyeball's view of the proceedings.

A tall, dark-haired man with a deep bass voice stepped to the center of the conclave, his back to the fire. He was dressed in a tailored, dark blue, double-breasted suit with a conservative striped tie. "Gentlemen, gentlemen, may I have your attention. We've all enjoyed the small talk, but now it's time to get down to business. Please find a seat and get a final drink of your pick of poison. We'll get started in sixty seconds."

The bartender moved through the room taking orders as the hearty drinkers filled up. Conversation between various groups broke off as each man settled in the seat of his choice amid a final round of handshakes and greetings.

"I'd like to thank our chairman for his good taste in selecting such an unusual setting for this meeting. The beauty of these surroundings is an inspiration to our noble goals. Let's give our chairman a big hand."

The leader motioned to his left as each head turned right and acknowledged a man seated at the far right corner of the room. The chairman, whose face Wes couldn't see, nodded, and polite clapping followed.

"We'll be receiving several reports from those in charge of legislative control. Let's start first with a summary from the department responsible for monitoring international trade agreements."

A man to the speaker's right leaned forward and put his briefcase on the edge of the fireplace hearth. When he turned to face the group, Wes recognized him as the man who had pulled Henry's I.V. The man took out a stack of papers that were distributed to each person. "I think you'll see that we've done a superb job entangling the U.S. government in obligations that ensure a balance of trade deficit for the next hundred years," the man said.

Several in the group chuckled.

"Last month the trade deficit was about fifteen billion dollars, but we think we can push that total to thirty billion within six months after the elections in the fall."

"How?" a voice called out. "If that happens, won't people be worried and demand some answers from Washington?"

The man shrugged his shoulders. "Perhaps, but Americans are getting used to being a debtor nation. We already owe more money than any other country, and the new treaties coming before the Senate will obligate the U.S. government to even higher tariffs. Each one will be subject to international tribunals where every country will have an equal vote. That means our 260 million people will have no more voting power than countries with a few thousand citizens. There's no way the U.S. can prevail in an international dispute. It's one country, one vote, and no matter what, America loses and we win!"

Polite clapping greeted the statement, and the man who presented the report sat back down. The meeting host stood again as an attendant nearby threw another log on the fire. Flames leaped upward and cinders scattered, forcing the moderator to step back for a moment until the intense heat from the newly stoked fire died down.

"Next, we'll see what's going on in the currency market. Who has that report?"

"I do," said a man with a clipped British accent. He was dressed in brown Irish tweed and held a pipe in one hand. "How would you chaps like to see a major recall of American currency?" he asked as he lifted his left eyebrow mischievously.

Audible oohs and aahs were heard as those present nodded affirmatively to each other. The Englishman put one foot on the edge of the hearth and rested an elbow on his knee. He turned the pipe upside down and tapped it in the direction of the fire, then put the pipe in the far right corner of his mouth.

"We all know that counterfeiting is a big problem," he said. "If the United States and major Western countries decided that counterfeiting had become so severe they needed to call in their currencies, they could crank up their printing presses and print as much money as they wanted. Worldwide inflation would reach a scale never before seen. In the end, the only thing left of value would be what we control—land, food commodities, livestock, and . . ."

"Gold!" several in the group cried out simultaneously to the accompaniment of cheers.

"By Jove, I think you've got it," the Englishman said as he tilted his head back and took several puffs on his pipe. "But you are missing an important ingredient. What we need is legislation in the U.S. Senate making it illegal to purchase gold bullion. If certain people like us already have a hoard of gold, the hyper-inflation created by the currency recall would make them rich. And who will introduce that legislation in the Senate?"

"Bill Baldwin, Bill Baldwin, Bill Baldwin!" the group chanted as if they were cheering a quarterback who had thrown the winning touchdown in the fourth quarter.

Baldwin moved to the center of the gathering, smiled, and shook one hand after another. He looked like he savored the moment. He nodded several times in appreciation and put his hands forward to hush them. "Thank you for that warm reception." He turned to the moderator. "And thank you, Mr. Albright, for inviting me to be part of this historic gathering."

Albright! Wes was stunned. *Baldwin is deferring to the man who molested his children!*

Baldwin continued. "I assure you that when I am elected on November 8 I won't disappoint you. Within thirty days of my victory, I will introduce a Senate bill that will make acquiring gold bullion a criminal offense. In the meantime, keep those planes loaded with bales coming into Colorado. The more gold we can stockpile, the better."

Wes looked down at Taylor, who glanced upward with a knowing look on his face. *So that's what was in those bales Andrew Patterson saw being unloaded,* Wes thought. *Not cocaine! Gold.*

The group, all except for the chairman, stood up. The men raised their glasses in a unanimous toast. As the applause continued, the chairman rose slowly and stepped toward Baldwin. Everyone moved back a few paces and grew quiet.

"Mr. Baldwin, we are most grateful for your pledge on behalf of our worthy goals," the chairman said seriously. "But how can we be certain you will still abide by our wishes once you're in office? You wouldn't be the first man we got elected who later turned on us. Power corrupts, and the influence of Washington, D.C. has a way of inflating the egos of elected officials who forget how they got there."

Baldwin appeared incensed. "Sir, you have my word," he insisted.

"Your word isn't good enough," the chairman retorted gruffly. "There must be no doubts!"

"What do you want? My firstborn child?" Baldwin asked jokingly.

"Yes. Precisely."

Baldwin stepped back slightly, visibly shaken. "You're kidding," he responded with an edge to his voice.

"Henry is too great a liability. He's your son, and he's also your enemy. If he's persuaded to join the Taylor camp, the Restore Our Heritage Crusade will have enough ammunition to get you defeated. We can't take that risk."

The others sat down and left center stage to Baldwin and the chairman. For a moment neither said a word. Then Baldwin protested again. "You can't be serious. Are you actually asking me to murder my own son?"

"Murder? Who said anything about murder? We both know his life right now is very fragile. He might not survive no matter what the doctors do. I'm suggesting that something might be done to hasten the inevitable. His room is guarded twenty-four hours a day, and you're the only one who can come and go without suspicion. If he isn't put out of his misery mercifully, we might all suffer. Henry suspects there is more to your election than the issues of abortion and homosexuality. If he gets out of that hospital and has five months to cause trouble, all the plans we've talked about tonight will come to nothing. Your bid for the Senate will be defeated. Baldwin, it's your career in politics or your son. Make your choice."

"Judge Hoffman, you can't expect me to kill my own son!"

The chairman turned around slowly and walked back to his seat. Wes clearly saw his face.

"You can do it, Mr. Baldwin," Hoffman assured him. "Look to the source where you've always drawn your strength. Look to the eye of the Alliance."

Baldwin's body shook as if he were resisting some compelling force. Then his head tilted back and he gazed upward toward the log beams. Dancing in the air above his head were the laser-projected Order of the New Alliance triangles. In the center was something Wes hadn't seen that day in Baldwin's office—an eye that looked human!

31

ad Judge Russell Hoffman pushed
Baldwin too far, asking him to mur-
der his son? Wes wondered. He watched Baldwin for his reaction, but
Baldwin was mesmerized by the triangles and the lifelike eye at the center.
His body shivered with spasms, and his eyes rolled back in his head. Then
he stiffened, and his head dropped so his chin almost touched his
collarbone.

Baldwin's eyes closed for a moment, and when they opened, he looked
directly at Judge Hoffman. "Okay, I'll do it."

Like a robot, Baldwin stepped between the chairs and headed toward
the rear exit of the room. No one spoke. Judge Hoffman wrinkled his bushy
eyebrows and pointed at Dave Kelly with his index finger. He motioned
with his thumb toward Baldwin.

"McCormick will be here with the helicopter to pick me up in a few
minutes. I'll see you back in Denver," Hoffman said.

In an instant, Kelly pulled his massive frame from the chair and walked
briskly after Baldwin. As Kelly moved across the room Hoffman said in a
menacing voice, "Make sure he doesn't change his mind, David. Give him
a little scare!"

Wes tapped Taylor and gently closed the door. Taylor stood up and stepped back. "We're better get to that gondola first so we can see what's going to happen," he whispered.

Wes and Taylor rushed through the kitchen, across the cafeteria, and out the front door. Then they raced through the trees next to the pathway, toward the gondola, without looking back. They heard Kelly and Baldwin, just behind them, shouting angrily at each other as they walked quickly down the path. When they reached the gondola terminal, Wes and Taylor scurried inside and crouched in a darkened corner where Baldwin and Kelly couldn't see them. Their angry voices pierced the night with curses as they came closer and closer.

My dictation recorder! It was in Wes's coat pocket where he always kept it. *If they yell that loud inside here, the steel roof of this building will act like an echo chamber to amplify every word. I'll record what they say as evidence!*

Wes took the Dictaphone from the pocket of his jacket, and with his right hand ran his finger along the side to find the play and record button. He switched the button to the record position, and the tiny red ON light glowed in the darkness. He slipped the device back into his pocket just as Baldwin and Kelly stepped inside the gondola terminal. The moon and the reflected light from the gondola equipment controls gave off just enough illumination so that Wes and Taylor could see what was happening.

Kelly and Baldwin squared their shoulders and faced each other with their feet apart. "I said I'd handle it, so stay out of it!" Baldwin insisted. "Back off!" Baldwin's face was pinched with anger. He had lost his composure and was yelling and swinging his fists to emphasize his words.

Kelly stepped toward Baldwin and shoved him with a stiff arm to his left shoulder. Baldwin staggered back slightly. "You're nothing without the Alliance, and you know it," Kelly declared with a look of superiority. "You can't win without them, and I won't allow you to do anything that might lose this election. The only part of politics you care about is money and ego, but this campaign means more than that to me. The success of our gay rights movement hinges on your victory. That's the *gold* that matters to me. If we lose this state, our national agenda will be set back. You're going to be a good boy and do what you're told."

"Look," Baldwin retorted, "you can't make your problems with your old man my problems. He knew you weren't a man in high school, and he pushed you to pretend to be one out on the college football field. Both of you ignored the truth. You didn't make it in professional football, and you can't get even with your father now by going to bed with one of your boyfriends. I know you've got a score to settle, but let's get this straight right now. I'll take care of Henry my way. I'm not about to risk going to jail for murder so you can get your cheap thrills!"

Baldwin's comments enraged Kelly. He clenched his fists but then looked down and took one step back from Baldwin. "Let's not get into a contest about what a real man is. You should ask yourself who wears the pants in your family. Who really plays hardball in matters of life and death? Maybe we should have Candy get rid of Henry. She can fill those pants pretty well!"

"What's that supposed to mean?" Baldwin said, visibly shaken.

"Oh, am I upsetting you, Billy boy? You and I both know what our friend Alex Lewis was talking about the night he shot himself." Kelly put his fingers against his lips. "Candy was with Rebecca the day she supposedly committed suicide. Your wife was horrified to have a lesbian for a daughter because it didn't fit in with her country club image. So she *eliminated* Rebecca from her life as a form of mercy killing. Candy ripped Rebecca to shreds emotionally and made her feel worse than the scum she already thought she was. In the end, I'm sure Rebecca thought she was doing the family a favor when Candy pushed her from that cliff.

"That's all Hoffman is telling you to do. It's a small price to pay so that two 'grieving' parents can get on with what they do best, acquiring fame and fortune."

Baldwin stepped back in the direction of a gondola. He frantically began pushing it on the rail toward the haul-rope. He was gasping for breath, and tears were streaming down his face. "I've heard enough. I'm getting out of here before I do something I'll regret."

Kelly grabbed Baldwin's arm and smiled in his face. "I'm going to take care of Henry myself. We've come too far to risk everything on how you handle things. You're getting weak and emotional. Your acting couldn't fool me. You were faking your trance back at the lodge."

"You stay out of it!" Baldwin said and jerked his arm free from Kelly's grasp.

Kelly's hand went to his belt, and his eyes turned steely. "You're not going to take things into your hands; I am!" His words were clipped but calm, as he pulled out a pistol and pointed it directly at Baldwin. "I won't take the chance that you could walk away with my sweet dreams." Kelly waved the gun in Baldwin's face.

"Kelly, turn around!" Taylor yelled as he leaped from his hiding place. He pointed his gun at Kelly's chest.

"Well, if it isn't one of the ten most-wanted cowards!" Kelly smiled as if he welcomed this confrontation. "So you like the smell of gunpowder, huh? A man who shoots doctors really shouldn't be playing with guns. You're too much of a coward anyway, but you got the blame. Oh, by the way, thanks to *Father* Vitali, that girl Molly was a setup. She wore a fancy piece of padding under her dress, not a baby, you bleeding heart." He looked down at his gun. "A friend of mine who was hiding in the bushes shot Dr. Bowman on Baldwin's orders. Too bad a thorough investigation wasn't done. It would have shown the angle of the bullet's entry and let you off the hook. But we wouldn't expect that kind of inquest from Sheriff McCormick, now would we?"

"The truth will come out," Taylor retorted and poked his gun toward Kelly.

"Truth? Doesn't that black book of yours say somewhere that perverts like me don't know about truth, that we've changed truth into a lie? So, what's one more little lie—like the lies McCormick and Hoffman will manufacture to explain what went on tonight. Didn't you know? Politics makes strange bedfellows," Kelly said as he laughed hysterically, amused at the cleverness of his pun. The shrill sound of Kelly's laugh distracted Taylor, and he lowered his gun.

Suddenly Kelly fired. The blast exploded from his gun barrel and lit up the terminal. The backfire reverberated thunderously against the cement and steel. Taylor spun backward from the close range of the impact to his right shoulder. His pistol flew from his hands as he slammed against a gondola cabin. He screamed and slumped to the floor, writhing in agony. Baldwin froze, his eyes wide as Kelly walked over to Taylor and stood above him with a smirk. Kelly kicked Taylor a couple of times and watched his victim cry out. Kelly picked up Taylor's gun and threw it out the terminal's open entry. He turned again to face Baldwin.

"Are you crazy?" Baldwin yelled. "You really are sick, aren't you? Now you and I are even more indebted to the Alliance than . . ."

Bang! Kelly fired directly at Baldwin, who was blown across the room by the blast and landed on his face near a pair of abandoned skis and poles that had most likely been leaned against the wall at the end of last season. His body jerked spasmodically, and he screamed out in torment.

"Dad, I did my best. I tried to please you," Baldwin pleaded. He stopped momentarily and took in a deep, raspy breath. It sounded like the bullet had pierced a lung. "I would have been a senator. You would have been proud . . ." The sound of death rattled in his throat. Blood filled his lungs, and he gasped for air. His body quivered one last time and went limp.

Kelly's head flew back, and he let out a hideous laugh that rang off the terminal walls like something from the pit of hell.

The wind blew cold through the terminal and carried the smell of blood to Wes's nostrils. Still hiding, undetected, he looked at Kelly with disbelief. He truly was a madman. Wes wanted to rush to Taylor, but he had to take care of Kelly first.

Wes sat in the shadows and sized up the situation. He remembered the days on the football field at Clarion College. It was Kelly who did the tackling then and always knocked the wind out of Wes. He seemed to enjoy putting his head down at the last minute and sticking his helmet into Wes's stomach. Wes never realized then how coldhearted Kelly really was.

Kelly walked around the terminal, surveying the scene. He ambled over near Taylor and aimed his pistol again, this time at Taylor's head. Wes lunged from his crouching position, wrapped his arms around Kelly's knees, and stuck his head in Kelly's stomach. Kelly's stocky frame couldn't withstand the charge. He wobbled off balance and fell, gasping for breath. Wes threw himself on top of Kelly and grappled for the gun. His hand felt the warm barrel. In one swift motion he jerked the pistol from Kelly's hand and threw it outside into the darkness where Kelly had flung Taylor's gun.

Kelly couldn't focus on Wes in the dark and yelled, "I'll kill you, too, whoever you are!" He thrashed from side to side, trying to throw off his assailant and regain his breath. Then light from the control room shined on Wes's face. "Bryant! What are you doing here? Listen, man, you don't understand. Let go of me, and I'll explain."

Wes held Kelly's throat in his hands, and his adrenaline pumped as Kelly's words made him angrier. He squeezed tighter.

"You're killing me, Wes," Kelly wheezed. Wes realized his stranglehold and started to let up. As he did Kelly reached up to poke out his eyes.

Wes's fist slammed into Kelly's face; blood streamed from his nose. Kelly was momentarily stunned. Then his knee caught Wes in the stomach and sent him sprawling across the floor. In a desperate attempt to catch his breath, Wes's body cramped into a fetal position. He fought to stay conscious and prepared for another assault.

Kelly staggered to his feet and wiped the blood from his face with his shirtsleeve. As Wes gasped for air Kelly spotted the pair of skis and poles that leaned against the wall. He grabbed one of the skis, wielded it like a club over his head, and ran toward Wes. His eyes were wide with rage. "That's the last time I'll stop at just knocking the wind out of you!" he howled.

Kelly swung the ski's sharp steel edge toward Wes's head. At the last second, Wes rolled to one side and jumped to his feet. *Crash!* The ski slammed into the cement and splintered its fiberglass sheathing. In frustration, Kelly threw the shattered ski aside and grabbed its companion. He swung the ski wildly back and forth like a scythe trying to take Wes's head off. The oscillating ski gave Kelly a six-foot radius to lash out at Wes, forcing him backward. Wes ducked behind a half-dozen gondola cabins dangling from a side rail and used them as a shield. Metal clanged against metal as Kelly swung at the cabins in his attempt to strike Wes.

Wes spotted the metal ski poles still propped against the wall, and grabbed one in his right hand. He lunged forward like a fencer holding a foil. He threatened Kelly by stabbing the pole in the air. Wes's weapon was the only protection he had to ward off the ski onslaught. Each time Kelly swung the ski, Wes lifted his pole with both hands to blunt the impact.

Clang! Thud! Blow after blow, Kelly sliced the ski against Wes's ski pole and sent slivers of metal flying in Wes's face. Between blows, Wes wrapped the wrist strap of the pole tightly around his forearm to keep from losing his grip as he flailed away defensively. Kelly's fury pushed Wes backward toward the entry end of the terminal.

Wes was only twenty feet away from death. Whoever designed the gondola system placed the drive terminal on a rock promontory to maximize the vertical drop for skiers. The exit end of the terminal was flat, but the end where the gondola cabins entered was a straight drop into a crevice a hundred feet below. If Kelly's ski didn't get him, the fall would.

Kelly knew this, too, and changed the strategy of his attack to save energy. He no longer flailed away erratically but measured each swing of the ski to drive Wes further backward. He grunted every time he swung. Then Wes looked past Kelly for a moment and saw Taylor staggering to his feet. Kelly was so intent on driving Wes toward the precipice, he was oblivious to what was going on behind him. He swung the ski again and again in arcs that steadily inched forward. His face was drenched in sweat, and he panted loudly.

Taylor somehow managed to stand on both feet, though his right side was drenched in blood. He reached for the remaining ski pole and held it in his left hand like a spear, the sharp end pointing toward Kelly's back. Wes realized his best chance was to keep attention focused on his retreat, so he kept an eye on how far he was from the edge, a tactic that brought homicidal delight to Kelly.

"Nobody will ever find you at the bottom of those rocks," Kelly taunted Wes, "at least not until ski season returns. By then the mountain lions will have shredded your worthless carcass."

Wes kept one eye on Kelly and the other on Taylor, who carefully moved forward from side to side, inching closer to Kelly. "Baldwin's dead. And so are your dreams of a gay-rights revolution!" Wes shot back.

"We'll find another sucker who'll believe our party line. There are a thousand political wanna-bes who'd jump at the chance to run for office," Kelly said as he stopped swinging for a moment. "Who knows, maybe I'll take a stab at it, with you and Taylor out of the way."

"Not if they find this!" With his free hand, Wes reached toward his coat pocket and patted it. "My Dictaphone is right here, and it has been recording everything since you walked in this terminal. It's all on here, and it's your ticket to the slammer. I have your admission of how Dr. Bowman was shot and your explanation of Rebecca's death. This recording will expose the Order of the New Alliance."

"Give me that thing!" Kelly screamed as he dropped the ski and lunged forward.

It was the moment Taylor had waited for. Kelly's concentration on the Dictaphone caused him to step slightly off balance and made an attack from the rear more effective. With all of his remaining energy, Taylor grabbed the pole near the sharp end with his good arm, and with his wounded arm he steadied the pole at the other end.

"*Aaargh!*" Taylor let out a scream that made Kelly freeze in his tracks. Giving it everything he had, Taylor ran toward Kelly and plunged the pointed end of the ski pole into Kelly's back. The pole tip punctured Kelly's back near his spine deep enough to momentarily embed itself. As he thrust in the pole, Taylor collapsed on the floor.

In anger, Kelly picked up the ski again and unleashed a ferocious swing. "I should have killed you long ago, you scrawny little homophobe!"

Wes ducked and threw himself at Kelly's knees like a blocking back taking out a defensive end. Kelly's lunge toward Wes and the impact of Wes's block, spun Kelly toward the edge of the terminal's entry. He tried to stop his momentum by flailing his arms, but his leather-soled shoes kept sliding across the frost-dampened floor until he was airborne.

All was quiet for a moment, and Wes waited to hear Kelly's cries as he plunged into the abyss below. Instead, Wes heard a voice faintly cry out. "Help me. Do something. I can't hang on much longer!"

Wes crawled toward the edge, favoring his bad knee; he saw the fingers of Kelly's right hand clasped on to the concrete ledge of the terminal floor. Kelly's body dangled in midair, and his arm and legs flapped in desperation.

"Bryant, you can save me! Don't let me die."

"Do it!" Wes heard Taylor's voice from behind him. "Try to pull him back up if you can."

Wes inched as close to the edge as possible and grasped Kelly's forearm with his hand. He hooked his feet around a gondola guide that ran along the floor.

"I've got your arm. Don't let go while I try to pull you back inside."

Wes strained every muscle in his body and bent his legs to pull Kelly back in the terminal. Slowly Kelly started to inch upward. He swung his body slightly, trying to get a leg high enough to fling it over the edge. Once, twice, three times he tried, to no avail. The fourth time he managed to plant the heel of his left shoe on the edge. With one final pull of Wes's arm, Kelly hurled himself back onto the terminal floor.

Kelly lay there bleeding and exhausted. Wes relaxed for a moment. Suddenly he felt Kelly's hands on his throat. His attacker showed no signs of gratefulness as his thumbs pressed inward on Wes's windpipe. "Give me that dictation machine!" he screamed.

Wes fumbled inside his pocket. Somehow he managed to pop open the door that held the recording cassette, flick out the cassette with his finger, close the door, and pull out the dictation unit, without the cassette.

"You want it; here it is!" Wes croaked with what little air he had left in his lungs. He waved the Dictaphone in Kelly's face, then threw it toward the terminal's ledge. The Dictaphone skidded across the floor, and Kelly dived, flat on his stomach, in its direction. His right arm stretched out for the recording device just as it slid off the edge and dropped into the void. Kelly's momentum carried him farther than he intended, and this time no hand grasped the ledge of the floor.

"No! No-o-o-o!" he screamed as he plunged headfirst over the edge. His shrieks bounced off the mountain's rock walls and echoed far into the night. Wes lay there waiting for the thud of Kelly's body as it struck the rocks below, but there was no sound.

"We've got to get out of here," Taylor groaned.

Wes climbed to his feet and walked toward where Taylor lay. He slung Taylor's uninjured arm over his neck, dragged Taylor's almost lifeless body toward a gondola cabin, and placed him on one of the seats. Then he laboriously pushed the cabin off the rail on to the still-moving haul-rope and jumped inside. Slowly the cabin looped around the bull-wheel and headed toward the terminal exit.

Taylor's blood-soaked body lay in an unconscious heap on the downhill seat of the cabin. Wes fell exhausted onto the other seat. Blood from Kelly's wound covered Wes's face and hands. Cold air coagulated the blood that matted his hair. He took off his jacket to use it as a towel. As he did, his hand passed across the Dictaphone tape, still in his pocket.

Suddenly, Wes heard a roaring overhead. He looked up and saw a helicopter lifting off from the top of Vail Mountain. For a moment the helicopter hovered above the gondola and shined a bright searchlight directly in Wes's eyes. The rotor blades sent gusts of wind across the mountain and rocked the cabin. Wes drew a hand to his face to shield against the searchlight's glare and strained his eyes to get a good look. He saw a symbol on the side of the helicopter that made his heart sink. The sign was more than an abstract emblem. It was a presence that had lurked in the shadows of his political nightmare—the symbol of three interlocking triangles.

Slowly, the helicopter ascended and disappeared into the darkness.

Epilogue

Election Day, Tuesday, November 8.

"Is there any popcorn left?" Wes called out. "I need to keep my energy up to watch TV."

"The waitresses are busy right now," Annette answered from the kitchen with a touch of good-humored sarcasm. "If you men are too lazy to come and get it, we could deliver for a slight service charge."

"I'll get the popcorn," Henry Baldwin said as he got up from his chair. He picked up a pair of crutches. "Maybe they'll be intimidated by a handicapped man and feel sorry for us," he joked.

"Not handicapped for long," Wes insisted. "From what Jennifer tells us, the doctor says you'll be off those crutches in a week or so."

"It can't happen soon enough for me. The nerve that bullet pinched still makes my right leg go limp occasionally. The physical therapist wants me to start putting my full weight on it as soon as I can stand the pain. He says that using the leg is the best way to get it back to normal."

"Sit down," Jennifer said with mock irritation as she emerged from the kitchen. She carried an overflowing bowl of Orville Redenbacker's best. "Mom and I want you and Dad to stay by the TV so you can keep us posted on the election. This is the big night we've all waited for, and I want to

---

know the minute the early precinct results start coming in, especially the returns on the Senate race."

Jennifer set the popcorn bowl on a glass-topped coffee table in front of them. She leaned down to affectionately kiss Henry. "You keep that leg rested," she said with a wink. "You'll need all the strength you can muster to walk down the aisle at our wedding. Remember, it's only four weeks away."

Jennifer's face glowed as Henry reached out and warmly squeezed her hand. "And you, Dad, eat all the popcorn you want. You'll need the energy to give me away without falling to pieces."

Wes couldn't imagine himself being any happier—unless his favored candidate, former Colorado state representative Zachary Broe, won the U. S. Senate seat by a landslide. Baldwin's death had thrown the senatorial race wide open. Both major parties had scrambled to repackage their candidates over the summer in time for the traditional Labor Day campaign kickoff. Broe and his liberal opponent, Matthew Woodruff, were running even, according to the latest pre-election polls. With Baldwin and his left-of-center sloganeering out of the headlines, the contestants were able to spend more time debating topics of local state interest, education, land use, and business development.

"With about 20 percent of the votes counted, Woodruff has a slight lead in the race. Returns on the referendum mandating a mill levy for the creation of a northeast Colorado parks district are . . ."

"I heard something about the Senate race. What's the latest?" Jennifer asked as she ran back into the living room and bounded in front of the TV.

Wes hit the remote control and temporarily muted the voice of the blow-dried, fixed-smile anchorman, Tom Benton, who earnestly peered into the camera.

Wes dodged his head from side to side trying to see past Jennifer. "Don't worry," he said, slightly irritated by her obstruction. "We'll call you from the kitchen as soon as we hear anything conclusive."

"Sorry, Dad," Jennifer said as she stepped out of Wes's line of sight.

"This is the first time I've ever been involved in the political process, and I've worked so hard on the Broe campaign."

"I understand your enthusiasm," Wes said, "but it's not like Woodruff is a Bill Baldwin kind of guy."

The mere mention of Baldwin's name sent a shiver through the room. Baldwin's legacy underscored Shakespeare's observation that "the evil men do, lives after them." The Abortion Liberty League seized upon the killing of Dr. Bowman to demand greater restrictions on abortion protests even though Stanley Taylor was exonerated. The Gay and Lesbian Caucus had enough friends in the media to twist the truth about Kelly's death to make him into a martyr.

Zachary Broe countered all those lies with his campaign pledge to restore family values in a nondiscriminatory atmosphere. Wes could still remember Broe's last campaign speech when he had said, "Traditional morality is essential to democracy. Faith in God and faith in the family is what's right with America. Let's work together for a country of safe neighborhoods, strong families, sound schools, and a government of citizen legislators with limited terms who will eventually live under the laws they have passed for others."

If Broe won by a whisker, his ability to advance a strong moral agenda might be in question. What Wes wanted was a clear mandate from the people that would give Broe the clout he needed to walk into Washington and pursue a bold course of action.

"With 40 percent of the precincts reporting and the latest results of our exit polls in, we are now in a position to project a winner in the state's most-watched race."

"Come here quickly, Annette and Jennifer, I think we finally have some results," Wes said. He watched the digits on the computerized readout crawl across the bottom of the TV screen and tally the votes. Annette and Jennifer rushed into the living room and plopped down on the couch.

The announcer's hand went to his ear to reposition the earplug feeding audio from his producer. His eyes rolled away from the screen as he concentrated on the instructions from the newsroom. "Before giving you those results, we are first going directly to the campaign headquarters of Matthew Woodruff, where our political consultant, Anne Alexander, is standing by. Anne?"

The camera focused on a smartly dressed correspondent who looked fresh out of journalism school. Her perky attitude seemed out of place with the seriousness of the evening. "Tom, I'm standing in the lobby of the Mile-High Hotel, where supporters of Matthew Woodruff have gathered for an announcement. Wait a minute. I think I see candidate Woodruff headed our way."

Alexander ignored the camera momentarily and waved frantically to get Woodruff's attention. The candidate, who looked emotionally exhausted, still managed a campaign-perfect smile as he leaned down toward Alexander's microphone.

"I understand you're about to enter the grand ballroom and address your supporters," the reporter said. "Can you give us an idea of what you will say?"

Woodruff turned serious. "I'm going to thank them for their gallant efforts on behalf of our candidacy, and I'm going to offer my congratulations to Mr. Broe."

Whatever else Woodruff said was drowned out by Jennifer's screams of delight. She jumped to her feet, threw popcorn in the air, and danced around Henry's chair.

"Calm down," Wes instructed. "It looks like they're switching to Broe's campaign headquarters."

Without any intervening correspondent to provide an explanation, the camera zeroed in on Broe, who stood confidently behind a lectern with a sign reading, "Forward to the future by reclaiming the past." Broe was flanked on both sides by his wife, three children, and extended family members, some of whom Wes recognized.

Broe held up his hands to get the attention of the crowd and smiled broadly. Jennifer ceased her victory demonstration and knelt down next to Henry's chair.

"Friends and supporters, just moments ago Matthew Woodruff called me to concede the election and offer me his best wishes. He asked me to tell all of you that he is prepared to cooperate in every way possible so that Colorado's senatorial representation will have the full support of all citizens from this great state."

Broe's supporters burst into cheers as Annette reached out to take Wes's hand. He knew more than anyone in the room that Broe's success had been bought with blood, and Wes's enthusiasm for Broe was tempered by those memories. He recalled Henry's painful recovery from the gunshot wound and Stanley Taylor's convalescence while he recuperated from David Kelly's attempt on his life. Wes couldn't understand why Henry was so torn up over the loss of his father, a man who was willing to sacrifice both of his own children. Henry had some healing to do, and Wes tried to understand his grieving.

Broe continued his speech. "The achievement we celebrate tonight is an affirmation of time-honored values and the belief that every American should be judged on the basis of his or her character and hard work, not on gender, race, or religion. I pledge to you a better America where playgrounds will once again be safe havens for our children, where babies will be welcomed by loving parents instead of being illegitimate accidents, and where our offspring will be considered a blessing, not a tax burden to the government."

"Yes! Yes!" Jennifer shouted.

Broe went on. "For too long the heavy hand of Uncle Sam has waged war on the most decent among us, those who uphold moral character, those who oppose the approval of aberrant behavior, and those who believe that crisis pregnancy centers are preferable to exterminating the unborn.

"I reach out to all the citizens of this state and promise that you will not be judged by your passions or preferences but by your actions and conduct. I do not say that God is on my side; but in the words of Abraham Lincoln, I declare, 'I know that the Lord is always on the side of right, but it is my constant anxiety and prayer that I and this nation should be on the Lord's side.' Thank you, God bless you, and watch what happens when we get to Washington!"

Everyone in the room clapped as Wes hit the OFF button on the TV remote control. He had had his fill of politics since last April 22, and he wanted to savor this moment without it being marred by the cynical analysis or some network television pundit.

The front doorbell rang.

"Who could that be at this time of night? Were you expecting anyone?" Annette asked.

Wes nodded his head as he rose from his chair and headed to the door.

"Wes, it's a great night for Colorado!" Stanley Taylor said. He carried a large paper bag in his arms. "I wanted to get right here after the good news was announced."

"Glad you stopped by," Wes said, inviting him in. "The night wouldn't be complete without our celebrating what's happened tonight."

"Hey, have you heard the latest?" Taylor asked. "I just picked it up on the car radio coming over. Election central is predicting a landslide for Broe, 60 percent or more of the vote!"

"It's the outcome we hoped for!" Wes said. "Can I take your coat?"

"No thanks. The family is waiting for me. I just wanted to stop by and deliver this little victory gift," he said, referring to the bag he held.

"Please come in for just a moment, " Annette insisted. "Jennifer and Henry would be so disappointed if they didn't get to see you."

After a round of greetings, Taylor opened the sack and pulled out two bottles of bubbly. "Nonalcoholic," he said. "A night like this deserves champagne, but I wanted you to stay sober so you could enjoy every minute," Taylor laughed.

"How's the shoulder?" Henry asked.

"Great. The doctor says I'll be pitching balls as Little League coach by summer. How's your leg?"

"I'll be off these things soon," Henry said as he pointed to his crutches.

"I can only stay a minute," Taylor insisted, "but I didn't want this night to pass without sharing its joy with all of you, and especially you, Wes.

Everyone here knows you saved my life, and I want to say again how much I appreciate your bravery. I also want to thank you one last time in case we don't see each other for a while."

"Why? Where are you going?" Wes asked.

"Washington, D.C. Zachary Broe has asked me to be his personal assistant on human life issues, including crisis pregnancy intervention. What we've tried to do here in Colorado, we can now accomplish on a nationwide scale."

"Congratulations," Jennifer said.

"The credit belongs to the Lord," Taylor said humbly. He reached in his pocket and took out a small object. He leaned toward Wes and reached out with both hands toward his shirt. "Wear this in memory of those we have yet to save."

We looked down to the left side of his chest just above his shirt pocket, where Stanley Taylor had pinned two tiny, silver baby's feet.